ALFRED HITCHCOCK PRESENTS:
STORIES THAT GO BUMP
IN THE NIGHT

ALFRED HITCHCOCK

Presents: STORIES THAT GO BUMP IN THE NIGHT

 Random House, New York

Library of Congress Cataloging in Publication Data
Main entry under title:

Alfred Hitchcock presents stories that go bump in the night.

   1. Detective and mystery stories, American. 2. Detective and mystery stories, English. I. Hitchcock, Alfred, 1899-   II. Title: Stories that go bump in the night.
PZ1.A3978   [PS648.D4]   823'.0872   77-3047
ISBN 0-394-41216-8

Manufactured in the United States of America
9 8 7 6 5 4 3 2
First Edition

Acknowledgments

"Edward the Conqueror" by Roald Dahl. Reprinted by permission of Alfred A. Knopf, Inc. Copyright 1953 by Roald Dahl. From *Kiss, Kiss* by Roald Dahl. This story first appeared in *The New Yorker*.

"By the Scruff of the Soul" by Dorothy Salisbury Davis. Reprinted by permission of the author. Copyright © 1962, 1963 by Dorothy Salisbury Davis. First published in *Ellery Queen's Mystery Magazine,* 1963.

"The Valentine Murder" by Mignon G. Eberhart. Reprinted by permission of Brandt & Brandt. Copyright 1954 by Mignon G. Eberhart.

"Hey, Look at Me!" by Jack Finney. Reprinted by permission of Harold Matson Co., Inc. Copyright © 1968 by Jack Finney. Published in *Playboy Anthology,* 1968.

"Muldoon and the Numbers Game" by Robert L. Fish. Reprinted by permission of the author and the author's agent, Robert P. Mills, Ltd. Copyright © 1974 by Robert L. Fish. Published in *The Saturday Evening Post.*

"The Guide's Story" by Dion Henderson. Reprinted by permission of Larry Sternig Literary Agency. Copyright © 1968 by H.S.D. Publications. Published in *Alfred Hitchcock Mystery Magazine.*

"Woodrow Wilson's Necktie" by Patricia Highsmith. Reprinted by permission of McIntosh and Otis, Inc. Copyright © 1972 by Patricia Highsmith. First appeared in *Ellery Queen's Mystery Magazine,* March 1972.

"Something for the Dark" by Edward D. Hoch. Reprinted by permission of the author and Larry Sternig Literary Agency. Copyright © 1968 by H.S.D. Publications.

"The Grey Shroud" by Antony Horner. Reprinted by permission of the author.

"The Gentleman Caller" by Veronica Parker Johns. Reprinted by permission of the author. Copyright © 1955 by Veronica Parker Johns. First published in *Ellery Queen's Mystery Magazine,* 1955.

"The Coconut Trial" by Don Knowlton. Reprinted by permission of National City Bank of Cleveland, Executor of the Estate of Donald S. Knowlton, by C. G. Martis, Vice President. Copyright © 1966 by Donald S. Knowlton. First appeared in *Ellery Queen's Mystery Magazine,* February 1966.

"Man in a Trap" by John D. MacDonald. Reprinted by permission of John D. MacDonald. Copyright © 1958 by John D. MacDonald. Published in *Ellery Queen Mystery Magazine,* 1958.

"The Bearded Lady" by John D. MacDonald. Reprinted by permission of Harold Ober Associates Incorporated. Copyright 1948, renewed in 1976 by Kenneth Millar. First published in *American Magazine,* October 1948.

"Dead Game" by Harold Q. Masur. Reprinted by permission of the author. Copyright © 1975 by H.S.D. Publications, Inc.

"No Such Thing As a Vampire" by Richard Matheson. Reprinted by permission of Harold Matson Co., Inc. Copyright © 1967 by Richard Matheson. Published in *Playboy,* 1967.

"A Piece of the World" by Steve O'Connell. Reprinted by permission of Larry Sternig Literary Agency. Copyright © 1965 H.S.D. Publications. Published in *Alfred Hitchcock Mystery Magazine,* June 1965.

"Easy Mark" by Talmage Powell. Reprinted by permission of the author and his agents, Scott Meredith Literary Agency, Inc., 845 Third Avenue, New York, New York 10022. Copyright © 1971 by Davis Publications, Inc. First published in *Alfred Hitchcock Mystery Magazine.*

"Proof of Guilt" by Bill Pronzini. Reprinted by permission of the author. Copyright © 1973 by Bill Pronzini. First published in *Ellery Queen's Mystery Magazine,* June 1963.

"The Operator" by Jack Ritchie. Reprinted by permission of Larry Sternig Literary Agency. Copyright © 1963 H.S.D. Publications. Published in *Alfred Hitchcock Mystery Magazine,* June 1963.

"An Evening in Soho" by Nancy C. Swoboda. Reprinted by permission of the author.

"The Other Celia" by Theodore Sturgeon. Reprinted by permission of the author and the author's agent, Kirby McCauley. Copyright © 1957 by Theodore Sturgeon.

"Wile Versus Guile" by Arthur Train. Reprinted by permission of Charles Scribner's Sons. Copyright 1919 by Curtis Publishing Co. Reprinted from *Tut and Mr. Tut* by Arthur Train.

The editor gratefully acknowledges the invaluable assistance of Harold Q. Masur in the preparation of this volume

Contents

Introduction

Good evening.

Once again I act as your guide on a tour through the felonious world of fictitious villainy. First, however, you must allow me to apologize for the title of this volume. I do so at the risk of offending my publisher, a corporate entity composed of many worthy ladies and gentlemen, all engaged in a highly esteemed enterprise—the production of books and the preservation of man's knowledge. As corporate objectives go, perhaps one of the most exalted.

Unfortunately, it is not always a profitable venture. Authors and editors must be compensated, likewise printers, binders and distributors, with a modest lagniappe for stockholders, to say nothing of extortionate tax-collectors and rapacious landlords.

As a consequence, occasional books must be published that will induce the public to part with its cash. Readers frequently do this for the privilege of being transported into a world of vicarious adventure. And my publisher informs me that a title often helps the process along. I sincerely hope he is right. In a long career I have never spurned financial rewards. Only radicals and pedants equate success with mediocrity.

Readers associate my name with stories that chill and thrill, hence the title of this book. It is not, however, entirely accurate. Oh, yes, there are tales here that should make you perspire and tremble. Nevertheless, I do have a lighter side. Occasionally I relish a smile or a chuckle. And in gathering this collection I came across several yarns that amused me, and since I am the editor I willy-nilly include them on the theory that a chortle now and then is more beneficent than an apple a day or a massive vitamin shot.

I want my readers to live and prosper and return again when my next collection is due.

ALFRED HITCHCOCK PRESENTS:
STORIES THAT GO BUMP
IN THE NIGHT

The Damned Thing

Ambrose Bierce

By the light of a tallow candle which had been placed on one end of a rough table, a man was reading something written in a book. It was an old account book, greatly worn; and the writing was not very legible, for the man sometimes held the page close to the flame of the candle to get a stronger light on it. The shadow of the book would then throw into obscurity half of the room, darkening a number of faces and figures; for besides the reader, eight other men were present.

Seven of them sat against the rough log walls, silent, motionless, and, the room being small, not very far from the table. By extending an arm any one of them could have touched the eighth man, who lay on the table, face upward, partly covered by a sheet, his arms at his sides. He was dead.

The person reading was the coroner. It was by virtue of his office that he had possession of the book in which he was reading; it had been found among the dead man's effects—in his cabin, where the inquest was now taking place.

When the coroner had finished reading, he put the book into his breast pocket. At that moment the door was pushed open and a young man entered. He, clearly, was not of mountain birth and breeding: he was clad as those who dwell in cities. His clothing was dusty, however, as from travel. He had, in fact, been riding hard to attend the inquest.

The coroner nodded; no one one else greeted him.

The young man smiled. "I am sorry to have kept you," he said. "I went away, not to evade your summons, but to send to my newspaper an account of what I suppose I am called back to relate."

The coroner smiled.

"The account that you sent to your newspaper," he said, "probably differs from that which you will give here under oath."

"That," replied the other, rather hotly and with a visible flush, "is as you please. I have a copy of what I sent. It was not written as news, for it is incredible, but as fiction. It may go as a part of my testimony under oath."

"But you say it is incredible."

"That is nothing to you, if I also swear it is true."

The coroner was silent for a time, his eyes upon the floor. The men about the sides of the cabin talked in whispers, but seldom withdrew their gaze from the face of the corpse. Presently the coroner lifted his eyes and said: "We will resume the inquest."

The men removed their hats. The witness was sworn.

"What is your name?" the coroner asked.

"William Harker."

"Age?"

"Twenty-seven."

"You knew the deceased, Hugh Morgan?"

"Yes."

"You were with him when he died?"

"Near him."

"How did that happen—your presence, I mean?"

"I was visiting him at his place, to shoot and fish. Part of my purpose, however, was to study him and his odd, solitary way of life. He seemed a good model for a character in fiction. I sometimes write stories."

"I sometimes read them."

"Thank you."

"Stories in general—not yours."

Some of the jurors laughed.

"Relate the circumstances of this man's death," said the coroner. "You may use any notes you please."

The witness understood. He held a manuscript near the candle and, turning the leaves until he found the passage that he wanted, began to read.

". . . The sun had hardly risen when we left the house. We were looking for quail, each with a shotgun, but we had only one dog. Morgan said that our best ground was beyond a certain ridge that he pointed out, and we crossed it by a trail through the chaparral. On the other side was comparatively level ground, thickly covered with wild oats. As we emerged from the chaparral Morgan was but a few yards in advance. Suddenly we heard, at a little distance to our right and partly in front, a noise as of some animal thrashing about in the bushes, which we could see were violently agitated.

" 'We've startled a deer,' I said. 'I wish we had brought a rifle.'

"Morgan, who had stopped and was intently watching the agitated chaparral, said nothing, but had cocked both barrels of his gun and was holding it in readiness to aim. I thought him a trifle excited, which surprised me, for he had a reputation for exceptional coolness, even in moments of sudden and imminent peril.

" 'Oh, come,' I said. 'You are not going to fill up a deer with quail-shot, are you?'

"Still he did not reply; but catching sight of his face as he turned it slightly toward me, I was struck by the intensity of his look. Then I understood that we had serious business in hand, and my first conjecture was that we had 'jumped' a grizzly. I advanced to Morgan's side, cocking my gun as I moved.

"The bushes were now quiet and the sound had ceased, but Morgan was as attentive to the place as before.

" 'What is it? What the devil is it?' I asked.

" 'That Damned Thing!' he replied, without turning his head. His voice was husky and unnatural. He trembled visibly.

"I was about to speak further, when I observed the wild oats near the place of the disturbance moving in the most inexplicable way. I can hardly describe it. The grain seemed to be stirred by a streak of wind, which not only bent it, but pressed it down —crushed it so that it did not rise; and this movement was slowly prolonging itself directly toward us.

"Nothing that I had ever seen had affected me so strangely as this unfamiliar and unaccountable phenomenon, yet I am unable to recall any sense of fear. However, the apparently causeless movement of the grain, and the slow, undeviating approach of the line of disturbance were distinctly disquieting.

"My companion appeared actually frightened, and I could hardly credit my senses when I saw him suddenly lift his gun to his shoulder and fire both barrels at the agitated grain! Before the smoke of the discharge had cleared away, I heard a loud savage cry—a scream like that of a wild animal. Flinging his gun on the ground, Morgan sprang away and ran swiftly from the spot. At the same instant I was thrown violently to the ground by the impact of something unseen in the smoke—some soft, heavy substance that seemed thrown against me with great force.

"Before I could get on my feet and recover my gun, which seemed to have been struck from my hands, I heard Morgan crying out as if in mortal agony, and mingling with his cries were such hoarse, savage sounds as one hears from fighting dogs. Inexpressibly terrified, I struggled to my feet and looked in the direction of Morgan's retreat; may Heaven in mercy spare me from another sight like that!

"At a distance of less than thirty yards was my friend, down upon one knee, his head thrown back at a frightful angle, hatless, his long hair in disorder, and his whole body in violent movement from side to side, backward and forward. His right arm was lifted and seemed to lack the hand—at least, I could see none. The other arm was invisible.

"At times, as my memory now reports this extraordinary scene, I could discern but a part of his body; it was as if he had been partly blotted out—I cannot otherwise express it—then a shifting of his position would bring it all into view again.

"All this must have occurred within a few seconds, yet in that time Morgan assumed all the postures of a determined wrestler vanquished by superior weight and strength. I saw nothing but him, and him not always distinctly. During the entire incident his shouts and curses were heard, as if through an enveloping uproar of such sounds of rage and fury as I had never heard from the throat of man or brute!

"For a moment only I stood irresolute, then throwing down

my gun I ran forward to my friend's assistance. I had a vague belief that he was suffering from a fit, or some form of convulsion. Before I could reach his side, he was prone and quiet.

"All sounds had ceased, but with a feeling of such terror as even these awful events had not inspired I now saw again the mysterious movement of the wild oats, prolonging itself from the trampled area about the prostrate man toward the edge of the wood. It was only when it had reached the wood that I was able to withdraw my eyes and look at my companion. He was dead."

The coroner rose from his seat and stood beside the dead man. Lifting an edge of the sheet he pulled it away, exposing the entire body, altogether naked and showing in the candle-light a claylike yellow. It had, however, broad marks of bluish black, obviously caused by extravasated blood from contusions. The chest and sides looked as if they had been beaten with a bludgeon. There were dreadful lacerations; the skin was torn in strips and shreds.

The coroner moved round to the end of the table and undid a silk handkerchief which had been passed under the chin and knotted on the top of the head. When the handkerchief was drawn away, it exposed what had been the throat. Some of the jurors who had risen to get a better view repented their curiosity and turned away their faces. Witness Harker went to the open window and leaned across the sill, faint and sick.

Dropping the handkerchief upon the dead man's neck, the coroner stepped to a corner of the room and from a pile of clothing produced one garment after another, each of which he held up a moment for inspection. All were torn, and stiff with blood.

"Gentlemen," the coroner said, "we have no more evidence, I think. Your duty has been already explained to you; if there is nothing you wish to ask, you may go outside and consider your verdict."

The foreman rose—a tall, bearded man of sixty. "I should like to ask one question, Mr. Coroner," he said. "What asylum did yer witness escape from?"

"Mr. Harker," said the coroner, gravely and tranquilly, "from what asylum did you last escape?"

Harker flushed crimson again but said nothing, and the seven jurors rose and solemnly filed out of the cabin.

"If you have finished insulting me, sir," said Harker, as soon as he and the officer were left alone with the dead man, "I suppose I am at liberty to go?"

"Yes."

Harker started to leave, but paused, with his hand on the door latch. The habit of his profession was strong in him—stronger than his sense of personal dignity. He turned about and said:

"The book that you have there—I recognize it as Morgan's diary. You seemed greatly interested in it; you read in it while I was testifying. May I see it? The public would like—"

"The book will cut no figure in this matter," replied the official, slipping it into his coat pocket; "all the entries in it were made before the writer's death."

As Harker passed out of the house, the jury reentered and stood about the table, on which the now covered corpse showed under the sheet with sharp definition. The foreman seated himself near the candle, produced from his breast pocket a pencil and scrap of paper, and wrote rather laboriously the following verdict, which with various degrees of effort all signed:

"We, the jury, do find that the remains come to their death at the hands of a mountain lion, but some of us thinks, all the same, they had fits."

In the diary of the late Hugh Morgan are certain interesting entries, which may possibly have some scientific value. At the inquest upon his body, the book was not put in evidence; possibly the coroner thought it not worth while to confuse the jury. The date of the first of the entries cannot be ascertained; the upper part of the leaf is torn away; the part of the entry remaining follows:

". . . would run in a half-circle, keeping his head turned always toward the center, and again he would stand still, barking furiously. At last he ran away into the brush as fast as he could go. I thought at first that he had gone mad, but on returning to the house found no other alteration in his manner than what was obviously due to fear of punishment.

"Can a dog see with his nose? Do odors impress some cerebral center with images of the thing that emitted them . . . ?

"Sept. 2—Looking at the stars last night, as they rose above the crest of the ridge east of the house, I observed them successively disappear—from left to right. Each was eclipsed but an instant, and only a few at the same time, but along the entire length of the ridge all that were within a degree or two of the crest were blotted out. It was as if something had passed along between me and them; but I could not see it, and the stars were not thick enough to define its outline. Ugh! I don't like this. It worries me."

Several weeks' entries are missing, three leaves being torn from the book.

"Sept. 27—It has been about here again—I find evidences of its presence every day. I watched again all last night in the same cover, gun in hand, double-charged with buckshot. In the morning the fresh footprints were there, as before. Yet I would have sworn that I did not sleep—indeed, I hardly sleep at all. It is terrible, insupportable! If these amazing experiences are real, I shall go mad; if they are fanciful, I am mad already.

"Oct. 3—I shall not go—it shall not drive me away. No, this is *my* house, *my* land. God hates a coward. . . .

"Oct. 5—I can stand it no longer; I have invited Harker to pass a few weeks with me—he has a level head. I can judge from his manner if he thinks me mad.

"Oct. 7—I have the solution of the mystery; it came to me last night—suddenly, as by revelation. How simple—how terribly simple!

"There are sounds that we cannot hear. At either end of the scale are notes that stir no chord of that imperfect instrument, the human ear. They are too high or too grave. I have observed a flock of blackbirds occupying an entire tree-top—the tops of several trees—and all in full song. Suddenly—in a moment—at absolutely the same instant—all spring into the air and fly away. How? They could not all see one another—whole tree-tops intervened. At no point could a leader have been visible to all.

"There must have been a signal of warning or command, high and shrill above the din, but by me unheard. I have observed, too, the same simultaneous flight when all were silent, among not only blackbirds, but other birds—quail, for example, widely separated by bushes—even on opposite sides of a hill.

"It is known to seamen that a school of whales basking or sporting on the surface of the ocean, miles apart, with the convexity of the earth between, will sometimes dive at the same instant—all gone out of sight in a moment. The signal has been sounded—too grave for the ear of the sailor at the masthead and his comrades on the deck—who nevertheless feel its vibrations in the ship, as the stones of a cathedral are stirred by the bass of the organ.

"As with sounds, so with colors. At each end of the solar spectrum the chemist can detect the presence of what are known as 'actinic' rays. They represent colors—integral colors in the composition of light—which we are unable to discern. The human eye is an imperfect instrument; its range is but a few octaves of the real 'chromatic scale.' I am not mad; there are colors that we cannot see.

"And, God help me! the Damned Thing is of such a color!"

Edward the Conqueror

Roald Dahl

Louisa, holding a dishcloth in her hand, stepped out the kitchen door at the back of the house into the cool October sunshine.

"Edward!" she called. "*Ed-ward!* Lunch is ready!"

She paused a moment, listening; then she strolled out onto the lawn and continued across it—a little shadow attending her —skirting the rose bed and touching the sundial lightly with one finger as she went by. She moved rather gracefully for a woman who was small and plump, with a lilt in her walk and a gentle swinging of the shoulders and the arms. She passed under the mulberry tree onto the brick path, then went all the way along the path until she came to the place where she could look down into the dip at the end of this large garden.

"*Edward!* Lunch!"

She could see him now, about eighty yards away, down in the dip on the edge of the wood—the tallish narrow figure in khaki slacks and dark-green sweater, working beside a big bonfire with a fork in his hands, pitching brambles onto the top of the fire. It was blazing fiercely, with orange flames and clouds of milky smoke, and the smoke was drifting back over the garden with a wonderful scent of autumn and burning leaves.

Louisa went down the slope toward her husband. Had she wanted, she could easily have called again and made herself

11

heard, but there was something about a first-class bonfire that impelled her toward it, right up close so she could feel the heat and listen to it burn.

"Lunch," she said, approaching.

"Oh, hello. All right—yes. I'm coming."

"*What* a good fire."

"I've decided to clear this place right out," her husband said. "I'm sick and tired of all these brambles." His long face was wet with perspiration. There were small beads of it clinging all over his moustache like dew, and two little rivers were running down his throat onto the turtleneck of the sweater.

"You better be careful you don't overdo it, Edward."

"Louisa, I do wish you'd stop treating me as though I were eighty. A bit of exercise never did anyone any harm."

"Yes, dear, I know. Oh, Edward! Look! Look!"

The man turned and looked at Louisa, who was pointing now to the far side of the bonfire.

"Look, Edward! The cat!"

Sitting on the ground, so close to the fire that the flames sometimes seemed actually to be touching it, was a large cat of a most unusual color. It stayed quite still, with its head on one side and its nose in the air, watching the man and woman with a cool yellow eye.

"It'll get burnt!" Louisa cried, and she dropped the discloth and darted swiftly in and grabbed it with both hands, whisking it away and putting it on the grass well clear of the flames.

"You crazy cat," she said, dusting off her hands. "What's the matter with you?"

"Cats know what they're doing," the husband said. "You'll never find a cat doing something it doesn't want. Not cats."

"Whose is it? You ever seen it before?"

"No, I never have. Damn peculiar color."

The cat had seated itself on the grass and was regarding them with a sidewise look. There was a veiled inward expression about the eyes, something curiously omniscient and pensive, and around the nose a most delicate air of contempt, as though the sight of these two middle-aged persons—the one small, plump, and rosy, the other lean and extremely sweaty—were a matter of some surprise but very little importance. For a cat, it certainly had an unusual color—a pure silvery gray with no blue in it at all—and the hair was very long and silky.

Louisa bend down and stroked its head. "You must go home," she said. "Be a good cat now and go on home to where you belong."

The man and wife started to stroll back up the hill toward the house. The cat got up and followed, at a distance first, but edging closer and closer as they went along. Soon it was alongside them, then it was ahead, leading the way across the lawn to the house, and walking as though it owned the whole place, holding its tail straight up in the air, like a mast.

"Go home," the man said. "Go on home. We don't want you."

But when they reached the house, it came in with them, and Louisa gave it some milk in the kitchen. During lunch, it hopped up onto the spare chair between them and sat through the meal with its head just above the level of the table, watching the proceedings with those dark-yellow eyes which kept moving slowly from the woman to the man and back again.

"I don't like this cat," Edward said.

"Oh, I think it's a beautiful cat. I do hope it stays a little while."

"Now, listen to me, Louisa. The creature can't possibly stay here. It belongs to someone else. It's lost. And if it's still trying to hang around this afternoon, you'd better take it to the police. They'll see it gets home."

After lunch, Edward returned to his gardening. Louisa, as usual, went to the piano. She was a competent pianist and a genuine music-lover, and almost every afternoon she spent an hour or so playing for herself. The cat was now lying on the sofa, and she paused to stroke it as she went by. It opened its eyes, looked at her a moment, then closed them again and went back to sleep.

"You're an awfully nice cat," she said. "And such a beautiful colour. I wish I could keep you." Then her fingers, moving over the fur on the cat's head, came into contact with a small lump, a little growth just above the right eye.

"Poor cat," she said. "You've got bumps on your beautiful face. You must be getting old."

She went over and sat down on the long piano bench, but she didn't immediately start to play. One of her special little pleasures was to make every day a kind of concert day, with a carefully arranged program which she worked out in detail before she began. She never liked to break her enjoyment by having to stop while she wondered what to play next. All she wanted was a brief pause after each piece while the audience clapped enthusiastically and called for more. It was so much nicer to imagine an audience, and now and again while she was playing—on the lucky days, that is—the room would begin to swim and fade and darken, and she would see nothing but row upon row of seats and a sea of white faces upturned toward her, listening with a rapt and adoring concentration.

Sometimes she played from memory, sometimes from music. Today she would play from memory; that was the way she felt. And what should the program be? She sat before the piano with her small hands clasped on her lap, a plump rosy little person with a round and still quite pretty face, her hair done up in a neat bun at the back of her head. By looking slightly to the right, she could see the cat curled up asleep on the sofa, and its silvery-gray coat was beautiful against the purple of the cushion. How about some Bach to begin with? Or, better still, Vivaldi. The Bach adaptation for organ of the D minor Concerto Grosso. Yes—that first. Then perhaps a little Schumann. *Carnaval?* That would be fun. And after that—well, a touch of Liszt for a change. One of the *Petrarch Sonnets.* The second one —that was the loveliest—the E major. Then another Schumann, another of his gay ones—*Kinderscenen.* And lastly, for the encore, a Brahms waltz, or maybe two of them if she felt like it.

Vivaldi, Schumann, Liszt, Schumann, Brahms. A very nice programme, one that she could play easily without the music. She moved herself a little closer to the piano and paused a moment while someone in the audience—already she could feel that this was one of the lucky days—while someone in the audience had his last cough; then, with the slow grace that accompanied nearly all her movements, she lifted her hands to the keyboard and began to play.

She wasn't, at that particular moment, watching the cat at all —as a matter of fact she had forgotten its presence—but as the first deep notes of the Vivaldi sounded softly in the room, she became aware, out of the corner of one eye, of a sudden flurry, a flash of movement on the sofa to her right. She stopped playing at once. "What is it?" she said, turning to the cat. "What's the matter?"

The animal, who a few seconds before had been sleeping peacefully, was now sitting bolt upright on the sofa, very tense, the whole body aquiver, ears up and eyes wide open, staring at the piano.

"Did I frighten you?" she asked gently. "Perhaps you've never heard music before."

No, she told herself. I don't think that's what it is. On second thought, it seemed to her that the cat's attitude was not one of fear. There was no shrinking or backing away. If anything, there was a leaning forward, a kind of eagerness about the creature, and the face—well, there was a rather an odd expression on the face, something of a mixture between surprise and shock. Of course, the face of a cat is a small and fairly expressionless thing, but if you watch carefully the eyes and ears working together, and particularly that little area of mobile skin below the ears and slightly to one side, you can occasionally see the reflection of very powerful emotions. Louisa was watching the face closely now, and because she was curious to see what would happen a second time, she reached out her hands to the keyboard and began to play Vivaldi.

This time the cat was ready for it, and all that happened to begin with was a small extra tensing of the body. But as the music swelled and quickened into that first exciting rhythm of the introduction to the fugue, a strange look that amounted almost to ecstasy began to settle upon the creature's face. The ears, which up to then had been pricked up straight, were gradually drawn back, the eyelids drooped, the head went over to one side, and at that moment Louisa could have sworn that the animal was actually *appreciating* the work.

What she saw (or thought she saw) was something she had noticed many times on the faces of people listening very closely to a piece of music. When the sound takes complete hold of them and drowns them in itself, a peculiar, intensely ecstatic look comes over them that you can recognize as easily as a smile. So far as Louisa could see, the cat was now wearing almost exactly this kind of look.

Louisa finished the fugue, then played the siciliana, and all the way through she kept watching the cat on the sofa. The final proof for her that the animal was listening came at the end, when the music stopped. It blinked, stirred itself a little, stretched a leg, settled into a more comfortable position, took a quick glance round the room, then looked expectantly in her direction. It was precisely the way a concertgoer reacts when the music momentarily releases him in the pause between two movements of a symphony. The behavior was so thoroughly human it gave her a queer agitated feeling in the chest.

"You like that?" she asked. "You like Vivaldi?"

The moment she'd spoken, she felt ridiculous, but not—and this to her was a trifle sinister—not quite so ridiculous as she knew she should have felt.

Well, there was nothing for it now except to go straight ahead with the next number on the program, which was *Carnaval.* As soon as she began to play, the cat again stiffened and sat up straighter; then, as it became slowly and blissfully saturated with the sound, it relapsed into that queer melting mood of ecstasy that seemed to have something to do with drowning and with dreaming. It was really an extravagant sight—quite a comical one, too—to see this silvery cat sitting on the sofa and being carried away like this. And what made it more screwy than ever, Louisa thought, was the fact that this music, which the animal seemed to be enjoying so much, was manifestly too *difficult,* too *classical,* to be appreciated by the majority of humans in the world.

Maybe, she thought, the creature's not really enjoying it at all. Maybe it's a sort of hypnotic reaction, like with snakes. After all, if you can charm a snake with music, then why not a cat? Except that millions of cats hear the stuff every day of their lives, on radio and gramophone and piano, and, as far as she knew, there'd never yet been a case of one behaving like this. This one was acting as though it were following every single note. It was certainly a fantastic thing.

But was it not also a wonderful thing? Indeed it was. In fact, unless she was much mistaken, it was a kind of miracle, one of those animal miracles that happen about once every hundred years.

"I could see you *loved* that one," she said when the piece was over. "Although I'm sorry I didn't play it any too well today. Which did you like best—the Vivaldi or the Schumann?"

The cat made no reply, so Louisa, fearing she might lose the attention of her listener, went straight into the next part of the program—Liszt's second *Petrarch Sonnet.*

And now an extraordinary thing happened. She hadn't played more than three or four bars when the animal's whiskers began perceptibly to twitch. Slowly it drew itself up to an extra height, laid its head on one side, then on the other, and stared into space with a kind of frowning concentrated look that seemed to say, "What's this? Don't tell me. I know it so well, but just for the moment I don't seem to be able to place it." Louisa was fascinated, and with her little mouth half open and half smiling, she continued to play, waiting to see what on earth was going to happen next.

The cat stood up, walked to one end of the sofa, sat down again, listened some more; then all at once it bounded to the floor and leaped up onto the piano bench beside her. There it sat, listening intently to the lovely sonnet, not dreamily this time, but very erect, the large yellow eyes fixed upon Louisa's fingers.

"Well!" she said as she struck the last chord. "So you came up to sit beside me, did you? You like this better than the sofa? All right, I'll let you stay, but you must keep still and not jump about." She put out a hand and stroked the cat softly along the back, from head to tail. "That was Liszt," she went on. "Mind you, he can sometimes be quite horribly vulgar, but in things like this he's really charming."

She was beginning to enjoy this odd animal pantomime, so she went straight on into the next item on the program, Schumann's *Kinderscenen.*

She hadn't been playing for more than a minute or two when she realized that the cat had again moved, and was now back in its old place on the sofa. She'd been watching her hands at the time, and presumably that was why she hadn't even noticed its going; all the same, it must have been an extremely swift and silent move. The cat was still staring at her, still apparently attending closely to the music, and yet it seemed to Louisa that there was not now the same rapturous enthusiasm there'd been during the previous piece, the Liszt. In addition, the act of leaving the stool and returning to the sofa appeared in itself to be a mild but positive gesture of disappointment.

"What's the matter?" she asked when it was over, "What's wrong with Schumann? What's so marvelous about Liszt?" The cat looked straight back at her with those yellow eyes that had small jet-black bars lying vertically in their centers.

This, she told herself, is really beginning to get interesting—a trifle spooky, too, when she came to think of it. But one look at the cat sitting there on the sofa, so bright and attentive, so obviously waiting for more music, quickly reassured her.

"All right," she said. "I'll tell you what I'm going to do. I'm going to alter my program specially for you. You seem to like Liszt so much, I'll give you another."

She hesitated, searching her memory for a good Liszt; then softly she began to play one of the twelve little pieces from *Der Weihnachtsbaum*. She was now watching the cat very closely, and the first thing she noticed was that the whiskers again began to twitch. It jumped down to the carpet, stood still a moment, inclining its head, quivering with excitement, and then, with a slow, silky stride, it walked around the piano, hopped up on the bench, and sat down beside her.

They were in the middle of all this when Edward came in from the garden.

"Edward!" Louisa cried, jumping up. "Oh, Edward, darling! Listen to this! Listen what's happened!"

"What is it now?" he said. "I'd like some tea." He had one of those narrow, sharp-nosed, faintly magenta faces, and the sweat was making it shine as though it were a long wet grape.

"It's the cat!" Louisa cried, pointing to it sitting quietly on the piano bench. "Just *wait* till you hear what's happened!"

"I thought I told you to take it to the police."

"But, Edward, *listen* to me. This is *terribly* exciting. This is a *musical* cat."

"Oh, yes?"

"This cat can appreciate music, and it can understand it too."

"Now stop this nonsense, Louisa, and let's for God's sake have some tea. I'm hot and tired from cutting brambles and building bonfires." He sat down in an armchair, took a cigarette from a box beside him, and lit it with an immense patent lighter that stood near the box.

"What you don't understand," Louisa said, "is that something extremely exciting has been happening here in our own house

while you were out, something that may even be ... well ...
almost momentous."

"I'm quite sure of that."

"Edward, *please!*"

Louisa was standing by the piano, her little pink face pinker
than ever, a scarlet rose high up on each cheek. "If you want
to know," she said, "I'l tell you what I think."

"I'm listening, dear."

"I think it might be possible that we are at this moment
sitting in the presence of—" She stopped, as though suddenly
sensing the absurdity of the thought.

"Yes?"

"You may think it silly, Edward, but it's honestly what I
think."

"In the presence of whom, for heaven's sake?"

"Of Franz Liszt himself!"

Her husband took a long slow pull at his cigarette and blew
the smoke up at the ceiling. He had the tight-skinned, concave
cheeks of a man who has worn a full set of dentures for many
years, and every time he sucked at a cigarette, the cheeks went
in even more, and the bones of his face stood out like a skele-
ton's. "I don't get you," he said.

"Edward, listen to me. From what I've seen this afternoon
with my own eyes, it really looks as though this might actually
be some sort of reincarnation."

"You mean this lousy cat?"

"Don't talk like that, dear, please."

"You're not ill, are you, Louisa?"

"I'm perfectly all right, thank you very much. I'm a bit confused—I don't mind admitting it, but who wouldn't be after
what's happened? Edward, I swear to you—"

"What *did* happen, if I may ask?"

Louisa told him, and all the while she was speaking, her
husband lay sprawled in the chair with his legs stretched out in
front of him, sucking at his cigarette and blowing the smoke up
at the ceiling. There was a thin cynical smile on his mouth.

"I don't see anything very unusual about that," he said when
it was over. "All it is—it's a trick cat. It's been taught tricks,
that's all."

"Don't be so silly, Edward. Every time I play Liszt, he gets all excited and comes running over to sit on the stool beside me. But only for Liszt, and nobody can teach a cat the difference between Liszt and Schumann. You don't even know it yourself. But this one can do it every single time. Quite obscure Liszt, too."

"Twice," the husband said. "He's only done it twice."

"Twice is enough."

"Let's see him do it again. Come on."

"No," Louisa said. "Definitely not. Because if this *is* Liszt, as I believe it is, or anyway the soul of Liszt or whatever it is that comes back, then it's certainly not right or even very kind to put him through a lot of silly undignified tests."

"My dear woman! This is a *cat*—a rather stupid gray cat that nearly got its coat singed by the bonfire this morning in the garden. And anyway, what do you know about reincarnation?"

"If his soul is there, that's enough for me," Louisa said firmly. "That's all that counts."

"Come on then. Let's see him perform. Let's see him tell the difference between his own stuff and someone else's."

"No, Edward. I've told you before, I refuse to put him through any more silly circus tests. He's had quite enough of that for one day. But I'll tell you what I *will* do. I'll play him a little more of his own music."

"A fat lot that'll prove."

"You watch. And one thing is certain—as soon as he recognizes it, he'll refuse to budge off that bench where he's sitting now."

Louisa went to the music shelf, took down a book of Liszt, thumbed through it quickly, and chose another of his finer compositions—the B minor Sonata. She had meant to play only the first part of the work, but once she got started and saw how the cat was sitting there literally quivering with pleasure and watching her hands with that rapturous concentrated look, she didn't have the heart to stop. She played it all the way through. When it was finished, she glanced up at her husband and smiled. "There you are," she said. "You can't tell me he wasn't absolutely *loving* it."

"He just likes the noise, that's all."

"He was *loving* it. Weren't you, darling?" she said, lifting the cat in her arms. "Oh, my goodness, if only he could talk. Just

think of it, dear—he met Beethoven in his youth! He knew
Schubert and Mendelssohn and Schumann and Berlioz and
Grieg and Delacroix and Ingres and Heine and Balzac. And let
me see ... My heavens, he was Wagner's father-in-law! I'm
holding Wagner's father-in-law in my arms!"

"Louisa!" her husband said sharply, sitting up straight. "Pull
yourself together." There was a new edge to his voice now, and
he spoke louder.

Louisa glanced up quickly. "Edward, I do believe you're jealous!"

"Oh, sure, sure I'm jealous—of a lousy gray cat!"

"Then don't be so grumpy and cynical about it all. If you're
going to behave like this, the best thing you can do is to go back
to your gardening and leave the two of us together in peace.
That will be best for all of us, won't it, darling?" she said, addressing the cat, stroking its head. "And later on this evening,
we shall have some more music together, you and I, some more
of your own work. Oh, yes," she said, kissing the creature several times on the neck, "and we might have a little Chopin, too.
You needn't tell me—I happen to know you adore Chopin. You
used to be great friends with him, didn't you, darling? As a
matter of fact—if I remember rightly—it was in Chopin's apartment that you met the great love of your life, Madame Something-or-Other. Had three illegimate children by her, too,
didn't you? Yes, you did, you naughty thing, and don't go trying
to deny it. So you shall have some Chopin," she said, kissing the
cat again, "and that'll probably bring back all sorts of lovely
memories to you, won't it?"

"Louisa, stop this at once!"

"Oh, don't be so stuffy, Edward."

"You're behaving like a perfect idiot, woman. And anyway,
you forget we're going out this evening, to Bill and Betty's for
canasta."

"Oh, but I couldn't *possibly* go out now. There's no question
of that."

Edward got up slowly from his chair, then bent down and
stubbed his cigarette hard into the ashtray. "Tell me something," he said quietly. "You don't really believe this—this
twaddle you're talking, do you?"

"But of *course* I do. I don't think there's any question about it now. And, what's more, I consider that it puts a tremendous responsibility upon us, Edward—upon both of us. You as well."

"You know what I think," he said. "I think you ought to see a doctor. And damn quick, too."

With that, he turned and stalked out of the room, through the French windows, back into the garden.

Louisa watched him striding across the lawn toward his bonfire and his brambles, and she waited until he was out of sight before she turned and ran to the front door, still carrying the cat.

Soon she was in the car, driving to town.

She parked in front of the library, locked the cat in the car, hurried up the steps into the building, and headed straight for the reference room. There she began searching the cards for books on two subjects—REINCARNATION and LISZT.

Under REINCARNATION she found something Called *Recurring Earth-Lives—How and Why,* by a man called F. Milton Willis, published in 1921. Under LISZT she found two biographical volumes. She took out all three books, returned to the car, and drove home.

Back in the house, she placed the cat on the sofa, sat herself down beside it with her three books, and prepared to do some serious reading. She would begin, she decided, with Mr. F. Milton Willis's work. The volume was thin and a trifle soiled, but it had a good heavy feel to it, and the author's name had an authoritative ring.

The doctrine of reincarnation, she read, states that spiritual souls pass from higher to higher forms of animals. "A man can, for instance, no more be reborn as an animal than an adult can re-become a child."

She read this again. But how did he know? How could he be so sure? He couldn't. No one could possibly be certain about a thing like that. At the same time, the statement took a great deal of the wind out of her sails.

"Around the center of consciousness of each of us, there are, besides the dense outer body, four other bodies, invisible to the eye of flesh, but perfectly visible to people whose faculties of perception of superphysical things have undergone the requisite development. . . ."

She didn't understand that one at all, but she read on, and —

soon she came to an interesting passage that told how long a soul usually stayed away from the earth before returning in someone else's body. The time varied according to type, and Mr. Willis gave the following breakdown:

Drunkards and the unemployable	40/50	years
Unskilled laborers	60/100	"
Skilled workers	100/200	"
The bourgeoisie	200/300	"
The upper-middle classes	500	"
The highest class of gentleman		
farmers	600/1000	"
Those in the Path of Initiation	1500/2000	"

Quickly she referred to one of the other books, to find out how long Liszt had been dead. It said he died in Bayreuth in 1886. That was sixty-seven years ago. Therefore, according to Mr. Willis, he'd have to have been an unskilled laborer to come back so soon. That didn't seem to fit at all. On the other hand, she didn't think much of the author's methods of grading. According to him, "the highest class of gentleman farmer" was just about the most superior being on the earth. Red jackets and stirrup cups and the bloody, sadistic murder of the fox. No, she thought, that isn't right. It was a pleasure to find herself beginning to doubt Mr. Willis.

Later in the book, she came upon a list of some of the more famous reincarnations. Epictetus, she was told, returned to earth as Ralph Waldo Emerson. Cicero came back as Gladstone, Alfred the Great as Queen Victoria, William the Conqueror as Lord Kitchener. Ashoka Vardhana, King of India in 272 B.C., came back as Colonel Henry Steel Olcott, an esteemed American lawyer. Pythagoras returned as Master Koot Hoomi, the gentleman who founded the Theosophical Society with Mme Blavatsky and Colonel H. S. Olcott (the esteemed American lawyer, alias Ashoka Vardhana, King of India). It didn't say who Mme Blavatsky had been. But "Theodore Roosevelt," it said, "has for numbers of incarnations played great parts as a leader of men. . . . From him descended the royal line of ancient Chaldea, he having been, about 30,000 B.C., appointed Governor of Chaldea by the Ego we know as Caesar who was then ruler of

Persia. . . . Roosevelt and Caesar have been together time after time as military and administrative leaders; at one time, thousands of years ago, they were husband and wife. . . ."

That was enough for Louisa. Mr. F. Milton Willis was clearly nothing but a guesser. She was not impressed by his dogmatic assertions. The fellow was probably on the right track, but his pronouncements were extravagant, especially the first one of all, about animals. Soon she hoped to be able to confound the whole Theosophical Society with her proof that man could indeed reappear as a lower animal. Also that he did not have to be an unskilled laborer to come back within a hundred years.

She now turned to one of the Liszt biographies, and she was glancing through it casually when her husband came in again from the garden.

"What are you doing now?" he asked.

"Oh—just checking up a little here and there. Listen, my dear, did you know that Theodore Roosevelt once was Caesar's wife?"

"Louisa," he said, "look—why don't we stop this nonsense? I don't like to see you making a fool of yourself like this. Just give me that goddamn cat and I'll take it to the police station myself."

Louisa didn't seem to hear him. She was staring openmouthed at a picture of Liszt in the book that lay on her lap. "My God!" she cried. "Edward, look!"

"What?"

"Look! The warts on his face! I forgot all about them! He had these great warts on his face and it was a famous thing. Even his students used to cultivate little tufts of hair on their own faces in the same spots, just to be like him."

"What's that got to do with it?"

"Nothing. I mean not the students. But the warts have."

"Oh, Christ," the man said. "Oh, Christ God Almighty."

"The cat has them, too! Look, I'll show you."

She took the animal onto her lap and began examining its face. "There! There's one! And there's another! Wait a minute! I do believe they're in the same places! Where's that picture?"

It was a famous portrait of the musician in his old age, showing the fine powerful face framed in a mass of long gray hair that covered his ears and came halfway down his neck. On the face itself, each large wart had been faithfully reproduced, and there were five of them in all.

"Now, in the picture there's *one* above the right eyebrow." She looked above the right eyebrow of the cat. "Yes! It's there! In exactly the same place! And another on the left, at the top of the nose. That one's there, too! And one just below it on the cheek. And two fairly close together under the chin on the right side. Edward! Edward! Come and look! They're exactly the same."

"It doesn't prove a thing."

She looked up at her husband who was standing in the center of the room in his green sweater and khaki slacks, still perspiring freely. "You're scared, aren't you, Edward? Scared of losing your precious dignity and having people think you might be making a fool of yourself just for once."

"I refuse to get hysterical about it, that's all."

Louisa turned back to the book and began reading some more. "This is interesting," she said. "It says here that Liszt loved all of Chopin's works except one—the Scherzo in B flat minor. Apparently he hated that. He called it the 'Governess Scherzo,' and said that it ought to be reserved solely for people in that profession."

"So what?"

"Edward, listen. As you insist on being so horrid about all this, I'll tell you what I'm going to do. I'm going to play this Scherzo right now and you can stay here and see what happens."

"And then maybe you will deign to get us some supper."

Louisa got up and took from the shelf a large green volume containing all of Chopin's works. "Here it is. Oh yes, I remember it. It *is* rather awful. Now, listen—or, rather, watch. Watch to see what he does."

She placed the music on the piano and sat down. Her husband remained standing. He had his hands in his pockets and a cigarette in his mouth, and in spite of himself he was watching the cat, which was now dozing on the sofa. When Louisa began to play, the first effect was as dramatic as ever. The animal jumped up as though it had been stung, and it stood motionless for at least a minute, the ears pricked up, the whole body quivering. Then it became restless and began to walk back and forth along the length of the sofa. Finally, it hopped down onto the floor, and with its nose and tail held high in the air, it marched slowly, majestically, from the room.

"There!" Louisa cried, jumping up and running after it. "That does it! That really proves it!" She came back carrying the cat which she put down again on the sofa. Her whole face was shining with excitement now, her fists were clenched white, and the little bun on top of her head was loosening and going over to one side. "What about it, Edward? What d'you think?" She was laughing nervously as she spoke.

"I must say it was quite amusing."

"*Amusing!* My dear Edward, it's the most wonderful thing that's ever happened! Oh, goodness me!" she cried, picking up the cat again and hugging it to her bosom. "Isn't it marvelous to think we've got Franz Liszt staying in the house?"

"Now, Louisa. Don't let's get hysterical."

"I can't help it, I simply can't. And to *imagine* that he's actually going to live with us for always!"

"I beg your pardon?"

"Oh, Edward! I can hardly talk from excitement. And d'you know what I'm going to do next? Every musician in the whole world is going to want to meet him, that's a fact, and ask him about the people he knew—about Beethoven and Chopin and Schubert—"

"He can't talk," her husband said.

"Well—all right. But they're going to want to meet him anyway, just to see him and touch him and to play their own music to him, modern music he's never heard before."

"He wasn't that great. Now, if it had been Bach or Beethoven ..."

"Don't interrupt, Edward, please. So what I'm going to do is to notify all the important living composers everywhere. It's my duty. I'll tell them Liszt is here, and invite them to visit him. And you know what? They'll come flying in from every corner of the earth!"

"To see a gray cat?"

"Darling, it's the same thing. It's *him*. No one cares what he *looks* like. Oh, Edward, it'll be the most exciting thing there ever was!"

"They'll think you're mad."

"You wait and see." She was holding the cat in her arms and

petting it tenderly but looking across at her husband, who now walked over to the French windows and stood there staring out into the garden. The evening was beginning, and the lawn was turning slowly from green to black, and in the distance he could see the smoke from his bonfire rising straight up in a white column.

"No," he said, without turning round, "I'm not having it. Not in this house. It'll make us both look perfect fools."

"Edward, what do you mean?"

"Just what I say. I absolutely refuse to have you stirring up a lot of publicity about a foolish thing like this. You happen to have found a trick cat. O.K.—that's fine. Keep it, if it pleases you. I don't mind. But I don't wish you to go any further than that. Do you understand me, Louisa?"

"Further than what?"

"I don't want to hear any more of this crazy talk. You're acting like a lunatic."

Louisa put the cat slowly down on the sofa. Then slowly she raised herself to her full small height and took one pace forward. "*Damn* you, Edward!" she shouted, stamping her foot. "For the first time in our lives something really exciting comes along and you're scared to death of having anything to do with it because someone may laugh at you! That's right, isn't it? You can't deny it, can you?"

"Louisa," her husband said. "That's quite enough of that. Pull yourself together now and stop this at once." He walked over and took a cigarette from the box on the table, then lit it with the enormous patent lighter. His wife stood watching him, and now the tears were beginning to trickle out of the inside corners of her eyes, making two little shiny rivers where they ran through the powder on her cheeks.

"We've been having too many of these scenes just lately, Louisa," he was saying. "No, no, don't interrupt. Listen to me. I make full allowance for the fact that this may be an awkward time of life for you, and that—"

"Oh, my God! You idiot! You pompous idiot! Can't you see that this is different, this is—this is something miraculous? Can't you see *that?*"

At that point, he came across the room and took her firmly by the shoulders. He had the freshly lit cigarette between his lips, and she could see faint contours on his skin where the heavy perspiration had dried in patches. "Listen," he said. "I'm hungry. I've given up my golf and I've been working all day in the garden, and I'm tired and hungry and I want some supper. So do you. Off you go now to the kitchen and get us both something good to eat."

Louisa stepped back and put both hands to her mouth. "My heavens!" she cried. "I forgot all about it. He must be absolutely famished. Except for some milk, I haven't given him a thing to eat since he arrived."

"Who?"

"Why, *him*, of course. I must go at once and cook something really special. I wish I knew what his favorite dishes used to be. What do you think he would like best, Edward?"

"*Goddamn* it, Louisa!"

"Now, Edward, please. I'm going to handle this *my* way just for once. You stay here," she said, bending down and touching the cat gently with her fingers. "I won't be long."

Louisa went into the kitchen and stood for a moment, wondering what special dish she might prepare. How about a soufflé? A nice cheese soufflé? Yes, that would be rather special. Of course, Edward didn't much care for them, but that couldn't be helped.

She was only a fair cook, and she couldn't be sure of always having a soufflé come out well, but she took extra trouble this time and waited a long while to make certain the oven had heated fully to the correct temperature. While the soufflé was baking and she was searching around for something to go with it, it occurred to her that Liszt had probably never in his life tasted either avocado pears or grapefruit, so she decided to give him both of them at once in a salad. It would be fun to watch his reaction. It really would.

When it was all ready, she put it on a tray and carried it into the living-room. At the exact moment she entered, she saw her husband coming in through the French windows from the garden.

"Here's his supper," she said, putting it on the table and turning toward the sofa. "Where is he?"

Her husband closed the garden door behind him and walked across the room to get himself a cigarette.

"Edward, where is he?"

"Who?"

"You know who."

"Ah, yes. Yes, that's right. Well—I'll tell you." He was bending forward to light the cigarette, and his hands were cupped around the enormous patent lighter. He glanced up and saw Louisa looking at him—at his shoes and the bottoms of his khaki slacks, which were damp from walking in long grass.

"I just went out to see how the bonfire was going," he said.

Her eyes traveled slowly upward and rested on his hands.

"It's still burning fine," he went on. "I think it'll keep going all night."

But the way she was staring made him uncomfortable.

"What is it?" he said, lowering the lighter. Then he looked down and noticed for the first time the long thin scratch that ran diagonally clear across the back of one hand, from the knuckle to the wrist.

"*Edward!*"

"Yes," he said, "I know. Those brambles are terrible. They tear you to pieces. Now, just a minute, Louisa. What's the matter?"

"*Edward!*"

"Oh, for God's sake, woman, sit down and keep calm. There's nothing to get worked up about. Louisa! Louisa, *sit down!*"

By the Scruff of the Soul

Dorothy Salisbury Davis

Most people, when they go down from the Ragapoo Hills, never come back; or if they do, for a funeral maybe—weddings don't count for so much around here any more either—you can see them fidgeting to get away again. As for me, I'm one of those rare birds they didn't have any trouble keeping down on the farm after he'd seen Paree.

It's forty years since I've seen the bright lights, but I don't figure I've missed an awful lot. Hell, I can remember the Ku Klux Klan marching right out in the open. My first case had to do with a revenue agent—I won it, too, and we haven't had a government man up here since. And take the League of Nations—I felt awful sorry in those days for Mr. Wilson though I didn't hold with his ideas.

Maybe things have changed, but sometimes I wonder just how much. This bomb I don't understand, fallout and all, but I've seen what a plague of locusts can do to a wheat field and I don't think man's ever going to beat nature when it comes to pure, ornery destruction. I could be wrong about that. Our new parson says I am and he's a mighty knowing man. Too knowing, maybe. I figure that's why the Synod shipped him up to us in Webbtown.

As I said, I don't figure I'm missing much. There's a couple of television sets in town and sometimes of an evening I'll sit for an hour or so in front of whichever one of them's working best. One of them gets the shimmies every time the wind blows and the other don't bring in anything except by way of Canada. Same shows but different commercials. That kind of tickles me, all them companies advertising stuff you couldn't buy if you wanted to instead of stuff you wouldn't want if you could buy it.

But, as you've probably guessed by now, I'd rather talk than most anything, and since you asked about The Red Lantern, I'll tell you about the McCracken sisters who used to run it—and poor Old Matt Sawyer.

I'm a lawyer, by the way. I don't get much practice up here. I'm also Justice of the Peace. I don't get much practice out of that either, but between the two I make a living. For pleasure I fish for trout and play the violin, and at this point in my life I think I can say from experience that practice ain't everything.

I did the fiddling at Clara McCracken's christening party, I remember, just after coming home from the first World War. Maudie was about my age then, so's that'd make a difference of maybe twenty years between the sisters, and neither chit nor chizzler in between, and after them, the whole family suddenly dies out. That's how it happens up here in the hills: one generation and there'll be aunts and uncles galore, and the next, you got two maiden ladies and a bobtailed cat.

The Red Lantern Inn's boarded up now, as you saw, but it was in the McCracken family since just after the American Revolution. It was burned down once—in a reprisal raid during the War of 1812, and two of the McCrackens were taken hostage. Did you know Washington, D.C. was also burned in reprisal? It was. At least that's how they tell it over in Canada—for the way our boys tore up the town they call Toronto now. You know, history's like a story in a way: it depends on who's telling it.

Anyways, Maudie ran the inn after the old folks died, and she raised Clara the best she could, but Clara was a wild one from the start. We used to call her a changeling: one minute she'd be sitting at the stove and the next she'd be off somewhere in the hills. She wasn't a pretty girl—the jutting McCracken jaw spoiled that—but there were times she was mighty feminine, and many a lad got thorny feet chasing after the will-o'-the-wisp.

As Clara was coming to age, Maudie used to keep a birch stick behind the bar, and now and then I dare say she'd use it, though I never saw it happen but once myself. But that birch stick and Old Faithful, her father's shotgun, stood in the corner side by side, and I guess we made some pretty rude jokes about them in those days. Anyways, Maudie swore to tame the girl and marry her to what she called a "settled" man.

By the time Clara was of a marrying age, The Red Lantern was getting pretty well rundown. And so was Maudie. She wasn't an easy woman by any calculation. She had a tongue you'd think was sharpened on the grindstone and a store of sayings that'd shock you if you didn't know your Bible. The inn was peeling paint and wanting shutters to the northeast, which is where they're needed most. But inside, Maudie kept the rooms as clean and plain as a glass egg. And most times they were about as empty.

It was the taproom kept the sisters going. They drew the best beer this side of Cornwall, England. If they knew you, that is. If they didn't know you, they served you a labeled bottle, stuff you'd recognize by the signboard pictures. About once a month, Maudie had to buy a case of that—which gives you an idea how many strangers stopped over in Webbtown. We had more stores then and the flour mill was working, so the farmers'd come in regular. But none of them were strangers. You see, even to go to Ragapoo City, the county seat, you've got to go twenty miles around—unless you're like Clara was, skipping over the mountain.

Matt Sawyer came through every week or two in those days and he always stopped at Prouty's Hardware Store. Matt was a paint salesman. I suppose he sold Prouty a few gallons over the years. Who bought it from Prouty, I couldn't say. But Prouty liked Matt. I did myself when I got to know him. Or maybe I just felt sorry for him.

It was during the spring storms, this particular day. The rain was popping blisters on Main Street. Most everyone in Webbtown seems to have been inside looking out that day. Half the town claimed afterwards to have seen Matt come out of Prouty's raising his black umbrella over Maudie's head and walking her home. I saw them myself, Maudie pulling herself in and Matt half in and half out. I know for a fact she'd never been under an umbrella before in her life.

Prouty told me afterwards he'd forgot she was in the store when he was talking to Matt: Maudie took a mighty long time making up her mind before buying anything. Like he always did, Prouty was joshing Matt about having enough money to find himself a nice little woman and give up the road. Maudie wasn't backward. She took a direct line: she just up and asked Matt since he had an umbrella, would he mind walking her home. Matt was more of a gentleman than anybody I ever knew. He said it would be a pleasure. Maybe it was, but that was the beginning of the doggonedest three-cornered courtship in the county history. And it's all documented today in the county court records over in Ragapoo City. But I'm getting ahead of myself.

I've got my office in my hat, you might say, and I hang that in rooms over Kincaid's Drug Store. I was standing at the window when Matt and Maudie came out of Prouty's. I remember I was trying to tune my violin. You can't keep a fiddle in tune weather like that. I played kind of ex tempore for a while, drifting from one thing to another—sad songs mostly, like "The Vacant Chair." *We shall meet but we shall miss him . . . there will be one vacant chair.* I got myself so depressed I hung up the fiddle and went down to The Red Lantern for a glass of Maudie's Own.

Well, sure enough, there was Matt Sawyer sitting at the bar advising Maudie on the costs of paint and trimming and how to estimate the amount of paint a place the size of The Red Lantern would need. Now I knew Maudie couldn't afford whitewash much less the high-class line of stuff Matt represented. But there she was, leaning on the bar, hand in chin and her rump in the air like a swaybacked mule. She drew me a beer and put a head on Matt's. Then she went back to listening to him.

I don't know how long it took me to notice what was really going on: I'm slow sometimes, but all this while Clara was standing on a stool polishing a row of fancy mugs Maudie kept on a ledge over the back mirror. The whole row of lights was on under the ledge and shining double in the mirror. Hell, Matt Sawyer wasn't actually making sense at all, what he was saying in facts and figures. He was just making up words to keep old Maudie distracted—he thought—and all the while him gazing up at Clara every chance he'd get. I might as well be honest with you: it was looking at Clara myself I realized what was going on in that room. The way she was reaching up and down in front of that mirror and with a silk petticoat kind of dress on, you'd have sworn she was stark naked.

Well, sir, just think about that. Matt, being a gentleman, was blushing and yearning—I guess you'd call it that—but making conversation all the time; and Maudie was conniving a match for Clara with a man who could talk a thousand dollars' worth of paint without jumping his Adam's apple. I'll say this about Maudie: for an unmarried lady she was mighty knowing in the fundamentals. Clara was the only innocent one in the room, I got to thinking.

All of a sudden Maudie says to me, "Hand, how's your fiddle these days?"

"It's got four strings," I said.

"You bring it up after supper, hear?" It was Maudie's way never to ask for something. She told you what you were going to do and most often you did it. Clara looked round at me from that perch of hers and clapped her hands.

Maudie laid a bony finger on Matt's hand. "You'll stay to supper with us, Mr. Sawyer. Our Clara's got a leg of lamb in the oven like you never tasted. It's home hung and roasted with garden herbs."

Now I knew for a fact the only thing Clara ever put in the oven was maybe a pair of shoes to warm them of a winter's morning. And it was just about then Clara caught on, too, to what Maudie was maneuvering. Her eyes got a real wild look in them, like a fox cornered in a chicken coop. She bounded down and across that room . . .

I've often wondered what would've happened if I hadn't spoken then. It gives me a cold chill thinking about it—words said with the best intentions in the world. I called out just as she got to the door: "Clara, I'll be bringing up my fiddle."

I don't suppose there ever was a party in Webbtown like Maudie put on that night. Word got around. Even the young folks came that mightn't have if it was spooning weather. Maudie wore her best dress—the one she was saving, we used to say, for Clara's wedding and her own funeral. It was black, but on happier occasions she'd liven it up with a piece of red silk at the collar. I remember Prouty saying once that patch of red turned Maudie from a Holstein into a Guernsey. Prouty, by the way, runs the undertaking parlor as well as the hardware store.

I near split my fingers that night fiddling. Maudie tapped a special keg. Everybody paid for his first glass, but after that she put the cash box away and you might say she drew by heart.

Matt was having a grand time just watching mostly. Matt was one of those creamy-looking fellows, with cheeks as pink as winter apples. He must've been fifty but there wasn't a line or wrinkle in his face. And I never seen him without his collar and tie on. Like I said, a gentleman.

Clara took to music like a bird to wing. I always got the feeling no matter who was taking her in or out she was actually dancing alone; she could do two steps to everybody else's one. Matt never took his eyes off her, and once he danced with her when Maudie pushed him into it.

That was trouble's start—although we didn't know it at the time. Prouty said afterwards he did, but Prouty's a man who knows everything after the fact. That's being an undertaker, I dare say. Anyway, Matt was hesitating after Clara—and it was like that, her sort of skipping ahead and leading him on, when all of a sudden, young Reuben White leaped in between them and danced with Clara the way she needed to be danced with.

Now Reuben didn't have much to recommend him, especially to Maudie. He did an odd job now and then—in fact, he hauled water for Maudie from the well she had up by the brewhouse back of Maple Tree Ridge. And this you ought to know about Maudie if you don't by now—anybody she could boss around, she had no use for.

Anyways, watching that boy dance with Clara that night should've set us all to thinking, him whirling her and tossing her up in the air, them spinning round together like an August twister. My fiddle's got a devil in it at a time like that. Faster and faster I was bowing, till plunk I broke a string, but I went right on playing.

Matt fell back with the other folks, clapping and cheering, but Maudie I could see going after her stick. I bowed even faster, seeing her. It was like a race we were all in together. Then all of a sudden, like something dying high up in the sky and falling mute, my E string broke and I wasn't playing any more. In the center of the tavern floor Clara and Reuben just folded up together and slumped down into a heap.

Everybody was real still for about a half a minute. Then Maudie came charging out, slashing the air with that switch of hers. She grabbed Clara by the hair—I swear she lifted the girl to her feet that way and flung her towards the bar. Then she turned on Reuben. That boy slithered clear across the barroom floor, every time just getting out of the way of a slash from Maudie's stick. People by then were cheering in a kind of rhythm—for him or Maudie, you couldn't just be sure, and maybe they weren't for either. "Now!" they'd shout at every whistle of the switch. "Now! Now! *Now!*"

Prouty opened the door just when Reuben got there, and when the boy was out Prouty closed it against Maudie. I thought for a minute she was going to turn on him. But she just stood looking and then burst out laughing. Everybody started clouting her on the back and having a hell of a time.

I was at the bar by then and so was Matt. I heard him, leaning close to Clara, say, "Miss Clara, I never saw anything as beautiful as you in all my life."

Clara's eyes snapped back at him but she didn't say a word.

Well, it was noon the next day before Matt pulled out of town, and sure enough, he forgot his umbrella and came back that night. I went up to The Red Lantern for my five o'clock usual, and him and Maudie were tête à tête, as they say, across the bar. Maudie was spouting the praises of her Clara—how she could sew and cook and bake a cherry pie, Billy Boy. The only attention she paid me was as a collaborating witness.

I'll say this for Clara: when she did appear, she looked almost civilized, her hair in a ribbon, and her wearing a new striped skirt and a grandmother blouse clear up to her chin. That night, by glory, she went to the movie with Matt. We had movies every night except Sundays in those days. A year or so ago, they closed up the Bellevue altogether. Why did she go with him? My guess is she wanted to get away from Maudie, or maybe for Reuben to see her dressed up that way.

The next time I saw all of them together was Decoration Day. Matt was back in town, arranging his route so's he'd have to stop

over the holiday in Webbtown. One of them carnival outfits had
set up on the grounds back of the schoolhouse. Like I said
before, we don't have any population to speak of in Webbtown,
but we're central for the whole valley, and in the old days
traveling entertainers could do all right if they didn't come too
often.

There was all sorts of raffle booths—Indian blankets and kew-
pie dolls, a shooting gallery and one of those things where you
throw baseballs at wooden bottles and get a cane if you knock
'em off. And there was an apparatus for testing a man's muscle:
you know, you hit the target on the stand with a sledgehammer
and then a little ball runs up a track that looks like a big ther-
mometer and registers your strength in pounds.

I knew there was a trick to it no matter what the barker said
about it being fair and square. Besides, nobody cares how strong
a lawyer is as long as he can whisper in the judge's ear. I could
see old Maudie itching herself to have a swing at it, but she
wasn't taking any chance or giving Matt the wrong impression
about either of the McCracken girls.

Matt took off his coat, folded it, and gave it to Clara to hold.
It was a warm day for that time of year and you could see where
Matt had been sweating under the coat, but like I said, he was
all gentleman. He even turned his back to the ladies before
spitting on his hands. It took Matt three swings—twenty-five
cents worth—but on the last one that little ball crawled the last
few inches up the track and just sort of tinkled the bell at the
top. The womenfolk clapped, and Matt put on his coat again,
blushing and pleased with himself.

I suppose you've guessed that Reuben showed up then. He
did, wearing a cotton shirt open halfway down to his belly.

"Now, my boy," the barker says, "show the ladies, show the
world that you're a man! How many?"

Reuben sniggled a coin out of his watch pocket, and mighty
cocky for him, he said, "Keep the change."

Well, you've guessed the next part, too: Reuben took one
swing and you could hear that gong ring out clear across the
valley. It brought a lot of people running and the carnival man
was so pleased he took out a big cigar and gave it to Reuben.
"That, young fellow, wins you a fifty-cent Havana. But I'll send
you the bill if you broke the machine, ha! ha!"

Reuben grinned and took the cigar, and strutting across to Clara, he made her a present of it. Now in Matt's book, you didn't give a lady a cigar, no, sir. Not saying a word, Matt brought his fist up with everything he had dead to center under Reuben's chin. We were all of us plain stunned, but nobody more than Reuben. He lay on the ground with his eyes rolling round in his head like marbles.

You'd say that was the blow struck for romance, wouldn't you? Not if you knew our Clara. She plopped down beside Reuben like he was the dying gladiator, or maybe just something she'd come on helpless in the woods. It was Maudie who clucked and crowed over Matt. All of a sudden Clara leaped up —Reuben was coming round by then—and she gave a whisk of that fancy skirt and took off for the hills, Maudie bawling after her like a hogcaller. And at that point, Reuben scrambled to his feet and galloped after Clara. It wasn't long till all you could see of where they'd gone was a little whiff of dust at the edge of the dogwood grove. I picked up the cigar and tried to smoke it afterwards. I'd have been better off on a mixture of oak leaf and poison ivy.

Everything changed for the worse at The Red Lantern after that. Clara found her tongue and sassed her sister, giving Maudie back word for word, like a common scold. One was getting mean and the other meaner. And short of chaining her, Maudie couldn't keep Clara at home any more, not when Clara wanted to go.

Matt kept calling at The Red Lantern regularly, and Maudie kept making excuses for Clara's not being there. The only times I'd go to the inn in those days was when I'd see Matt's car outside. The place would brighten up then, Maudie putting on a show for him. Otherwise, I'd have as soon sat in Prouty's cool room. It was about as cheerful. Even Maudie's beer was turning sour.

Matt was a patient man if anything, and I guess being smitten for the first time at his age he got it worse than most of us would: he'd sit all evening just waiting a sight of that girl. When we saw he wasn't going to get over it, Prouty and I undertook one day in late summer to give him some advice. What made us think we were authorities, I don't know. I've been living with my fiddle for years and I've already told you what Prouty'd been living with. Anyways, we advised Matt to get himself some hunting clothes—the season was coming round—and to put away that doggone collar and tie of his and get out in the open country where the game was.

Matt tried. Next time he came to Webbtown, as soon as he put in at The Red Lantern, he changed into a plaid wool shirt, brand-new khaki britches, and boots laced up to his knees, and with Prouty and me cheering him on, he headed for the hills. But like Cox's army, or whoever it was, he marched up the hill and marched down again.

But he kept at it. Every weekend he'd show up, change, and set out, going farther and farther every time. One day, when the wind was coming sharp from the northeast, I heard him calling out up there: "Clara . . . Clara . . ."

I'll tell you, that gave me a cold chill, and I wished to the Almighty that Prouty and I had minded our own business. Maudie would stand at the tavern door and watch him off, and I wondered how long it was going to take for her to go with him. By then, I'd lost whatever feeling I ever had for Maudie and I didn't have much left for Clara either. But what made me plain sick one day was Maudie confiding in me that she was thinking of locking Clara in her room and giving Matt the key. I said something mighty close to obscene such as I'd never said to a woman before in my life and walked out of the tavern.

It was one of those October days, you know, when the clouds keep building up like suds and then just seem to wash away. You could hear the school bell echo, and way off the hawking of the wild geese, and you'd know the only sound of birds till spring would be the lonesome cawing of the crows. I was working on a couple of things I had coming up in Quarter Sessions Court when Prouty pounded up my stairs. Prouty's a pretty dignified man who seldom runs.

"Hank," he said, "I just seen Matt Sawyer going up the hill. He's carrying old man McCracken's shotgun."

I laughed kind of, seeing the picture in my mind. "What do you think he aims to do with it?"

"If he was to fire it, Hank, he'd be likely to blow himself to eternity."

"Maybe the poor buzzard'd be as well off," I said.

"And something else, Hank—Maudie just closed up the tavern. She's stalking him into the hills."

"That's something else," I said, and reached for my pipe.

"What are we going to do?" Prouty fumbled through his pockets for some matches for me. He couldn't keep his hands still.

"Nothing," I said. "The less people in them hills right now the better."

Prouty came to see it my way, but neither one of us could do much work that afternoon. I'd go to the window every few minutes and see Prouty standing in the doorway. He'd look down toward The Red Lantern and shake his head, and I'd know Maudie hadn't come back yet.

Funny, how things go on just the same in a town at a time like that. Tom Kincaid, the druggist, came out and swept the sidewalk clean, passed the time of day with Prouty, and went inside again. The kids were coming home from school. Pretty soon they were all indoors doing their homework before chore time. Doc Sissler stopped at Kincaid's—he liked to supervise the making up of his prescriptions. It was Miss Dorman, the schoolteacher, who gave the first alarm. She always did her next day's lessons before going home, so it was maybe an hour after school let out. I heard her scream and ran to the window.

There was Matt coming down the street on Prouty's side, trailing the gun behind him. You could see he was saying something to himself or just out loud. I opened my window and shouted down to him. He came on then across the street. His step on the stair was like the drum in a death march. When he got to my doorway he just stood there saying, "I killed her, Hank. I killed her dead."

I got him into a chair and splashed some whiskey out for him. He dropped the gun on the floor beside him and I let it lie there, stepping over it. By then Prouty had come upstairs, and by the time we got the whiskey inside Matt, Luke Weber, the constable, was there.

"He says he killed somebody," I told Weber. "I don't know who."

Matt rolled his eyes towards me like I'd betrayed him just saying what he told me. His face was hanging limp and white as a strung goose. "I know Matt Sawyer," I added then, "and if there was any killing, I'd swear before Jehovah it must've been an accident."

That put a little life back in him. "It was," he said, "it was truly." And bit by piece we got the story out of him.

"I got to say in fairness to myself, taking the gun up there wasn't my own idea," he started. "Look at me, duded up like this—I had no business from the start pretending I was something I wasn't."

"That was me and Hank's fault," Prouty said, mostly to the constable, "advising him on how to court Miss Clara."

He didn't have to explain that to Weber. Everybody in town knew it.

"I'm not blaming either one of you," Matt said. "It should've been enough for me, chasing an echo every time I thought I'd found her. And both of them once sitting up in a tree laughing at me fit to bust and pelting me with acorns . . ."

We knew he was talking about Reuben and Clara. It was pathetic listening to a man tell that kind of story on himself, and I couldn't help but think what kind of an impression it was going to make on a jury. I had to be realistic about it: there's some people up here would hang a man for making a fool of himself where they'd let him go for murder. I put the jury business straight out of my mind and kept hoping it was clear-cut accident. He hadn't said yet who was dead, but I thought I knew by then.

"Well, I found them for myself today," he made himself go on, "Clara and Reuben, that is. They were cosied in together in the sheepcote back of Maudie's well. It made me feel ashamed just being there and I was set to sneak away and give the whole thing up for good. But Maudie came up on me and took me by surprise. She held me there—by the scruff of the soul, you might say—and made me listen with her to them giggling and carrying on. I was plain sick with jealousy, I'll admit that.

"Then Maudie gave a shout: 'Come out, you two! Or else we'll blow you out!' Something like that.

"It was a minute or two: nothing happened. Then we saw Reuben going full speed the other way, off towards the woods.

" 'Shoot, Matt, now!' That's what Maudie shouted at me. 'You got him clear to sight.' But just then Clara sauntered out of the shelter towards us—just as innocent and sweet, like the first time I ever laid eyes on her."

I'm going to tell you, Prouty and me looked at each other when he said that.

The constable interrupted him and asked his question straight: "Did she have her clothes on?"

"All but her shoes. She was barefoot and I don't consider that unbecoming in a country girl."

"Go on," Weber told him.

Matt took a long drag of air and then plunged ahead. "Maudie kept hollering at the boy—insults, I guess—I know I'd have been insulted. Then he stopped running and turned around and started coming back. I forget what it was she said to me then —something about my manhood. But she kept saying, 'Shoot, Matt! Shoot, shoot!' I was getting desperate, her hounding me that way. I slammed the gun down between us, butt-end on the ground. The muzzle of it, I guess, was looking her way. And it went off.

"It was like the ground exploding underneath us. Hell smoke and brimstone—that's what went through my mind. I don't know whether it was in my imagination—my ears weren't hearing proper after all that noise—but like ringing in my head I could hear Clara laughing, just laughing like hysterics . . . And then when I could see, there was Maudie lying on the ground. I couldn't even find her face for all that was left of her head."

We stood all of us for a while after that. Listening to the tick of my alarm clock on the shelf over the washstand, I was. Weber picked up the gun then and took it over to the window where he examined the breech.

Then he said, "What did you think you were going to do with this when you took it from the tavern?"

Matt shook his head. "I don't know. When Maudie gave it to me, I thought it looked pretty good on me in the mirror."

I couldn't wait to hear the prosecutor try that one on the jury.

Weber said, "We better get on up there before dark and you show us how it happened."

We stopped by at Prouty's on the way and picked up his wicker basket. There wasn't any way of driving beyond the dogwood grove. People were following us by then. Weber sent them back to town and deputized two or three among them to be sure they kept the peace.

We hadn't got very far beyond the grove, the four us, just walking, climbing up, and saying nothing. Hearing the crows a-screaming not far ahead gave me a crawling stomach. They're scavengers, you know.

Well, sir, down the hill fair-to-flying, her hair streaming out in the wind, came Clara to meet us. She never hesitated, throwing herself straight at Matt. It was instinct made him put his arms out to catch her and she dove into them and flung her own arms around his neck, hugging him and holding him, and saying things like, "Darling Matt . . . wonderful Matt. I love Matt." I heard her say that.

You'd have thought to see Matt; he'd turned to stone. Weber was staring at them, a mighty puzzled look on his face.

"Miss Clara," I said, "behave yourself."

She looked at me—I swear she was smiling—and said, "You hush, old Hank, or we won't let you play the fiddle at our wedding."

It was Prouty said, hoisting his basket up on his shoulders, "Let's take one thing at a time."

That got us started on our way again, Clara skipping along at Matt's side, trying to catch his hand. Luke Weber didn't say a word.

I'm not going into the details now of what we saw. It was just about like Matt had told it in my office. I was sick a couple of times. I don't think Matt had anything left in him to be sick with. When it came to telling what had happened first, Clara was called on to corroborate. And Weber asked her, "Where's Reuben now, Miss Clara?"

"Gone," she said, "and I don't care."

"Didn't care much about your sister either, did you?" Weber drawled, and I began to see how really bad a spot old Matt was in. There was no accounting Clara's change of heart about him —except he'd killed her sister. The corroborating witness we needed right then was Reuben White.

Prouty got Weber's go-ahead on the job he had to do. I couldn't help him though I tried. What I did when he asked it, was go up to Maudie's well to draw him a pail of water so's he could wash his hands when he was done. Well, sir, I'd have been better off helping him direct. I couldn't get the bucket down to where it would draw the water.

After trying a couple of times, I called out to Weber asking if he had a flashlight. He brought it and threw the beam of light down into the well. Just above the water level a pair of size-twelve shoes were staring up at us—the soles of them like Orphan Annie's eyes.

There wasn't any doubt in our minds that what was holding them up like that was Reuben White, headfirst in the well.

The constable called Clara to him and took a short-cut in his questioning.

"How'd it happen, girl?"

"I guess I pushed him," Clara said, almost casual.

"It took a heap of pushing," Weber said.

"No, it didn't. I just got him to look down and then I tumbled him in."

"Why?"

"Matt," she said, and smiled like a Christmas cherub.

Matt groaned, and I did too inside.

"Leastways, it come to that," Clara explained. Then in that quick-changing way of hers, she turned deep serious. "Mr. Weber, you wouldn't believe me if I told you what Reuben White wanted me to do with him—in the sheepcote this afternoon."

"I might," Luke Weber said.

I looked at Prouty and drew my first half-easy breath. I could see he felt the same. We're both old-fashioned enough to take warmly to a girl's defending her virtue.

But Weber didn't bat an eye, "And where does Matt here come in on it?" he said.

"I figure he won't ever want me to do a thing like that," Clara said, and gazed up at old stoneface with a look of pure adoration.

"Where was Matt when you . . . tumbled Reuben in?" Weber asked, and I could tell he was well on his way to believing her.

"He'd gone down the hill to tell you what'd happened to Sister Maudie."

"And when was it Reuben made this—this proposal to you?" Weber said. I could see he was getting at the question of premeditation. Luke Weber's a pretty fair policeman.

"It was Matt proposed to me," Clara said. "That's why I'm going to marry him. Reuben just wanted ..."

Weber interrupted. "Why, if he wasn't molesting you just then, and if you'd decided to marry Matt Sawyer, why did you have to kill him? You must've known a well's no place for diving."

Clara shrugged her pretty shoulders. "By then I was feeling kind of sorry for him. He'd have been mighty lonesome after I went to live with Matt."

Well, there isn't much more to tell. We sort of disengaged Matt, you might say. His story of how Maudie died stood up with the coroner, Prouty and I vouching for the kind of man he was. I haven't seen him since.

Clara—she'll be getting out soon, coming home to the hills, and maybe opening up The Red Lantern again. I defended her at the trial, pleading temporary insanity. Nobody was willing to say she was insane exactly. We don't like saying such things about one another up here. But the jury agreed she was a temporary sort of woman. Twenty years to life, she got, with time off for good behavior.

You come around some time next spring. I'll introduce you.

Murder on
St. Valentine's Day

Mignon G. Eberhart

I looked at the lacy object on my desk. *"What is this?"*

The young assistant cashier replied, "It's a handkerchief. Possibly intended for the Valentine trade," he hazarded thoughtfully. "It's shaped like a heart."

"I can see that!"

The handkerchief was undoubtedly heart-shaped and outlined with lace. Written on it in bright red were words and numerals. I touched the writing cautiously.

The assistant cashier said, "It's not blood. It's lipstick."

"I'm not so old I don't know lipstick when I see it," I said stiffly.

"Yes, sir," he said hurriedly. "I mean, no, sir. Shall I tell them to cash it?"

I debated, seething with exasperation. For the thing was, incredibly, a check—and a check for $20,000. It was made out to one Ronald Murch and it was signed by Clarissa Hartridge, and Clarissa was one of my widows.

I hasten to say that I am, and, *Deo volente,* intend to remain, a bachelor. My name is James Wickwire. I am a senior vice president at the bank within whose sedate walls I have spent most of my life.

Clarissa was one of my widows only in the sense that her estate, along with that of sundry other widows, was in my care.

One way and another, my widows have caused me considerable mental anguish, due in the main to their recurrent impulses to invest money in nonexistent oil wells, or to finance expeditions for the discovery of buried pirate treasure.

Up to that day, however, Clarissa had given me very little anxiety. She had kept well within her income, never made mistakes in subtraction, and was an extremely charming and pretty woman.

Consequently I had felt deeply grateful to her, and enjoyed dining with her, and a Miss Gray who shared her house, once or twice a year in the comfortable certainty that Clarissa would not ask me to balance her checkbook.

But this fantastic check was not merely an illusion shattered for me. It represented a large share of Clarissa's capital. The walls of the bank did not in fact rock, but I myself was shaken to the core. It was all too clear that something had happened to Clarissa and it was quite as clear what that something was. For my widows do not invariably remain widows. Sometimes they follow the same remarkable quality of impulse in choosing second husbands that they do in choosing investments.

"You say this Ronald Murch is out there now?" I asked the assistant cashier.

"Yes, sir. Young. Dark. Handsome. Presented the check as cool as you please. They brought it to me and I thought you'd better see it."

"Of course." I tapped the lacy edge of the handkerchief. Young, dark, and handsome! Clarissa was fifty if she was a day, and if I'd had my fingers on her plump little neck just then I really think I'd have twisted it. Instead I told my secretary to get Mrs. Hartridge on the telephone and then, perceiving the inquisitive gleam in the assistant cashier's pale blue eyes, I told him he could go and I'd see to it. He looked frustrated but went away.

Clarissa came on the phone and began at once to speak. "James, I know why you're calling me," she said airily. "It's all right about the check. Cash it."

I daresay I uttered a rather strangled sound. She said coolly, "Have you got a cold, James?"

"No! What is the meaning . . ."

"I'm buying a formula for face cream."

"*Face*—Clarissa, this is capital!"

She laughed lightly. "Of course. I sold those Turnpike bonds."

A choking sensation gripped me. She said, "Oh, by the way, James. Can you return that check to me yourself? After you've cashed it, I mean. I don't want it to go through all that routine in the bank."

"I can understand that!" I said acidly, but she had hung up.

When I had got control of myself I sent for Mr. Ronald Murch, who was still waiting. He was, indeed, dark, young, and handsome with a charm which raked my already lacerated nerves. And to my intense surprise a young lady with a great many golden curls and a sallow but heavily made-up face was hanging fondly on his arm. He introduced her.

"This is Miss April Moon."

The young lady gave me a coquettish smile. "Soon to be Mrs. Ronald Murch," she said, and hugged his arm. "We just got the license."

I was rather taken aback, since I had believed Clarissa destined for this dubious honor. Ronald Murch nodded at the heart-shaped handkerchief with its red writing. "That does look rather silly, doesn't it?" he said.

"May I ask why it is written in this remarkable way?"

For an instant something puzzled flashed in his dark eyes. "It was a whim of Clarissa's—I mean Mrs. Hartridge's. Just an impulse. She said it was suitable—lipstick, cosmetics. You see?"

"I can't say that I do," I replied shortly.

Miss April Moon giggled. "What does it matter how the old girl wanted to write it! It's legal. He gets the cash. She gets her formula. We get married."

He drew a folded paper from an inner pocket and waved it at me. "This is my new formula for face cream."

I reached automatically for the paper but he returned it quickly to his pocket. "Sorry," he said, "but it's a secret. I developed it myself. Believe me, it's an oil well."

The words struck a sensitive nerve within me. I said icily, "Does Mrs Hartridge know of your approaching marriage?"

Miss Moon giggled. Mr. Murch assumed a businesslike air.

"That has nothing to do with you, Mr. Wickwire. If you have any doubt about this check kindly phone Mrs. Hartridge."

So I was obliged to give directions to the effect that the absurd check was to be cashed. I also saw to it that the handkerchief itself was given to me. I placed it in my desk, and there was nothing further that I could do. Clarissa's instructions had been definite. I had already exceeded such small authority as I had. And Clarissa was in love. I know little of women, but I know when I'm licked.

Scarcely an hour later Clarissa telephoned me. "James," she said, "he's dead! Ronald Murch. He's been shot. Right in my library. The police are here. They say he's been murdered. Please come!"

Clarissa's neat if unpretentious little house in the East Nineties was surrounded by policemen. Once inside the living room, a police lieutenant fell upon me, questioned me exhaustively, then told me the circumstances of the murder.

"He's in there," he said, nodding toward the tiny library which adjoined the living room. The door was open; a cluster of men, some in uniform and some in plain-clothes, moved apart a little and I could see feet in highly polished black oxfords, at an odd angle on the rug. I could not see the rest of the body.

"Shot twice," the lieutenant said. "One got him through the heart. Mrs. Hartridge claims she heard the shots and thought it was a backfire from the street. After a time she came downstairs. Saw the guy in there, on the rug. Dead as a duck. Says she phoned to the police right away. She was alone in the house."

There were no servants in the household, but there was Miss Gray. I said, "There's a Miss Gray who lived with Mrs. Hartridge—"

The lieutenant interrupted. "She's gone shopping. She hasn't come back yet."

"Did you find the murder gun?" I asked.

He nodded solemnly. "That's the clincher. The gun belonged to Mrs. Hartridge. She says it was her husband's. Kept in a drawer of the table in the hall. Says she hasn't touched it, knows nothing of it. There were no fingerprints. Probably she wore gloves."

"Do you mean to say you suspect Mrs. Hartridge?"

"Who else?" he said, and rose as if to end the interview.

"Wait," I said hurriedly. "She had no motive, no reason—"

He gave me a cold and skeptical look. "Listen. The guy had twenty thousand dollars in his pocket. Mrs. Hartridge admits that she gave him a check for the cash this morning. He had a key to this house in his pocket—a key to *this* house. She's an elderly widow with money. *And* he had another girl!" He eyed me triumphantly. "There was a marriage license in his pocket. What does it look like to you?"

It looked extremely serious, and I swallowed hard. "What about the girl?"

"*She* didn't kill him. We traced her right away. She's at a beauty shop getting her hair curled and she's been there for an hour. I've sent a squad car for her."

I could not comprehend Miss Moon's unbridled desire for still more curls, but I did comprehend the solid nature of her alibi. I said, "Didn't Mrs. Hartridge tell you that she gave him the twenty thousand dollars for the purchase of a face cream formula?"

He laughed shortly. "Oh, sure. She also admitted that she'd picked him up on the street! Didn't know anything about his background! Claims she didn't know he was going to be married! Probably that's not the first money she's given him. By the way—you say you're her banker—we'll have to take a look through her canceled checks."

And I'd be obliged to give them a check written in lipstick on a heart-shaped handkerchief. It seemed wiser to tell him of it at once, give him Murch's own explanation for it, and—if possible—thus minimize its disastrous effect. So, very carefully, I related the whole incident.

But the lieutenant was again triumphant. He smacked Clarissa's little Pembroke table with a fist which nearly broke it. "That proves it! She was in love with the guy. You're a banker. Did you ever get a check written like that before?"

I was obliged to confess I hadn't. "It was an impulse," I told him again. "Lipstick—cosmetic business—there's a connection. He said he had the face cream formula. It was in his pocket."

He shook his head. "He was lying to you. So was she because she knew you'd question that check. She wouldn't have wanted you to know her real reason for giving him that money. There's no formula. I went through his pockets myself." He looked at the door as another policeman entered. "What is it, Jake?"

It was Clarissa's friend and housemate, Miss Gray, returned from her shopping trip and horrified. They ushered her into the room and let me remain while they questioned her.

Naturally I listened with some interest. I knew Miss Gray, of course. She was a pleasant, rather plain young woman, although she looked handsomer than usual that morning for the light from the window fell directly upon her, revealing a dazzling complexion which seemed to make her dark eyes glow. She wore a neat gray suit and hat and clutched a black handbag.

She knew Mr. Murch, of course, she told the lieutenant; he had been a frequent guest of Clarissa's. She had gone shopping that morning. When asked if she had talked to anyone who could identify her, she grasped the intent of the question at once, with a flash of her dark eyes. But she said that she doubted it very much. She had made only one purchase, stockings, and that was not a charge; she had paid cash. The box of stockings was on the table in the hall. Most of the morning she had simply strolled, window shopping.

The lieutenant pounced: "Mrs. Hartridge was very fond of Ronald Murch, wasn't she? In fact, there was quite a romance going on there. Tell us the truth, Miss Gray."

She rose angrily, her eyes blazing. "That is outrageous! How dare you suggest such a thing!"

"Suppose I say that we have proof of it. Suppose I say that Mrs. Hartridge quarreled with him over a girl and shot him?"

"Then I'd say you don't know what you're talking about! There was nothing like that between them—nothing! I'll swear to it in court if it comes to that."

I interposed. "A formula for face cream seems to have disappeared, Miss Gray. Do you mind if the lieutenant—er—searches your handbag?"

She lifted her eyebrows but gave her handbag to the lieutenant, who searched it rapidly, returned it to her, and said to me, "I tell you there's no such formula, Mr. Wickwire. See here, you go and talk to Mrs. Hartridge. Get her to confess. It'll save trouble all the way around. Jake—" The policeman stepped forward. "Take him to her."

I followed Jake's broad blue back up the little stairway to Clarissa's room. Another policeman, at a word from Jake, permitted me to enter it, and Clarissa came quickly to me. "James! I believe they think I shot him!"

She was very pretty, with blue eyes, brown hair, and an astonishing complexion—so lovely, indeed, and so much more youthful than I remembered it, that my anxiety was sharpened.

It has always been said that love beautifies a woman, and certainly she looked glowing and younger than her years. On the other hand she certainly showed no signs of grief, or, indeed, of any sort of emotion. But, of course, murderers are said to be remarkably callous and cold-blooded.

I said gloomily, "You'd better tell me all about it."

She did. Her story differed in no detail from the one she had told the police. When I asked her how young Murch had got a key to the front door, her blue eyes widened. "I don't know! I didn't give him a key."

I didn't, I couldn't believe her. "Clarissa, when and where did you meet this young man?"

This, too, squared with the lieutenant's account. She said, with deplorable candor, it was in a taxi. "That is, I was waiting for a taxi, and so was he. It was raining. A taxi came along and he offered it to me and, of course, I had to ask him to share it. We were going the same way. By the way, James, the formula for the face cream is mine. I paid for it, remember, and he had come to deliver it to me. So be sure you claim it for me."

"Clarissa, are you telling the truth about this formula?"

"Certainly!" Her eyes snapped and she swished past me into a dressing room and back again. She had a white jar with a black top, unlabeled, in her hand. She held it under my nose. "This is the cream!"

I thrust it away with some force. After a moment I said, "Clarissa, *why* did you write that check in lipstick?"

She sniffed the cream, absently. "I'd never have thought of it myself. But then I realized it was an excellent idea."

I caught her by the shoulders. "*Who* thought of it? *Who* suggested it? Young Murch?"

She told me.

I went downstairs at once, and as I got to the foot of the stairs the door opened and April Moon, sobbing wildly between two policemen, surged into the hall. The lieutenant and Miss Gray emerged from the library. And there was only one course for me to take.

A flat parcel, wrapped and tied, lay on the hall table. I snatched it up. Miss Gray hurled herself upon me like a tiger defending its young. Miss Moon screamed. I thrust the flat parcel at the lieutenant and dived behind him, evading Miss Gray's fingers. Miss Gray whirled around and made for the door where the two policemen seized her.

The formula for the face cream was neatly tucked into the folds of a pair of stockings.

I explained it, although, of course, it was perfectly clear. "It's an excellent face cream. They've both been using it. Mrs. Hartridge and—" I nodded at Miss Gray whose flawless complexion was now a blazing white, as her eyes were blazing black. "Both of them wanted it. Miss April Moon only wanted the money."

"I've never used it!" Miss Moon cried. "It's no good. Ronald told me so. He said it was only a mixture of junk! He said it was a trick to get money from—" She clapped both hands over her mouth.

I said to the lieutenant, "The formula is, in fact, excellent. Obviously Murch didn't know that—he hit on it by chance. He meant merely to use the formula as an excuse to get money from Mrs. Hartridge. But both Miss Gray and Mrs. Hartridge have developed beautiful complexions by using the cream.

"Mrs. Hartridge made a deal with Murch for its purchase. He was to deliver the formula to her this morning. Miss Gray knew that it was her last chance to get the formula for herself. So she determined upon a subtle but rather neat plan."

"Huh?" The lieutenant was perplexed.

"It occurred to her to suggest a romance between Mrs. Hartridge and young Murch. It was a perfect set-up. Elderly widow with money; charming and poor young man. When Mrs. Hartridge was actually about to write a check to Murch for the formula, Miss Gray suggested that she write it in lipstick, on a heart-shaped handkerchief, as a good omen to the cosmetic business. Mrs. Hartridge—er—did so.

"Miss Gray knew the police would eventually see the check,

which was sufficiently out-of-the-ordinary to attract attention. She denied the romance, indignantly, knowing that her defense of Mrs. Hartridge would incline you to exonerate Miss Gray—for if she had shot him, she reasoned, you would expect her to leap at the suggestion of Mrs. Hartridge's guilt."

"But—" the lieutenant said, "how did she find out—"

I replied, "I suggest that Miss Gray knew Murch was to come to the house. I suggest that she returned quietly, waited for him, let him in, took him to the library—and cold-bloodedly shot him.

"Then she had to hurry. She put her own house key in his pocket—to add to the theory of a romance—snatched the formula and, probably, escaped by the kitchen door. She hid the formula in the parcel with the stockings merely, I think, because it struck her as a hiding place which was likely to be overlooked.

"So when that occurred to me, I snatched the stockings, because—well, you see if there had been nothing of importance in the parcel she would have done nothing. Instead of that—"

Something tingled on my cheek; I dabbed at it with my handkerchief which came away with streaks of red on it from the scratches left by Miss Gray's fingernails.

Not long ago I dined with Clarissa in her new and magnificent penthouse. As possibly everyone knows, she has made an enormous amount of money from her astute marketing of a face cream called, simply but suitably, Clarissa's Cream. Perhaps much of the success she has had in its merchandising is due to its trademark—which is a gay, red and white photograph of a heart-shaped handkerchief. It proved to be one of those extraordinary flukes of genius in advertising.

"So that," I said, "is why you wanted the check in good condition."

She smiled at me. "James," she said, "I have so much money. You must tell me all about investments."

I looked at her elegant gown, her matchless pearls, the sapphires and diamonds on her hands. "No, my dear," I said. "You tell me."

Hey, Look At Me!

Jack Finney

About six months after Maxwell Kingery died, I saw his ghost walking along Miller Avenue in Mill Valley, California. It was 2:20 in the afternoon, a clear sunny day, and I saw him from a distance which I later paced off; it was less than fifteen feet. There is no possibility that I was mistaken about who—or what —I saw, and I'll tell you why I'm sure.

My name is Peter Marks, and I'm the book editor of a San Francisco newspaper. I live in Mill Valley a dozen miles from San Francisco, and I work at home most days; from about nine till around two or three in the afternoon. My wife is likely to need something from the store by then, so I generally walk downtown, nearly always stopping in at Myer's bakery, which has a lunch counter. Until he died, I often had coffee there with Max Kingery, and we'd sit at the counter for half an hour and talk.

He was a writer, so it was absolutely inevitable that I'd be introduced to him soon after he came to Mill Valley. A lot of writers live here, and whenever a new one arrives people love to introduce us and then stand back to see what will happen. Nothing much ever does, though once a man denounced me right out on the sidewalk in front of the Redhill liquor store. "Peter Marks? The book critic?" he said, and when I nodded, he said, "You, sir, are a puling idiot who ought to be writing 'News of Our Pets' for *The Carmel Pine Cone* instead of critizing the work of your betters." Then he turned, and—this is the word—stalked off, while I stood staring after him, smiling. I'd panned two of his books, he'd been waiting for Peter Marks ever since, and was admirably ready when his moment came.

But all Max Kingery said, stiffly, the day we were introduced, was, "How do you do," then he stood there nodding rapidly a number of times, finally remembering to smile; and that's all I said to him. It was in the spring, downtown in front of the bank, I think, and Max was bareheaded, wearing a light-brown shabby-looking topcoat with the collar turned up. He was a black-haired, black-eyed man with heavy black-rimmed glasses, intense and quick-moving; it was hard for him to stand still there. He was young but already stooped, his hair thinning. I could see this was a man who took himself seriously, but his name rang no bell in my mind and we spoke politely and parted quickly; probably forever if we hadn't kept meeting in the bakery after that. But we both came in for coffee nearly every afternoon, and after we'd met and nodded half a dozen times we were almost forced to sit together at the counter and try to make some conversation.

So we slowly became friends; he didn't have many. After I knew him I looked up what he'd written, naturally, and found it was a first novel which I'd reviewed a year before. I'd said it showed promise, and that I thought it was possible he'd write a fine novel someday, but all in all it was the kind of review usually called *mixed,* and I felt awkward about it.

But I needn't have worried. I soon learned that what I or anyone else thought of his book was of no importance to Max; he knew that in time I and everyone else would have to say that Maxwell Kingery was a very great writer. Right now not many people, even here in town, knew he was a writer at all, but that was OK with Max; he wasn't ready for them to know. Someday not only every soul in Mill Valley but the inhabitants of remote villages in distant places would know he was one of the important writers of his time, and possibly of all time. Max never said any of this, but you learned that he thought so and that it wasn't egotism. It was just something he knew, and maybe he was right. Who knows how many Shakespeares have died prematurely, how many young geniuses we've lost in stupid accidents, illnesses and wars?

Cora, my wife, met Max presently, and because he looked thin, hungry and forlorn—as he was—she had me ask him over for a meal, and pretty soon we were having him often. His wife had died about a year before we met him. (The more I learned about Max, the more it seemed to me that he was one of the occasional people who, beyond all dispute, are plagued by simple bad luck all their lives.) After his wife died, and his book had failed, he moved from the city to Mill Valley, and now he lived alone working on the novel which, with the others to follow, was going to make him famous. He lived in a mean, cheap little house he'd rented, walking downtown for meals. I never knew where he got whatever money he had; it wasn't much. So we had him over often so Cora could feed him, and, once he was sure he was welcome, he'd stop in of his own accord, if his work was going well. And nearly every day I saw him downtown, and we'd sit over coffee and talk.

It was seldom about writing. All he'd ever say about his own work when we met was it was going well or that it was not, because he knew I was interested. Some writers don't like to talk about what they're doing, and he was one; I never even knew what his book was about. We talked about politics, the possible futures of the world, and whatever else people on the way to becoming pretty good friends talk about. Occasionally he read a book I'd reviewed, and we'd discuss it and my review. He was always polite enough about what I did, but his real attitude showed through. Some writers are belligerent about critics, some are sullen and hostile, but Max was just contemptuous. I'm sure he believed that all writers outranked all critics— well or badly, they actually do the deed which we only sit and carp about. And sometimes Max would listen to an opinion of mine about someone's book, then he'd shrug and say, "Well, you're not a writer," as though that severely limited my understanding. I'd say, "No, I'm a critic," which seemed a good answer to me, but Max would nod as though I'd agreed with him. He liked me, but to Max my work made me only a hanger-on, a camp follower, almost a parasite. That's why it was all right to accept free meals from me; I was one of the people who live off the work writers do, and I'm sure he thought it was only my duty, which I wouldn't deny, to help him get his book written. Reading it would be my reward.

But, of course, I never read Max' next book or the others that were to follow it; he died that summer, absolutely pointlessly. He caught flu or something; one of those nameless things everyone gets occasionally. But Max didn't always eat well or live sensibly, and it hung on and turned into pneumonia, though he didn't know that. He lay in that little house of his waiting to get well, and didn't. By the time he got himself to a doctor, and the doctor got him to a hospital and got some penicillin in him, it was too late and Max died in Marin General Hospital that night.

What made it even more shocking to Cora and me was the way we learned about it. We were out of town on vacation 600 miles away in Utah when it happened, and didn't know about it. (We've thought over and again, of course, that if only we'd been home when Max took sick we'd have taken him to our house and he'd never have gotten pneumonia, and I'm sure it's true; Max was just an unlucky man.) When we got home, not only did we learn that Max was dead but even his funeral, over ten days before, was already receding into the past.

So there was no way for Cora and me to make ourselves realize that Max was actually gone forever. You return from a vacation and slip back into an old routine so easily sometimes it hardly seems you'd left. It was like that now, and walking into the bakery again for coffee in the afternoons it seemed only a day or so since I'd last seen Max here, and whenever the door opened I'd find myself glancing up.

Except for a few people who remembered seeing me around town with Max, and who spoke to me about him now, shaking their heads, it didn't seem to me that Max' death was even discussed. I'm sure people had talked about it to some extent at least, although not many had known him well or at all. But other events had replaced that one by some days. So to Cora and me Max' absence from the town didn't seem to have left any discernible gap in it.

Even visiting the cemetery didn't help. It's in San Rafael, not Mill Valley, and the grave was in a remote corner; we had to climb a steep hill to reach it. But it hardly seemed real; there was no marker, and we had to count in from the road to even locate it. Standing there in the sun with Cora, I felt a flash of resentment against his relatives, but then I knew I shouldn't. Max had a few scattered cousins or something in New Jersey and Pennsylvania. The last time he'd known any of them at all well they'd been children, and he hadn't corresponded with them since. Now they'd sent a minimum of money to California to pay expenses, more from family pride than for Max, I expect, and none of them had come themselves. You couldn't blame them, it was a long way and expensive, but it was sad; there'd been only five people at the funeral. Max had never been in or even seen this cemetery, and standing at the unmarked grave, the new grass already beginning, I couldn't get it through my head that it had anything much to do with him.

He just vanished from the town, that's all. His things—a half-finished manuscript, portable typewriter, some clothes and half a ream of unused yellow paper—had been shipped to his relatives. And Max, with a dozen great books hidden in his brain, who had been going to be famous, was now just gone, hardly missed and barely remembered.

Time is the great healer, it makes you forget; sometimes it makes you forget literally and with great cruelty. I knew a man whose wife ran away, and he never saw her again. He missed her so much he thought he could never for a moment forget it. A year later, reading in his living room at night, he became so absorbed in his book that when he heard a faint familiar noise in the kitchen he called out without looking up from his book and asked his wife to bring him a cup of tea when she came back into the room. Only when there was no answer did he look up from his complete forgetfulness; then his loss swept over him worse than ever.

About six months after Max died, I finished my day's work and walked downtown. This was in January, and we'd just had nearly a month of rain, fog and wet chill. Then California did what it does several times every winter and for which I always forgive it anything. The rain stopped, the sun came out, the sky turned an unclouded blue, and the temperature went up into the high 70s. Everything was lush from the winter rains and there was no way to distinguish those three or four days from summer, and I walked into town in shirt-sleeves. And when I started across Miller Avenue by the bus station heading for Myer's bakery across the street and saw Max Kingery over there walking toward the corner of Throckmorton just ahead, I wasn't surprised but just glad to see him. I think it was because this was like a continuation of the summer I'd known him, the interval following it omitted; and because I'd never really had proof that he died. So I walked on, crossing the street and watching Max, thin, dark and intense; he didn't see me. I was waiting till I got close enough to call to him and I reached the middle of the street and even took a step or two past it before I remembered that Max Kingery was dead. Then I just stood there, my mouth hanging open, as Max or what seemed to be Max walked on to the corner, turned, and moved on out of sight.

I went on to the bakery then and had my coffee; I had to have something. I don't know if I could have spoken, but I didn't have to; they always set a cup of coffee in front of me when I came in. My hand shook when I lifted the cup, and I spilled some, and if it had occurred to me I'd have gone to a bar instead and had several drinks.

If you ever have some such experience you'll learn that people resist believing you as they resist nothing else; you'll resist it yourself. I got home and told Cora what had happened; we sat in the living room and this time I did have a drink in my hand. She listened; there really wasn't much to say, I found, except that I'd seen Max Kingery walking along Miller Avenue. I couldn't blame Cora; my words sounded flat and foolish as I heard them. She nodded and said that several times she'd seen dark, preoccupied, thin young men downtown who reminded her a little of Max. It was only natural; it was where we'd so often run into him.

Patiently I said, "No, listen to me, Cora. It's one thing to see someone who reminds you of someone else; from a distance, or from the back, or just as he disappears in a crowd. But you cannot possibly mistake a stranger when you see him close up and see his face in full daylight for someone you know well and saw often. With the possible exception of identical twins, there was no such resemblances between people. That was Max, Cora, Max Kingery and no one else in the world."

Cora just sat there on the davenport continuing to look at me; she didn't know what to say. I understood, and felt half sorry for her, half irritated. Finally—she had to say *something*—she said, "Well . . . what was he wearing?"

I had to stop and think. Then I shrugged. "Well, just some kind of pants; I didn't notice the shoes; a dark shirt of some kind, maybe plaid, I don't know. And one of those round straw hats."

"Round straw hats?"

"Yeah, you know. You see people wearing them in the summer. I think they buy them at carnivals or somewhere. With a peak. Shaped like a baseball cap only they're made of some kind of shiny yellow straw. Usually the peak is stitched around the rim with a narrow strip of red cloth or braid. This one was, and it had a red button on top, and"—I remembered this suddenly, triumphantly—"it had his initials on the front! Big red initials, *M. K.*, about three inches high, stitched into the straw just over the peak in red thread or braid or something."

Cora was nodding decisively. "That proves it."

"Of course! It—"

"No, no," she said irritably. "It proves that it *wasn't* Max; it couldn't be!"

I don't know why we were so irritable; fear of the unnatural, I suppose. "And just how does it prove that?"

"Oh, Pete! Can you *imagine* Max Kingery of all people wearing a hat like that? You've got to be"—she shrugged, hunting for the word—"some kind of extrovert to wear silly hats. Of all people in the world who would *not* wear a straw baseball cap with a red button on the top and three-inch-high *initials* on the front . . ." She stopped, looking at me anxiously, and after a moment I had to agree.

"Yeah," I said slowly. "He'd be the last guy in the world to wear one of those." I gave in then; there wasn't anything else to do. "It must have been someone else. I probably got the initials wrong; I saw what I thought they ought to be instead of what they were. It would *have* to be someone else, naturally, cap or no cap." Then the memory of what I'd seen rose up in my mind again clear as a sharply detailed photograph, and I said slowly, "But I just hope you see him sometime, that's all. Whoever he is."

She saw him ten days later. There was a movie at the Sequoia we wanted to see, so we got our sitter, then drove downtown after supper; the weather was clear and dry but brisk, temperature in the middle or high thirties. When we got to the box office, the picture was still on with twenty minutes to go yet, so we took a little walk first.

Except for the theater and a bar or two, downtown Mill Valley is locked up and deserted at night. But most of the display windows are left lighted, so we strolled along Throckmorton Avenue and began looking into them, beginning with Gomez Jewelry. We were out of sight of the theater here, and as we moved slowly along from window to window there wasn't another human being in sight, not a car moving, and our own footsteps on the sidewalk—unusually loud—were the only sound. We were at The Men's Shop looking in at a display of cuff links, Cora urging me once more to start wearing shirts with French cuffs so I could wear links in my sleeves, when I heard footsteps turn a corner and begin approaching us on Throckmorton, and I knew it was Max.

I used to say that I'd like to have some sort of psychical experience, that I'd like to see a ghost, but I was wrong. I think it must be one of the worst kinds of fear. I now believe it can drive men insane and whiten their hair, and that it has. It's a nasty fear, you're so helpless, and it began in me now, increasing steadily, and I wanted to spare Cora the worst of it.

She was still talking, pointing at a pair of cuff links made from old cable-car tokens. I knew she'd become aware of the footsteps in a moment and turn to see whoever was passing. I had to prepare her before she turned and saw Max full in the face without warning, and—not wanting to—I turned my head slowly. A permanent awning projects over the storefronts along here, and the light from the windows seemed to be confined under it, not reaching the outer edge of the walk beyond the awning. But there was a three-quarter moon just rising above the trees that surround the downtown area, and by that pale light I saw Max walking briskly along that outer edge of sidewalk beside the curb, only a dozen yards away now. He was bareheaded and I saw his face sharp and clear, and it was Max beyond all doubt. There was no way to say anything else to myself.

I slipped my hand under Cora's coat sleeve and began squeezing her upper arm, steadily harder and harder, till it must have approached pain—and she understood, becoming aware of the footsteps. I felt her body stiffen and I wished she wouldn't but knew she had to—she turned. Then we stood there as he walked steadily toward us in the moonlight. My scalp stirred, each hair of my head moved and tried to stand. The skin all over my body chilled as the blood receded from it. Beside me Cora stood shivering, violently, and her teeth were chattering, the only time in my life I've ever heard the sound. I believe she would have fallen except for my grip on her arm.

Courage was useless, and I don't claim I had any, but it seemed to me that to save Cora from some unspeakable consequence of fear beyond ability to bear it that I had to speak and that I had to do it casually. I can't say why I thought that, but as Max approached—his regular steadily advancing steps the only sound left in the world now, his white face in the moonlight not ten feet away—I said, "Hello, Max."

At first I thought he wasn't going to answer or respond in any way. He walked on, eyes straight ahead, for at least two more steps, then his head turned very slowly as though the effort were enormous, and he looked at us as he passed with a terrible sadness lying motionless in his eyes. Then, just as slowly, he turned away again, eyes forward, and he was actually a pace or two beyond us when his voice—a dead monotone, the effort tremendous—said, "Hello," and it was the voice of despair, absolute and hopeless.

The street curves just ahead, he would disappear around its bend in a moment, and as I stared after him, in spite of the fear and sorrow for Max, I was astounded at what I saw now. There is a kind of jacket which rightly or wrongly I associate with a certain kind of slouching, thumbs-hooked-in-the-belt juvenile exhibitionist. They are made of some sort of shiny sateen-like cloth, always in two bright and violently contrasting colors—the sleeves yellow, the body a chemical green, for example—and usually a name of some sort is lettered across the back. Teenage gangs wear them, or used to.

Max wore one now. It was hard to tell colors in the moonlight, but I think it was orange with red sleeves, and stitched on the back in a great flowing script that nearly covered it was *Max K.*

Then he was gone, around the corner, his fading footsteps continuing two, three, four or five times as they dwindled into silence.

I had to support Cora, and her feet stumbled as we walked to the car. In the car she began to cry, rocking back and forth, her hands over her face. She told me later that she'd cried from grief at feeling such fear of Max. But it helped her, and I drove us to lights and people then; to a crowded bar away from Mill Valley in Sausalito a few miles off. We sat and drank then, several brandies each, and talked and wondered and asked each other the same questions but had no answers.

I think other people saw Max in Mill Valley during those days. One of the local cabdrivers who park by the bus station walked up to me one day; actually he strolled, hands in pockets, making a point of seeming very casual. He said, "Say, that friend of yours, that young guy used to be around town that died?" There was caution in his voice, and he stood watching me closely as I answered. I nodded and said yeah to show that I understood who he meant. "Well, did he have a brother or something?" the driver said, and I shook my head and said not that I knew of. He nodded but was unsatisfied, still watching my face and waiting for me to offer something more but I didn't. And I knew he'd seen Max. I'm sure others saw him and knew who it was, as Cora and I did; it isn't something you mention casually. And I suppose there were those who saw him and merely recognized him vaguely as someone they'd seen around town before.

I walked over to Max' old house a day or so after we'd seen him; by that time, of course, I knew why he'd come back. The real-estate office that had it listed for rental again would have let me have the key if I'd asked; they knew me. But I didn't know what I could tell them as a reason for going in. It was an old house, run down, too small for most people; not the kind that rents quickly or that anyone bothers guarding too diligently. I felt sure I could get in somewhere, and on the tiny back porch, shielded from view, I tried the kitchen window and it opened and I climbed in.

The few scraps of furniture that had come with the place were still there, in the silence: a wooden table and two chairs in the tiny kitchen which Max had hardly used; the iron single bed in the bedroom; the worn-out musty-smelling davenport and matching chair in the living room and the rickety card table beside the front windows where Max had worked. What little I found, I found lying on the floor beside the table; two crumbled-up wads of the yellow copy paper Max had used.

I opened them up, but it's hard to describe what was written on them. There were single words and what seemed to be parts of words and fragments of sentences and completely unreadable scribblings, all written in pencil. There was a word that might have been *forest* or *foreign;* the final letters degenerated into a scrawl as though the hand holding the pencil had begun to fall away from the paper before it could finish. There was an unfinished sentence beginning, *She ran to,* and the stroke crossing the t wavered on partway across and then down the sheet till it ran off the bottom. There is no use describing in detail what is on those two crumpled sheets; there's no sense to be made of it, though I've often tried. It looks, I imagine, like the scrawlings of a man weak from fever and in delirium: as though every squiggle and wobbly line were made with almost-impossible effort. And I'm sure they were. It is true that they might be notes jotted down months earlier when Max was alive and which no one bothered to pick up and remove; but I know they aren't. They're the reason Max came back. They're what he tried to do, and failed.

I don't know what ghosts are or why, in rare instances, they appear. Maybe all human beings have the power, if they have the will, to reappear as Max and a few others have done occasionally down through the centuries. But I believe that to do so takes some kind of terrible and unimaginable expenditure of psychic energy. I think it takes such a fearful effort of will that it is beyond our imagining; and that only very rarely is such an incredible effort made.

I think a Shakespeare killed before *Hamlet, Othello* and *Macbeth* were written might have put forth such effort and returned. And I know that Max Kingery did. But there was almost nothing left over to do what he came back for. Those meaningless fragments were the utmost he could accomplish. His appearances were at the cost of tremendous effort, and I think that to even turn his head and look at us in addition, as he did the night we saw him, and then to actually pronounce an audible word besides, were efforts no one alive can understand.

It was beyond him, he could not return and then write the books that were to have made the name of Max Kingery what he'd been certain it was destined to be. And so he had to give up; we never saw Max again, though we saw two more places he'd been.

Cora and I were driving to San Rafael over the county road. You can get there on a six-lane highway now, 101, that slices straight through the hills, but this was once part of the only road between the two towns and it winds a lot around and between the Marin County hills, under the trees. It's a pleasant narrow little two-lane road, and we like to take it once in a while; I believe it's still the shortest route to San Rafael, winding though it is. This was the end of January or early in February, I don't remember. It was early in the week, I'd taken the day off, and Cora wanted something at Penney's so we drove over.

Twenty or thirty feet up on the side of a hill about a mile outside Mill Valley there's an outcropping of smooth-faced rock facing the road, and Cora glanced at it, exclaimed and pointed, and I jammed on the brakes and looked up where she was pointing. There on the rock facing the public road, painted in great four-foot letters, was *Max Ki,* the lines crude and uneven, driblets of paint running down past the bottoms of letters, the final stroke continuing on down the face of the rock until the paint or oil on the brush or stick had run thin and faded away. We knew Max had painted it—his name or as much of it as he could manage—and staring up at it now, I understood the loud jacket with *Max K* on its back, and the carnival straw hat with the big red initials.

For who *are* the people who paint their names or initials in public places and on the rocks that face our highways? Driving from San Francisco to Reno through the Donner Pass you see them by the hundreds, some painted so high that the rocks must have been scaled, dangerously, to do it. I used to puzzle over them; to paint your name or initials up there in the mountains wasn't impulse. It took planning. You'd have to drive over a hundred miles with a can of paint on the floor of the car. Who would do that? And who would wear the caps stitched with initials and the jackets with names on their backs? It was plain to me now; they are the people, of course, who feel that they have no identity. And who are fighting for one.

They are unknown, nearly invisible, so they feel; and their names or initials held up to the uninterested eyes of the world are silent shouts of, *'Hey, look at me!'* Children shout it incessantly while acquiring their identities, and if they never acquire one maybe they never stop shouting. Because the thing they do must always leave them with a feeling of emptiness. Initials on their caps, names on their jackets, or even painted high on a cliff visible for miles, they must always feel their failure to leave a real mark, and so they repeat it again and again. And Max who had to be someone, who *had* to be, did as they did, finally, from desperation. To have never been anyone and to be forgotten completely was not to be borne. At whatever cost he too had to try to leave his name behind him, even if he were reduced to painting it on a rock.

I visited the cemetery once more that spring; plodding up the hill, eyes on the ground. Nearing the crest I looked up, then stopped in my tracks, astounded. There at the head of Max' grave stood an enormous gray stone, the biggest by far of any in sight, and it was made not of concrete or pressed stone but of the finest granite. It would last a thousand years, and cut deeply into its face in big letters was MAXWELL KINGERY, AUTHOR.

Down in his shop outside the gates I talked to the middle-aged stonecutter in the little office at the front of the building; he was wearing a work apron and cap. He said, "Yes, certainly I remember the man who ordered it; black hair and eyes, heavy glasses. He told me what it should say, and I wrote it down. Your name's Peter Marks, isn't it?" I said it was, and he nodded as though he knew it. "Yes, he told me you'd be here, and I knew you would. Hard for him to talk; had some speech impediment, but I understood him." He turned to a littered desk, leafed through a little stack of papers, then found the one he wanted, and slid it across the counter to me. "He said you'd be in and pay for it; here's the bill. It's expensive but worth it, a fine stone and the only one here I know of for an author."

For several moments I just stood there staring at the paper in my hand. Then I did the only thing left to do, and got out one of the checks I carry in my wallet. Waiting while I wrote, the stonecutter said politely, "And what do you do, Mr. Marks; you an author, too?"

"No," I said, signing the check, then I looked up smiling. "I'm just a critic."

Muldoon and the Numbers Game

Robert L. Fish

A few of those who believed in the powers of old Miss Gilhooley said she did it with ESP, but the majority claimed she had to be a witch, she having come originally from Salem, which she never denied. The ones who scoffed, of course, said it was either the percentages, or just plain luck. But the fact was, she could see things—in cloud formations, or in baseball cards, or in the throwing of bottle caps, among other things—that were truly amazing.

Muldoon was one of those who believed in old Miss Gilhooley implicitly. Once, shortly after his Kathleen had passed away three years before, old Miss Gilhooley, reading the foam left in his beer glass, told him to beware of a tall, dark woman, and it wasn't two days later that Mrs. Johnson, who did his laundry, tried to give him back a puce striped shirt as one of his own that Muldoon wouldn't have worn to a Chinese water torture. And not long after, old Miss Gilhooley, reading the lumps on his skull after a brawl at Maverick Station, said he'd be taking a long voyage over water, and the very next day didn't his boss send him over to Nantasket on a job, and that at least halfway across the bay?

So, naturally, being out of work and running into old Miss Gilhooley having a last brew at Casey's Bar & Grill before taking the bus to her sister's in Framingham for a week's visit, Muldoon wondered why he had never thought of it before. He therefore took his beer and sat down in the booth across from the shawled old Miss Gilhooley and put his problem directly to her.

"The unemployment's about to run out, and it looks like nobody wants no bricks laid no more, at least not by me," he said simply. "I need money. How do I get some?"

Old Miss Gilhooley dipped her finger in his beer and traced a pattern across her forehead. Then she closed her eyes for fully a minute by the clock before she opened them.

"How old's your mother-in-law?" she asked in her quavering voice, fixing Muldoon with her steady eyes.

Muldoon stared. "Seventy-four." he said, surprised. "Just last month. Why?"

"I don't rightly know," old Miss Gilhooley said slowly. "All I know is I closed me eyes and asked meself, 'How can Muldoon come up with some money?' And right away, like in letters of fire across the insides of me eyeballs, I see, 'How old is Vera Callahan?' It's got to mean something."

"Yeah," Muldoon said glumly. "But what?"

"I'll miss me bus," said old Miss Gilhooley, and came to her feet, picking up her ancient haversack. "It'll come to you, don't worry." And with a smile she was through the door.

Seventy-four, Muldoon mused as he walked slowly toward the small house he now shared with his mother-in-law. You'd think old Miss Gilhooley might have been a little more lavish with her clues. She'd never been that cryptic before. Seventy-four! Suddenly Muldoon stopped dead in his tracks. There was only one logical solution, and the more he thought about it, the better it looked. Old Miss Gilhooley and Vera Callahan had been lifelong enemies. And his mother-in-law had certainly mentioned her life insurance policy often enough when she first used it ten years before as her passport into the relative security of the Muldoon ménage. And, after all, seventy-four was a ripe old age, four years past the biblical threescore and ten, not to mention being even further beyond the actuarial probabilities.

Muldoon smiled at his own brilliance in solving the enigma so quickly. Doing away with his mother-in-law would be no chore. By Muldoon's figuring, she had to weigh in at about a hundred pounds dripping wet and carrying an anvil in each hand. Nor, he conceded, would her passing be much of a loss. She did little except creep between bed and kitchen and seemed to live on tea. Actually, since the poor soul suffered such a wide variety of voiced ailments, the oblivion offered by the grave would undoubtedly prove welcome.

He thought for a moment of checking with the insurance company as to the exact dollar value of his anticipated inheritance, but then concluded it might smack of greediness. It might also look a bit peculiar when the old lady suffered a fatal attack of something-or-other so soon after the inquiry. Still, he felt sure it would be a substantial amount; old Miss Gilhooley had never failed him before.

When he entered the house, the old lady was stretched out on the couch, taking her afternoon nap (she slept more than a cat, Muldoon thought) and all he had to do was to put one of the small embroidered pillows over her face and lean his two hundred pounds on it for a matter of several minutes, and that was that. She barely wriggled during the process. Muldoon straightened up, removed the pillow, and gazed down. He had been right; he was sure he detected a grateful expression on the dead face. He fluffed the pillow up again, placed it in its accustomed location, and went to call the undertaker.

It was only after all decent arrangements had been made, all hard bargaining concluded, and all the proper papers signed, that Muldoon called the insurance company—and got more than a slight shock. His mother-in-law's insurance was for four hundred dollars, doubtless a princely sum when her doting parents had taken it out a matter of sixty years before, but rather inadequate in this inflationary age. Muldoon tried to cancel the funeral, but the undertaker threatened suit, not to mention a visit from his nephew, acknowledged dirty-fight champion of all South Boston. The additional amount of money Muldoon had to get up to finally get Vera Callahan underground completely wiped out his meager savings.

So that, obviously, was not what old Miss Gilhooley had been hinting at, Muldoon figured. He was not bitter, nor was his faith impaired; the fault had to be his own. So there he was with the numbers again. Seventy-four ... seventy-four.... Could they refer to the mathematical possibilities? Four from seven left three—but three what? Three little pigs? Three blind mice? Three blind pigs? He gave it up. On the other hand, four plus seven equaled . . .

He smote himself on the head for his previous stupidity and quickly rubbed the injured spot, for Muldoon was a strong man with a hand like the bumper on a gravel truck. Of course! *Seven and four added up to eleven. ELEVEN!* And—Muldoon told himself with authority—if that wasn't a hint to get into the floating crap game that took place daily, then his grandfather came from Warsaw.

So Muldoon took out a second mortgage on his small house, which netted him eight hundred dollars plus change, added to that the two hundred he got for his three-and-a-half-year-old, secondhand-to-begin-with car, and with the thousand dollars in big bills in his pocket, made his way to Casey's Bar & Grill.

"Casey!" he asked in his ringing voice, "Where's the floating game today?"

"Callahan Hotel," Casey said, rinsing glasses. "Been there all week. Room Seventy-Four."

Muldoon barely refrained from smiting himself on the head again. How dumb could one guy be? If only he'd asked before, he would not have had to deal with that thief of an undertaker, not to mention the savings he's squandered—although in truth he had to admit the small house was less crowded with the old lady gone.

"Thanks," he said to Casey, and hurried from the bar.

The group standing around the large dismountable regulation crap table in Room Seventy-Four of the Callahan Hotel, was big and tough, but Muldoon was far from intimidated. With one thousand dollars in his pocket and his fortune about to be made, Muldoon felt confidence flowing through him like a fourth beer. He nodded to one of the gamblers he knew there and turned to the man next to him, tapping him on the shoulder.

"Got room for one more?" he asked.

"Hunnert dollars minimum," the man said without looking up from the table. "No credit."

Muldoon nodded. It was precisely the game he wanted. "Who's the last man?" he asked.

"Me," the man said, and clamped his lips shut.

Muldoon took the money from his pocket and folded the bills lengthwise gambler-fashion, wrapping them around one finger, awaiting his turn. When at last the dice finally made their way to him, Muldoon laid a hundred-dollar bill on the table, picked up the dice, and shook them next to one ear. They made a pleasant, ivory sound. A large smile appeared on Muldoon's face.

"Seven and four are me lucky numbers," he announced. "Same as them that's on the door of this room, here. Now, if a guy could only roll an eleven *that* way!"

"He'd end up in a ditch," the back man said expressionlessly. "You're faded—roll them dice. Don't wear 'em out."

Muldoon did not wear out the dice. In fact, he had his hands on them exactly ten times, managing to throw ten consecutive craps, equally divided between snake-eyes and boxcars. They still speak of it at the floating crap game; it seems the previous record was only five and the man who held it took the elevator to the roof—they were playing at some hotel up in Copley Square that day—and jumped off. Muldoon turned the dice over to the man to his right and wandered disconsolately out of the hotel.

Out in the street Muldoon ambled along a bit aimlessly, scuffing his heavy work brogans against anything that managed to get in his way; a tin can, a broken piece of brick he considered with affectionate memory before he kicked it violently; a crushed cigarette pack. He tried for an empty candy wrapper but with his luck missed. Seventy-four! *Seventy-four!* What in the bleary name of Eustice Q. Peabody could the blaggety numbers mean? (The Sisters had raised Muldoon strictly; no obscenity passed his lips.) He tried to consider the matter logically, forcing his temper under control. Old Miss Gilhooley had never failed him, nor would she this time. He was simply missing the boat.

Seventy-four? Seventy-*four?* The figures began to take on a certain rhythm, like the *Punch, brother, punch with care* of Mark Twain. Muldoon found himself trying to march to it. Seven-ty-four! Seven*ty*-four! He shook his head; it lacked beat. Seventy-four-hup! No. Seven-*ty*-four-*hup!* Better but still not it. The old lady had been seventy-four and now she was zero. He tried that. Seventy-four-zero! Seventy-four-zero-hup! Almost it but not quite. Seven-four-zero-hup! Seven-four-zero, *hup!* Got it! Muldoon said to himself, deriving what little satisfaction he could from the cadence, and marched along swinging. Seven-four-zero, *hup!*

And found himself in front of Casey's Bar & Grill, so he went inside and pulled a stool up to the deserted bar.

"Beer," he said.

"How'd you do in the game?" Casey asked.

"Better give me a shot with that beer," Muldoon said by way of an answer. He slugged the shot down, took about half his beer for a chaser, and considered Casey as he wiped his mouth. "Casey," he said earnestly, really wanting to know, "what do the numbers seven and four mean to you?"

"Nothing," Casey said.

"How about seven, four, and zero?"

"Nothing," Casey said. "Maybe even less."

"How about backwards?" Muldoon asked in desperation, but Casey had gone to the small kitchen in the rear to make himself a sandwich during the slack time, and Muldoon found himself addressing thin air. He tossed the proper amount of change on the counter and started for the door. Where he ran into a small man named O'Leary, who ran numbers for the mob. It wasn't what he preferred, but it was a living.

"Wanna number today, Mr. Muldoon?" O'Leary asked.

Muldoon was about to pass on with a shake of his head, when he suddenly stopped. A thrill went through him from head to foot. Had he been in a cartoon a light bulb would have lit up in a small circle over his head. Not being in a cartoon, he kicked himself, his heavy brogan leaving a bruise that caused him to limp painfully for the next three weeks.

Good Geoffrey T. Soppingham! He must have been blind! Blind? Insane! What possible meaning could numbers have, if not *that they were numbers?* Just thinking about it made Muldoon groan. If he hadn't killed the old lady and gotten into that stupid crap game, at this moment he could be putting down roughly fifteen hundred bucks on Seven-Four-Zero. Fifteen-hundred dollars at five-hundred-to-one odds! Still, if he hadn't smothered the old lady, he'd never have come up with the zero, so it wasn't a total loss. But the floating game had been completely unnecessary.

Because now Muldoon didn't have the slightest doubt as to what the numbers meant.

"Somethin' wrong. Mr. Muldoon?" O'Leary asked, concerned with the expression on Muldoon's face.

"No!" Muldoon said, and grasped the runner by the arm, drawing him back into Casey's Bar & Grill, his hand like the clamshell bucket of a steam shovel on the smaller man's bicep. He raised his voice, bellowing. "*Casey!*"

Casey appeared from the kitchen, wiping mayonnaise from his chin. "Don't shout," he said. "What do you want?"

Muldoon was prying his wedding ring from his finger. He laid it down on the bar. "What'll you give me for this?"

Casey looked at Muldoon as if the other man had suddenly gone mad. "This ain't no hockshop, Muldoon," he said.

But Muldoon was paying no attention. He was slipping his wristwatch and its accompanying stretch band over his thick fingers. He placed the watch down on the bar next to the ring.

"One hundred bucks for the lot," he said simply. "A loan, is all. I'll pay it back tonight." As Casey continued to look at him with fishy eyes, Muldoon added in a quiet, desperate voice, "I paid sixty bucks each for them rings; me and Kathleen had matching ones. And that watch set me back better than a bill-and-a-half all by itself, not to mention the band, which is pure Speidel. How about it?" A touch of pleading entered his voice. "Come on; we been friends a long time."

"Acquaintances," Casey said, differentiating, and continued to eye Muldoon coldly. "I ain't got that much cash in the cash register right now."

"Jefferson J. Billingsly the cash register," Muldoon said, irked. "You got that much and more in your pants pocket."

Casey studied the other a moment longer and then casually swept the ring and the watch from the counter into his palm, and pocketed them. From another pocket he brought out a wallet that looked like it was suffering from mumps. He began counting out bills.

"Ninety-five bucks," he said. "Five percent off the top, just like the Morris Plan."

Muldoon was about to object, but time was running out.

"Someday we'll discuss this transaction in greater detail, Casey," he said. "Out in the alley," and he turned to O'Leary, grasping both of the smaller man's arms for emphasis. "O'Leary I want ninety-five bucks on number seven-four-zero. Got it? *Seven-Four-Zero!* Today!"

"*Ninety-five bucks?*" O'Leary was stunned. "I never wrote no slip bigger than a deuce in my life, Mr. Muldoon," he said. He thought a moment. "No, a fin," he said brightly, but then his face fell. "No a deuce. I remember now, the fin was counterfeit. . . ."

"You're wasting time," Muldoon said in a dangerous voice. He suddenly realized he was holding the smaller man several inches from the floor, and lowered him. "Will they pay off? That's the question," he said in a quieter voice, prepared for hesitation.

"Sure they pay off, Mr. Muldoon," O'Leary said, straightening his sleeves into a semblance of their former shape. "How long you figure they stay alive, they start welching?"

"So long as they know it," Muldoon said, and handed over the ninety-five bucks. He took his receipt in return, checked the number carefully to make sure O'Leary had made no mistake, and slipped the paper into his pocket. Then he turned to Casey.

"A beer," he said in a voice that indicated their friendship had suffered damage. "And take it out of that five bucks you just stole!"

. . .

Muldoon was waiting in a booth at Casey's Bar & Grill at seven o'clock P.M., which was the time the runners normally had the final three figures of the national treasury balance—which was the Gospel by St. Carlo Gambino that week. Muldoon knew that straight cash in hand would not be forthcoming; after all, he was due a matter of over forty-seven-thousand dollars. Still he'd take a check. If he hadn't gotten into that crap game, he'd have been rich—or, more probably, in a ditch like the man had mentioned this afternoon. Who was going to pay off that kind of loot? No mob in Boston, that was sure. Better this way, Muldoon thought. Forty-seven grand was big enough to be the year's best advertisement for the racket, but still it was enough by their standards for the mob to loosen up.

It was a nice feeling being financially secure after the problems of the past few years, and he certainly had no intention of splurging. All honest debts would be cleared up, of course, and he'd have to buy himself some wheels—a compact, nothing fancy—but the rest would go into the bank. At five percent it wouldn't earn no fortune, he knew, but it would still be better than a fall off a high scaffold onto a low sidewalk.

He reached for his beer and saw old Miss Gilhooley walking through the door. Had a week passed so quickly? He supposed it must have; what with the funeral, and one thing and another, the time had flown. He waved her over and called out to Casey to bring old Miss Gilhooley anything her heart desired.

Old Miss Gilhooley settled herself in the booth across from him and noted the expression on his face. "So you figured it out, Muldoon," she said.

"Not right off," Muldoon admitted. "To be honest, it just come to me this afternoon. But better late than never; at least it come." He leaned over over the table confidentially. "It was the numbers, see? The seven and the four for her age, plus the zero at the end, because whether you heard or not, that's what the poor soul is now."

Old Miss Gilhooley sipped the beer Casey had brought, and nodded. "That's what I figured," she said, "especially after seeing O'Leary in me dreams three nights running, and me old enough to be his mother."

"And I can't thank you enough—" Muldoon started to say, and then paused, for O'Leary had just burst through the door of the bar like a Roman candle, and was hurrying over to them, brushing people aside. His eyes were shining.

"Mr. Muldoon! Mr. Muldoon!" O'Leary cried excitedly. "I never seen nothin' like it in all me born days! And on a ninety-five dollar bet!"

Muldoon grinned happily.

"Only one number away!" O'Leary cried, still impressed by his close brush with fame. "Tough you had Seven-Four-Zero. Seven-Five-Zero wins!"

O'Leary sighed, and then put the matter from his mind. After all, life had to go on. "Wanna number for tomorrow, Mr. Muldoon?"

"No," Muldoon said in a dazed tone, and turned to old Miss Gilhooley who was making strange noises. But they were not lamentations for Muldoon; to Muldoon's surprise the old lady was cackling like a fiend.

"That Vera Callahan!" she said triumphantly. "I always *knew* she lied about her age!"

The Capture

James Hay, Jr.

Vinal sat in a plain deal chair near the cold fireplace, his body leaning slightly forward, his hands resting lightly upon his knees. With the exception of two brief interruptions he had been in that position for more than twelve hours, but there was in the lines of his still figure that which suggested desperate expectancy, incessant alertness.

At eleven o'clock that morning he had risen from the chair by inches and tiptoed to the window and, gently pulling aside the thick, dirty curtain, had looked out through a chink in the closed shutters to glance at the two policemen patrolling the pavement outside. In that journey he had not made a sound. Not a board had creaked. There had not been even so much as the scraping of one part of his clothing against another. And again at five o'clock in the afternoon, creeping, a master of silence, he had repeated the pilgrimage and had seen the same patrol. At the back of the house, he knew, was a third blue-coated man.

On the far side of the room was a door and beyond that door were Pole and Dowell, two of the men who had murdered old Sothoron and old Sothoron's wife. He knew they were there. How he knew it he could not have explained. So far as his trained senses had been able to discover, there had come from

79

the next room during his long wait the sound of neither voice nor motion. He simply felt that they were on the other side of the wall.

He had acted on the supposition that they would do what thousands of others of their kind had done, double on their tracks and return, if possible, to their old refuge. He had figured that if they could enter the house in spite of the one policeman at the rear and the two at the front, he in his pursuit of them could accomplish the same feat.

As he thought of this deduction on his part, and its impending result, he experienced the greatest excitement he ever allowed himself to feel. It was only a question of minutes, at most not more than an hour, before he would have the laugh on the police commissioner. He would make Finkman and his men look like fools; and the famous Bloomer agency, with its cocksure chief, would find itself cheated of its prize at the very time when the city and the entire country expected it to turn its best trick. He liked neither the commissioner nor Finkman nor the Bloomers. They had never given him a fair chance, and he had a nice sense of revenge. Single-handed he would deliver two of the three murderers to justice that evening.

If he had waited a lifetime he could not have had a better setting for the drama he was about to enact. The newspapers the next morning would grip the imagination of the whole country and lead it irresistibly into the dark room of that miserable house in which he now sat. Because the public mind had been inflamed by the recitals of the outrage, it would read eagerly, even delightedly, the details of the capture of the criminals.

For three days the search for the murders had spread out, spun itself into a mighty web. The furor had been created because of the prominence of the victims, not because of any particular brutality in the commission of the crime. While one man had watched outside the other two had crept into the bedroom, chloroformed the husband and the wife and ransacked the house. To all intents and purposes, so far as the burglars were concerned, the double murder had been an accident. Instead of stupefying, as they had intended, they had killed.

But immediately the authorities and the newspapers had come forward with the cry: "The chloroform gang!" They recognized in the tragedy the work of the Chloroform Colonel and his two associates, Dowell and Pole. And because the owners of millions had been done to death, he, Vinal, sat there in the cold, dark room and calculated to a nicety the details of every move he must make to accomplish this triumph unaided, to achieve it in such a way that he—he alone—would stand head and shoulders above the mass of men who made the pursuit of crime their profession.

He had entered the house before daylight that morning, coming up like a specter out of the wet blackness of the back alley, slipping past the sleepy policeman and disappearing into the areaway in perfect silence. His progress on stockinged feet from the basement to the fourth story of the rickety house had been as quiet as death and laborious enough to wring the sweat from his body.

And yet he should have had no real fear of interruption. The police, having searched the place from top to bottom two days before, had contented themselves with placing the three pickets on the outside—in case the murderers should seize on the perilous chance of doubling back. And if his marvelous intuition had served him right and any of the three had returned to wait for a last play for freedom, they would have made no outcry if he had stumbled against them. They would have realized the futility of further resistance. The average crook, dislodged from his last ditch, makes no fight. In view of these things his care, his fear of outside interference and his incredible patience were sure signs of the eagerness with which he looked forward to the capture.

The time had come for him to act, to put into execution the plan which he had elaborated. On the other side of the flimsy door there were only two men. He knew this. In the first place the Colonel, their leader, would never have beaten back aimlessly to an old haunt. Rather than pen himself up in a place in which either starvation or a second search would end his career, he would make a daring try for more open ground. Realizing that all the machinery of the law was combing clean the retreats of the city, he would strive in every way to get beyond the scope of such a chase. Only the lower intelligence of Pole and Dowell would hold out to them the promise of ultimate escape by such a ruse.

The room was very cold. Vinal wanted to shiver, but checked the impulse. In all the time he had been there he had not moved a muscle unnecessarily. The darkness was in the shuttered, curtained house like a tangible, palpable object. It seemed a solid, oblong formation against which the glare of the street lights beat in vain. And the silence inside was almost as bad. In that vast, crashing, shrieking city it was a separate thing, unchanged and unmoved by the ordinary uproar humanity makes at night. It began to get on his nerves, until he mentally took hold of himself and assured himself that there was nothing uncanny in the affair. It was simply a matter of one man sitting moveless and soundless in one room and two other men equally moveless, equally silent, in the other.

He got to his feet—and it took him two full minutes to reach an upright position—his hands held slightly away from his sides. He moved his fingers, crooking them and straightening them out methodically time and again to get out of them the stiffness that had been caused by the cold. He raised his right foot and put it forward through the darkness in one long step, but when he placed it on the bricks of the hearth nearby it was with a motion as soft as the falling of down. Once on the hearth and away from the danger of creaking boards, he began to rise slowly and repeatedly on the balls of his feet in such a way that the exertion called into play all the muscles of his legs. He did this fifty times, more rapidly toward the last, and always continuing the movements of his fingers.

He went through with it scientifically, utilizing the knowledge he had gained in the gymnasium. He had begun to roll his head from side to side when he noticed that his neck, unshaven for thirty-six hours, rasped against his collar. With slow deftness and short, tedious movement he took off his cravat and, leaning over, placed it carefully on the bricks to one side. He did not drop it. The collar was more difficult. He moistened his fingers with saliva and applied them many times to the buttonholes. When he slipped the first flap from its holding the buttonhole was as soft and wet as if it had been dipped in a river.

His straining ears, ready to receive every sound, could not

hear his own work. Outside there was the constant chorus of the city, punctuated now and then by the shrill horn of an automobile or the wail of wheels against the cold steel rails on the Elevated, and continuously there came up from the pavement directly underneath the monotonous pit-pat of the brogans of the slowly promenading policemen. Several times he heard voices guying the officers.

"Watch the Sherlock Holmeses doing a marathon!" one of the street gamins called out.

And another:

"Why don't you go down to the station and wait for 'em to walk in?"

But there was no sound from the next room. He had taken off the collar and laid it down beside the cravat when the thought came to him: "Suppose they're not there!" He paused, still bowed over, and listened as if to reassure himself. He heard nothing. And yet the old intuition came back to him. They were there. That was the only explanation of why the newsboys at that very moment were crying the extras telling of their remarkable escape. They must be there. They would have thought of no other place when the chase behind them had grown too hot.

He did not falter once in his infinite precaution, his far-reaching calculation of just what each muscle would do, of how he must place each hand and each foot to avoid even the chance of noise. The slightest thing, he knew, would split that block of silence like the thundering blow of a trip-hammer. The blackness pressed upon him and stung him as if he had been made up of the ends of live wires, wires which, in his unnatural imagination, he thought would carry straight to the ears of the two in the other room the ghost of any sound. But he forced himself to calmness. He could not afford nervousness.

As plainly as if it had been in the room he suddenly heard the rattle of the knob of the door of the house. One of the policemen, varying the monotony of his vigil, had rattled it aimlessly. In an instant he became one degree more alert. The eager desire of his mind sharpened still more his hearing. There had come from the other room a sound. He listened—listened—listened hungrily, painfully. The noise was not repeated. It had not been enough, in the first place, to make a scratch on the hard block of the silence which hemmed him in. And yet he was sure, certain.

He leaned over again and, resting his left hand on the bricks, thrust his right slowly into the fireplace and up the chimney the fraction of an inch. He wanted some of the soot, but none of it must be dislodged and fall into the fireplace. He put the soot with well-considered smears upon his cheeks and nose and fore-head. Then, regaining his upright posture, he slowly turned up the soft collar of his coat and buttoned the garment tightly about his slender figure.

He stood hesitant once more, cataloguing in his mind all the things he had done, the limbering and softening of the muscles and ligaments of his body, the removal of his collar and tie, the disfiguring of his face—this being done for two reasons: The blackness of the soot would remove the possibility of his face looming up like a white blur before the men he intended to capture; also, if they discovered him too soon, he would stand a chance to fraternize with them as being, like them, a fugitive. That idea struck him as grimly ludicrous. What would they, the murderers, think if they became convinced that he, fleeing because of some minor offense, was closeted with them in their last house of refuge?

With soft touches he felt that the revolver in the right-hand outer pocket of his coat was as it should be and that the one on the other side was convenient to his immediate reach. He was ready, he told himself. Finkman and the Bloomers, he reflected, could not have prepared themselves one-half so well for what he was about to do.

Vinal was not a coward. No man with fear in his heart ever could have gone through with that day's watching. But as he put out his right foot and started on that long, apparently intermi-nable journey across the short expanse of flooring between him and the door, the slightest noise of his own making would have thrown him into a panic. Keyed up to an abnormal pitch, his nerves raw from their tension, he was emotionally wide open to any impression, any idea, any happening foreign to his defi-nite undertaking.

It was as if he carried in the balls of his feet premonition of noise. In his trip to the door he traveled at right angles to the boarding of the floor, and he knew that in order to avoid the creaking of the planks he must follow the line of one of the crosspieces underneath the boarding. He found this by instinct and he kept to it unswervingly in his progress.

His sense of direction was extraordinary, weird; the more so because every step he made was almost a half-circle, since he did not dare to tip forward in the ordinary manner. In each groping stride his foot went out to one side from him and forward at the same time, so as to avoid the danger of one trousers leg brushing against the other. And he was guided entirely by the mental picture of what he had seen grayly when the daylight had been sifting through the chinks of the shutters—by that and by the instinctive accuracy with which his light, catlike feet followed the safe part of the flooring.

Within a yard of the door, he stopped midway in the act of letting his weight swing with wearisome slowness from his right foot to his left. He had had neither food nor drink for twenty-four hours, and in the anguished nervousness of his progress he had allowed his mouth to slacken, half-open. It was like that of a runner who, nearing the close of a race, gasps for breath. And all of a sudden he realized that the inhalations went into his lungs with what threatened to be the sound of a low whistle. He closed his lips and hung motionless, balanced halfway in his stride. He listened. There was nothing except the roar of the city—that and the pit-pat of the policemen's feet.

He put out his hand and moved it forward slowly, slowly as the ages.

The tips of his fingers thrilled and pulsated as if the nerves were not covered by the epidermis. And when they touched the doorjamb he had to hold himself together to keep from starting suddenly, so hard and abrupt seemed the touch when they struck against the woodwork.

Very slowly, almost imperceptibly, his long, lean figure crouched forward more and more until his ear was on a level with the keyhole. He waited five minutes—eight minutes—ten minutes. His hearing was reinforced by his hope of discovering them and his fear of their discovering him. All his senses reached forward into that other room. So great was his concentration that the noises of the city and the echoes of the footsteps down below were at last a million miles away.

He could see the two men exactly as they had been pictured

in the newspapers—Pole, little, round-shouldered, pusillani-
mous; and Dowell, heavy-set, broad-shouldered, bull-necked.
Now, more than ever, he knew that they were there—Pole
bunched up, terror-stricken, white-lipped, and Dowell a big,
immovable lump. But he could not understand why he did not
hear their breathing. It was natural that they should not move
about. Their consuming fear of discovery would account for
this. And yet the fact that they made no sounds whatever was
beyond him. If they were breathing, he felt, the sound of it must
come to him in that virgin silence.

Then he heard. It was a whisper, low, guarded, but to him it
sounded like the crack of a gun, so much so that instinctively
and in silent swiftness he put his hands to his revolver pockets.

He listened.

"If they get the Colonel we've got a chance."

He knew that the voice was Pole's. It was a whisper, but to
his ears, incredibly trained, it had in it all the characteristics of
a voice. It sounded like the talk of a little, shrill-toned man.

"They won't get him." Dowell's whisper in reply was like
Dowell, slow and heavy.

The silence closed in again.

"For God's sake, we've got to do something! We'll starve to
death here."

Pole's whisper, so low that it seemed scarcely to make a ripple
on the ocean of stillness, was freighted nevertheless with a
coward's despair.

Vinal, exerting himself as if he wrestled with ten men, had
heard every syllable of what had been said. He found himself
balanced on his toes, his right arm straightened out behind him,
his left pointed forward and downward, as if he were poised
agilely and perfectly for instant movement. He hung, light as
a feather, in the silence, and yet his muscles were so tense that
he looked, too, like a man supporting tremendous weight.

"Don't talk." Dowell ended the whispering.

Vinal put his hand on the doorknob. His fingers touched it as
lightly as grains of dust, and, while all his consciousness was
centered on the gigantic task of turning it without noise, somewhere in the back of his mentality he was cursing the necessity
of fooling with a thing so pregnant in its possibilities for the ruin
of his plan.

It seemed to him afterward that he used up a year of his life in turning the knob. At every fraction of the turn he paused, knowing that, if he went the thousandth of a second faster, the inevitable grating of the latch would follow. He was seized by an insane desire to wrench the door open and charge in with thunderous noise, discharging his guns and shouting at the top of his voice. The silence—silence which was necessary to him —was growing too big, too mysterious for him. It was a torture that multiplied itself every moment.

When he had the latch free of the hasp, there came a repetition of the careful tactics he had already followed. Just as there had been a certainty that the lock would creak, there was the dead-sure thing that the hinges would cry out if urged by more than snail-like motion. As the door opened he began to calculate through his sense of touch just when to bring it to a stop, and to go through again the crucifying process of letting the latch creep back to the point from which he had started it. While he did this he could hear the breathing of the two men, and gradually, by painful degrees, he began to sense their positions in the room. They were nearer to the window than he had thought and they faced the window. That was the first piece of good fortune he had had. He could work on them from behind.

He took his hand from the knob and the door was still. He took one slow step into the room. It was a motion that required minutes. Three times the ball of his foot touched the flooring and drew back. Each time he knew that, if he had put the weight of ten pounds on that step, the flimsy flooring would have cried out. At the fourth attempt he felt safe—and he could not have explained the feeling to save his soul.

"I wish I had some water," Pole's little whisper rang out.

Involuntarily there flashed through Vinal's mind a story he had read years before of the carrying power of certain actors' voices. Pole, he thought, undoubtedly would have made a good actor.

Before he took the next step he got both the pistols from his pockets and held them ready. He was possessed by a mania for speed, a wild desire to make a rush, to liberate his muscles from the captivity of care, to throw from his limbs the manacles of tediousness. But as he went forward, gaining at every step a clearer consciousness of where the two men sat, he did not hurry in the slightest. Each contraction of his muscles was as slow as it had been at the hearth in the other room. And even at this moment, when the whole fabric of his success hung on the slender chain of a few silent seconds, he thought with astonishment of how perfectly his mind controlled every smallest atom of his body.

The climax came exactly as he had planned it. He ended the torture of slowness with a rush of motion and cut the stillness with a whisper. With one lightning-like sweep the revolvers flashed through two feet of space and came down, muzzles forward, on the backs of the two men's necks. He could tell by the way the flesh at the end of the right-hand revolver gave way that the little Pole shrank down in his chair as far as he could. The left-hand gun met the thickness of Dowell's neck and moved only a few inches.

"If you make a sound I'll pull the trigger!" he said, and he put the threat in a murmur scarcely louder than had been the whispers he had heard.

For nearly half a minute the group was motionless—only Pole's breathing began to come and go with a hissing sound.

Finally Dowell broke the stillness.

"What do you want?" he asked aloud, but in a subdued tone.

"Don't do that again!" Vinal's whisper was sharp enough to be like a blow. "I want you both. I've got you. Now listen. There's another man in this house, and if you make a sound he may make a getaway. You are going with me quietly—or get shot."

There began in Pole's throat what would have developed into a whimper, but Vinal stopped it with his thumb.

"Now," he whispered his directions, "I'll guide you out of this room through the next into the hall and down to the front door. You go the way these guns press you."

Dowell had made no sign of emotion, except that his breathing was faster. Both he and Pole rose to their feet and turned as Vinal indicated with the revolvers. To be more certain in his guidance he had thrust the muzzles of the revolvers inside their collars.

"Where are your shoes?" he asked, whispering softly.

It was Dowell who replied:

"Over in the corner."

"They are not in the way? We won't stumble against them?"

"No."

He was still desirous of silence. Nobody must enter the house to interfere with his work, his capture. He would deliver them at the front door, on the pavement, to the sleepy policemen. But the three could not traverse three flights of stairs without some noise, and this angered him. Whenever his captives made a board creak he gouged them mercilessly with the revolvers; but he did not whisper.

Quietly, with reasonable quickness, they reached the vestibule. Pole, weak and small, was flinching under every thrust of the revolver against his collarbone. Occasionally he trembled violently. Dowell, knowing that the game was up, went deliberately, almost calmly, as directed by the cold steel inside his collar.

Once or twice Vinal was seized by the impulse he had felt upstairs to shriek, to cry out, to end the thing with a storm of blows and shots. He had been tortured past human endurance ever since entering the house. But whenever he felt the impulse to give way the thought of Finkman and his men, of the Bloomer operators and of the commissioner himself nerved him on for the few remaining minutes.

At the door he flashed his hand from Pole's shoulder and left the revolver hanging in the little man's collar. It was only for the two seconds required to snap back the latch and fling open the door. He grasped the revolver again and thrust the two men before him into the brilliantly lighted street.

"Here!" he called out imperiously. "Come here, you men! Here they are! Grab 'em!"

Pole and Dowell stood blinking in the light and the two policemen sprang forward, willing but dazed. One of them, the fellow with a red mustache, paused before he leaped, and blew his whistle.

In the twinkling of an eye they had the two captives. As if by magic the street was filled with flying feet and excited cries. Men and women ran from all directions, and on the crest of the wave came other policemen, forming quickly a circle round the two white-faced silent men.

Vinal, with blackened face, shouted excitedly to the red-mustached policeman:

"Got 'em upstairs! Did it all myself! Why, you poor fools—you and your detectives—they've been up there all day!"

Two of the officers rushed into the house to search it again. Another put in a call for a patrol wagon.

From the crowd that was closing more tightly all the time about the captives and the police rang yells and jeers:

"Chickens come home to roost!"

"Oh, you chloroform!"

"Where's de guy dat nipped 'em?"

"Ain't dat little gink a nice lookin' slice of pie!"

When the wagon, carrying its new load of captive wretchedness, rumbled over the cobblestones to the stationhouse five blocks away the spectators followed only to be stopped at the doorway.

Inside, the desk sergeant was inclined to get out of the situation all the pleasure possible. He grinned affably at Dowell and Pole, who stood near the railing while their clothing was being searched by rough and ready hands.

"I guess the Bloomers got you," he commented. "Well, it'll be quick work with you! As soon as we get the Colonel the three of you will hang—hang nice and high."

This was too much for the nerves of the little, ratlike Pole. He burst into wild hysterical laughter, and fell forward against the desk, beating his skinny hands on the hardwood. He began to shriek, and one of the policemen put a hand over his mouth.

He wrenched his head away.

"Aw!" he squeaked, the tears streaming down his face. "You poor fools! The Colonel's got a big start on you! The man who brought us down the steps was the Colonel. That was Vinal himself. He's made another getaway!"

The Guide's Story

Dion Henderson

The bank was robbed on the Monday morning after the deer season opened. That was what made it possible, the hunting season, and the snow, which had started on Friday. The town began to fill up with hunters, but then on Saturday when the hunting should have been splendid, the wind shifted, bringing rain, and the back roads turned to mire. Sunday was miserable, with gray scudding clouds and intermittent sleet, but then it got colder and the wind came up strongly in the north. By Monday morning there was driving snow and the hunters stayed.

Joe Grignon, an expert guide, was sitting at the far end of the bar drinking coffee when the three men came into the Lumberjacks' Retreat.

"Hey," one of them said, "you hear about the bank robbery?"

They stomped and brushed futilely, the snow melting too quickly and leaving dark wet patches on the red coats. All three wore hunting clothes. So did the men at the bar, except that most of the hunting coats were hung on chairs or piled on benches in the back room. Most of the hunters did not know one another, but they were very friendly. Everyone is always friendly on the first weekend of deer season, but perhaps most friendly when the weather is bad, preventing competition.

The bar was lined with men, a few still in red coats but the rest, in wool shirts, talking now about the bank robbery; the tables at the side of the barroom were full, and the booths behind, and in the back room Lou Adonis had put plywood across the pool tables and covered it with oilcloth so that there was more space to sit. Across the street there was a line of men two abreast standing dumbly in the snow waiting to get into Jack's Café, and up on East Main, Ma Hurley had declared a moratorium and sent all the girls over to the hotel to help cook and wait on table.

Joe Grignon sat at the far end of the bar with his coffee, listening to the talk. His red cap, with the green button of the guide's license, was pushed back so that his curly black hair hung down on his forehead. His scarlet coat, with the four black stripes that once meant it was worth four prime beaver in trade goods, hung dry on the back rest.

There was a momentary small space beside him and a man smelling of freshly oiled leather and new duck and aftershave lotion edged into it. Lou Adonis brought him a beer, looked at Joe Grignon's coffee cup and moved away.

"Well," the man said cheerfully, "at least there's a little excitement today."

Joe Grignon sighed. "There is, from time to time. If one is patient."

"But not a bank robbery."

"No. But usually by now there are several search parties for city hunters who have become lost."

"That's pretty exciting."

"Only for the man who is lost," Joe Grignon said. "Additionally, by this time there are usually a number of casualties."

"People getting shot accidentally?"

"There is always that question."

"That sounds pretty exciting."

"When the deceased was a dear friend of someone's wife it is occasionally interesting."

"Are they always deceased?"

"When they were a dear friend of someone's wife," Joe Grignon said. "Under such circumstances, the stray bullet is unfailingly accurate."

The man had been looking sidewise at Joe Grignon and now had identified the guide's license.

"This is a measure of the weather?"

"One other thing—no one has shot himself, either, so far—not pulling a loaded rifle from a car, nor climbing a fence. Only when the weather is superlatively bad does no one shoot himself."

"I see," the man said, smiling now. "And what does all this mean as far as tomorrow's hunting is concerned?"

"Tell me," Joe Grignon said, "what is your line of work?"

"I am a dentist in Chicago."

"Excellent. It happens that I have a wisdom tooth that is a great nuisance. What do you recommend?"

"Well, I could give you an appointment, and you could come to my office. I would be glad to look at it."

"Just so," Joe Grignon said, "and I am a guide. If you would put a hundred dollars on the bar, I would be glad to discuss hunting with you for one full day. But it will have to be next year because I do not have any appointments open this season."

"Excuse me," the man said. "I did not mean to be rude."

"Of course not. It was entirely accidental."

After the dentist left, Joe Grignon sat at the bar, with the little space beside him. He could see down the length of the bar through the front window, past the moving silhouette of Lou Adonis, and the stationary silhouette of the palms in the window. Outside, the sheriff's car lumbered heavily up the street, paused briefly and a man wearing a lynx parka over his blue uniform stepped out and walked awkwardly but expertly through the snow toward the Lumberjacks' Retreat. The snow in the street was nearly knee deep now, very wet, with the bottom inch or two watery slush so that it did not pack under traffic but sloshed to one side and formed again.

The man in the blue uniform dropped his parka on a pile of other coats and moved into the space beside Joe Grignon.

"You're a lousy policeman," Joe said. "Why aren't you out chasing bank robbers?"

"I'm not a policeman," John MacKenzie said. "I'm a game warden. The hell with bank robbers."

"Maybe the sheriff will say the hell with poachers, when the Indians start dropping dynamite in the Eau Bois next spring."

"The sheriff doesn't need help on bank robberies; he has the FBI."

"So," Grignon said. "They do not think you are a policeman either."

"They do not seem convinced that the sheriff is a policeman. I left when they discussed whether to give him permission to go to the bathroom."

"All right. The hell with bank robbers."

"Good," the game warden said. "Let's talk about hunting."

"What hunting?"

"Your party must be getting a little nervous. They have invested a lot of money in you, and there is no hunting."

Joe Grignon shrugged. "It doesn't matter. For their investment they are guaranteed a deer."

"Even if there is no hunting?"

"There is always a little hunting." Joe Grignon smiled disarmingly. "After all, I am a very dependable guide."

MacKenzie scowled.

"And now," Grignon said gaily, "you have visions of a hidden shack where I already have killed and dressed five fine bucks with impressive racks, in the event that there is no hunting."

"There are only four in your party, I heard," the game warden said, scowling.

"Five is to provide a choice," Grignon said. "Then there is one left over for Father Grenville's poor."

"Sure there is."

"One must never forget the church and its charitable works," Grignon said. "One never knows when there will be need for the prayers of little children."

"Let me catch you with five deer hanging up some place," the warden said stubbornly.

"That is the only way you'll catch me," Grignon said, still smiling. "If I let you."

"Everybody lies a little. A man from the city tried to check a jackass through Savage's Station yesterday. He said he thought he shot a mule deer."

"Sometimes it is hard to tell."

"A jackass from a mule deer?"

"No," Grignon said. "Whether a man lies a little."

MacKenzie still was considering the alternatives involved when someone new came in the front door. He was wearing a topcoat, a business suit soaked to the knees, and a smart felt hat, and when he took it off to shake away the snow he had a trim eastern haircut. He looked around the steamy haze of the bar-room, and when he saw the blue uniform at the end of the bar he came forward purposefully.

"A friend of yours, MacKenzie?"

"Maybe the sheriff has locked himself in the bathroom."

The young man stood very close behind them and said quietly, "Is this the guide?"

"Yes, sir," MacKenzie answered.

"Je suis Grignon," Grignon said.

"Does he speak English?"

"Very little," Grignon said. "Un petit."

"Good," the young man said seriously. "You may speak it now."

"Certainement."

The warden looked straight ahead out the window.

The young man said, "Someone left the bank in a great hurry this morning. It is why I am here."

Grignon said, "You mean the bank robber?"

"I am not prepared to discuss what has transpired," the young man said stiffly.

"Pardonnez mois."

"English, please."

"Excuse me. English it is."

"Very good. As I was saying, a man left the bank."

"You said that."

"Never mind. The point is, I would like to ask you a question."

"It is nearly noon."

"I am not authorized to buy you any lunch."

"Only to ask the question."

"That is correct."

"Excuse me," Grignon said, "but I have forgotten the question."

"I haven't asked it yet."

"Oh."

"Are you sure," the young man said to MacKenzie, "that this is the best guide in the country?"

"Yes," MacKenzie said.

"Merci," Joe Grignon said. "Beaucoup. And you are the finest game warden."

"He's the only game warden," the young man said. "My question is, how far could a man go on foot on a day like this?"

"After leaving the bank in a hurry?"

"All right, after leaving the bank in a hurry."

"Carrying money?"

"Say he was carrying money."

"A mile," Joe Grignon said. "Possibly two, if he were strong."

"Very good," the young man said. "Is there any place within that distance where he might successfully seclude himself?"

"Even three miles," Grignon said thoughtfully. "If the money were very light."

MacKenzie said warningly, "Answer the question."

"There is such a place," Grignon said. "Is there not, MacKenzie?"

"I know of no such place," the warden said.

The young man waited.

"It is just possible," Grignon said, "that in all the length and breadth of the Coupe de Foudre, Monsieur, from the Coteau des Gros Pins on the south, along the vast watershed of Les Guerrières and the twinkling waters of La Belle Lac des Mille et Une Lacs, to the forbidding frontier of Le Pay d'en Haut, there is one secluded place which is known to me but not to my good friend the warden."

"Yes," MacKenzie said, almost to himself. "Where he hangs the bloody deer."

The young man ignored MacKenzie.

"Take me there?"

"If you agree not to tell the warden."

"I cannot make any agreement like that."

Grignon shrugged. "Then let the warden take you."

"But you heard him. He does not know of any such place."

"Yes, I heard him."

"It is your duty," the young man said earnestly, staring at Grignon.

"That's different," Grignon said. "I am very public-spirited."

"Then you'll take me?"

"Of course. Since it is my duty."

"If I were you," the warden said, "I would not go."

"That is because you are not public-spirited," Grignon told him. "In addition, you have an evil mind."

"When?" the young man said. "When can we go?"

Grignon looked at his watch, then turned on his stool and squinted across the room at a calendar.

"Tomorrow," he said. "If it stops snowing. If not then, possibly next week. Certainly," he said, "in the spring."

The young man's face went through minute tightening stages before it turned red. "Thank you for your time," he said tightly.

When he was gone, Grignon laughed until he wept. MacKenzie sat staring stonily out the window. It was a great effort.

"You are pretty funny," he said. "But it will not be so funny for the man who robbed the bank."

"You have faith that they will catch him?"

"Of course," the warden said. "They always do. A man cannot get off the road in this weather, and the roads are so bad he cannot get away fast. They have all the roads blocked for a hundred miles, and when the snow stops they will have the airplanes up. Even if he gets away, they will have a thread from his hunting coat, or a couple of numbers from a license plate, or perhaps from his hunting license tag, and they will spend months quietly running things through the analyzers and computers and next year they will rap on someone's door and say politely, 'You're under arrest.' "

"The way you explain it," Grignon said, "it is all very complicated."

MacKenzie looked sidewise, suspiciously.

"It is fortunate that you became a game warden," Grignon said. "I do not think you have the head for this other work."

"You are not very much impressed."

"Un peu," Grignon said, "as they used to say back in the French seminar at the mission school."

"Sure they did."

"Suppose it were not so complicated," Grignon said. "Suppose a man were sitting at a bar somewhere, and it was very dull, and he thought it might be interesting to rob a bank."

"All right, suppose he were."

"Suppose he knew that Albert Tangora arrives at his bank an hour before the first teller, without fail."

"That is no great supposition. Everyone here knows about it."

"And it is Monday morning, and the night depository is very full, from the first weekend of deer hunting when there was no hunting, but only the saloons and the hotel and Ma Hurley's, and the bags in the night depository are full of dirty, wrinkled old money that does not at the moment have any recorded pedigree, being of all denominations and numbers and quite unrelated."

"You're right," MacKenzie said. "This is very interesting."

"So suppose this man at the crowded bar announces he must make a short trip to the washroom, and goes back through the arch, and from the great pile of hunting coats he selects one, and from another a stocking cap, and takes a cased rifle from the stack in the corner, and walks out the side door in the driving snow and up the alley to the bank."

MacKenzie did not say anything.

"And with the stocking cap pulled over his face, permitting him to see clearly through the yarn, he huddles at the front door of the bank in the snow, and taps on the glass, and Albert Tangora lifts the green shade and peeks out at him, seeing only a forlorn hunter huddling against the storm, what does he think?"

MacKenzie said. "You know what he would think, old Tangora. He would think about some poor devil needing to cash a check because he played poker too long, or went to sleep at Ma Hurley's, and he would twitch his nose and giggle and speculate on all the details while he stood peeking out under the shade."

"Just so. And then he would open the door," Grignon said. "Would he not?"

"Yes," MacKenzie said. "The old fool."

"Now," said Joe Grignon, "suppose that when he opened the door, the man outside came in very quickly with the wind and the snow and judiciously poked Albert Tangora in his fat belly with one end of the cased rifle, and when Albert bent over with a mighty grunt, the man then thumped him sufficiently on the head with the other end."

MacKenzie said thoughtfully, "It would not take a man long, then, to empty the money from the bags in the night depository, and to walk out."

"Locking the door behind him," said Joe Grignon. "And then walking rapidly with his head down against the snow, like a hundred other men in the same block on the same sidewalk, return down the alley, put the rifle in the stack, the coat on the bench and resume his place at the bar, all in less time than it would have taken for him to wait his turn there at the bathroom."

The warden looked hard out the window. The snow was beginning to let up. Several men at the bar began to talk about going hunting, and a few straggled after their coats. The warden sighed heavily. "It is too simple," he said. "Even if it were that simple, he eventually would start to spend the money and then he would be caught."

"I am not sure," Grignon said. "Suppose it were not the money, after all. Suppose when he returned with the coat pockets stuffed full of money, he took a handful and put it in this coat, and another handful in that coat, and so on. There must be fifty coats back there on the bench, to say nothing of those that are hung carefully on the racks."

"You make a joke of it," MacKenzie said, "but a bank robbery is not a joke. Whatever it is, it is no joke."

"Even so," Grignon was smiling. "Do you remember my grandfather?"

"The one who killed the bear with the hatchet?"

"Now you have it." Grignon still was smiling but he was very serious. "For this reason, he is very well remembered, even by those who have no idea whether he really killed the bear, even," he said slyly, "though I am not sure myself that there was any evidence at the time that would have stood up in court."

"Except the dead bear."

"Of course. There was the bear, in the one case. In another there might be something else."

"Money, for instance."

"You are very quick, for a Scotsman."

MacKenzie said nothing. He picked up his coffee cup, sipped, then made a small disgusted sound because the coffee was cold.

Grignon said gently, "When my grandfather was young, a man who felt himself different than other men did not have to talk about it. He could fight a bear, and there was no need for talk."

"Unless the bear won."

"The risk is essential," Grignon said. "Each man who would be daring must find the ultimate risk, in his own way."

Outside, the snow was definitely stopping, and hunters were beginning to leave. One stopped at the bar to pay for the last round of drinks, put his hand in the pocket of his red coat and took it out. Startled, he looked at the wad of ten and twenty dollar bills in his hand. Then, quickly, he took a ten from the wad and tossed it on the bar and left.

"After all," Joe Grignon said smiling. "What does money matter, so long as one has one's health, n'est ce pas?"

Woodrow Wilson's Necktie

Patricia Highsmith

The façade of MADAME THIBAULT'S WAXWORK HORRORS glittered and throbbed with red and yellow lights, even in the daytime. Knobs of golden balls—the yellow lights—pulsated amid the red lights, attracting the eye and holding it.

Clive Wilkes loved the place, the inside and the outside equally. Since he was a delivery boy for a grocery store, it was easy for him to say that a certain delivery had taken him longer than had been expected—he'd had to wait for Mrs. So-and-so to get home because the doorman had told him she was due back any minute, or he'd had to go five blocks to find some change because Mrs. Smith had had only a twenty-dollar bill. At these spare moments—and Clive managed one or two a week—he visited MADAME THIBAULT'S WAXWORK HORRORS.

Inside the establishment you went through a dark passage—to be put in the mood—and then you were confronted by a bloody murder scene on the left: a girl with long blonde hair was sticking a knife into the neck of an old man who sat at a kitchen table eating his dinner. His dinner consisted of two wax frankfurters and wax sauerkraut. Then came the Lindbergh kidnaping scene, with Hauptmann climbing down a ladder outside a nursery window; you could see the top of the ladder out the window, and the top half of Hauptmann's figure, clutching

101

the little boy. Also there was Marat in his bath with Charlotte nearby. And Christie with his stocking, throttling a woman.

Clive loved every tableau, and they never became stale. But he didn't look at them with the solemn, vaguely startled expression of the other people who looked at them. Clive was inclined to smile, even to laugh. They were amusing. So why not laugh?

Farther on in the museum were the torture chambers—one old, one modern, purporting to show Twentieth Century torture methods in Nazi Germany and in French Algeria. Madame Thibault—who Clive strongly suspected did not exist—kept up to date. There were the Kennedy assassinations and the Tate massacre, of course, and some murder that had happened only a month ago somewhere.

Clive's first definite ambition in regard to MADAME THIBAULT'S WAXWORK HORRORS museum was to spend a night there. This he did one night, providently taking along a cheese sandwich in his pocket. It was fairly easy to accomplish. Clive knew that three people worked in the museum proper—down in the bowels, as he thought of it, though the museum was on street level—while a fourth, a plumpish middle-aged man in a nautical cap, sold tickets at a booth in front. The three who worked in the bowels were two men and a woman; the woman, also plump and with curly brown hair and glasses and about forty, took the tickets at the end of the dark corridor, where the museum proper began.

One of the inside men lectured constantly, though not more than half the people ever bothered to listen. "Here we see the fanatical expression of the true murderer, captured by the supreme wax artistry of Madame Thibault"—and so on. The other inside man had black hair and black-rimmed glasses like the woman, and he just drifted around, shooing away kids who wanted to climb into the tableaux, maybe watching for pickpockets, or maybe protecting women from unpleasant assaults in the semidarkness. Clive didn't know.

He only knew it was quite easy to slip into one of the dark corners or into a nook next to one of the Iron Molls—maybe even into one of the Iron Molls; but slender as he was, the spikes might poke into him, Clive thought, so he ruled out this idea. He had observed that people were gently urged out around 9:15 P.M., as the museum closed at 9:30 P.M. And lingering as late as possible one evening, Clive had learned that there was a sort of cloakroom for the staff behind a door in one back corner, from which direction he had also heard the sound of a toilet flushing.

So one night in November, Clive concealed himself in the shadows, which were abundant, and listened to the three people as they got ready to leave. The woman—whose name turned out to be Mildred—was lingering to take the money box from Fred, the ticket seller, and to count it and deposit it somewhere in the cloakroom. Clive was not interested in the money. He was only interested in spending a night in the place and being able to boast he had.

"Night, Mildred—see you tomorrow," called one of the men.

"Anything else to do? I'm leaving now," said Mildred. "Boy, am I tired! But I'm still going to watch Dragon Man tonight."

"Dragon Man," the other man repeated, uninterested.

Evidently the ticket seller, Fred, left from the front of the building after handing in the money box, and in fact Clive recalled seeing him close up the front once, cutting the lights from inside the entrance door, then locking the door and barring it on the outside.

Clive stood in a nook by an Iron Moll. When he heard the back door shut and the key turn in the lock, he waited for a moment in delicious silence, aloneness, and suspense, and then ventured out. He went first, on tiptoe, to the room where they kept their coats, because he had never seen it. He had brought matches—also cigarettes, though smoking was not allowed, according to several signs—and with the aid of a match he found the light switch. The room contained an old desk, four metal lockers, a tin wastebasket, an umbrella stand, and some books in a bookcase against a grimy wall that had once been white. Clive slid open a drawer and found the well-worn wooden box which he had once seen the ticket seller carrying in through the front door. The box was locked. He could walk out with the box, Clive thought, but he didn't care to, and he considered this rather decent of himself. He gave the box a wipe with the side of his hand, not forgetting the bottom where his fingertips had touched. That was funny, he thought, wiping something he wasn't going to steal.

Clive set about enjoying the night. He found the lights and put them on so that the booths with the gory tableaux were all illuminated. He was hungry, took one bite of his sandwich, then put it back in the paper napkin in his pocket. He sauntered slowly past the John F. Kennedy assassination—Mrs. Kennedy and the doctors bending anxiously over the white table on which JFK lay. This time, Hauptmann's descent of the ladder made Clive giggle. Charles Lindbergh, Jr.'s face looked so untroubled that one would think he might be sitting on the floor of his nursery, playing with blocks.

Clive swung a leg over a metal bar and climbed into the Judd-Snyder tableau. It gave him a thrill to be standing right *with* them, inches from the throttling-from-behind which the lover of the woman was administering to the husband. Clive put a hand out and touched the red-paint blood that was seeming to come from the man's throat where the cord pressed deep. Clive also touched the cool cheekbones of the victim. The popping eyes were of glass, vaguely disgusting, and Clive did not touch those.

Two hours later he was singing church hymns, *Nearer My God to Thee* and *Jesus Wants Me for a Sunbeam.* Clive didn't know all the words. And he smoked.

By two in the morning he was bored and tried to get out by both the front door and back, but couldn't—both were barred on the outside. He had thought of having a hamburger at an all-night diner between here and home. However, his enforced incarceration didn't bother him, so he finished the now-dry cheese sandwich and slept for a bit on three straight chairs which he arranged in a row. It was so uncomfortable that he knew he'd wake up in a while, which he did—at 5:00 A.M. He washed his face, then went for another look at the wax exhibits. This time he took a souvenir—Woodrow Wilson's necktie.

As the hour of 9:00 approached—MADAME THIBAULT'S WAXWORK HORRORS opened at 9:30 A.M.—Clive hid himself in an excellent spot, behind one of the tableaux whose backdrop was a black-and-gold Chinese screen. In front of the screen was a bed and in the bed lay a wax man with a handlebar mustache, who was supposed to have been poisoned by his wife.

The public began to trickle in shortly after 9:30 A.M., and the taller, more solemn man began to mumble his boring lecture. Clive had to wait till a few minutes past ten before he felt safe enough to mingle with the crowd and make his exit, with Woodrow Wilson's necktie rolled up in his pocket. He was a bit tired, but happy—though on second thought, who would he tell about it? Joey Vrasky, that dumb cluck who worked behind the counter at Simmons' Grocery? Hah! Why bother? Joey didn't deserve a good story. Clive was half an hour late for work.

"I'm sorry, Mr. Simmons, I overslept," Clive said hastily, but he thought quite politely, as he came into the store. There was a delivery job awaiting him. Clive took his bicycle and put the carton on a platform in front of the handlebars.

Clive lived with his mother, a thin highly strung woman who was a saleswoman in a shop that sold stockings, girdles, and underwear. Her husband had left her when Clive was nine. She had no other children. Clive had quit high school a year before graduation, to his mother's regret, and for a year he had done nothing but lie around the house or stand on street corners with his pals. But Clive had never been very chummy with any of them, for which his mother was thankful, as she considered them a worthless lot. Clive had had the delivery job at Simmons' for nearly a year now, and his mother felt that he was settling down.

When Clive came home that evening at 6:30 P.M. he had a story ready for his mother. Last night he had run into his old friend Richie, who was in the Army and home on leave, and they had sat up at Richie's house talking so late that Richie's parents had invited him to stay over, and Clive had slept on the couch. His mother accepted this explanation. She made a supper of baked beans, bacon, and eggs.

There was really no one to whom Clive felt like telling his exploit of the night. He couldn't have borne someone looking at him and saying, "Yeah? So what?" because what he had done had taken a bit of planning, even a little daring. He put Woodrow Wilson's tie among his others that hung over a string on the inside of his closet door. It was a gray silk tie, conservative and expensive-looking. Several times that day Clive imagined one of the two men in the museum, or maybe the woman named Mildred, glancing at Woodrow Wilson and exclaiming, "Hey! What happened to Woodrow Wilson's tie, I wonder?"

Each time Clive thought of this he had to duck his head to hide a smile.

After twenty-four hours, however, the exploit had begun to lose its charm and excitement. Clive's excitement only rose again—and it could rise two or three times a day—whenever he cycled past the twinkling façade of MADAME THIBAULT'S WAXWORK HORRORS. His heart would give a leap, his blood would run a little faster, and he would think of all the motionless murders going on in there, and all the stupid faces of Mr. and Mrs. Johnny Q. Public gaping at them. But Clive didn't even buy another ticket—price 65 cents—to go in and look at Woodrow Wilson and see that his tie was missing and his collar button showing—his work.

Clive did get another idea one afternoon, a hilarious idea that would make the public sit up and take notice. Clive's ribs trembled with suppressed laughter as he pedaled toward Simmons', having just delivered a bag of groceries.

When should he do it? Tonight? No, best to take a day or so to plan it. It would take brains. And silence. And sure movements—all the things Clive admired.

He spent two days thinking about it. He went to his local snack bar and drank beer and played pinball machines with his pals. The pinball machines had pulsating lights too—*More Than One Can Play* and *It's More Fun To Compete*—but Clive thought only of MADAME THIBAULT'S as he stared at the rolling, bouncing balls that mounted a score he cared nothing about. It was the same when he looked at the rainbow-colored jukebox whose blues, reds, and yellows undulated, and when he went over to drop a coin in it. He was thinking of what he was going to do in MADAME THIBAULT'S WAXWORK HORRORS.

On the second night, after a supper with his mother, Clive went to MADAME THIBAULT'S and bought a ticket. The old guy who sold tickets barely looked at people, he was so busy making change and tearing off the stubs, which was just as well. Clive went in at 9:00 P.M.

He looked at the tableaux, though they were not so fascinating to him tonight as they had been before. Woodrow Wilson's tie was still missing, as if no one had noticed it, and Clive chuckled over this. He remembered that the solemn-faced pickpocket-watcher—the drifting snoop—had been the last to leave the night Clive had stayed, so Clive assumed he had the keys, and therefore he ought to be the last to be killed.

The woman was the first. Clive hid himself beside one of the Iron Molls again, while the crowd ambled out, and when Mildred walked by him, in her hat and coat, to leave by the back door, having just said something to one of the men in the exhibition hall, Clive stepped out and wrapped an arm around her throat from behind.

She made only a small *ur-rk* sound.

Clive squeezed her throat with his hands, stopping her voice. At last she slumped, and Clive dragged her into a dark, recessed corner to the left of the cloakroom. He knocked an empty cardboard box of some kind over, but it didn't make enough noise to attract the attention of the two men.

"Mildred gone?" one of the men asked.

"I think she's in the office."

"No, she's not." The owner of the voice had already gone into the corridor where Clive crouched over Mildred and had looked into the empty cloakroom where the light was still on. "She's left. Well, I'm calling it a day too."

Clive stepped out then and encircled this man's neck in the same manner. The job was more difficult, because the man struggled, but Clive's arm was thin and strong; he acted with swiftness and knocked the man's head against the wooden floor.

"What's going on?" The thump had brought the second man.

This time Clive tried a punch to the man's jaw, but missed and hit his neck. However, this so stunned the man—the little solemn fellow, the snoop—that a quick second blow was easy, and then Clive was able to take him by the shirtfront and bash his head against the plaster wall which was harder than the wooden floor. Then Clive made sure that all three were dead. The two men's heads were bloody. The woman was bleeding slightly from her mouth. Clive reached for the keys in the second man's pockets. They were in his left trousers pocket and with them was a penknife. Clive also took the knife.

Then the taller man moved slightly. Alarmed, Clive opened the pearl-handled penknife and plunged it into the man's throat three times.

Close call, Clive thought, as he checked again to make sure they were all dead. They most certainly were, and that was

most certainly real blood, not the red paint of MADAME THI-
BAULT'S WAXWORK HORRORS. Clive switched on the lights for
the tableaux and went into the exhibition hall for the interesting task of choosing exactly the right places for the three
corpses.

The woman belonged in Marat's bath—not much doubt
about that. Clive debated removing her clothing, but decided
against it, simply because she would look much funnier sitting
in a bath wearing a fur-trimmed coat and hat. The figure of
Marat sent him off into laughter. He'd expected sticks for legs,
and nothing between the legs, because you couldn't see any
more of Marat than from the middle of his torso up; but Marat
had no legs at all and his wax body ended just below the waist
in a fat stump which was planted on a wooden platform so that
it would not topple. This crazy waxwork Clive carried into the
cloakroom and placed squarely in the middle of the desk. He
then carried the woman—who weighed a good deal—onto the
Marat scene and put her in the bath. Her hat fell off, and he
pushed it on again, a bit over one eye. Her bloody mouth hung
open.

Good lord, it *was* funny!

Now for the men. Obviously, the one whose throat he had
knifed would look good in the place of the old man who was
eating wax franks and sauerkraut, because the girl behind him
was supposed to be stabbing him in the throat. This took Clive
some fifteen minutes. Since the figure of the old man was in a
seated position, Clive put him on the toilet off the cloakroom.
It was terribly amusing to see the old man seated on the toilet,
throat apparently bleeding, a knife in one hand and a fork in the
other. Clive lurched against the door jamb, laughing loudly, not
even caring if someone heard him, because it was so comical it
was even worth getting caught for.

Next, the little snoop. Clive looked around him and his eye
fell on the Woodrow Wilson scene which depicted the signing
of the armistice in 1918. A wax figure sat at a huge desk signing
something, and that was the logical place for a man whose head
was almost split open. With some difficulty Clive got the pen out
of the wax man's fingers, laid it on one side on the desk, and
carried the figure—it didn't weigh much—into the cloakroom,
where Clive seated him at the desk, rigid arms in an attitude

of writing. Clive stuck a ballpoint pen into his right hand. Now for the last heave. Clive saw that his jacket was now quite spotted with blood and he would have to get rid of it, but so far there was no blood on his trousers.

Clive dragged the second man to the Woodrow Wilson tableau, lifted him up, and rolled him toward the desk. He got him onto the chair, but the head toppled forward onto the green-blottered desk, onto the blank wax pages, and the pen barely stood upright in the limp hand.

But it was done. Clive stood back and smiled. Then he listened. He sat down on a straight chair and rested for a few minutes, because his heart was beating fast and he suddenly realized that every muscle in his body was tired. Ah, well, he now had the keys. He could lock up, go home, and have a good night's rest, because he wanted to be ready to enjoy tomorrow.

Clive took a sweater from one of the male figures in a log-cabin tableau of some kind. He had to pull the sweater down over the feet of the waxwork to get it off, because the arms would not bend; it stretched the neck of the sweater, but he couldn't help that. Now the wax figure had a sort of bib for a shirtfront, and naked arms and chest.

Clive wadded up his jacket and went everywhere with it, erasing fingerprints from whatever he thought he had touched. He turned the lights off, made his way carefully to the back door, locked and barred it behind him, and would have left the keys in a mailbox if there had been one; but there wasn't, so he dropped the keys on the rear doorstep. In a wire rubbish basket he found some newspapers; he wrapped up his jacket in them and walked on with it until he found another wire rubbish basket, where he forced the bundle down among candy wrappers, beer cans, and other trash.

"A new sweater?" his mother asked that night.

"Richie gave it to me—for luck."

Clive slept like the dead, too tired to even laugh again at the memory of the old man sitting on the toilet.

The next morning Clive was standing across the street when the ticket seller arrived just before 9:30 A.M. By 9:35 A.M. only four people had gone in; but Clive could not wait any longer, so he crossed the street and bought a ticket. Now the ticket seller was doubling as ticket taker, and telling people, "Just go on in. Everybody's late this morning."

The ticket man stepped inside the door to put on some lights, then walked all the way into the place to put on the display lights for the tableaux, which worked from switches in the hall that led to the cloakroom. And the funny thing, to Clive who was walking behind him, was that the ticket man didn't notice anything odd, didn't even notice Mildred in her hat and coat sitting in Marat's bathtub.

The other customers so far were a man and a woman, a boy of fourteen or so in sneakers, alone apparently, and a single man. They looked expressionlessly at Mildred in the tub as if they thought it quite "normal," which would have sent Clive into paroxysms of mirth, except that his heart was thumping madly and he could hardly breathe for the suspense. Also, the man with his face in franks and sauerkraut brought no surprise either. Clive was a bit disappointed.

Two more people came in, a man and a woman.

Then at last, in front of Woodrow Wilson tableau, there was a reaction. One of the women, clinging to her husband's arm, asked. "Was someone shot when the armistice was signed?"

"I don't know. I don't *think* so," the man replied vaguely.

Clive's laughter pressed like an explosion in his chest; he spun on his heel to control himself, and he had the feeling he knew *all* about history, and that no one else did. By now, of course, the real blood had turned to a rust color. The green blotter was now splotched, and blood had dripped down the side of the desk.

A woman on the other side of the room, where Mildred was, let out a scream.

A man laughed, but only briefly.

Suddenly everything happened. A woman shrieked, and at the same time a man yelled, "My God, it's *real!*"

Clive saw a man climbing up to investigate the corpse with his face in the frankfurters.

"The blood's *real!* It's a *dead* man!"

Another man—one of the public—slumped to the floor. He had fainted.

The ticket seller came bustling in. "What's the trouble here?"

"Coupla corpses—*real* ones!"

Now the ticket seller looked at Marat's bathtub and fairly jumped into the air with surprise, "Holy Christmas! *Holy cripes!*—it's *Mildred!*"

"And this one!"

"And the one here!"

"My God, got to—got to call the police!" said the ticket seller. One man and woman left hurriedly. But the rest lingered, shocked, fascinated.

The ticket seller had run into the cloakroom, where the telephone was, and Clive heard him yell something. He'd seen the man at the desk, of course, the wax man, and the half body of Marat on the desk.

Clive thought it was time to drift out, so he did, sidling his way through a group of people peering in the front door, perhaps intending to come in because there was no ticket seller.

That was good. Clive thought. That was all right. Not bad. Not bad at all.

He had not intended to go to work that day, but suddenly he thought it wiser to check in and ask for the day off. Mr. Simmons was of course as sour as ever when Clive said he was not feeling well, but as Clive held his stomach and appeared weak, there was little old Simmons could do. Clive left the grocery. He had brought with him all his ready cash, about $23.

Clive wanted to take a long bus ride somewhere. He realized that suspicion might fall on him, if the ticket seller remembered his coming to MADAME THIBAULT'S often, or especially if he remembered Clive being there last night; but this really had little to do with his desire to take a bus ride. His longing for a bus ride was simply, somehow, irresistible. He bought a ticket westward for $8 and change, one way. This brought him, by about 7:00 P.M., to a good-sized town in Indiana, whose name Clive paid no attention to.

The bus spilled a few passengers, Clive included, at a terminal, where there was a cafeteria and a bar. By now Clive was curious about the newspapers, so he went to the newsstand near the street door of the cafeteria. And there were the headlines:

Triple Murder in Waxworks
Mass Murder in Museum
Mystery Killer Strikes: Three Dead in Waxworks

Clive liked the last one best. He bought the three newspapers, and stood at the bar with a beer.

"This morning at 9:30 A.M., ticket-man Fred J. Carmody and several of the public who had come to see Madam Thibault's Waxwork Horrors, a noted attraction of this city, were confronted by three genuine corpses among the displays. They were the bodies of Mrs. Mildred Veery, 41; George P. Hartley, 43; and Richard K. McFadden, 37, all employed at the waxworks museum. The two men were killed by concussion and stabbing, and the woman by strangulation. Police are searching for clues on the premises. The murders are believed to have taken place shortly before 10:00 P.M. last evening, when the three employees were about to leave the museum. The murderer or murderers may have been among the last patrons of the museum before closing time at 9:30 P.M. It is thought that he or they may have concealed themselves somewhere in the museum until the rest of the patrons had left . . ."

Clive was pleased. He smiled as he sipped his beer. He hunched over the papers, as if he did not wish the rest of the world to share his pleasure, but this was not true. After a few minutes Clive stood up and looked to the right and left to see if anyone else among the men and women at the bar was also reading the story. Two men were reading newspapers, but Clive could not tell if they were reading about him, because their newspapers were folded.

Clive lit a cigarette and went through all three newpapers to see if any clue to him was mentioned. He found nothing. One paper said specificially that Fred. J. Carmody had not noticed any person or persons entering the museum last evening who looked suspicious.

". . . Because of the bizarre arrangement of the victims and of the displaced wax figures in the exhibition, in whose places the victims were put, police are looking for a psychopathic killer. Residents of the area have been warned by radio and television to take special precautions on the streets and to keep their houses locked."

Clive chuckled over that one. Psychopathic killer! He was sorry about the lack of detail, the lack of humor in the three reporters' stories. They might have said something about the old guy sitting on the toilet. Or the fellow signing the armistice with the back of his head bashed in. Those were strokes of genius. Why didn't they appreciate them?

When he finished his beer, Clive walked out onto the sidewalk. It was now dark and the streetlights were on. He enjoyed looking around in the new town, looking into shop windows. But he was aiming for a hamburger place, and he went into the first one he came to. It was a diner made up to look like a crack railway car.

Clive ordered a hamburger and a cup of coffee. Next to him were two Western-looking men in cowboy boots and rather soiled broad-brimmed hats. Was one a sheriff, Clive wondered? But they were talking, in a drawl, about acreage somewhere. Land. They were hunched over hamburgers and coffee, one so close that his elbow kept touching Clive's. Clive was reading his newspapers all over again and he had propped one against the napkin container in front of him.

One of the men asked for a napkin and disturbed Clive, but Clive smiled and said in a friendly way, "Did you read about the murders in the waxworks?"

The man looked blank for a moment, then said, "Yep, saw the headlines."

"Someone killed the three people who worked in the place. Look." There was a photograph in one of the papers, but Clive didn't much like it because it showed the corpses lined up on the floor. He would have preferred Mildred in the bathtub.

"Yeah" said the Westerner, edging away from Clive as if he didn't like him.

"The bodies were put into a few of the exhibits. Like the wax figures. They say that, but they don't show a picture of it," said Clive.

"Yeah," said the Westerner, and went on eating.

Clive felt let down and somehow insulted. His face grew a little warm as he stared back at his newspapers. In fact, anger was growing quickly inside him, making his heart go faster, as it always did when he passed MADAME THIBAULT'S WAXWORK HORRORS, though now the sensation was not at all pleasant.

Clive put on a smile, however, and turned to the man on his left again. "I mention it, because I did it. That's my work there." He gestured toward the picture of the corpses.

"Listen, boy," said the Westerner casually, "you just keep to yourself tonight. Okay? We ain't botherin' you, so don't you go botherin' us." He laughed a little, glancing at his companion.

His friend was staring at Clive, but looked away at once when Clive stared back.

This was a double rebuff, and quite enough for Clive. He got out his money and paid for his unfinished food with a dollar bill. He left the change and walked to the sliding-door exit.

"But y'know maybe that guy ain't kiddin'!" Clive heard one of the men say.

Clive turned and said, "I *ain't* kiddin'!" Then he went out into the night.

Clive slept at a Y.M.C.A. The next day he half expected he would be picked up by a passing cop on the beat, but he wasn't. He got a lift to another town, nearer his hometown. The day's newspapers brought no mention of his name, and no mention of clues. In another café that evening, almost the identical conversation took place between Clive and a couple of fellows his own age. They didn't believe him. It was stupid of them, Clive thought, and he wondered if they were pretending? Or lying?

Clive hitched his way home and headed for the police station. He was curious as to what *they* would say. He imagined what his mother would say after he confessed. Probably the same thing she had said to her friends sometimes, or that she'd said to a policeman when he was sixteen and had stolen a car.

"Clive hasn't been the same since his father went away. I know he needs a man around the house, a man to look up to, imitate, you know. That's what people tell me. Since he was fourteen Clive's been asking me questions like, " 'Who am I, anyway?' and 'Am I a person, mom?' " Clive could see and hear her in the police station.

"I have an important confession to make," Clive said to a deskman in the front.

The man's attitude was rude and suspicious, Clive thought, but he was told to walk to an office, where he spoke with a police officer who had gray hair and a fat face. Clive told his story.

"Where do you go to school, Clive?"

"I don't. I'm eighteen." Clive told him about his job at Simmons' Grocery.

"Clive, you've got troubles, but they're not the ones you're talking about," said the officer.

Clive had to wait in a room, and nearly an hour later a psychiatrist was brought in. Then his mother. Clive became more and more impatient. They didn't believe him. They were saying his was a typical case of false confession in order to draw attention to himself. His mother's repeated statements about his asking questions like "Am I a person?" and "Who am I?" only seemed to corroborate the opinions of the psychiatrist and the police.

Clive was to report somewhere twice a week for psychiatric therapy.

He fumed. He refused to back to Simmons' Grocery, but found another delivery job, because he liked having a little money in his pocket, and he was fast on his bicycle and honest with the change.

"You haven't *found* the murderer, have you?" Clive said to the police psychiatrist. "You're all the biggest bunch of jackasses I've ever seen in my life!"

The psychiatrist said soothingly, "You'll never get anywhere talking to people like that, boy."

Clive said, "Some perfectly ordinary strangers in Indiana said, 'Maybe that guy ain't kidding.' They had more sense than *you!*"

The psychiatrist smiled.

Clive smoldered. One thing might have helped prove his story—Woodrow Wilson's necktie, which still hung in his closet. But these dumb clucks damned well didn't deserve to see that tie. Even as he ate his suppers with his mother, went to the movies, and delivered groceries, he was planning. He'd do something more important next time—like starting a fire in depths of a big building or planting a bomb somewhere or taking a machinegun up to some penthouse and letting 'em have it down on the street. Kill a hundred people at least, or a thousand. They'd have to come up in the building to get him. *Then* they'd know. *Then* they'd treat him like somebody who really existed, like somebody who deserved a wax model of himself in MADAME THIBAULT'S WAXWORK HORRORS.

Something for the Dark

Edward D. Hoch

The monthly editorial sessions were held in the cork-walled conference room at *Neptune Magazine,* and for Steve Foley they were often the most interesting part of the office routine. He hadn't yet been on the *Neptune* editorial staff long enough to be bored by the individual mannerisms of the dozen or so men and women who lounged about the massive oak table, and it was one of the few times during the month when he felt he was actually contributing something toward the finished product on the printed page.

Steve was still under thirty when he'd joined *Neptune* a year earlier. In his position as associate feature editor he was surprised even to be included in the editorial planning sessions, but Mike Eldon, ashen-haired editor-in-chief, was a man who liked to have a full staff around the polished oak table. He'd brought the magazine a long way since the day when it was founded as "a monthly compendium of fable, fashion and food for those who travel the seven seas." Today *Neptune* devoted more space to fact than fiction, and most of it was likely to take place on solid ground. If its emphasis was still on "the adventure of travel," both "adventure" and "travel" were interpreted in their broadest meanings.

"People," Mike Eldon said, hitting the polished surface with

116

his fist, "that's what the readers care about, and that's what sells copies. No more stories about some mountain in the Andes. Now we do stories on the people who climb that mountain!"

It was a stock speech, and he repeated it in some form or another at almost every meeting, but no one could deny that it was mainly this philosophy which had helped boost *Neptune's* lagging circulation from 875,000 to nearly two million in three short years.

"The October issue," Mike Eldon said, tapping the table with his rubber-tipped pencil. It was still early summer, but in the magazine business you always live in the future. "Halloween. You know, something for the dark."

Steve Foley raised a finger. "I've got a funny one on my desk right now. Came in from an agent. A man and his wife, on a camping trip a few months ago, claim they were attacked by some sort of great winged creature that even carried off their dog." He'd been about to reject the thing, but now it just might have possibilities.

Eldon frowned down the table at him. "That's a bit out of *Neptune's* line. Still, it might be what we're looking for." He turned to the art director. "Harry, could you do a full page, in color, of a winged creature? A *great* winged creature? With red eyes, maybe? Probably something like those old illustrations of the Jabberwock in *Through the Looking-Glass*. Was it a Jabberwock by any chance, Steve?"

"I'm just as skeptical as you are, but do you want something for October or don't you?"

"I want something our readers will *believe*—at least enough to scare them a little." He sighed and stopped tapping the pencil. "All right, what the hell! Look into it, Steve. Talk to the people and see if there's any truth at all in it. You've got ten days before we lock up the issue. If it looks good to you, we'll run it. But take a camera along. Get some pictures of where it happened—whatever it was."

That was how it started.

Steve Foley phoned the agent who had submitted the article, a little Frenchman with a slight accent who worked out of his apartment on Central Park West. "Pete, this is Steve over at *Neptune.*" Everyone called him Pete, because it was easier than

trying to pronounce his real name. "It's about this flying creature article you sent us, by a fellow named Walter Wangard."
"Oh, yes."
"What do you know about him? Any truth to it?"
"I couldn't tell you. He's written a few outdoor items—hunt-
ing, fishing, camping. I think I've sold two or three for him. I'm
not getting rich on it."
"Ever met him? Is he a phony?"
"Doesn't seem like it from his letters. He and his wife live in
a little town near the Pennsylvania border, not far from where
they saw the creature. He's a tire salesman, but he likes the
outdoors."
"I guess I'll have to go see him," Steve said.
"You're going to buy it?"
"Probably, if they're not complete nuts. I want to get some
pictures too."
"Want me to go along?" the agent offered.
"Not necessary. Just let them know I'm coming. I'll drive over
this weekend, maybe."
He left early on Saturday morning while the summer heat
still smoldered unleashed. He was halfway across New Jersey by
ten o'clock, and was pulling into the Wangards' driveway at
noon. Their house was a little white frame place in a little white
frame town, sleepy in the summer except when the city cars
drove through on the way to the lake. There was a church across
the street, and a wedding was in progress. Steve stood for a
moment watching the clouds of colored confetti shower down
on the squealing bride and happy groom. Some things were the
same everywhere, he decided, and lit a cigarette before turning
toward the white frame house.
He had time for just a few puffs before he discarded it and
pressed the doorbell. The woman who came through the dim
living room to the latched screen door was younger than he'd
expected, with long blonde hair and a good figure. He guessed
her to be about his own age, certainly no more than thirty.
"Hello. I'm Steve Foley from *Neptune Magazine.* I believe your
husband is expecting me."
"Oh, yes, Mr. Foley." He stepped in as she unlatched the
door. "This is quite a treat for us, having an editor drive all the
way from New York. I'm Lynn Wangard, Walt's wife."

As if on cue, her husband appeared, tucking the ends of a clean sport shirt into his pants. He was what Steve might have expected—medium height, running just a bit to overweight and thinnish hair, with a ruddy complexion that reflected the outdoor life in a summertime along the Pennsylvania border. "Glad to meet you, Mr. Foley," he said briskly. "My agent told us to expect you."

Steve sat down, trying to feel at ease, telling himself that they seemed friendly enough, yet feeling oddly bothered by something. "We're seriously considering using the account of your experiences in the October issue," he told them. "We just wanted to talk to you in person and perhaps get a few pictures out where it happened."

Lynn Wangard gave a little shiver of anticipation. "We haven't been back there since. It was the most horrible thing that ever happened to me, in my whole life. It was almost like a dream, a terrible nightmare."

"Of course I've read your article," Steve told Wangard, "but I'd appreciate hearing it from your wife again, just briefly, to refresh my memory a little bit, you see."

Walt Wangard smiled thinly. "Or to compare our stories? I assure you they agree."

"Walt!" She seemed to speak a bit sharply. "I'd be glad to tell him about it." Then, turning to Steve, she began. "Actually, it's a very short story. It was the middle of May, and it was the first time we'd been camping this season. The weather was good— a warm evening with lots of stars—but we'd chosen a camping spot a mile or so away from the main area. We don't have any children, and we're always just as happy off by ourselves, away from the other campers. Besides, our dog Jake used to bark a lot at night—you know, just baying at the moon like dogs are supposed to do."

"What kind of dog was he?" Steve asked.

She seemed startled. "A beagle. Surely that was in Walt's article."

"I'd forgotten." He lit another cigarette. "Sorry I interrupted you."

"Anyway, we were sitting around the little fire having a few drinks. Jake was off prowling in the underbrush somewhere, and there were the usual night sounds from the woods. I began to feel strange, and so did Walt. It's hard to explain—it was as if we were no longer alone there. All of a sudden the woods were menacing, the trees seemed to take on a life of their own. There was a noise above us, a sort of flapping. I was frightened, but Walt thought it was just an owl."

"I was the first to see it," Walt said. "I can still remember those red eyes, as big as fists."

"I started to scream," Lynn Wangard continued. "I screamed and I screamed. It was a great scaly thing, with wings a good twelve feet across. It came crashing through the trees above us, all red eyes and dripping mouth. It was horrible . . ."

"No chance the other campers were playing some sort of a trick on you?" Steve asked.

"Mr. Foley, it was *alive*! Walt ran for the gun he'd brought along, a single-shot rifle he fooled around with sometimes. He fired once and was reloading when—when Jake ran up barking at the thing."

"Just where was it then?"

"Above our heads, in the low branches."

"Your bullet missed him, Mr. Wangard?"

He rubbed his stubbled chin, and thought about it. "No. No, I just don't think it hurt him. I have another rifle that I use for hunting, but I hadn't brought it that weekend. The single-shot gun is old and the sights are no good on it, but I do think I must have hit him. At that range I couldn't miss."

"We could almost feel its breath on our faces," Lynn Wangard went on. "I don't know just what happened next, but suddenly Jake stopped barking and—and I guess the creature had him. The thing went away after that, and took Jake along."

"That's it," Wangard said. "That's the way it happened. We drove down the road to warn the other campers, but nobody else saw a thing. The sheriff got out of bed to chase around after it the rest of the night, but he didn't see anything either. We made the newspapers, though; even a paragraph on the last page of *The New York Times*. A week or so later an old widow with a farm near the spot reported that something was bothering her cows. Said they hadn't been giving as much milk lately. Thought it might be they'd been scared by our creature."

Steve hadn't bothered to take notes, because it had all been in the article. They seemed to be telling the truth, and even if they weren't, that wasn't really his concern. Mike Eldon's only stipulation was that they not be obvious crackpots or fakes. They seemed to be neither one. "Could I see the place, get some pictures?" he asked.

"We'll drive you over," Wangard said, getting to his feet. "It's only about a forty-minute ride from here."

The wedding party from the church across the street had gone now, leaving only a tired janitor to sweep up the flecks of colored confetti. Steve sat in the back seat as they drove him down the main street of the town, across jolting railway tracks, and into the rich farmland of the countryside. It took just over a half-hour to reach the state park, a solid rise of timberland that cut through the oatfields and across the horizon like some unexpected curtain. The afternoon warmth had spread itself across the landscape, and here in the park even the Saturday bustle of playing children was muted by the heat. Only at the carefully supervised swimming pool did the noise level give evidence of youthful joy.

"It was out this way," Lynn told him as they turned off the main pavement onto a well-traveled dirt road. Some campers were in the area now, and they waved as campers will, perhaps expecting someone they knew. Finally Walt Wangard brought the car to a stop and they got out, under a great old oak that might have been standing in William Penn's day.

"That was the tree." Wangard pointed up at it. "The creature came down right about here and snatched up Jake."

Steve nodded and got out the little German camera he'd brought from the office. He snapped pictures of the tree, and pictures of Walt and Lynn by the tree, then general pictures of the area. The place seemed awfully harmless in the summer sunshine. "Do you have a photo of the dog that I could have?" he asked.

"I think there's one in our scrapbook—" Lynn began, and then suddenly choked off her words. Something had happened to her husband.

Walt Wangard had toppled against the tree, his face screwed into a mask of sheer terror. "No, no!" he muttered, clawing at the bark. "It's coming again, coming . . ." He screamed.

Steve felt the chill on his spine as he followed Lynn's terrified gaze to the treetops, but there was nothing to be seen. Perhaps they were all crazy. Perhaps the world was crazy. Steve shot one quick picture of the huddled man against the tree and then ran over to help Lynn with him.

"I can't understand it," she said, truly frightened now. "He's never been like this before."

"Let's get him into the car, away from this place."

Wangard was shivering, almost beside himself with fear, as they half-carried him to the car. Steve sat with him in the back while Lynn turned the vehicle toward home. The day was no longer a sunny summer afternoon. Something cold and dark and unknown had thrust itself upon them.

Steve remained at a nearby motel overnight, and on Sunday morning he phoned Mike Eldon at his home, filling him in quickly on the previous day's events. "The whole thing might have been an act for my benefit," he concluded, "but if it was, he did a damned good job of it."

"You think they really saw this creature?"

"Who knows? I talked with a few neighbors last night, and they confirmed the story as much as they could. The dog certainly did vanish that night, and it hasn't been seen since."

Eldon sighed into the phone. "What about Wangard? How is he?"

"All right. He'd pretty much snapped out of it by the time we got him back to the house. He can't understand what happened to him."

"You got some pictures?"

"Yes."

"It doesn't seem that you can do too much there. Might as well come back tonight."

Steve hesitated and then said, "I'd like to stay over one more night if the expense account can stand it. There's something strange about the whole business."

"All right. One more night."

Steve hung up and strolled out to the street. Townspeople, dressed up for church, hurried past. He watched them, then followed along for a ways until he reached the Wangards' street. Services were just letting out at the little church across from their house, and he waited on the sidelines until a youngish blond minister finished greeting his parishioners.

Steve introduced himself. "I was wondering about the Wangards' experience," he said, getting quickly to the point. "What do people think of it? How has it affected the town?"

The minister looked even younger than Steve, and he spoke with a touch of New England accent that seemed surprising. For a moment, Steve had forgotten that a good many men had followed Franklin's early path from Boston to Philadelphia. "They're good people," he told Steve, smiling up at the sun. "Whatever happened to them, whatever was out there, I believe they told the truth."

"But what does the town believe?"

The blond minister shrugged. "The Wangards are dismissed as harmless. The creature in the woods is only another form of flying saucer, after all."

"And how has this affected them?"

The minister seemed thoughtful. A woman passed and called, "Good afternoon, Dr. Reynolds!"

"Good afternoon, Sarah." The smile came automatically to his face, but lingered a bit longer than necessary. He was a pastor who knew his people. Then he answered Steve's question. "Oddly enough, I believe it has brought them closer together. It's no secret that there was actually some talk of divorce before all this happened."

"I see," Steve said. Then, "What do *you* think it was, Dr. Reynolds? Not a flying saucer, certainly."

"No."

"The devil, perhaps?"

The blond minister smiled slightly. "Perhaps. I would never be one to deny it."

Steve Foley thanked him and strolled away. The sun was high in a cloudless sky, and he was thinking it would be a good day for a picnic.

He spent the afternoon with the Wangards, lunching on a rough wooden picnic table in the back yard. Walt seemed completely recovered from his seizure of the previous afternoon, and the three of them sat chatting about the town and its people.

"The woman who saw your creature," Steve said. "Is she worth talking to?"

"She never really said she saw it," Lynn said. "Just that something was bothering her cows. It could have been a small bear. We've had them in the area before."

"The woman's something of a crackpot," Walt agreed. "You'll get nothing you can use out of her."

Steve nodded. "Then I guess I'll get back to New York in the morning since my work's about over."

"You're staying another night?"

"It's a long trip back in the dark. I'd rather start in the morning."

He left them in the late afternoon, while the sun was still bright in the western sky. Back at the motel, he read over the manuscript from Walter Wangard once more, waiting until the sky began to turn a mottled, midnight blue. Then he got into the car and drove out to the park, to the camping area where Walter and Lynn Wangard had met their creature.

The place was different by dark, a silent world where only the occasional sounds of the night creatures intruded upon the subdued campers and stray lovers. Steve passed a few parked cars, pulled off the road into the shielding foliage, then found a parking space of his own near the big tree Lynn and Walt had shown him.

He took a flashlight with him when he left the car, but he didn't know exactly what he was seeking. It was just an idea, the beginnings of an idea . . .

Then he heard it, a great whirring of wings from somewhere above. The thing in the tree had been disturbed by his presence. He crouched against the trunk, shooting his flashlight beam into the upper branches.

Something flew down at him, blinded by the light, but swerved away at the final instant, chasing its shadow back into the depth of the forest.

It was an owl—large and probably very old, but still an owl.

Steve relaxed a bit and directed the beam of light toward the ground. He began to walk in an ever-widening circle until he'd gone some thirty feet from the tree, in the direction away from the camp site. Then he dropped to his hands and knees to study the earth. Hard to tell after two or three months, but the soil might have been disturbed, the grass uprooted since its spring growth. Perhaps the breath of the winged creature had scorched it. Or perhaps . . .

Steve started to scoop the earth away with his hands, then went back to the car and brought a tire iron from the trunk. It took him ten minutes to funnel a hole a foot deep in the hard soil. That was all he needed. He'd found Jake, the missing dog.

He drove back into town then, not to the motel but to the little house across from the church, where Walt and Lynn Wangard lived. The place was in darkness when he reached it a little before midnight. He had to ring the bell four times before Lynn appeared at the door, her face a frightened mask, pale and distorted in fear.

"Come quickly!" she gasped. "He's killed himself!"

Steve followed her up the stairs, close on her heels as she snapped on the lights. Finally, at the bathroom door, she flicked the last light switch and stepped aside. Walt Wangard was sitting on the toilet seat with his head and hands in the sink. He was bleeding from both wrists.

"Call an ambulance!" Steve shouted over his shoulder. "There may still be time to save him!"

She ran out and he heard her dialing for help. In a few minutes the rising siren of an approaching ambulance cut through the outer night. When they arrived with a stretcher, Steve had already managed to stop the bleeding from both wrists.

"I'm going with him," Lynn said. "In the ambulance." Her face was a twisted, frightened thing, hardly recognizable.

"Wait," Steve insisted. "I'll drive you to the hospital." His hand was heavy on her shoulder. He stepped onto the front porch and said a few words to the ambulance driver.

She was waiting when he returned to the living room, lit now only by a single shaded lamp. "Why wouldn't you let me go? Why?"

"Because we have to talk, Mrs. Wangard. We have to talk about your monstrous winged creature."

She fumbled for a cigarette. "My husband's dying, Mr. Foley."

"Let's hope not."

She blew out the cigarette smoke, nervous, unsure of herself. "What do you want me to say?"

"I want the truth. I found the dog tonight, Mrs. Wangard. Where he'd been buried."

She sighed and stubbed out the cigarette in a sudden motion of resignation. "All right, all right. There never was a creature. Walt made the whole thing up for the story. He killed the dog and buried it. When you started asking too many questions he tried to kill himself tonight. Is that what you wanted to hear?"

"No," Steve said softly. It was almost over now, nearly at an end, and for an instant he wondered what he was doing there, standing in the dimly-lit living room of this little house and playing God. "There is a creature, Mrs. Wangard. There was one that night. Your husband saw it."

"What did you just tell those men who took him to the hospital?" she asked suddenly.

"I told them to pump his stomach," Steve said. He felt very tired. "To get out whatever you fed him."

"What are you talking about?"

"Mrs. Wangard, did you walk into the bathroom, find your husband bleeding to death in the sink, and then *turn the light off* as you left? Is that what you want me to believe?"

"I . . ."

"You've been trying to kill him for two months, and I hope to God you haven't succeeded tonight."

For an instant he thought she would throw herself at him, perhaps clawing at his eyes with the unleashed fury of some jungle cat, but the moment passed, and the fight seemed to drain away from her face. She sank back onto the sofa and said, very quietly, "You really believe that?"

"You know a lot about drugs, don't you? Maybe you were a nurse once, or you have a boy-friend who's a doctor. Maybe you just read a lot. That night of the camping weekend you fed him a hallucinogen or psychedelic drug of some sort, didn't you?"

"You're doing the talking, mister."

"It might have been LSD, but more likely it was DMT—dimethyltryptamine—a more intense form that concentrates and compresses the hallucinations into a half-hour period. He might have done almost anything during that half-hour, even accidentally killed himself. As it was, he saw an owl or some other bird and imagined a great winged beast. You told the same story, and even killed the dog and buried it to back up the tale. The way it worked out was just as good for your plans. He could be killed by the 'beast' at a later date, or a suicide could be arranged. Either way, you'd be in the clear. Of course he wrote the story about his experience, and then you had to wait. You didn't know what might happen, but I suppose you felt that its publication would strengthen your hand. Walt Wangard would be judged either a crazed suicide or the victim of some unknown creature, whichever way you wanted to play it."

"You figured all that out?"

"I had help. The thought of a drug crossed my mind the first time I read Walt's article. It sounded so much like an LSD-created experience. Even if I were right, though, it could have gone either way—either one of you could have administered the drug to the other, and then simply matched your story to the drug-inspired hallucination. But when Walt had his attack in the park yesterday, I knew. Drugs like LSD and DMT sometimes cause repeat hallucinations days, weeks, or months after the initial effects have worn off. Our visit to that spot triggered just such a reaction in Walt. Later, when I heard you two had been talking about divorce before all this happened, I had a semblance of motive. What was it, money? I suppose you wanted it all, instead of just some alimony."

She wasn't looking at him. She was staring at the floor. "You're too late, you know. He's dead."

"If he is, you're in extra big trouble lady. They'll find the sleeping potion or whatever it was in his stomach. They'll know you knocked him out before propping him up in the bathroom and cutting his wrists. After yesterday in the park, you figured you had to do something fast. The time seemed right for it, while I was on the scene to testify to his mental unbalance."

Steve had gotten to his feet, and she asked, "Where are you going now?"

"To the hospital. To see how he is. Do you want to come?"

She shivered, curling into herself on the couch. "No. I don't think so."

He left her there with herself, because he was not a policeman. Someone would come for her later.

As he walked quickly out of the silent house and along the dark street, he saw a queer shape pass across the face of the moon. To some it might have seemed like a great winged creature, but he knew it was only a cloud.

The Gray Shroud

Anthony Horner

Baker's heart sank as he looked out of the window. Visibility was pretty poor already. He could only just see the buildings across the road. He licked his lips nervously.

"I expect the buses will be delayed, won't they?"

The head cashier snorted. "Delayed? They won't run in this." He pulled his watch out of his pocket and frowned at it.

"Ten to six. Might as well get along, I suppose. Take me an hour to walk. You'll see to the door, won't you?" He put on his hat and coat. "Good night, Baker."

Baker watched his figure recede down the passage and fought back an impulse to rush after him. He lived in the opposite direction. Company as far as the corner would provide scant comfort. After that, Baker would be on his own.

On his own. The three words vibrated through his brain and he found himself gripping the edge of his desk. As he let go he watched the sweat marks evaporate.

And precious little sympathy he'd get from Miriam. He could picture her irritable expression. "I suppose you had to wait for it to lift," she'd say crossly. "Why, you're like a great baby about fog."

He wouldn't say anything of course. He never did, these days.

128

Once or twice, just after they were married, he'd tried to get her to understand. But she had only stared at him.

"Phobias?" she'd said. "I don't know what you're talking about. Normal, healthy men don't have phobias."

Baker got up and peered out of the window. If anything, it was thicker than ever. He shivered and reached reluctantly for his coat. He dare not drag it out any longer; the caretaker locked the main door at six-thirty.

Outside, the fog wrapped him in a cocoon of anguish. Within twenty minutes, he was hopelessly lost. As he had known he would be. He stood still and the physical oppression made him cry aloud. He started to run, hands outstretched—a gesture more supplicatory than defensive. He ran awkwardly, head tucked well into his collar. Twice he cannoned into people, the impetus of his loping gait carrying him forward. Then a malignant pillar-box struck at him from the gloom, and he reeled into the gutter.

He had no idea how long it was before he saw the glimmer of light. But the relief when it turned out to be a small pub was overwhelming. He leaned against the bar, gulping brandy and staring at the landlord who sat stolidly reading the evening paper.

The only other customer was a small fusty-looking individual, wearing a tweed cap and steel-rimmed spectacles. Decidedly commonplace—save for the fact that he was idly screwing one of his fingers on and off.

Baker didn't really see him until he'd finished his second brandy. For a moment he stared, eyes bulging. Then the rational explanation swept over him with a surge of relief. A false finger! But how damnably realistic!

He was raising his glass to his mouth when the man slowly started to unscrew each of the other fingers in turn. A false *hand*!

Baker put his glass down on the bar. The man looked up and Baker nodded towards the "hand." "Rather unusual, isn't it?"

The other looked puzzled. "Unusual? Why?"

"Well, false fingers on a false hand. What's the point of them?"

The man stared at him. Then he turned to look at the landlord who had put down the paper and was listening. "False?"

he repeated, and there was a bewildered note in his voice as he turned back to Baker. "What do you mean—false?"

But before Baker could give vent to his rising exasperation, the landlord methodically unscrewed his left wrist and laid it on the bar.

Baker stared at the grotesque object, lying there like an inflated glove. The hammering in his brain told him that this could not be happening—that it was a trick—an optical illusion. He groped for sanity, forcing his lips into a smile. But their deliberate scrutiny began to tell on his nerves, and he dashed out of the bar.

Although the fog was as thick as ever, he must have run for nearly a quarter of a mile before his breath gave out. He leant against a wall, panting. The unaccustomed brandy had left a raw taste in his mouth and his head was beginning to ache. He cursed the fog and the chill wind. The oaths triggered off all the strange obscenities that had lain dormant in his mind for years. The sense of isolation lent him courage and he strode along, swearing out loud, until at last, dazed and breathless, he sank on to a seat in a bus shelter.

A thin tremor of normalcy filtered into his body. The fog was lifting—that gray obscurity that had shrouded his whole life. He blinked at the scurries of mist that no longer seemed to exacerbate his every sense. Rising swiftly to his feet, he was appalled to see that it was half past nine. He wouldn't be home before eleven. Miriam would be in bed. She was a firm believer in her eight hours.

The long walk did a lot to clear his head. Even the horror of the public-house assumed a more reasonable shape. A hallucination, perhaps? Some form of self-hypnosis? No matter, it had gone, and with it his lifelong claustrophobia.

He let himself into the silent house. The cold supper looked singularly unattractive and he went upstairs. Undressing swiftly in the dark, he clambered in beside Miriam.

It must have been ten minutes or more before something penetrated his consciousness. Miriam wasn't snoring. Baker wondered idly whether she had found a cure without telling him. He switched on the light.

For a moment, he gazed at the smooth bareness of his wife's neck without fully taking in the screw-thread where it ended so abruptly. Then, he turned to look at the dressing-table. Her head was there, lying on its side, the curlers still neatly in position.

Baker tried to struggle out of bed as the first wave of hysteria caught him by the throat, and he was still half-laughing, half-screaming, when a merciful blackness enveloped him.

But not before he had glimpsed on the dressing-table, nestling incongruously amongst the pots of foundation-creams and powders, a dainty little oil-can.

The Gentleman Caller

Veronica Parker Johns

Miss Emmy Rice, who didn't look a day over seventy-five, lifted a lid to sniff the fragrance of bubbling beef stew. Beef it really was this time—not scraps conned from a kindly butcher but nuggets of succulent beef bought with twice-counted pennies. The young man, the light of her fast-dimming life, was coming to dinner.

Lowering the gas, she glanced at the turnip watch which had belonged to her father and now hung on the hook of an abandoned birdcage. It was a quarter to six. The guest, Gerald, would appear in fifteen minutes if he continued to indulge his admirable habit of punctuality, which seemed an anachronism in this impolite world. Nightly, for weeks, he had joined her at precisely eight o'clock on the park bench facing the river, since that first evening when the unlikely had happened; then, observing his unease, his need, Miss Emmy had defied convention and struck up a conversation with a member of the opposite sex.

Combing her wispy hair, fluffing it deceptively into a net, she recalled the details of that encounter. It was strange how she could remember almost everything that related to Gerald although frequently she forgot her own name and address and had to consult the paper pinned inside her handbag for that data. Once, in one of those sudden flashes of lucidity which in the pattern of her vagueness were now the exception, not the rule, she had heard her landlady remark of her that she had lost contact with reality. Indeed, it was quite the contrary. Reality had lost contact with her. Until that night on the bench—how long ago was it, as though time mattered?

She digressed from the sweet recollection of her meeting with Gerald to think spitefully of her landlady. A lot *she* knew, nagging Emmy constantly to part with some of the magazines which crowded the nine by twelve bed- dining- living-room. "Dust catchers," Mrs. Martin complained, jabbing at a tottering pile of them with an angry carpet sweeper, "full of outdated news, which could be news to nobody." Emmy had primly replied that they were pretty and that was enough for her.

"Pretty!" Mrs. Martin snorted antagonistically. "I'd like to know what's pretty about *Time* magazine for February five of 'forty-eight."

Miss Emmy had not demeaned herself to retort. She chuckled now, content that she had not yielded to pressure, in which event she might have missed the 'fifty-three issue of *Life* with the picture that looked like Gerald.

It wasn't really Gerald, of course. Gerald's hair was red whereas the man in the photograph was obviously a towhead. Gerald sported a mustache as dashingly as ever was done in the nineties; she was sure it did not conceal a mouth as weak as this other's. Still, there was something about the eyes and the corners of them, the deep cleft chin and the jawline, which had made her tear out the picture and squirrel it away in a bureau drawer.

Spiritually there was no comparison between Gerald and the young man who had achieved national notoriety, who was a thief and an escaped convict. Some time, just for a joke, she would show Gerald the clipping and they would have a good laugh over it, but not tonight. Tonight she wanted everything to be just perfect.

There had been a girl with him that first evening, a flashy, cheap-looking hussy not worth the apologies he was lavishing upon her. The girl had grumbled about something, her shrill voice fairly drowning out Gerald's placatory murmurings, while Miss Emmy stood tentatively behind the bench which years of occupancy had led her to think of as her own. Before she had decided to assert squatters' rights, the baggage had flounced off, happily never to reappear in that vicinity.

Miss Emmy, then, had spoken to the distraught young man, making a diversionary remark about the number of cars there were on the streets nowadays, had he noticed, and wasn't it a caution? It was an observation she often made, always with an air of well-bred surprise and moderate disapproval because she always *was* surprised to notice that the horseless carriage had entirely taken over.

"I shudder to think," she murmured, illustrating her reaction with a Delsarte gesture, "what became of all the horses. They seem to have vanished from the face of the earth."

"Lady," he said, not turning toward her, "it should happen to the nags I bet on."

Young people talked differently nowadays, she knew, and this was the only thing Gerald had ever said to her which might be considered coarse or common. After that he turned and looked at her, long and silently. He stared at the pink straw hat which obligingly lent itself to an endless routine of retrimming, at the mined-diamond pinky ring, the paired gold bangles, the pince-nez on a thin gold pully pinned to her crepe dress.

Gerald's blue eyes were set a little too close together for him to be as handsome as she pretended. Their gaze had grown so intense that for a second or two she regretted the impulse which had led her to speak to him. Then, in some recess of his ordered mind, Gerald pushed a button marked *Charm*. A smile flooded his face.

"I bet you've driven many a spanking pair in your day, ma'am," he said.

"When I was little," she told him, "I used to have a pony."

She told him lots more, then and later, to which he listened with rapt attention. He was such an audience as she had believed no longer existed. People, it seemed, did not have the time or simply weren't interested in the things she found absorbing. Gerald's attitude was refreshingly different.

Which was why she had invited him to dinner tonight. No other man had been permitted to enter her tiny home. Mrs. Martin had had fits trying to find a lady electrician when the ceiling light blew out, and there was a cracked pane in the window because of the shortage of female glaziers. Gerald would be the first man ever to put foot in Emmy's room.

It was precisely six when the downstairs bell of the converted brownstone rang sharply. Emmy went to the top of the top flight of steps to welcome her gentleman caller.

Gerald had brought a bottle of port and three sweetheart roses. Her eyes brimmed with tears as she filled a vase from the bathroom which she shared with four other roomers. Meticulously she rinsed dusty wineglasses, her hands trembling with the long-forgotten ecstasy of receiving a gift of posies.

She hurried, an onset of panic nearly convincing her that she had invented the whole thing, that there was no Gerald, that these receptacles were being prepared for wine and flowers that were dust and ashes. Her imagination had played similarly plausible pranks on her only recently.

She had found things in her room the presence of which she could not possibly explain. On the other hand she kept losing things, or thought she kept losing things she had never owned. There had been that frightful row with the woman in the room adjoining hers about a saucepan. Mrs. Martin had meddled in that affair, proving to her own if not Miss Emmy's satisfaction that the pan belonged to the neighbor. There was definitely a new dimension in Miss Emmy's life in which fact and fancy were interchangeable.

It was an area, she was aware, in which she must tread gently, for Mrs. Martin was always ready to pounce upon her. Mrs. Martin had indicated that she could very well do without a tenant who was so unclear about what was and wasn't. One false step, Emmy knew, would send her hurtling into that "Institution" in which, the landlady often stated behind a not too carefully cupped hand, she ought to be.

Back in her room she was pleased to discover that Gerald abided in the factual world. He was whistling a waltz as he uncorked the port. She set down the wet glasses and started looking for the dish towel. By the time she had found it, wrapped in crumpled newspaper in a compartment of the desk, he had already done the honors with a clean handkerchief.

"Thank you," she said humbly. "I don't know what gets into

me. It seems almost as if I take great pains to hide things even from myself."

She meant objects like the towel, and the nightgown for which she had to hunt an average of fifteen minutes every night, but under the stimulus of Gerald's sympathy she broadened the field to include all those secret things about herself that currently worried her.

"I'm not as sharp as I used to be," she asserted boldly, glad at last to have said it aloud.

"You're bright as a dollar," Gerald protested, "and a grand cook, by the smell of that stew." With a gallant bow he handed her one of the filled wineglasses, saying, "Do you know what it means to me, a home-cooked meal?"

"I hope you enjoy it."

She sipped the port, saying it tasted strong, did he suppose she should? "I'm not used to it now, although they did say I had quite a head when I was a girl. Did I tell you about that young man wining and dining me at the Hotel Brevoort?"

"No," Gerald lied. This would make seven times he had heard it.

She had just reached the part about the champagne in the slipper, an apocryphal bit which by now she found wholly convincing, when her eyelids began to droop.

"You must forgive an old lady," she said breathlessly. "Just a cat nap. I take them often. Ten minutes or so and I'm fit as a fiddle."

In an instant she was asleep, bolt upright. Gerald reached for the bottle and poured himself two in quick succession. It wasn't exactly his kind of liquor, but it was better than nothing. He was hungry and the stew *did* smell good, but that could wait. Waiting was a thing he did well because he had had plenty of practice.

Nevertheless, after a quarter of an hour he grew restless. The straight-backed chair on which he sat was uncomfortable. The room was small, like a cell, and seemed to be growing smaller. He got up and twiddled the knob of the early model radio. Sound filled the small room but the old lady slept on. He tuned in a rhumba full blast and walked over to her, mockingly pantomiming an invitation to dance. But she did not stir. Maybe she's dead already, he thought, shrugging; just my luck.

She was not. A few minutes later, she awoke with a start.
"My goodness!" she exclaimed, stumbling over to the stove.
"Phew! Why didn't you turn it off. Didn't you smell it?"
"Smell what?"
"Scorching. I smelled it so hard it woke me up. Always did
have a keen sense of smell. My eyesight's failing and my
hearing's gone off badly, but," she tapped her highbridged nose,
"my smeller's still A number one. When I was a girl Papa used
to say he'd hire me out as one of the bloodhounds in an Uncle
Tom troupe. Joking, of course."

Papa would have been beside himself to hear the reception
given his sally by Gerald. Gerald laughed until he sounded as
if he were having hysterics and momentarily she expected hammering on the common wall of her neighbor's room.

She managed to salvage enough of the stew, which was delicious. After dinner they went out and sat on their bench for a
while and watched the boats go up and down the river.

He didn't mention the will until the third visit.

She'd served meat loaf that night, counter scraps eked out
with bread crumbs. She knew she was overspending, but she
didn't give it too much thought. Chiefly what she thought was
that few people get a chance to live more than once—that very
few elderly ladies, their friends gone on before them, ever
found a whole new life on a riverside bench.

He called her "Aunty" by now; he had appointed himself her
favorite nephew. "I want to talk to you about something," he
announced after the dinner dishes had been washed and put
away. "It's rather a touchy subject. I don't want to hurt your
feelings."

"You're not going away?" she asked, panicky, that being the
worst thing she could think of.

"No," he said soberly. "It's not me. It's you. You'll be going
away some day, maybe sooner than we think."

"Me?" She chuckled. "I never go anywhere."

"I'm referring," there was tremolo in his voice, "to that last,
long journey."

His mien was so funereal that she could not miss the point.

Comfortingly she told him that she would be ready when the
call came to join her family and friends Beyond.

"That's not what I'm getting at," he said. "Look, I guess the best way to say this is just to say it right out. I've been reading a book about wills. Have you made one?"

"No, I haven't. I didn't think I had enough to bother."

"You have plenty of nice things," he contradicted, fingering a chipped Meissen shepherdess. "You have your treasures. You want to make sure, don't you, the right people get them afterwards?"

She saw the wisdom of this. She supposed that if she left no specific instructions Mrs. Martin would simply come in and pirate everything.

Gerald hung the smile on his face. "Don't go thinking your favorite nephew is only fixing it so he will inherit your fortune," he teased.

"Fortune?" she echoed, bewildered. "I'm sure I've got no fortune. Papa lost almost everything and Mama's last illness ate up the rest."

"Don't kid me." There was dust from the shepherdess on the finger with which he stroked her cheek. "Until I came into your life you were what the newspapers call a 'recluse.' Recluses always have millions in banknotes stashed away between the pages of old magazines. It's expected."

"Not me," she insisted. "All I have is a few little shares of Consolidated Gas and American Telephone. They're very nice to me, the companies. They send me money every now and again. It's what I live on.

"Sometimes," she added shyly, "they send me an envelope and I think it's money but it turns out to be some kind of paper to sign, a p-r-o-x-y, something I don't understand. The next thing I don't understand, will you explain to me?"

"Sure thing, Aunty, glad to oblige. But about a will, that stock is something you should say who gets it."

"There isn't anyone," she mused. "No one I can remember seeing for a long, long time."

The tremolo came back to Gerald's voice: "When the angels gather you to them I'd like to have a momentum of our happy hours together. That watch, for instance. Boy, that's a beaut!"

Momentum, she thought. Momentum. It sounded queer, and somehow wrong. Words did that nowadays—they stood on their heads and did not seem to mean what they used to.

Gerald removed the watch from the birdcage hook, whistled at it appreciatively.

"It was Papa's," she told him. "I'll write your name on the back of it. I do that. I'll show you."

She darted about the room, exhibiting tiny scraps of adhesive on which she had written names, stuck to the backs of pictures and the bases of bric-a-brac.

Gerald wasn't sure the bits of adhesive would have any legal value.

"But lawyers cost money," she protested. "I couldn't afford one."

"It so happens you don't need one. I read this here book about wills very carefully, and I took the liberty of drawing you up a proper one. It's simple. I'll go over it with you, and if it's okay you can sign it in front of a couple of witnesses. Think we could dig up some people here in the house?"

"Mrs. Martin usually has a few friends over. I could go downstairs with you when you leave. It's good of you to do this. Since Papa's been gone there hasn't been a man around to take care of my affairs."

"A pleasure," he assured her.

He drew a single typed sheet from his pocket, unfolded it, and began to read: " 'I give, devise, and bequeath all my property, whether real, personal, or mixed wheresoever located to,' " he raised his head, "what's the name of your church?"

"My church? I've got it here somewhere. I go every Sunday, at least I used to." She rummaged through the desk, came up with a dog-eared Gift Offering envelope which she handed to him. Gerald copied the name in ink in a space he had reserved.

"Paragraph Two," he intoned. "There are only two, and this one I'll mostly have to fill in, subject to your approval."

He leaned closer to the lamp and started reading again:

" 'The sole exception to the foregoing is that I give, devise, and bequeath to my dear friend, Gerald Musgrove, the following.' "

He began to scrawl on a piece of scrap paper, dictating the words aloud to himself: " 'the solid gold watch which belonged to Papa. Also,' " he glanced at her, grinning mischievously, the corners of his eyes crinkled with stifled laughter, " 'also all the cash money found within my room, whatsoever sum that may be.' "

"Oh, go 'long with you!" She giggled, pushing his shoulder affectionately. "You're such a josher. I told you there's nothing."

He allowed his laughter to break free and she joined in with him, saying as she dabbed at her streaming eyes that he ought to take more, that he really should have the stock because he would know what to do with the papers the companies sent out. He wasn't too well off, she could tell, although he brought her flowers and wine and that pint of vanilla ice cream last night. He really and truly ought not to be so unselfish.

"Honestly, Aunty," he argued. "The watch and the money is all I want. And I don't really want that, not for a long, long while. I'd much rather have my sweet little aunty among the living."

She dozed off as he carefully copied his notes on the original document. When she awoke they went downstairs together. Mrs. Martin had a parlorful of guests who watched Miss Emmy flourishingly sign her last will and testament. Then Mrs. Martin and that dyed blonde from across the street with whom she was so chummy affixed their signatures as witnesses.

As she passed the parlor door again, after bidding Gerald good night, she could hear them cackling in there and she thought she knew the source of the merriment. They must think she was giving herself unholy airs, making a will when she was churchmouse poor.

They couldn't know she had something they'd give their wordly goods to get: a touch of magic. Brothers and sisters she had none, but miraculously she had sprouted a nephew who now looked after her.

When she woke up the next morning it was to the frightening suspicion that she was in for an illness. She'd never had a sick day in her life, never an ache or a pain, yet she felt dizzy and headachy and not up to snuff at all.

There was a funny smell in the room, one she couldn't seem to place. The window was closed, although she couldn't imagine why she had shut it last night.She tottered over to it. As she threw it open, the cracked pane with its gaping hole rattled menacingly. She wondered if Gerald were handy enough about the house to fix it. Papa used to be able to do things like that. She must remember to call Gerald's attention to it and ask him.

As she dressed she decided to give Mrs. Martin one last chance to find a glazier and save Gerald the trouble. On her way out to market she stopped at the parlor door and had already started to knock when she heard the landlady on the telephone.

"Honest to Pete," she was saying. "I'd sell the house like a shot if I could find a buyer. Furniture and all. The real estate man's already got the papers drawn up."

She must have met attempted dissuasion at the other end of the line, for she listened a moment before resuming:

"I know I get a pretty penny in rentals and the janitor does all the heavy work, except Miss Emmy's room which she used to be so fussy about letting a man into, but it's getting on my nerves. Especially with these plainclothes cops hanging around watching. Won't tell me *what* they're watching for, but it's plain that one of the tenants is up to no good.

"I suspect it's that pretty second-floor parlor front. I've always thought she had entirely too many uncles visiting her all the time. If you ask me, that girl is uncled to death. But she pays in advance, and I've looked the other way. Now I don't know—"

There was another long pause. Miss Emmy raised a hand again to knock, then realized she had forgotten what she wanted to ask. All she could think of was how wonderful it would be if Mrs. Martin did sell the house and someone really nice replaced her as landlady.

She kept returning to that dream throughout the day. Anyone, she felt sure, would be an improvement on the incumbent, yet she tried casting this and that person she knew in the role, mentally auditioning them. By late afternoon she was convinced that the delightful possibility was a *fait accompli*, warranting some special sort of celebration.

She dressed herself elegantly, pinning a lavender bow in her hair. From the bureau drawer she took the picture that looked like Gerald. One of the boxes under the bed contained a number of broken picture frames, one of which did nicely. In its split corner she tucked a bouquet of artificial daisies. It looked very pretty on the mantel.

That evening Gerald was punctual but not alone. With him was the baggage Emmy had not seen since the first evening. Emmy almost wept with disappointment.

"I thought you wouldn't mind," he said nonchalantly, and she wondered how he could possibly have been so in error. "I brought my Cousin Mildred along. She's heard me rave about you and she's anxious to meet you."

The girl stepped into the room, although with wholly pseudo-daintiness she seemed to hold herself apart from it. Her plucked eyebrows rose critically as she looked about. The snapping eyes lit upon the picture on the mantel and suddenly her voluptuous mouth tautened.

"What's that doing there?"

"Nothing," said Emmy truthfully. "I just thought it looked like Gerald."

"Well, it doesn't a bit," said Mildred. "Get rid of it."

Emmy blinked back the tears so as not to give the girl the satisfaction. She had never been spoken to in such a tone. She had done nothing. She had behaved, as always, like a perfect lady.

Mildred repeated the command, "Get rid of it!"

"Mildred, dear!" Gerald was once more placatory. With a creature like that, Miss Emmy supposed, it was the only tack to take if one wanted to remain friendly cousins. "It doesn't matter. Let it be."

"Okay," contemptuously. "It's no skin off my—"

"Darling, don't!" He turned to their hostess. "Is dinner nearly ready?" he asked. "I'm starving. Don't worry about is there enough for Mildred. She eats like a bird."

Fortunately there was enough. Emmy's appetite was uncustomarily pawky. With the girl there the vibrations in the room were all wrong, and no amount of effort on Gerald's part could bring them into tune. The washing up, usually a happy affair with one assistant, became an unwieldy maneuver with two, and Emmy was worn out by the whole dismal business when she returned to her rocking chair beside the window.

"Don't she remind you of Whistler's mother?" Gerald cooed dotingly.

"Sure," said Mildred. "Real quaint."

Miss Emmy promptly went to sleep.

The room was dusky when she awoke, lit only by the small bulb in the kitchen unit. Mildred had her hand inside the stove. Gerald yanked it out of there, twisting the wrist a little so that she dropped the screwdriver, or whatever it was she'd been holding.

"Don't be such a milktoast," Mildred squeaked. "Suppose she *has* got the keenest nose in town. If we turn it so little every night it'll be weeks before—Wouldn't it be better just to open the burners all the way just before we leave?"

"She'd smell it," Gerald said. "She'd turn it off, and then where would you be?"

"All right, then—let her get used to it gradual. Turn the control valve a little at a time, but does it have to be *this* little?"

Mildred's voice had risen. "Shut up, kid," Gerald implored, glancing toward the chair. "You'll wake her up."

Miss Emmy pretended she was still asleep, to spare him the embarrassment of knowing she had witnessed his cousin's inexcusable behavior. Not having been born yesterday she knew what the wretched girl was up to, and she knew now what the funny smell in the room was, the intensification of which had just awakened her.

This hateful young person was wasting the gas just to run up the bill. True, the smell had been in the room before Mildred entered it, but there was probably some mechanical reason for that which was beyond Emmy's power to figure out.

Gerald was trying to make her stop. She was glad to see him showing some backbone, but she did not propose to let him carry the burden alone. She had stock in the Gas Company. They wouldn't approve of someone who wasted their commodity. Yes, she would tell them what was going on, and she would let Mildred know she was on to her shenanigans.

As a prelude Emmy yawned extravagantly.

"I think I'll just go downtown tomorrow and pay a visit to the Company," she said pointedly. "I haven't been there for a long time. It's way far down somewhere." She waved an arm. "It'll take all morning, but I'll find it, you can be sure."

"That's right, Aunty," said Gerald, coming over to her. "Go ahead and live it up a little little."

Miss Perkins, who had not even been born 'way back when the Consolidated Edison Company was known as Consolidated Gas, took her job with it most conscientiously. Every day provided fresh problems, but she had rarely had one so provocative as the one now being presented by the little old lady who sat at her desk.

Miss Emma T. Rice, owner of ten shares of Consolidated Gas, was either nutty as a fruitcake or terribly careless in her choice of friends, one of whom seemed to be trying to murder her by slow leak. It wasn't the Gas Company's baby, but someone had to look into it, the police or the Department of Welfare. Miss Perkins would not sleep a wink until she was sure that another person's bedroom wasn't filling with gas, barely perceptibly, until enough had accumulated to cause death. If the story were an hallucination, then the poor darling needed help of another sort.

"I'll take care of it," Miss Perkins promised, cutting short the third reprise.

"Pray do." Emmy shivered in her black going-downtown coat which was too warm for the day but too sleazy for the air-conditioned office. "We must stop this thievery, this willful waste of something that belongs to the Company and to me. It isn't Mildred's to throw away that way."

"It certainly is not," agreed Miss Perkins as she reached for a telephone.

It was a long trip home and when Emmy got there all she wanted was to crawl upstairs and lie down for a few minutes. But as luck would have it, Mrs. Martin intercepted her in the downstairs hall.

"Your niece was here this morning," she said. " I let her use my key to get into your room."

Emmy was in no mood to stand there and talk such nonsense. It just went to show how much Mrs. Martin knew. Miss Emmy had no niece.

Without bothering to answer she started up the steps.

"You've forgotten to pay your rent again," Mrs. Martin

nagged after her. "You've skipped a week. I'd appreciate your giving me this week's and next's at your earliest convenience."

Emmy marched resolutely upward. Although her pillow looked inviting she was determined to gather the rent money before resting.

This was never a simple operation. To outwit pilferers she banked her small funds in various corners of the room, in an assortment of envelopes and old bread wrappers, or she tucked them between the pages of magazines or into the top of the sugar bowl.

Her method of making withdrawals was to search thoroughly, find all she could, spread it on the bed, count it, and then subtract the amount needed for the rent or whatever else had to be paid. Today she was astonished to discover that she had much more than usual, a great deal more than last time. In fact, the excess was so striking she was half inclined to think that someone, unknown to her, had been taking advantage of the excellent hiding places her room afforded. Miss Saucepan, perhaps, or Miss Bang-on-the-wall, the annoying neighbor.

But if anyone on the top floor might be presumed to be wealthy it was far most likely to be Miss Emmy. She came of a much older family, and it might very well be that she had always had this much money and had simply forgotten it. Certainly she would not mention her doubts to anyone lest she receive that suspicious glance, that tacit implication that Miss Emmy was slightly tibble-dotty and maybe ought to be put away somewhere.

But Gerald, that dear boy—he had *known.* He'd said she had a fortune. He had called her a recluse, a type which *ipso facto* has a roomful of banknotes. And, bless him, here they were. How exciting that Gerald should be so right, when she could have sworn . . .

After a while she went downstairs with the money.

It was so late when she returned that there was barely time to prepare Gerald's dinner, much less stretch out and relax. But the day which had been so unlike the average still had another surprise for her.

A strange man was waiting for her in the upstairs hall.

"Where the heck have you been, lady?" he asked irritably.

She was conscience-stricken. This must be the man from the Gas Company. She had asked them to send someone, then had not been here to receive him.

"I had to go out again," she apologized. "Something unexpected came up and I had to attend to it right away."

She opened the door, waving him toward the best chair by way of mollification. Then it occurred to her that his first interest was undoubtedly the stove, so she waved him toward that.

The man obeyed neither signal. He walked to the mantel and stood with arms akimbo before the picture which was not of Gerald.

"Some character!" he remarked.

"You know him?" she asked delightedly. "He resembles a gentleman friend of mine who will be here any minute. If you're still here you can tell me if they really do look alike. That Mildred," she uttered the name with fastidious distaste, "doesn't seem to think that they do."

"Neither did the lieutenant," the man said cryptically. "Mind if I open the window? The smell of gas in here is fierce."

He didn't wait for a reply. "You're lucky that pane's broken," he observed. "Yes, our friend had us guessing. He's grown that mustache, dyed his hair, and taken off a good deal of weight. The boss is a bug about false arrest, and he just wasn't sure.

"What stumps him is—here's a big-time crook. After he gets out he should live like a king, but our boy clerks in a grocery store and lives in a crummy fleabag. His girl's got runs in her stockings, though she looks like the kind that likes nice things when she can get them.

"We keep a tail on him for weeks, hoping to catch him spending more than he can reasonably explain having, but he doesn't step out of line once. He acts like a law-abiding citizen. He doesn't even spit on the sidewalk. And he not only helps old ladies across the street but escorts them upstairs. Then you give us the break we need, by going to Con Edison.

"This patrolman is sent over to check on your story. I'm standing around outside, like always, and I walk up to him to break the monotony, to find out what else is cooking in the house. When he tells me, I go right over and get a warrant for attempted homicide."

"That's nice," she said vaguely. "I'm sure you deserve it." He frowned at her, then shook his head.

"I decide to make the pinch here," he continued, "so's you could identify him without having to go to the station. I've got a grandma myself. We won't have to bother you any more, ma'am, soon's we get his prints. We'll make it as painless on you as possible. Is that okay?"

How the man did chatter on, Emmy thought, saying anxiously, "I'm afraid I haven't been listening. I guess my mind's on the dinner I should be preparing. My guest will be here any minute. Isn't there something you want to do to the stove?"

He had a nice smile. "I'll wait," he said courteously. "It'll be a pleasure to meet him."

Miss Emmy began to peel potatoes. The man from the Gas Company rocked contentedly in the chair by the window.

Gerald was his usual punctual self. She went to the door to greet him, her heart springing as always at the sight of him. He scowled when he saw the man in the rocker and turned away as though about to leave in anger. Was he jealous? she wondered, almost unbearably flattered. But he couldn't have left just then even if he had wanted to, because two men were coming up the stairs abreast, cutting off his path.

"Is this the man?" the visitor in the rocker demanded. "Is this the one you heard talking over by the stove last night, ma'am, planning a little surprise party for you?"

"Yes," she said proudly. "This is Gerald."

There was something metallic in the gasman's hand—a tool for fixing the stove, she supposed. But she was wrong, because suddenly the thing was snapped about Gerald's wrist.

"Take him away, boys," he told the others.

And then, in spite of all the confusion, she understood. The Gas Company was going to punish Gerald for something that wasn't his fault at all, was wholly Mildred's. And Emmy herself was to blame for their learning about it in the first place. She wished there were some way she could make amends.

Perhaps there was. "Could I speak to you privately?" she asked the gasman, drawing him deeper into the room, although the others had already reached the lower landing. She had no wish to embarrass Gerald further.

"I found today I had quite a bit more money tucked away

here than I'd thought," she broached the subject delicately. "It might help him."

She unsnapped her handbag, which was capacious but quite inadequate to restrain its contents; the bills burst forth like feathers from a ruptured pillow.

"Great jumping wheels of fire," said the gasman, and he began counting.

She kept asking him if there was enough to buy Gerald's freedom, but he paid no attention to her. He just shook his head and whistled as if he had never seen that much money before.

At last he found his tongue. "It's practically the whole payroll from that factory stick-up," he exclaimed. "The job our boy did time for. All that's missing is a measly few hundred."

"You need a few hundred more?" she asked, panicky. "I'm afraid I haven't got it."

"You will have—and lots more," he said, patting her shoulder. "There's a ten thousand dollar reward for recovering this loot, ma'am. And it's all yours."

"Oh, dear," she said, trying to keep all these figures straight. "But if you need more, that ten thousand won't help Gerald. I've already spent that much today. You see, I bought this house right out from under Mrs. Martin. I know the real estate man won't give me back any of the money."

She dabbed at her teary eyes and sniffed disconsolately.

"Poor Gerald," she sighed. "Such a good boy, and I can't do a thing for him. Well, anyhow" she brightened, "some day he'll have Papa's watch to remember me by."

The Coconut Trial

Don Knowlton

When you're sitting at a bar—well, I don't know, but it's a queer thing—people talk with you. Rather, I should say, they talk *at* you. They say things they'd never tell their wives or their bosses or anybody else. People, I mean, you don't know, you've never seen before and you'll never see again. I think the anonymity of the situation has something to do with it.

Anyhow, there I was, in a bar on lower Broadway. It was a seedy bistro. There were all sorts of old stickers and placards on the walls, and the bartender looked as if he hadn't shaved in a week. Why was I there? Well, why was the young man on my left there? We were both getting quietly and steadily drunk. I guess there is no accounting for human behavior.

Well, this boy on my left—I call him a boy, but he was bigger than I am—this boy had volunteered the information that he was in the Navy, and currently on leave. He was a good-looking kid, and all of a sudden he began to talk. I realized afterward that what he told me must have been on his mind for a long time, but he probably hadn't dared tell it to his shipmates or to his folks back home; not just because they wouldn't believe it, but because it made him look silly. The reason he got into the mess, that is.

"You see," he began, "there we were on the destroyer, anchored about a mile off that island. They were playing war games and we were supposed to meet up with a tanker at that exact spot on that exact date, only something got fouled up and the tanker didn't get there. We learned all about it, of course, by radio, and we were told to stay right where we were; the tanker would show up the next day.

"Now that island was something. It was just a volcano. Not a big one, but a perfect one, like you see sometimes on Japanese screens. And there were little wisps of smoke coming out of the top of it.

"Around the edges of the island, along the sea, there were a few stretches of level land, and one of them stuck way out into the ocean. It was just a big finger of sand. Well, on that finger there was growing a row of coconut palms. They stood out against the horizon like evenly spaced sentinels.

"Well, I'd been brought up in Connecticut, and until that moment I'd never even *seen* a palm tree, much less a coconut palm. And I wanted to get close enough to take a good look. Oh, I suppose it sounds funny, but put it the other way round. Suppose a native of New Guinea saw snow for the first time; I'll bet he'd want to get near enough so he could actually feel it with his hands.

"Anyhow, Bill Scott and I got permission to take a dinghy and row over to that line of coconut palms.

"We anchored the dinghy instead of pulling it part-way onto the beach, because we weren't sure about the tides. And then we went to look at those trees. Of course, that sort of thing may be old hat to you; but I tell you, I got a big kick out of those trunks that just went up and up without a single branch, with a big tuft of palm leaves on the very top and a cluster of nuts hanging just beneath them.

"There was one coconut on the ground, and I picked it up. Bill thought maybe he could knock another down with a stone, and he was looking around for a rock the right size when all of a sudden we were surrounded. In no time at all about twenty men had made a circle around us. Some had guns, some had spears, and some had knives. And they were all pointed at *us*."

The boy stopped talking for a moment, and sipped reflectively at his bourbon and water.

"Well!" he said. "The surprise was that there were men there at all. Because we'd assumed, all of us on the destroyer, that the island, with that live volcano on it, was uninhabited.

"What kind of men? Thinking about it afterwards, I'd say they were a mixture from 'way back—so far back that now they all looked pretty much alike. There was some Polynesian there, and some Negro, and some Malayan, and a tinge of Japanese, and at some time there must have been a white man in somebody's family tree.

"They weren't big men. They were brown, they didn't wear any clothes to speak of, and they obviously meant business. They jabbered in their own tongue, whatever it was, which of course we couldn't understand a word of, but we *could* understand what they wanted—which was for us to get going along a trail that led to the interior of the island. Which we did.

"After going through a sort of tunnel under big trees we came out to a little clearing. I wouldn't have thought there was that much land between the base of the volcano and the ocean, but there was. In the middle of that clearing there was a—well, I wouldn't call it a house exactly. I would hardly call it a shack, because part of it didn't have any walls, but it *did* have a roof, and it *did* have a porch. I could see women moving around in the back of the place but what struck us was the man who was sitting on the porch.

"He was a white man, though much tanned, of course; and he was old. His hair was snow-white. He must have once had a powerful build; but now his shoulders had shrunk and he had a paunch. But it was his face that held us. His brow was clear; but the lines on his cheeks were so deep that he looked—well, perhaps ravaged is the word. As if he had been driven by something or had suffered from something.

"Well, he got up from his chair and he listened patiently while all those natives chattered at him like monkeys and made threatening gestures at us. He answered them in their own language. Then he turned to us and he said—I'll try to remember his exact words—he said, 'You are charged with trespassing and stealing. These are serious offenses. You will therefore be subjected to a trial, which will be held immediately. I shall be the presiding judge, and I shall also act as interpreter for both sides.'

"With that he started up a little hill, with everybody following. He took us into a little open place in the forest, and there, believe it or not, was a big high chair. To its right, facing it, were two benches; and to its left, facing it, were two low chairs.

"The judge took the high chair and indicated that we were to sit in the two low ones. Then he motioned toward the benches, and twelve of the natives sat down there, six on each bench. All this time we had been talking our heads off, explaining how and why we had come to the island, but the judge paid not the slightest attention, so far as we could tell; and no wonder, because it sounded perfectly silly. And would those natives believe that two men had come ashore just to look at a coconut tree? When *they* had *lived* with and under coconut trees all their lives?"

"Did the judge tell you anything before the trial started?" I asked.

"He certainly did. He put himself down in that big chair with all the dignity in the world, and then he made us a speech. He said, 'You will be tried, in accordance with the rules of common law, by a jury of your peers. You may not consider them such, but on the basis of my past experience with the human race I can assure you they are. I have appointed counsel for the prosecution, and counsel for the defense. Before the trial begins I shall translate your explanation, as you gave it to me on the way up here, to both of them. After they have made their respective pleas I shall instruct the jury, who will then retire to arrive at their verdict.'

"So the trial began. Counsel for the prosecution turned out to be one of the most bloodthirsty villains I have ever seen in my life. He did not speak long, but he spoke violently; and we could see some of the jurors nodding their heads. When he had finished, the judge turned to us.

" 'For your benefit,' he said, 'I shall give you the substance of the case for the prosecution. Trespassing is not allowed on this island; and stealing is a capital crime. The prosecution accuses you of both, since, when you were apprehended, one of you had a coconut in his hand and the other was about to knock one off a tree. The prosecutor asks for the death penalty. This, I might add, is usually carried out on this island by burning at the stake, since the natives prefer roasted meat to boiled. I might also

mention that the prosecutor bases his case on a sound premise
—that ignorance of the law is no excuse.' "

"My God!" I exclaimed. "Didn't you have the guts scared out
of you?"

"Of course we did! But then counsel for the defense got up.
He was a little chap, with a sort of wily, persuasive voice. Besides trying to make a case, I suspect that he even contrived to
get into his appeal something about the quality of mercy. Anyhow, when he got through the judge again turned to us.

" 'Your counsel,' he explained, 'has hit upon a most ingenious
defense. He admits the trespassing; he admits your intent to
steal the coconuts. But, he says, you assumed that the island was
uninhabited—and how could anyone trespass on an island
owned or occupied by nobody? As to ignorance of the law being
no defense, there again he admits the correctness of the con-
cept. But, he says, since you thought there was nobody on the
island, you naturally assumed that there were no laws of which
to be ignorant. And finally he mentioned—just casually, you
understand—that the ship from which you had come is a war-
ship of the United States of America . . . I shall now charge the
jury.'

"Which he proceeded to do. What he told them I don't know
—he didn't translate that for us. Then he sat down and the jury
solemnly filed back behind a group of palms and went into a
huddle. After about ten minutes they came back and sat down
again on the benches.

"There was an exchange between the judge and one of the
jurymen, which I assume was: Have you reached a verdict? Yes,
we have. What is your verdict?—and then the verdict was pro-
nounced. And *that* the judge did translate for us.

" 'The verdict,' he declared, 'is *not* guilty. Gentlemen, I congratulate you.'

"And then he walked down the path with us, back to our boat.
It was lucky we had anchored it, because the tide had changed
and it was now about fifty yards offshore. We would have to
swim for it.

"It was just as we were about to plunge into the water—*not*,
by the way, taking a coconut with us—that Bill Scott couldn't
contain himself any longer.

" 'Say,' he said to the judge, "Who are you, anyhow? And why and how did you ever come to this island?' "

The lined face of the old judge took on a look that was positively terrifying.

" 'Why and how I came here," he said, 'is something I shall never tell a living soul. As to who I am—or rather, I should say, who I *was*—'

"And suddenly his face softened.

" 'Well, boys,' he said, 'I will give you just one clue. I trust you have noticed that this is a *volcanic* island.'

"And with that he turned back up the path, and we swam to our dinghy.

"Next morning the tanker caught up with us, and we refueled, and were on our way again. But do you know, it took me a whole day before I caught on as to who that fellow was?"

"What fellow?" I asked.

"Why, the judge! The last thing he said was that it was a volcanic island. That did it."

"Well, who was he?"

"Judge Crater, of course."

Man in a Trap

John D. MacDonald

When Joe Conroy walked from the supermarket to his parked car with the bag of groceries on a late Saturday afternoon, he looked at the black sky in the west and hoped the rain would hold off until he could get the grass cut. He was a gangling, freckled man, part owner and manager of a small and profitable trucking line. He put the groceries in the back on the floor and got behind the wheel.

As he looked back over his left shoulder, preparing to back out, the car door on the other side opened. He turned his head in time to see a big man step into the car quickly and pull the door shut.

The man was blond and in his twenties. His forehead and nose were peeling from recent sunburn. His features were heavy and brutal. He wore jeans, a pale blue sports shirt, and a cheap-looking dark blue corduroy jacket. He held a small automatic pistol in his right hand. He held it low, with the barrel aimed at Joe Conroy's waist. He brought a whisky smell into the car, and a smell of perspiration.

"What do you want?" Joe asked, and was pleased because his voice sounded a lot more calm than he felt.

The man moved closer and suddenly slapped the barrel against the point of Joe's knee. It hurt.

155

"Hey!"

"This real, ole buddy. You just drive. Go west on Oak and turn north at the boulevard light. Take it nice and easy and careful. I'm a nervous man today."

"You can get in a lot of—"

"No talk. Drive."

Joe did as he was told. He had long since decided he was not the hero type. When they said hands up, Joe's hands would go up. When they said turn around, he'd turn around. A big dead hero would be no help to Marty and the kids.

There was a curiously unreal flavor about the situation. It was something you knew could happen. But it never did. Until right now. Bang on the brakes and bust his head against the windshield. Sure. And if you lived maybe they'd let you keep the slugs they took out of you. On the mantel, mounted in plastic.

"How far?"

The gun barrel hit him on the knee again. "Just drive, dad." The blond man was as tensely alert as an animal.

Joe saw where he had made a mistake when he had dreamed up such an incident. You imagined the criminal would be somebody you could reason with. This man was big, ugly, irrational, and unpredictable.

Ten miles north of the city he said, "Turn in up there on the right. That Sundown Motel." After Joe had turned in, he said, "Now all the way to the end. Park on the far side of that Ford. Take the keys out and put them in my little hot hand. Okay. Now pick up your groceries. Use both hands. Now walk ahead of me right to that door. Number 20. Good. Now stand still. And don't try any funny stuff."

He rapped on the door, five sharp raps, closely spaced.

"Ray?" It was a woman's voice.

"Open up."

The door opened inward. Ray prodded him at the base of the spine with the gun barrel. "Go on in."

The woman backed away from the door, staring at Joe Conroy with surprise and, he thought, alarm. She was a lean-faced, full-mouthed blonde with a short hairdo. She wore a white blouse, and dark-red, shiny bullfighter pants. She was barefoot, and her ankles looked soiled. She had a very slim waist, long, heavy legs.

A man bounded off one of the beds and pushed the woman out of the way roughly. Ray had kicked the door shut. The man was about the same age as Ray. He had glossy black hair worn full and long, and sideburns down to the corners of a narrow jaw. He was in blue and white plaid underwear shorts. There was a half crescent of lipstick on his chin. His chest was hairless. His arms were long and powerful.

"Is there anything you can't foul up?" he demanded of Ray. "Just one lousy little thing?"

"Get off my back, Diz. I figured it all out."

"You're a big brain now, already."

"Look, Diz. I found a couple I could have took easy, so what happens? The car gets listed as hot maybe ten minutes later, and every prowl in town has it on the list and with the luck we've been running, they grab us off. So I figure this way. Take the car and the driver too. See? That means it isn't reported stole. Isn't that using the old head?"

Diz gave Ray a look of intense disgust. "That's using the old head," he said. He sat down on the bed, heavily, reached the bottle on the night stand and splashed whiskey into a glass.

"So what's the matter?" Ray demanded, looking from the girl to the man.

"Tell him, Lauralee," Diz said.

"This is the matter, lambie pie. Suppose it doesn't go real, real smooth. Suppose somebody has to go bang-bang. Then your new friend has a long talk with the fuzz. Descriptions, stupid."

Ray turned and stared indignantly at Joe Conroy. After a time his expression cleared. "So okay, then. Who's stupid? If the deal goes sour, then it don't make any difference we kill this one, too, does it?"

"If it's any help to you . . ." Joe said.

"Shut up!" Diz said. "Throw me his wallet, stupid."

"You stop climbing on my back," Ray grumbled. He took Joe's wallet out of his hip pocket and threw it to Diz.

Diz looked in it. "You're up to par, Ray. Four bucks." He took the identification cards out, and the photographs Joe carried. "Joseph T. Conroy," he said. "Hello, Joe. Wife and kids. And about two hours from now the wife gets so itchy she calls the cops. What the hell is the car? A thirty-seven jalopy or something?

"No, it's a good car, Diz, honest. Look out the window. It's a new four-door job with five thousand on it and a full tank. It ought to roll."

"Says here you're manager of Pyramid Trucking Lines, Conroy. Ever get called back to the office?"

"Sometimes."

Diz turned to Lauralee. "You hold stupid's hand while Joe and I wander up to the booth and make us a phone call." He put on trousers, shoes, and a jacket, slipped a gun into the jacket pocket. "Put that sack down someplace, Joe. Let's go."

Once they were outside he said, "Nothing funny now. I'm going to hear both ends of this little chat. You met a guy from the office. Something has come up. Make up something logical. You'll have to work late."

The booth was outside the motel office. Diz crowded in with Joe. The phone rang three times before Marty answered.

"Yes?"

"It's Joe, honey. Look, something came up. I checked at the terminal and I've got to go back for a while."

"Will you kids hush! I can't hear your father. Did you say you have to go back to work? What's the trouble?"

"Usual thing. Too many rigs down, and we'll have to dig up a lease someplace to keep from faulting on a contract."

"Did you get the groceries?"

"Yes."

"Well, can't you bring them home before you go back?"

"This is sort of an emergency, hon."

"You sound funny, Joe. Is anything wrong?"

"No. Everything is fine."

"Danny, stop screeching! Mommie can't hear. Will you be late?"

"I guess so."

"The Shermans were coming over after dinner."

"Well, you better call Liz and cancel, hon."

"You make sure you get something to eat, now. You're sure everything is all right?"

With enormous false heartiness he said, "Everything is dandy. I'm just a little worried about the contract. See you, honey."

"Goodbye, darling."

He was sweating as he hung up. The conversation had been like a little window open on a sane and normal world. As soon as he hung up he was back in a fantasy place inhabited by Diz, by Ray, and by Lauralee. He wiped his brow, waiting.

"That was just fine, Joe boy. You're being real cool. Now suppose she tries to phone you at the terminal? Think she will?"

"I . . . I guess she might. To remind me to eat."

"Then they better be ready to say you stepped out for a couple of minutes. Who can you call there?"

"Henry Gluckman, the dispatcher."

"Well, leave us do so, ole Joe."

Henry seemed baffled by Joe's request at first, and then he suddenly seemed to understand. "I get it, Mr. Conroy. Sure thing. Have a ball, Mr. Conroy."

Joe hung up and said, "He thinks I've got a woman lined up."

"It happens every day, Uncle Joe. Let's go back. I like you about a half step in front of me. Good."

They went back into the room. It was a setup usually called family accommodations. Two rooms and a bath. Ray was scowling down into a stiff highball. Diz went over and took it lightly out of his hand, and when Ray looked up in sharp annoyance, reaching to retrieve the glass, Diz said, "No more sauce, stupid. You might get another genius-type idea."

"I told him to lay off," Lauralee said.

"Shut up!" Ray barked at her.

"Watch Uncle Joe," Diz said. He went into the next room and came back with a roll of black tar tape. Joe Conroy was instructed to sit on the floor by the radiator, encircle a pipe with his arms, and clasp his hands. Diz wound his wrists and hands with the tape. Each encirclement made tighter pressure.

They don't do this, Joe thought. They tie you to a chair and you work the ropes loose. Nobody works this stuff loose. This is going to be a long day.

Once he was secure, they ignored him. They unfolded a road map on the bed and went over it carefully. Diz was the leader. He gave the orders. There was another piece of paper. Joe judged from the conversation that it was a sketch of a building.

"We spot the car here, motor running, lights out, Lauralee at the wheel. They close at eleven. They have the night deposit made up by midnight. Two of them take it in, the manager and some kind of clerk. They come out of the back. Their car is parked here. We'll be between the car and the hedge.

"Now get this, Ray. The minute we hit is when the fat one shoves the key in the car door. The other one will be holding the money bag. You come around the front, fast, gun in the left hand, blackjack in the right. And for God's sake, hit him right, not too hard and not too soft. I'll take the fat one.

"Then we unlock the car and dump them in so nobody sees them laying around. We throw the car keys into the yard and walk—get that—walk to Conroy's car. I'll take the wheel, Lauralee. You be ready to shove over. Ray, you'll have the money. You get in the back."

"How much do you think there'll be?" Lauralee asked with a husky wistfulness.

"From the business they do, someplace between fifteen and twenty-five thousand."

"It's about time," Ray mumbled.

"Six weeks and all we've done is pay expenses," Diz said. "Somebody is a jinx."

"Don't look at me," Ray said. "We did good until you picked her up, Diz."

"If I drop anybody, I drop you. Maybe I drop you after we split this one, stupid."

"I can do good by myself."

"You do fine. Big operations. Mug jobs."

Ray shrugged. "How about dads?"

"If it's smooth we leave him here and they find him when they come to change the sheets. If it goes sour . . . we decide later."

"I feel all empty in the middle," Lauralee said.

Diz rumpled her hair. "That's the name of the game, sweetheart. That's the kick."

She kissed him thoroughly, kneading his back. "How'll I look in mink?" she said.

"Like any other mink," Ray said.

Diz and the girl got up and went into the other room, arms around each other's waists. The door closed softly behind them. Ray got the bottle and poured himself a drink.

"From what I've heard—"

"Shut up, dad."

"I've heard that when you people team up with a woman, things go bad for you."

Ray got up and came around the bed. Holding his drink carefully so as not to spill it, he kicked Joe in the ribs with a full hard swing of his leg. Joe felt the bone go and the pain sickened him. It shamed him to sit on the floor and be kicked like an animal. And for the first time he felt a true and genuine anger.

Ray sat on the bed again. "Just don't talk," he said. "Just don't say word one."

Each time Joe drew breath pain was a knife in his side. I should have started being a man when I had the chance, Joe thought. That kick could have killed me. It could have driven a splintered edge of bone into the lungs. Then Diz would have been very happy with Ray. Delighted with him.

And he began to have a vague idea. As it took more definite shape, he liked it better. If he merely endured, the choice was not good. The men with the money would be armed and wary. This trio had the smell of defeat about them. If they killed one of the men, they would kill the other and come back and kill him. It would not go smoothly for them. Not with Ray drinking heavily. And the only chance seemed to be to increase the dissension between them.

He found the first step of his plan astoundingly hard to accomplish. He caught a fold of the inside of his cheek between his teeth, and for long moments he did not have the courage to do as he wished. Finally, bracing himself against the expected pain, he bit down as powerfully as he could and tasted the flow of blood into his mouth.

He chewed again and again, and then slumped over against the floor and made himself breathe in a heavy rasping way and let the blood run onto the floor. He kept his eyes closed. He heard Ray come over to him. The big hand took him by the shoulder and shook him roughly.

"Hey! Hey! Wake up!" Ray whispered.

Joe breathed in the same way. There was a long silence. Ray moved away from him.

"Hey, Diz."

"Go away, stupid."

"Diz, come here a minute."

"Shut up, Ray."

"Diz, you got to come here a minute."

Joe heard the door open finally and knew that they had come over to him.

"What the hell happened?" Diz demanded, his voice taut with anger.

"I just kicked him a little. One time. Honest. He was talking too much."

"Oh, you slob! Oh, you stupid, crazy jerk!"

Joe heard the quick suck of breath and knew the girl had come over and seen him. "He's ... bleeding."

"The genius kicked him. He probably busted up his insides. The guy may be dying."

"I ... I don't like this," Lauralee said. "I don't like it."

"A nice juicy kidnap murder," Diz said. "In this state they gas you. They drop it in a bucket under a chair."

"Honest, Diz, I only—"

There was a sudden brutal splat of fist on flesh and something heavy fell against a bed and slid sideways.

"You didn't have to do that," Ray said, his voice muffled.

"What're we gonna do?" Lauralee said, and Joe detected hysteria in her voice. He made his breathing more ragged.

"Lemme think," Diz said. "He may be going out right now."

"We ought to get a doctor," Lauralee said.

"That's a wonderful idea. That's a real good idea. The kind Ray has all the time."

"Maybe we ought to anyway cut him loose and put him on the bed," the girl said. "Look at him bleed!"

They unwound the tape from his hands. He kept himself utterly limp. They carried him to the bed and put him down clumsily.

"Go get a towel or something," Diz said.

"I just gave him one little kick in the ribs," Ray said wonderingly.

"Shut up. I got to think. If he dies, we'll have to get him out of here. He'll have to be dumped someplace."

"I didn't know I was going to get into anything like this. I don't like this," Lauralee whined.

"Maybe he's faking," Ray said. "Give me that cigarette, honey," Diz said.

Joe Conroy braced himself. He did not know where the pain would begin. It began on the back of his left hand. It was bright pain, fierce and sharp. He fought against the instinctive reflex. It lasted a little longer than forever, and finally stopped.

"He's not faking," Diz said. "He's in bad shape."

"If it's going to happen anyway, let's finish it," Ray said.

"No!" Lauralee cried.

"Shut up, honey. Who says it's going to happen anyway? I'm no doctor. You want a murder rap against you, Ray? Stop having ideas. Give me a chance to think."

"It's driving me nuts, listening to him," Ray said.

"Go in the other room and shut the door."

"I want to know what—"

"Move, will you!"

"Okay, okay, okay." Joe heard the door slam.

"What are you going to do?" the girl whispered nervously.

"Ray goofed it up. But I need him tonight. We can get along without you. You stay here with Conroy. Then we'll come back here. Dead or not, we'll take Conroy along. We'll find a side road and I'll have Ray help me drag him off in the brush. And . . . when I come back to the car, I'll be alone."

"No, Diz!"

"Think of a better way. I can leave the gun in Conroy's hand. It'll confuse the law. And we'll switch cars as soon as we can."

"I'm scared."

"Don't be scared. Diz will fix everything nice for baby."

It was a sizable slice of eternity before the two men left. He heard his car drive away. Diz, before he left, had taped Joe's wrists and ankles. Joe opened his eyes and groaned. The girl came over to the bed.

"Water," he gasped.

"Okay. I'll get some." She came back with a glass. She held his head up and held the glass to his lips. "You know, I was a nurse's aide once. I was going to go into nurse training, but it was too tough, you know what I mean? I'm sorry about Ray kicking you."

He clasped his fingers together. "Fix the pillow. Please," he gasped.

"Sure thing." She put the empty glass aside. Joe felt vastly guilty about what he was about to do. He had never struck a woman in his life. And he knew he could not be half-hearted about it.

His wrists were fastened together in front of him. She reached around him to tug at the pillow. He watched her chin carefully. When he judged it was in perfect position, he brought his clasped hands up as hard and as quickly as he could.

The force of the blow straightened her up and she fell against the other bed and bounced onto the floor. He swung his legs over the side of the bed and sat up. She came up onto her hands and knees, face bleared and dazed. As she started to push herself up, he struck her again, swinging his clasped hands sideways, striking the angle of her jaw.

He tried to hop to the door, but he lost his balance and fell. He wriggled the rest of the way, knelt and caught the knob, pulled himself up, unlocked the door, and hopped out into the night yelling as loudly as he could. He hopped four times and fell into the driveway, still hollering, as doors opened, and people were running . . .

At one in the morning, after the police surgeon had taped his cracked rib and packed the wound on the inside of his mouth, Detective Lieutenant Halverson, small and trim, came in as Joe Conroy was putting his shirt back on.

"Delivered the car to your wife. Told her I'd bring you home, but she's going to get a sitter somehow and come down for you."

"You got them, then."

Halverson leaned against a file cabinet and lit a cigarette. "Wouldn't have, if you hadn't overheard the name of the supermarket they were going to knock off. When we put the floods on them they got rattled. So the girl is in a cell, and the big blond punk is in the police morgue, and the one with the sideburns is on the operating table. We don't have the history yet, but it will be coming through soon. Now I've got time for your end of the story."

Joe told him—and the words came hard.

Halverson nodded when he finished. "Smart," he said.

"I'm a real hero," Joe said. "She was being a roadshow Florence Nightingale and I sucker-punched her beautifully."

"So you wish you'd tried to climb the boys instead, so Monday your wife could be picking out a box with bronze handles?"

"Not that. But ..."

"I know what you mean. Both papers want to talk to you. How will you handle it?"

"I managed to get away. That's enough."

And that's all he told them. But he told Marty all of it. And he didn't start to shake with reaction until he was at last home and safe, and then he took the pills he hadn't thought he would need.

Sunday, except for all the phone calls, was like any other Sunday. Almost like any other Sunday. Just like every day from now on would be almost like the days that had gone before. With one little exception. For Joe Conroy life had become a little more valuable because it could not so readily be taken for granted.

There was evil loose in the world, random and brutal as summer lightening. And this time his luck had been like a coin found in the street. He read the funnies to the kids, and, with an awkward gladness, kissed Marty more often than was his habit.

The Bearded Lady

Ross Macdonald

The unlatched door swung inward when I knocked. I walked into the studio, which was high and dim as a hayloft. The big north window in the opposite wall was hung with monkscloth draperies that shut out the morning light. I found the switch beside the door and snapped it on. Several fluorescent tubes suspended from the naked rafters flickered and burnt blue-white.

A strange woman faced me under the cruel light. She was only a charcoal sketch on an easel, but she gave me a chill. Her nude body, posed casually on a chair, was slim and round and pleasant to look at. Her face wasn't pleasant at all. Bushy black eyebrows almost hid her eyes. A walrus moustache bracketed her mouth, and a thick beard fanned down over her torso.

The door creaked behind me. The girl who appeared in the doorway wore a starched white uniform. Her face had a little starch in it, too, though not enough to spoil her good looks entirely. Her black hair was drawn back severely from her forehead.

"May I ask what you're doing here?"

"You may ask. I'm looking for Mr. Western."

"Really? Have you tried looking behind the pictures?"

"Does he spend much time there?"

"No, and another thing he doesn't do—he doesn't receive visitors in his studio when he isn't here himself."

"Sorry. The door was open. I walked in."

"You can reverse the process."

"Just a minute. Hugh isn't sick?"

She glanced down at her white uniform and shook her head.

"Are you a friend of his?" I said.

"I try to be." She smiled slightly. "It isn't always easy, with a sib. I'm his sister."

"Not the one he was always talking about?"

"I'm the only one he has."

I reached back into my mental grab bag of war souvenirs. "Mary. The name was Mary."

"It still is Mary. Are *you* a friend of Hugh's?"

"I guess I qualify. I used to be."

"When?" The question was brusque. I got the impression she didn't approve of Hugh's friends, or some of them.

"In the Philippines. He was attached to my group as a combat artist. The name is Archer, by the way. Lew Archer."

"Oh. Of course."

Her disapproval didn't extend to me, at least not yet. She gave me her hand. It was cool and firm, and went with her steady gaze. I said:

"Hugh gave me the wrong impression of you. I thought you were still a kid in school."

"That was four years ago, remember. People grow up in four years. Anyway, some of them do."

She was a very serious girl for her age. I changed the subject.

"I saw the announcement of his show in the L.A. papers. I'm driving through to San Francisco, and I thought I'd look him up."

"I know he'll be glad to see you. I'll go and wake him. He keeps the most dreadful hours. Sit down, won't you, Mr. Archer?"

I had been standing with my back to the bearded nude, more or less consciously shielding her from it. When I moved aside and she saw it, she didn't turn a hair.

"What next?" was all she said.

But I couldn't help wondering what had happened to Hugh

Western's sense of humor. I looked around the room for something that might explain the ugly sketch.

It was a typical working artist's studio. The tables and benches were cluttered with things that are used to make pictures: palettes and daubed sheets of glass, sketch pads, scratchboards, bleeding tubes of paint. Pictures in half a dozen mediums and half a dozen stages of completion hung or leaned against the burlap-covered walls. Some of them looked wild and queer to me, but none so wild and queer as the sketch on the easel.

There was one puzzling thing in the room, besides the pictures. The wooden doorframe was scarred with a row of deep round indentations, four of them. They were new, and about on a level with my eyes. They looked as if an incredible fist had struck the wood a superhuman blow.

"He isn't in his room," the girl said from the doorway. Her voice was very carefully controlled.

"Maybe he got up early."

"His bed hasn't been slept in. He's been out all night."

"I wouldn't worry. He's an adult after all."

"Yes, but he doesn't always act like one." Some feeling buzzed under her calm tone. I couldn't tell if it was fear or anger. "He's twelve years older than I am, and still a boy at heart. A middle-aging boy."

"I know what you mean. I was his unofficial keeper for a while. I guess he's a genius, or pretty close to it, but he needs somebody to tell him to come in out of the rain."

"Thank you for informing me. I didn't know."

"Now don't get mad at me."

"I'm sorry. I suppose I'm a little upset."

"Has he been giving you a bad time?"

"Not really. Not lately, that is. He's come down to earth since he got engaged to Alice. But he still makes the weirdest friends. He can tell a fake Van Gogh with his eyes shut, literally, but he's got no discrimination about people at all."

"You wouldn't be talking about me? Or am I having ideas of reference?"

"No." She smiled again. I liked her smile. "I guess I acted terribly suspicious when I walked in on you. Some pretty dubious characters come to see him."

"Anyone in particular?" I said it lightly. Just above her head I could see the giant fist-mark on the doorframe.

Before she could answer, a siren bayed in the distance. She cocked her head. "Ten to one it's for me."

"Police?"

"Ambulance. The police sirens have a different tone. I'm an X-ray technician at the hospital, so I've learned to listen for the ambulance. And I'm on call this morning."

I followed her into the hall. "Hugh's show opens tonight. He's bound to come back for that."

She turned at the opposite door, her face brightening. "You know, he may have spent the night working in the gallery. He's awfully fussy about how his pictures are hung."

"Why don't I phone the gallery?"

"There's never anybody in the office till nine." She looked at her unfeminine steel wristwatch. "It's twenty to."

"When did you last see him?"

"At dinner last night. We ate early. He went back to the gallery after dinner. He said he was only going to work a couple of hours."

"And you stayed here?"

"Until about eight, when I was called to the hospital. I didn't get home until quite late, and I thought he was in bed." She looked at me uncertainly, with a little wrinkle of doubt between her straight eyebrows. "Could you be cross-questioning me?"

"Sorry. It's my occupational disease."

"What do you do in real life?"

"Isn't this real?"

"I mean now you're out of the army. Are you a lawyer?"

"A private detective."

"Oh. I see." The wrinkle between her eyebrows deepened. I wondered what she'd been reading.

"But I'm on vacation." I hoped.

A phone burred behind her apartment door. She went to answer it, and came back wearing a coat. "It *was* for me. Somebody fell out of a loquat tree and broke a leg. You'll have to excuse me, Mr. Archer."

"Wait a second. If you'll tell me where the art gallery is, I'll see if Hugh's there now."

"Of course, you don't know San Marcos."

She led me to the French windows at the rear end of the hall. They opened on a blacktop parking space which was overshadowed on the far side by a large stucco building, the shape of a flattened cube. Outside the windows was a balcony from which a concrete staircase slanted down to the parking lot. She stepped outside and pointed to the stucco cube:

"That's the gallery. It's no problem to find, is it? You can take a shortcut down the alley to the front."

A tall young man in a black leotard was polishing a red convertible in the parking lot. He struck a pose, in the fifth position, and waved his hand:

"Bonjour, Marie."

"Bonjour, my phony Frenchman." There was an edge of contempt on her good humor. "Have you seen Hugh this morning?"

"Not I. Is the prodigal missing again?"

"I wouldn't say missing—"

"I was wondering where your car was. It's not in the garage." His voice was much too musical.

"Who's he?" I asked her in an undertone.

"Hilary Todd. He runs the art shop downstairs. If the car's gone, Hugh can't be at the gallery. I'll have to take a taxi to the hospital."

"I'll drive you."

"I wouldn't think of it. There's a cabstand across the street." She added over her shoulder: "Call me at the hospital if you see Hugh."

I went down the stairs to the parking lot. Hilary Todd was still polishing the hood of his convertible, though it shone like a mirror. His shoulders were broad and packed with shifting muscle. Some of the ballet boys were strong and could be dangerous. Not that he was a boy, exactly. He had a little round bald spot that gleamed like a silver dollar among his hair.

"Bonjour," I said to his back.

"Yes?"

My French appeared to offend his ears. He turned and straightened. I saw how tall he was, tall enough to make me feel squat, though I was over six feet. He had compensated for the bald spot by growing sideburns. In combination with his liquid eyes, they gave him a Latin look. Pig Latin.

"Do you know Hugh Western pretty well?"

"If it's any concern of yours."

"It is."

"Now why would that be?"

"I asked the question, sonny. Answer it."

He blushed and lowered his eyes, as if I had been reading his evil thoughts. He stuttered a little. "I—I—well, I've lived below him for a couple of years. I've sold a few of his pictures. Why?"

"I thought you might know where he is, even if his sister doesn't."

"How should I know where he is? Are you a policeman?"

"Not exactly."

"Not at all, you mean?" He regained his poise. "Then you have no right to take this overbearing attitude. I know absolutely nothing about Hugh. And I'm very busy."

He turned abruptly and continued his polishing job, his fine useless muscles writhing under the leotard.

I walked down the narrow alley which led to the street. Through the cypress hedge on the left, I caught a glimpse of umbrella tables growing like giant multicolored mushrooms in a restaurant patio. On the other side was the wall of the gallery, its white blankness broken by a single iron-barred window above the level of my head.

The front of the gallery was Greek-masked by a high-pillared porch. A broad flight of concrete steps rose to it from the street. A girl was standing at the head of the steps, half leaning on one of the pillars.

She turned towards me, and the slanting sunlight aureoled her bare head. She had a startling kind of beauty: yellow hair, light hazel eyes, brown skin. She filled her tailored suit like sand in a sack.

"Good morning."

She pretended not to hear me. Her right foot was tapping the pavement impatiently. I crossed the porch to the high bronze door and pushed. It didn't give.

"There's nobody here yet," she said. "The gallery doesn't open until ten."

"Then what are you doing here?"

"I happen to work here."

"Why don't you open up?"

"I have no key. In any case," she added primly, "we don't allow visitors before ten."

"I'm not a tourist, at least at the moment. I came to see Mr. Western."

"Hugh?" She looked at me directly for the first time. "Hugh's not here. He lives around the corner on Rubio Street."

"I just came from there."

"Well, he isn't here." She gave the words a curious emphasis. "There's nobody here but me. And I won't be here much longer if Dr. Silliman doesn't come."

"Silliman?"

"Dr. Silliman is our curator." She made it sound as if she owned the gallery. After a while she said in a softer voice: "Why are you looking for Hugh? Do you have some business with him?"

"Western's an old friend of mine."

"Really?"

She lost interest in the conversation. We stood together in silence for several minutes. She was tapping her foot again. I watched the Saturday-morning crowd on the street: women in slacks, women in shorts and dirndls, a few men in ten-gallon hats, a few in berets. A large minority of the people had Spanish or Indian faces. Nearly half the cars in the road carried out-of-state licenses. San Marcos was a unique blend of western border town, ocean resort, and artists' colony.

A small man in a purple corduroy jacket detached himself from the crowd and bounded up the steps. His movements were quick as a monkey's. His lined face had a simian look, too. A brush of frizzled gray hair added about three inches to his height.

"I'm sorry if I kept you waiting, Alice."

She made a *nada* gesture. "It's perfectly all right. This gentleman is a friend of Hugh's."

He turned to me. His smile went on and off. "Good morning, sir. What was the name?"

I told him. He shook my hand. His fingers were like thin steel hooks.

"Western ought to be here at any minute. Have you tried his flat?"

"Yes. His sister thought he might have spent the night in the gallery."

"Oh, but that's impossible. You mean he didn't come home last night?"

"Apparently not."

"You didn't tell me that," the blond girl said.

"I didn't know you were interested."

"Alice has every right to be interested." Silliman's eyes glowed with a gossip's second-hand pleasure. "She and Hugh are going to be married. Next month, isn't it, Alice? Do you know Miss Turner, by the way, Mr. Archer?"

"Hello, Mr. Archer." Her voice was shallow and hostile. I gathered that Silliman had embarrassed her.

"I'm sure he'll be along shortly," he said reassuringly. "We still have some work to do on the program for the private showing tonight. Will you come in and wait?"

I said I would.

He took a heavy key ring out of his jacket pocket and un-locked the bronze door, relocking it behind us. Alice Turner touched a switch which lit up the high-ceilinged lobby and the Greek statues standing like frozen sentinels along the walls. There were several nymphs and Venuses in marble, but I was more interested in Alice. She had everything the Venuses had, and the added advantage of being alive. She also had Hugh Western, it seemed, and that surprised me. He was a little old for her, and a little used. She didn't look like one of those girls who'd have to settle for an aging bachelor. But then Hugh Western had talent.

She removed a bundle of letters from the mail box and took them into the office which opened off the lobby. Silliman turned to me with a monkey grin.

"She's quite a girl, is she not? Trust Hugh to draw a circle around the prettiest girl in town. And she comes from a very good family, an excellent family. Her father, the Admiral, is one of our trustees, you know, and Alice has inherited his interest in the arts. Of course she has a more personal interest now. Had you known of their engagement?"

"I haven't seen Hugh for years, not since the war."

"Then I should have held my tongue and let him tell you himself."

As we were talking, he led me through the central gallery, which ran the length of the building like the nave of a church. To the left and right, in what would have been the aisles, the walls of smaller exhibition rooms rose halfway to the ceiling. Above them was a mezzanine reached by an open iron staircase.

He started up it, still talking: "If you haven't seen Hugh since the war, you'll be interested in the work he's been doing lately."

I was interested, though not for artistic reasons. The wall of the mezzanine was hung with twenty-odd paintings: landscapes, portraits, groups of semi-abstract figures, and more abstract still lifes. I recognized some of the scenes he had sketched in the Philippine jungle, transposed into the permanence of oil. In the central position there was a portrait of a bearded man whom I'd hardly have known without the label, "Self-Portrait."

Hugh had changed. He had put on weight and lost his youth entirely. There were vertical lines in the forehead, gray flecks in the hair and beard. The light eyes seemed to be smiling sardonically. But when I looked at them from another angle, they were bleak and somber. It was a face a man might see in his bathroom mirror on a cold gray hangover morning.

I turned to the curator hovering at my elbow. "When did he raise the beard?"

"A couple of years ago, I believe, shortly after he joined us as resident painter."

"Is he obsessed with beards?"

"I don't quite know what you mean."

"Neither do I. But I came across a funny thing in his studio this morning. A sketch of a woman, a nude, with a heavy black beard. Does that make sense to you?"

The old man smiled. "I've long since given up trying to make sense of Hugh. He has his own esthetic logic, I suppose. But I'd have to see this sketch before I could form an opinion. He may have simply been doodling."

"I doubt it. It was big, and carefully done." I brought out the question that had been nagging at the back of my mind. "Is there something the matter with him, emotionally? He hasn't gone off the deep end?"

His answer was sharp. "Certainly not. He's simply wrapped up in his work, and he lives by impulse. He's never on time for appointments." He looked at his watch. "He promised last night to meet me here this morning at nine, and it's almost nine-thirty."

"When did you see him last night?"

"I left the key of the gallery with him when I went home for dinner. He wanted to rehang some of these paintings. About eight or a little after he walked over to my house to return the key. We have only the one key, since we can't afford a watchman."

"Did he say where he was going after that?"

"He had an appointment, he didn't say with whom. It seemed to be urgent, since he wouldn't stop for a drink. Well." He glanced at his watch again. "I suppose I'd better be getting down to work, Western or no Western."

Alice was waiting for us at the foot of the stairs. Both of her hands gripped the wrought-iron bannister. Her voice was no more than a whisper, but it seemed to fill the great room with leaden echoes:

"Dr. Silliman, the Chardin's gone."

He stopped so suddenly I nearly ran into him. "That's impossible."

"I know. But it's gone, frame and all."

He bounded down the remaining steps and disappeared into one of the smaller rooms under the mezzanine. Alice followed him more slowly. I caught up with her:

"There's a picture missing?"

"Father's best picture, one of the best Chardins in the country. He loaned it to the gallery for a month."

"Is it worth a lot of money?"

"Yes, it's very valuable. But it means a lot more to Father than the money—" She turned in the doorway and gave me a closed look, as if she'd realized she was telling her family secrets to a stranger.

Silliman was standing with his back to us, staring at a blank space on the opposite wall. He looked badly shaken when he turned around.

"I *told* the board that we should install a burglar alarm—the insurance people recommended it. But Admiral Turner was the only one who supported me. Now of course they'll be blaming me." His nervous eyes roved around and paused on Alice. "And what is your father going to say?"

"He'll be sick." She looked sick herself.

They were getting nowhere, and I cut in: "When did you see it last?"

Silliman answered me. "Yesterday afternoon, about five-thirty. I showed it to a visitor just before we closed. We check the visitors very closely from the office, since we have no guards."

"Who was the visitor?"

"A lady—an elderly lady from Pasadena. She's above suspicion, of course. I escorted her out myself, and she was the last one in, I know for a fact."

"Aren't you forgetting Hugh?"

"By George, I was. He was here until eight last night. But you surely don't suggest that Western took it? He's our resident painter, he's devoted to the gallery."

"He might have been careless. If he was working on the mezzanine and left the door unlocked—"

"He always kept it locked," Alice said coldly. "Hugh isn't careless about the things that matter."

"Is there another entrance?"

"No," Silliman said. "The building was planned for security. There's only the one window in my office, and it's heavily barred. We do have an air-conditioning system, but the inlets are much too small for anyone to get through."

"Let's have a look at the window."

The old man was too upset to question my authority. He led me through a storeroom stacked with old gilt-framed pictures whose painters deserved to be hung, if the pictures didn't. The single casement in the office was shut and bolted behind a Venetian blind. I pulled the cord and peered out through the dusty glass. The vertical bars outside the window were no more than three inches apart. None of them looked as if it had been tampered with. Across the alley, I could see a few tourists obliviously eating breakfast behind the restaurant hedge.

Silliman was leaning on the desk, one hand on the cradle phone. Indecision was twisting his face out of shape. "I do hate to call the police in a matter like this. I suppose I must, though, mustn't I?"

Alice covered his hand with hers, the line of her back a taut curve across the desk. "Hadn't you better talk to Father first? He was here with Hugh last night—I should have remembered before. It's barely possible he took the Chardin home with him."

"Really? You really think so?" Silliman let go of the telephone and clasped his hands hopefully under his chin.

"It wouldn't be like Father to do that without letting you know. But the month is nearly up, isn't it?"

"Three more days." His hand returned to the phone. "Is the Admiral at home?"

"He'll be down at the club by now. Do you have your car?"

"Not this morning."

I made one of my famous quick decisions, the kind you wake up in the middle of the night reconsidering five years later. San Francisco could wait. My curiosity was touched, and something deeper than curiosity. Something of the responsibility I'd felt for Hugh in the Philippines, when I was the practical one and he was the evergreen adolescent who thought the jungle was as safe as a scene by Le Douanier Rousseau. Though we were nearly the same age, I'd felt like his elder brother. I still did.

"My car's around the corner," I said. "I'll be glad to drive you."

The San Marcos Beach Club was a long low building painted an unobtrusive green and standing well back from the road. Everything about it was unobtrusive, including the private policeman who stood inside the plate-glass doors and watched us come up the walk.

"Looking for the Admiral, Miss Turner? I think he's up on the north deck."

We crossed a tiled lanai shaded with potted palms, and climbed a flight of stairs to a sun deck lined with cabanas. I could see the mountains that walled the city off from the desert in the northeast, and the sea below with its waves glinting like blue fish scales. The swimming pool on the lee side of the deck was still and clear.

Admiral Turner was taking the sun in a canvas chair. He stood up when he saw us, a big old man in shorts and a sleeveless shirt. Sun and wind had reddened his face and crinkled the flesh around his eyes. Age had slackened his body, but there was nothing aged or infirm about his voice. It still held the brazen echo of command.

"What's this, Alice? I thought you were at work."

"We came to ask you a question, Admiral." Silliman hesitated, coughing behind his hand. He looked at Alice.

"Speak out, man. Why is everybody looking so green around the gills?"

Silliman forced the words out: "Did you take the Chardin home with you last night?"

"I did not. Is it gone?"

"It's missing from the gallery," Alice said. She held herself uncertainly, as though the old man frightened her a little. "We thought you might have taken it."

"Me take it? That's absurd! Absolutely absurd and preposterous!" The short white hair bristled on his head. "When was it taken?"

"We don't know. It was gone when we opened the gallery. We discovered it just now."

"God damn it, what goes on?" He glared at her and then he glared at me, from eyes like round blue gun muzzles. "And who the hell are you?"

He was only a retired admiral, and I'd been out of uniform for years, but he gave me a qualm. Alice put in:

"A friend of Hugh's, Father. Mr. Archer."

He didn't offer his hand. I looked away. A woman in a white bathing suit was poised on the ten-foot board at the end of the pool. She took three quick steps and a bounce. Her body hung jack-knifed in the air, straightened and dropped, cut the water with hardly a splash.

"Where is Hugh?" the Admiral said petulantly. "If this is some of his carelessness, I'll ream the bastard."

"Father!"

"Don't father me. Where is he, Allie? You ought to know if anyone does."

"But I don't." She added in a small voice: "He's been gone all night."

"He has?" The old man sat down suddenly, as if his legs were too weak to bear the weight of his feelings. "He didn't say anything to me about going away."

The woman in the white bathing suit came up the steps behind him. "Who's gone away?" she said.

The Admiral craned his wattled neck to look at her. She was worth the effort from anyone, though she wouldn't see thirty again. Her dripping body was tanned and disciplined, full in the right places and narrow in the others. I didn't remember her face, but her shape seemed familiar. Silliman introduced her as Admiral Turner's wife. When she pulled off her rubber cap, her red hair flared like a minor conflagration.

"You won't believe what they've been telling me, Sarah. My Chardin's been stolen."

"Which one?"

"I've only the one. The 'Apple on a Table'."

She turned on Silliman like a pouncing cat. "Is it insured?"

"For twenty-five thousand dollars. But I'm afraid it's irreplaceable."

"And who's gone away?"

"Hugh has," Alice said. "Of course it's nothing to do with the picture."

"You're sure?" She turned to her husband with an intensity that made her almost ungainly. "Hugh was at the gallery when you dropped in there last night. You told me so yourself. And hasn't he been trying to buy the Chardin?"

"I don't believe it," Alice said flatly. "He didn't have the money."

"I know that perfectly well. He was acting as agent for someone. Wasn't he, Johnston?"

"Yes," the old man admitted. "He wouldn't tell me who his principal was, which is one of the reasons I wouldn't listen to the offer. Still, it's foolish to jump to conclusions about Hugh. I was with him when he left the gallery, and I know for a fact he didn't have the Chardin. It was the last thing I looked at."

"What time did he leave you?"

"Some time around eight—I don't remember exactly." He seemed to be growing older and smaller under her questioning. "He walked with me as far as my car."

"There was nothing to prevent him from walking right back."

"I don't know what you're trying to prove," Alice said.

The older woman smiled poisonously. "I'm simply trying to bring out the facts, so we'll know what to do. I notice that no one has suggested calling in the police." She looked at each of the others in turn. "Well? Do we call them? Or do we assume as a working hypothesis that dear Hugh took the picture?"

Nobody answered her for a while. The Admiral finally broke the ugly silence. "We can't bring in the authorities if Hugh's involved. He's virtually a member of the family."

Alice put a grateful hand on his shoulder, but Silliman said uneasily, "We'll have to take some steps. If we don't make an effort to recover it, we may not be able to collect the insurance."

"I realize that," the Admiral said. "We'll have to take that chance."

Sarah Turner smiled with tight-lipped complacency. She'd won her point, though I still wasn't sure what her point was. During the family argument I'd moved a few feet away, leaning on the railing at the head of the stairs and pretending not to listen.

She moved towards me now, her narrow eyes appraising me as if maleness was a commodity she prized.

"And who are you?" she said, her sharp smile widening.

I identified myself. I didn't smile back. But she came up very close to me. I could smell the chlorine on her, and under it the not so very subtle odor of sex.

"You look uncomfortable," she said. "Why don't you come swimming with me?"

"My hydrophobia won't let me. Sorry."

"What a pity. I hate to do things alone."

Silliman nudged me gently. He said in an undertone: "I really must be getting back to the gallery. I can call a cab if you prefer."

"No, I'll drive you." I wanted a chance to talk to him in private.

There were quick footsteps in the patio below. I looked down and saw the naked crown of Hilary Todd's head. At almost the same instant he glanced up at us. He turned abruptly and started to walk away, then changed his mind when Silliman called down.

"Hello there. Are you looking for the Turners?"

"As a matter of fact, I am."

From the corner of my eye, I noticed Sarah Turner's reaction to the sound of his voice. She stiffened, and her hand went up to her flaming hair.

"They're up here," Silliman said.

Todd climbed the stairs with obvious reluctance. We passed him going down. In a pastel shirt and a matching tie under a bright tweed jacket he looked very elegant, and very self-conscious and tense. Sarah Turner met him at the head of the stairs. I wanted to linger a bit, for eavesdropping purposes, but Silliman hustled me out.

"Mrs. Turner seems very much aware of Todd," I said to him in the car. "Do they have things in common?"

He answered tartly: "I've never considered the question. They're no more than casual acquaintances, so far as I know."

"What about Hugh? Is he just a casual acquaintance of hers, too?"

He studied me for a minute as the convertible picked up speed. "You notice things, don't you?"

"Noticing things is my business."

"Just what is your business? You're not an artist?"

"Hardly. I'm a private detective."

"A detective?" He jumped in the seat, as if I had offered to bite him. "You're not a friend of Western's then? Are you from the insurance company?"

"Not me. I'm a friend of Hugh's, and that's my only interest in this case. I more or less stumbled into it."

"I see." But he sounded a little dubious.

"Getting back to Mrs. Turner—she didn't make that scene with her husband for fun. She must have had some reason. Love or hate."

Silliman held his tongue for a minute, but he couldn't resist a chance to gossip. "I expect that it's a mixture of love and hate. She's been interested in Hugh ever since the Admiral brought her here. She's not a San Marcos girl, you know." He seemed to take comfort from that. "She was a Wave officer in Washington during the war. The Admiral noticed her—Sarah knows how to make herself conspicuous—and added her to his personal staff. When he retired he married her and came here to live in his family home. Alice's mother has been dead for many years. Well, Sarah hadn't been here two months before she was making eyes at Hugh." He pressed his lips together in spinsterly disapproval. "The rest is local history."

"They had an affair?"

"A rather one-sided affair, so far as I could judge. She was quite insane about him. I don't believe he responded, except in the physical sense. Your friend is quite a demon with the ladies." There was a whisper of envy in Silliman's disapproval.

"But I understood he was going to marry Alice."

"Oh, he is, he is. At least he certainly was until this dreadful business came up. His—ah—involvement with Sarah occurred before he knew Alice. She was away at art school until a few months ago."

"Does Alice know about his affair with her stepmother?"

"I daresay she does. I hear the two women don't get along at all well, though there may be other reasons for that. Alice refuses to live in the same house; she's moved into the gardener's cottage behind the Turner house. I think her trouble with Sarah is one reason why she came to work for me. Of course, there's the money consideration, too. The family isn't well off."

"I thought they were rolling in it," I said, "from the way he brushed off the matter of the insurance. Twenty-five thousand dollars, did you say?"

"Yes. He's quite fond of Hugh."

"If he's not well heeled, how does he happen to have such a valuable painting?"

"It was a gift, when he married his first wife. Her father was in the French Embassy in Washington, and he gave them the Chardin as a wedding present. You can understand the Admiral's attachment to it."

"Better than I can his decision not to call in the police. How do you feel about that, doctor?"

He didn't answer for a while. We were nearing the center of the city and I had to watch the traffic. I couldn't keep track of what went on in his face.

"After all it *is* his picture," he said carefully. "And his prospective son-in-law."

"You don't think Hugh's responsible, though?"

"I don't know what to think. I'm thoroughly rattled. And I won't know what to think until I have a chance to talk to Western." He gave me a sharp look. "Are you going to make a search for him?"

"Somebody has to. I seem to be elected."

When I let him out in front of the gallery, I asked him where Mary Western worked.

"The City Hospital." He told me how to find it. "But you will be discreet, Mr. Archer? You won't do or say anything rash? I'm in a very delicate position."

"I'll be very suave and bland." But I slammed the door hard in his face.

There were several patients in the X-ray waiting room, in various stages of dilapidation and disrepair. The plump blonde at the reception desk told me that Miss Western was in the dark room. Would I wait? I sat down and admired the way her sunburned shoulders glowed through her nylon uniform. In a few minutes Mary came into the room, starched and controlled and efficient-looking. She blinked in the strong light from the window. I got a quick impression that there was a lost child hidden behind her façade.

"Have you seen Hugh?"

"No. Come out for a minute." I took her elbow and drew her into the corridor.

"What is it?" Her voice was quiet, but it had risen in pitch. "Has something happened to him?"

"Not to *him*. Admiral Turner's picture's been stolen from the gallery. The Chardin."

"But how does Hugh come into this?"

"Somebody seems to think he took it."

"Somebody?"

"Mrs. Turner, to be specific."

"*Sarah!* She'd say anything to get back at him for ditching her."

I filed that one away. "Maybe so. The fact is, the Admiral seems to suspect him, too. So much so that he's keeping the police out of it."

"Admiral Turner is a senile fool. If Hugh were here to defend himself—"

"But that's the point. He isn't."

"I've got to find him." She turned toward the door.

"It may not be so easy."

She looked back in quick anger, her round chin prominent. "You suspect him, too."

"I do not. But a crime's been committed, remember. Crimes often come in pairs."

She turned, her eyes large and very dark. "You do think something has happened to my brother."

"I don't think anything. But if I were certain that he's all right, I'd be on my way to San Francisco now."

"You believe it's as bad as that," she said in a whisper. "I've got to go to the police."

"It's up to you. You'll want to keep them out of it, though, if there's the slightest chance—" I left the sentence unfinished.

She finished it: "That Hugh is a thief? There isn't. But I'll tell you what we'll do. He may be up at his shack in the mountains. He's gone off there before without telling anyone. Will you drive up with me?" She laid a light hand on my arm. "I can go myself if you have to get away."

"I'm sticking around," I said. "Can you get time off?"

"I'm taking it. All they can do is fire me, and there aren't enough good technicians to go around. Anyway, I put in three hours' overtime last night. Be with you in two minutes."

And she was.

I put the top of the convertible down. As we drove out of the city the wind blew away her smooth glaze of efficiency, colored her cheeks and loosened her sleek hair.

"You should do this oftener," I said.

"Do what?"

"Get out in the country and relax."

"I'm not exactly relaxed, with my brother accused of theft, and missing into the bargain."

"Anyway, you're not working. Has it ever occurred to you that perhaps you work too hard?"

"Has it ever occurred to you that somebody has to work or nothing will get done? You and Hugh are more alike than I thought."

"In some ways that's a compliment. You make it sound like an insult."

"I didn't mean it that way, exactly. But Hugh and I are so different. I admit he works hard at his painting, but he's never tried to make a steady living. Since I left school, I've had to look after the bread and butter for both of us. His salary as resident painter keeps him in artist's supplies, and that's about all."

"I thought he was doing well. His show's had a big advance buildup in the L.A. papers."

"Critics don't buy pictures," she said bluntly. "He's having the show to try to sell some paintings, so he can afford to get married. Hugh has suddenly realized that money is one of the essentials." She added with some bitterness, "The realization came a little late."

"He's been doing some outside work, though, hasn't he? Isn't he a part-time agent or something?"

"For Hendryx, yes." She made the name sound like a dirty word. "I'd just as soon he didn't take any of that man's money."

"Who's Hendryx?"

"A man."

"I gathered that. What's the matter with his money?"

"I really don't know. I have no idea where it comes from. But he has it."

"You don't like him?"

"No. I don't like him, and I don't like the men who work for him. They look like a gang of thugs to me. But Hugh wouldn't notice that. He's horribly dense where people are concerned. I don't mean that Hugh's done anything wrong," she added quickly. "He's bought a few paintings for Hendryx on commission."

"I see." I didn't like what I saw, but I named it. "The Admiral said something about Hugh trying to buy the Chardin for an unnamed purchaser. Would that be Hendryx?"

"It could be," she said.

"Tell me more about Hendryx."

"I don't know any more. I only met him once. That was enough. I know that he's an evil old man, and he has a bodyguard who carries him upstairs."

"Carries him upstairs?"

"Yes. He's crippled. As a matter of fact, he offered me a job."

"Carrying him upstairs?"

"He didn't specify my duties. He didn't get that far." Her voice was so chilly it quick-froze the conversation. "Now could we drop the subject, Mr. Archer?"

The road had begun to rise towards the mountains. Yellow and black Slide Area signs sprang up along the shoulders. By holding the gas pedal nearly to the floor, I kept our speed around fifty.

"You've had quite a busy morning," Mary said after a while, "meeting the Turners and all."

"Social mobility is my stock in trade."

"Did you meet Alice, too?"

I said I had.

"And what did you think of her?"

"I shouldn't say it to another girl, but she's a lovely one."

"Vanity isn't one of my vices," Mary said. "She's beautiful. And she's really devoted to Hugh."

"I gathered that."

"I don't think Alice has ever been in love before. And painting means almost as much to her as it does to him."

"He's a lucky man." I remembered the disillusioned eyes of the self-portrait, and hoped that his luck was holding.

The road twisted and climbed through red clay cutbanks and fields of dry chaparral.

"How long does this go on?" I asked.

"It's about another two miles."

We zigzagged up the mountainside for ten or twelve minutes more. Finally the road began to level out. I was watching its edge so closely that I didn't see the cabin until we were almost on top of it. It was a one-story frame building standing in a little hollow at the edge of the high mesa. Attached to one side was an open tarpaulin shelter from which the rear end of a gray coupe protruded. I looked at Mary.

She nodded. "It's our car." Her voice was bright with relief.

I stopped the convertible in the lane in front of the cabin. As soon as the engine died, the silence began. A single hawk high over our heads swung round and round on his invisible wire. Apart from that, the entire world seemed empty. As we walked down the ill-kept gravel drive, I was startled by the sound of my own footsteps.

The door was unlocked. The cabin had only one room. It was a bachelor hodgepodge, untouched by the human hand for months at a time. Cooking utensils, paint-stained dungarees and painter's tools and bedding were scattered on the floor and furniture. There was an open bottle of whiskey, half empty, on the kitchen table in the center of the room. It would have been just another mountain shack if it hadn't been for the watercolors on the walls, like brilliant little windows, and the one big window which opened on the sky.

Mary had crossed to the window and was looking out. I moved up to her shoulder. Blue space fell away in front of us all the way down to the sea, and beyond to the curved horizon. San Marcos and its suburbs were spread out like an air map between the sea and the mountains.

"I wonder where he can be," she said. "Perhaps he's gone for a hike. After all, he doesn't know we're looking for him."

I looked down the mountainside, which fell almost sheer from the window.

"No," I said. "He doesn't."

The red clay slope was sown with boulders. Nothing grew there except a few dust-colored mountain bushes. And a foot, wearing a man's shoe, which projected from a cleft between two rocks.

I went out without a word. A path led round the cabin to the edge of the slope. Hugh Western was there, attached to the solitary foot. He was lying, or hanging, head down with his face in the clay, about twenty feet below the edge. One of his legs was doubled under him. The other was caught between the boulders. I climbed around the rocks and bent down to look at his head.

The right temple was smashed. The face was smashed; I raised the rigid body to look at it. He had been dead for hours, but the sharp strong odor of whiskey still hung around him.

A tiny gravel avalanche rattled past me. Mary was at the top of the slope.

"Don't come down here."

She paid no attention to the warning. I stayed where I was, crouched over the body, trying to hide the ruined head from her. She leaned over the boulder and looked down, her eyes bright black in her drained face. I moved to one side. She took her brother's head in her hands.

"If you pass out," I said, "I don't know whether I can carry you up."

"I won't pass out."

She lifted the body by the shoulders to look at the face. It was a little unsettling to see how strong she was. Her fingers moved gently over the wounded temple. "This is what killed him. It looks like a blow from a fist."

I kneeled down beside her and saw the row of rounded indentations in the skull.

"He must have fallen," she said, "and struck his head on the rocks. Nobody could have hit him that hard."

"I'm afraid somebody did, though." Somebody whose fist was hard enough to leave its mark in wood.

Two long hours later I parked my car in front of the art shop on Rubio Street. Its windows were jammed with Impressionist and Post-Impressionist reproductions, and one very bad original oil of surf as stiff and static as whipped cream. The sign above the windows was lettered in flowing script: *Chez Hilary.* The cardboard sign on the door was simpler and to the point; it said: *Closed.*

The stairs and hallway seemed dark, but it was good to get out of the sun. The sun reminded me of what I had found at high noon on the mesa. It wasn't the middle of the afternoon yet, but my nerves felt stretched and scratchy, as though it was late at night. My eyes were aching.

Mary unlocked the door of her apartment, stepped aside to let me pass. She paused at the door of her room to tell me there was whiskey on the sideboard. I offered to make her a drink. No, thanks, she never drank. The door shut behind her. I mixed a whiskey and water and tried to relax in an easy chair. I couldn't relax. My mind kept playing back the questions and the answers, and the questions that had no answers.

We had called the sheriff from the nearest firewarden's post, and led him and his deputies back up the mountain to the body. Photographs were taken, the cabin and its surroundings searched, many questions asked. Mary didn't mention the lost Chardin. Neither did I.

Some of the questions were answered after the county coroner arrived. Hugh Western had been dead since sometime between eight and ten o'clock the previous night; the coroner couldn't place the time more definitely before analyzing the stomach contents. The blow on the temple had killed him. The injuries to his face, which had failed to bleed, had probably been inflicted after death. Which meant that he was dead when his body fell or was thrown down the mountainside.

His clothes had been soaked with whiskey to make it look like a drunken accident. But the murderer had gone too far in covering, and outwitted himself. The whiskey bottle in the cabin showed no fingerprints, not even Western's. And there were no fingerprints on the steering wheel of his coupe. Bottle and wheel had been wiped clean.

I stood up when Mary came back into the room. She had brushed her black hair gleaming, and changed to a dress of soft black jersey which fitted her like skin. A thought raced through my mind like a nasty little rodent. I wondered what she would look like with a beard.

"Can I have another look at the studio? I'm interested in that sketch."

She looked at me for a moment, frowning a little dazedly. "Sketch?"

"The one of the lady with the beard."

She crossed the hall ahead of me, walking slowly and carefully as if the floor were unsafe and a rapid movement might plunge her into black chaos. The door of the studio was still unlocked. She held it open for me and pressed the light switch.

When the fluorescent lights blinked on, I saw that the bearded nude was gone. There was nothing left of her but the four torn corners of the drawing paper thumbtacked to the empty easel. I turned to Mary.

"Did you take it down?"

"No. I haven't been in the studio since this morning."

"Somebody's stolen it then. Is there anything else missing?"

"I can't be sure, it's such a mess in here." She moved around the room looking at the pictures on the walls and pausing finally by a table in the corner. "There was a bronze cast on this table. It isn't here now."

"What sort of a cast?"

"The cast of a fist. Hugh made it from the fist of that man—that dreadful man I told you about."

"What dreadful man?"

"I think his name is Devlin. He's Hendryx' bodyguard.

Hugh's always been interested in hands, and the man has enormous hands."

Her eyes unfocused suddenly. I guessed she was thinking of the same thing I was: the marks on the side of Hugh's head, which might have been made by a giant fist.

"Look." I pointed to the scars on the doorframe. "Could the cast of Devlin's fist have made these marks?"

She felt the indentations with trembling fingers. "I think so —I don't know." She turned to me with a dark question in her eyes.

"If that's what they are," I said, "it probably means that he was killed in this studio. You should tell the police about it. And I think it's time they knew about the Chardin."

She gave me a look of passive resistance. Then she gave in. "Yes, I'll have to tell them. They'll find out soon enough, anyway. But I'm surer now than ever that Hugh didn't take it."

"What does the picture look like? If we could find it, we might find the killer attached to it."

"You think so? Well, it's a picture of a little boy looking at an apple. Wait a minute: Hilary has a copy. It was painted by one of the students at the college, and it isn't very expert. It'll give you an idea, though, if you want to go down to his shop and look at it."

"The shop is closed."

"He may be there anyway. He has a little apartment at the back."

I started for the hall, but turned before I got there. "Just who is Hilary Todd?"

"I don't know where he's from originally. He was stationed here during the war, and simply stayed on. His parents had money at one time, and he studied painting and ballet in Paris, or so he claims."

"Art seems to be the main industry in San Marcos."

"You've just been meeting the wrong people."

I went down the outside stairs to the parking lot, wondering what that implied about her brother. Todd's convertible stood near the mouth of the alley. I knocked on the back door of the art shop. There was no answer, but behind the Venetian-blinded door I heard a murmur of voices, a growling and a twittering. Todd had a woman with him. I knocked again.

After more delay the door was partly opened. Todd looked out through the crack. He was wiping his mouth with a red-stained handkerchief. The stains were too bright to be blood. Above the handkerchief his eyes were very bright and narrow, like slivers of polished agate.

"Good afternoon."

I moved forward as though I fully expected to be let in. He opened the door reluctantly under the nudging pressure of my shoulder, and backed into a narrow passage between two wallboard partitions.

"What can I do for you, Mr.——? I don't believe I know your name."

Before I could answer, a woman's voice said clearly, "It's Mr. Archer, isn't it?"

Sarah Turner appeared in the doorway behind him, carrying a highball glass and looking freshly groomed. Her red hair was unruffled, her red mouth gleaming as if she had just finished painting it.

"Good afternoon, Mrs. Turner."

"Good afternoon, Mr. Archer." She leaned in the doorway, almost too much at ease. "Do you know Hilary, Mr. Archer? You should. Everybody should. Hilary's simply loaded and dripping with charm, aren't you, dear?" Her mouth curled in a thin smile.

Todd looked at her with hatred, then turned to me without changing his look. "Did you wish to speak to me?"

"I did. You have a copy of Admiral Turner's Chardin."

"A copy, yes."

"Can I have a look at it?"

"What on earth for?"

"I want to be able to identify the original. It's probably connected with the murder."

I watched them both as I said the word. Neither showed surprise.

"We heard about it on the radio," the woman said. "It must have been dreadful for you."

"Dreadful," Todd echoed her, injecting synthetic sympathy into his dark eyes.

"Worse for Western," I said, "and for whoever did it. Do you still think he stole the picture, Mrs. Turner?"

Todd glanced at her sharply. She was embarrassed, as I'd intended her to be. She dunked her embarrassment in her highball glass, swallowing deeply from it and leaving a red half-moon on its rim.

"I never thought he stole it," her wet mouth lied. "I merely suggested the possibility."

"I see. Didn't you say something about Western trying to buy the picture from your husband? That he was acting as agent for somebody else?"

"I wasn't the one who said that. I didn't know it."

"The Admiral said it then. It would be interesting to know who the other man was. He wanted the Chardin, and it looks to me as if Hugh Western died because somebody wanted the Chardin."

Todd had been listening hard and saying nothing. "I don't see any necessary connection," he said now. "But if you'll come in and sit down I'll show you my copy."

"You wouldn't know who it was that Western was acting for?"

He spread his palms outward in a Continental gesture. "How would I know?"

"You're in the picture business."

"I *was* in the picture business." He turned abruptly and left the room.

Sarah Turner had crossed to a portable bar in the corner. She was splintering ice with a silver-handled ice pick. "May I make you one, Mr. Archer?"

"No, thanks." I sat down in a cubistic chair designed for people with square corners, and watched her take half of her new highball in a single gulp. "What did Todd mean when he said he *was* in the picture business? Doesn't he run this place?"

"He's having to give it up. The boutique's gone broke, and he's going around testing shoulders to weep on."

"Yours?" A queer kind of hostile intimacy had risen between us, and I tried to make the most of it.

"Where did you get that notion?"

"I thought he was a friend of yours."

"Did you?" Her laugh was too loud to be pleasant. "You ask a great many questions, Mr. Archer."

"They seem to be indicated. The cops in a town like this are pretty backward about stepping on people's toes."

"You're not."

"No. I'm just passing through. I can follow my hunches."

"What do you hope to gain?"

"Nothing for myself. I'd like to see justice done."

She sat down facing me, her knees almost touching mine. They were pretty knees, and uncovered. I felt crowded. Her voice, full of facile emotion, crowded me more:

"Were you terribly fond of Hugh?"

"I liked him." My answer was automatic. I was thinking of something else: the way she sat in her chair with her knees together, her body sloping backward, sure of its firm lines. I'd seen the same pose in charcoal that morning.

"I liked him, too," she was saying. "Very much. And I've been thinking—I've remembered something. Something that Hilary mentioned a couple of weeks ago, about Walter Hendryx wanting to buy the Chardin. It seems Hugh and Walter Hendryx were talking in the shop—"

She broke off suddenly. She had looked up and seen Todd leaning through the doorway, his face alive with anger. His shoulders moved slightly in her direction. She recoiled, clutching her glass. If I hadn't been there, I guessed he would have hit her. As it was, he said in a monotone:

"How cozy. Haven't you had quite a bit to drink, Sarah darling?"

She was afraid of him, but unwilling to admit it. "I have to do something to make present company bearable."

"You should be thoroughly anesthetized by now."

"If you say so, darling."

She hurled her half-empty glass at the wall beside the door. It shattered, denting the wallboard and splashing a photograph of Nijinsky as the Faun. Some of the liquid splattered on Todd's blue suede shoes.

"Very nice," he said. "I love your girlish antics, Sarah. I also love the way you run at the mouth." He turned to me: "This is the copy, Mr. Archer. Don't mind her, she's just a weensy bit drunky."

He held it up for me to see, an oil painting about a yard square showing a small boy in a blue waistcoat sitting at a table. In the center of the linen tablecloth there was a blue dish containing a red apple. The boy was looking at the apple as if he intended to eat it. The copyist had included the signature and date: Chardin, 1744.

"It's not very satisfactory," Todd said, "if you've ever seen the original. But of course you haven't?"

"No."

"That's too bad. You probably never will now, and it's really perfect. Perfect. It's the finest Chardin west of Chicago."

"I haven't given up hope of seeing it."

"You might as well, old boy. It'll be well on its way by now, to Europe, or South America. Picture thieves move fast, before the news of the theft catches up with them and spoils the market. They'll sell the Chardin to a private buyer in Paris or Buenos Aires, and that'll be the end of it."

"Why 'they'?"

"Oh, they operate in gangs. One man can't handle the theft and the disposal of a picture by himself. Division of labor is necessary, and specialization."

"You sound like a specialist yourself."

"I am, in a way." He smiled obliquely. "Not in the way you mean. I was in museum work before the war."

He stooped and propped the picture against the wall. I glanced at Sarah Turner. She was hunched forward in her chair, still and silent, her hands spread over her face.

"And now," he said to me, "I suppose you'd better go. I've done what I can for you. And I'll give you a tip if you like. Picture thieves don't do murder, they're simply not the type. So I'm afraid your precious hypothesis is based on bad information."

"Thanks very much," I said. "I certainly appreciate that. Also your hospitality."

"Don't mention it."

He raised an ironic brow, and turned to the door. I followed him out through the deserted shop. Most of the stock seemed to be in the window. Its atmosphere was sad and broken-down, the atmosphere of an empty-hearted, unprosperous, second-hand Bohemia. Todd didn't look around like a proprietor. He had already abandoned the place in his mind, it seemed.

He unlocked the front door. The last thing he said before he shut it behind me was:

"I wouldn't go bothering Walter Hendryx about that story of

Sarah's. She's not a very trustworthy reporter, and Hendryx isn't as tolerant of interuders as I am."

So it was true.

I left my car where it was and crossed to a taxi stand on the opposite corner. There was a yellow cab at the stand, with a brown-faced driver reading a comic book behind the wheel. The comic book had dead women on the cover. The driver detached his hot eyes from its interior, leaned wearily over the back of the seat and opened the door for me. "Where to?"

"A man called Walter Hendryx—know where he lives?"

"Off of Foothill Drive. I been up there before. It's a two-fifty run, outside the city limits." His Jersey accent didn't quite go with his Sicilian features.

"Newark?"

"Trenton." He showed bad teeth in a good smile. "You want to make something out of it?"

"Nope. Let's go."

He spoke to me over his shoulder when we were out of the heavy downtown traffic. "You got your passport?"

"What kind of a place are you taking me to?"

"They don't like visitors. You got to have a visa to get in, and a writ of habeas corpus to get out. The old man's scared of burglars or something."

"Why?"

"He's got about ten million reasons, the way I hear it. Ten million bucks." He smacked his lips.

"Where did he get it?"

"You tell me. I'll drop everything and take off for the same place."

"You and me both."

"I heard he's a big contractor in L.A.," the driver said. "I drove a reporter up here a couple of months ago, from one of the L.A. papers. He was after an interview with the old guy, something about a tax case."

"What about a tax case?"

"I wouldn't know. It's way over my head, friend, all that tax business. I have enough trouble with my own forms."

"What happened to the reporter?"

"I drove him right back down. The old man wouldn't see him. He likes his privacy."

"I'm beginning to get the idea."

"You a reporter, too, by any chance?"

"No."

He was too polite to ask me any more questions.

We left the city limits. The mountains rose ahead, violet and unshadowed in the sun's lengthening rays. Foothill Drive wound through a canyon, across a high-level bridge, up the side of a hill from which the sea was visible like a low blue cloud on the horizon. We turned off the road through an open gate on which a sign was posted: *Trespassers Will Be Prosecuted.*

A second gate closed the road at the top of the hill. It was a double gate of wrought iron hung between a stone gatepost and a stone gatehouse. A heavy wire fence stretched out from it on both sides, following the contours of the hills as far as I could see. Hendryx' estate was about the size of a small European country.

The driver honked his horn. A thick-waisted man in a Panama hat came out of the stone cottage. He squeezed through a narrow postern and waddled up to the cab. "Well?"

"I came to see Mr. Hendryx about a picture."

He opened the cab door and looked me over, from eyes that were heavily shuttered with old scar tissue. "You ain't the one that was here this morning."

I had my first good idea of the day. "You mean the tall fellow with the sideburns?"

"Yeah."

"I just came from him."

He rubbed his heavy chin with his knuckles, making a rasping noise. The knuckles were jammed.

"I guess it's all right," he said finally. "Give me your name and I'll phone it down to the house. You can drive down."

He opened the gate and let us through into a shallow valley. Below, in a maze of shrubbery, a long, low house was flanked by tennis courts and stables. Sunk in the terraced lawn behind the house was an oval pool like a wide green eye staring at the sky. A short man in bathing trunks was sitting in a Thinker pose on the diving board at one end.

He and the pool dropped out of sight as the cab slid down the eucalyptus-lined road. It stopped under a portico at the side of the house. A uniformed maid was waiting at the door.

"This is further than that reporter got," the driver said in an undertone. "Maybe you got connections?"

"The best people in town."

"Mr. Archer?" the maid said. "Mr. Hendryx is having his bath. I'll show you the way."

I told the driver to wait, and followed her through the house. I saw when I stepped outside that the man on the diving board wasn't short at all. He only seemed to be short because he was so wide. Muscle bulged out his neck, clustered on his shoulders and chest, encased his arms and legs. He looked like a graduate of Muscle Beach, a subman trying hard to be a superman.

There was another man floating in the water, the blotched brown swell of his stomach breaking the surface like the shell-back of a Galápagos tortoise. Thinker stood up, accompanied by his parasitic muscles, and called to him:

"Mr. Hendryx!"

The man in the water rolled over lazily and paddled to the side of the pool. Even his head was tortoise-like, seamed and bald and impervious-looking. He stood up in the waist-deep water and raised his thin brown arms. The other man bent over him. He drew him out of the water and steadied him on his feet, rubbing him with a towel.

"Thank you, Devlin."

"Yessir."

Leaning far forward with his arms dangling like those of a withered, hairless ape, Hendryx shuffled towards me. The joints of his knees and ankles were knobbed and stiffened by what looked like arthritis. He peered up at me from his permanent crouch:

"You want to see me?" The voice that came out of his crippled body was surprisingly rich and deep. He wasn't as old as he looked. "What is it?"

"A painting was stolen last night from the San Marcos gallery: Chardin's 'Apple on a Table'. I've heard that you were interested in it."

"You've been misinformed. Good afternoon." His face closed like a fist.

"You haven't heard the rest of it."

Disregarding me, he called to the maid who was waiting at a distance: "Show this man out."

Devlin came up beside me, strutting like a wrestler, his great curved hands conspicuous.

"The rest of it," I said, "is that Hugh Western was murdered at the same time. I think you knew him?"

"I knew him, yes. His death is unfortunate. Regrettable. But so far as I know, it has nothing to do with the Chardin and nothing to do with me. Will you go now, or do I have to have you removed?"

He raised his cold eyes to mine. I stared him down, but there wasn't much satisfaction in that.

"You take murder pretty lightly, Hendryx."

"Mr. Hendryx to you," Devlin said in my ear. "Come on now, bud. You heard what Mr. Hendryx said."

"I don't take orders from him."

"I do," he said with a lopsided grin like a heat-split in a melon. "I take orders from him." His light small eyes shifted to Hendryx. "You want for me to throw him out?"

Hendryx nodded, backing away. His eyes were heating up, as if the prospect of violence excited him. Devlin's hand took my wrist. His fingers closed around it and overlapped.

"What is this, Devlin?" I said. "I thought Hugh Western was a pal of yours."

"Sure thing."

"I'm trying to find out who killed him. Aren't you interested? Or did you slap him down yourself?"

"The hell." Devlin blinked stupidly, trying to hold two questions in his mind at the same time.

Hendryx said from a safe distance: "Don't talk. Just give him a going-over and toss him out."

Devlin looked at Hendryx. His grip was like a thick handcuff on my wrist. I jerked his arm up and ducked under it, breaking the hold, and chopped at his nape. The bulging back of his neck was hard as a redwood bole.

He wheeled, and reached for me again. The muscles in his arm moved like drugged serpents. He was slow. My right fist found his chin and snapped it back on his neck. He recovered, and swung at me. I stepped inside of the roundhouse and hammered his rigid stomach, twice, four times. It was like knocking my fists against the side of a corrugated iron building. His great arms closed on me. I slipped down and away.

When he came after me, I shifted my attack to his head, jabbing with the left until he was off balance on his heels. Then I pivoted and threw a long right hook which changed to an uppercut. An electric shock surged up my arm. Devlin lay down on the green tiles, chilled like a side of beef.

I looked across him at Hendryx. There was no fear in his eyes, only calculation. He backed into a canvas chair and sat down clumsily.

"You're fairly tough, it seems. Perhaps you used to be a fighter? I've owned a few fighters in my time. You might have a future at it, if you were younger."

"It's a sucker's game. So is larceny."

"Larceny-farceny," he said surprisingly. "What did you say you do?"

"I'm a private detective."

"Private, eh?" His mouth curved in a lipless tortoise grin. "You interest me, Mr. Archer. I could find a use for you—a place in my organization."

"What kind of an organization?"

"I'm a builder, a mass-producer of houses. Like most successful entrepreneurs, I make enemies: cranks and bleeding hearts and psychopathic veterans who think the world owes them something. Devlin here isn't quite the man I thought he was. But you—"

"Forget it. I'm pretty choosy about the people I work for."

"An idealist, eh? A clean-cut young American idealist." The smile was still on his mouth; it was saturnine. "Well, Mr. Idealist, you're wasting your time. I know nothing about this picture or anything connected with it. You're also wasting *my* time."

"It seems to be expendable. I think you're lying, incidentally."

Hendryx didn't answer me directly. He called to the maid: "Telephone the gate. Tell Shaw we're having a little trouble with a guest. Then you can come back and look after this." He jerked a thumb at Muscle-Boy, who was showing signs of life.

I said to the maid: "Don't bother telephoning. I wouldn't stick around here if I was paid to."

She shrugged and looked at Hendryx. He nodded. I followed her out.

"You didn't stay long," the cab driver said.

"No. Do you know where Admiral Turner lives?"

"Curiously enough, I do. I should charge extra for the directory service."

I didn't encourage him to continue the conversation. "Take me there."

He let me out in a street of big old houses set far back from the sidewalk behind sandstone walls and high eugenia hedges. I paid him off and climbed the sloping walk to the Turner house. It was a weathered frame building, gabled and turreted in the style of the nineties. A gray-haired housekeeper who had survived from the same period answered my knock.

"The Admiral's in the garden," she said. "Will you come out?"

The garden was massed with many-colored begonias, and surrounded by a vine-covered wall. The Admiral, in stained and faded suntans, was chopping weeds in a flowerbed with furious concentration. When he saw me he leaned on his hoe and wiped his wet forehead with the back of his hand.

"You should come in out of the sun," the housekeeper said in a nagging way. "A man of your age—"

"Nonsense! Go away, Mrs. Harris." She went. "What can I do for you, Mr.——?"

"Archer. I guess you've heard that we found Hugh Western's body."

"Sarah came home and told me half an hour ago. It's a foul thing, and completely mystifying. He was to have married—"

His voice broke off. He glanced towards the stone cottage, at the rear of the garden. Alice Turner was there at an open window. She wasn't looking in our direction. She had a tiny paintbrush in her hand, and she was working at an easel.

"It's not as mystifying as it was. I'm starting to put the pieces together, Admiral."

He turned back to me quickly. His eyes became hard and empty again, like gun muzzles.

"Just who are you? What's your interest in this case?"

"I'm a friend of Hugh Western's, from Los Angeles. I stopped off here to see him, and found him dead. I hardly think my interest is out of place."

"No, of course not," he grumbled. "On the other hand, I don't believe in amateur detectives running around like chickens with their heads cut off, fouling up the authorities."

"I'm not exactly an amateur. I used to be a cop. And any fouling up there's been has been done by other people."

"Are you accusing me?"

"If the shoe fits."

He met my eyes for a time, trying to master me and the situation. But he was old and bewildered. Slowly the aggressive ego faded from his gaze. He became almost querulous.

"You'll excuse me. I don't know what it's all about. I've been rather upset by everything that's happened."

"What about your daughter?" Alice was still at the window, working at her picture and paying no attention to our voices. "Doesn't she know Hugh is dead?"

"Yes. She knows. You mustn't misunderstand what Alice is doing. There are many ways of enduring grief, and we have a custom in the Turner family of working it out of our system. Hard work is the cure for a great many evils." He changed the subject, and his tone, abruptly. "And what is your idea of what's happened?"

"It's no more than a suspicion, a pretty foggy one. I'm not sure who stole your picture, but I think I know where it is."

"Well?"

"There's a man named Walter Hendryx who lives in the foothills outside the city. You know him?"

"Slightly."

"He probably has the Chardin. I'm morally certain he has it, as a matter of fact, though I don't know how he got it."

The Admiral tried to smile, and made a dismal failure of it. "You're not suggesting that Hendryx took it? He's not exactly mobile, you know."

"Hilary Todd is very mobile," I said. "Todd visited Hendryx this morning. I'd be willing to bet even money he had the Chardin with him."

"You didn't see it, however?"

"I don't have to. I've seen Todd."

A woman's voice said from the shadow of the back porch: "The man is right, Johnston."

Sarah Turner came down the path towards us, her high heels spiking the flagstones angrily.

"Hilary did it!" she cried. "He stole the picture and murdered Hugh. I saw him last night at midnight. He had red mountain clay on his clothes."

"It's strange you didn't mention it before," the Admiral said dryly.

I looked into her face. Her eyes were bloodshot, and the eyelids were swollen with weeping. Her mouth was swollen, too. When she opened it to reply, I could see that the lower lip was split.

"I just remembered."

I wondered if the blow that split her lip had reminded her.

"And where did you see Hilary Todd last night at midnight?"

"Where?"

In the instant of silence that followed, I heard footsteps behind me. Alice had come out of her cottage. She walked like a sleepwalker dreaming a bad dream, and stopped beside her father without a word to any of us.

Sarah's face had been twisting in search of an answer, and found it. "I met him at the Presidio. I dropped in there for a cup of coffee after the show."

"You are a liar, Sarah," the Admiral said. "The Presidio closes at ten o'clock."

"It wasn't the Presidio," she said rapidly. "It was the bar across the street, the Club Fourteen. I had dinner at the Presidio, and I confused them—"

The Admiral brushed past her without waiting to hear more, and started for the house. Alice went with him. The old man walked unsteadily, leaning on her arm.

"Did you really see Hilary last night?" I asked her.

She stood there for a minute, looking at me. Her face was disorganized, raddled with passion. "Yes, I saw him. I had a date with him at ten o'clock. I waited in his flat for over two hours. He didn't show up until after midnight. I couldn't tell *him* that." She jerked one shoulder contemptuously toward the house.

"And he had red clay on his clothes?"

"Yes. It took me a while to connect it with Hugh."

"Are you going to tell the police?"

She smiled a secret and unpleasant smile. "How can I? I've got a marriage to go on with, such as it is."

"You told me."

"I like you." Without moving, she gave the impression of leaning towards me. "I'm fed up with all the little stinkers that populate this town."

I kept it cool and clean, and very nasty: "Were you fed up with Hugh Western, Mrs. Turner?"

"What do you mean?"

"I heard that he dropped you hard a couple of months ago. Somebody dropped *him* hard last night in his studio."

"I haven't been near his studio for weeks."

"Never did any posing for him?"

Her face seemed to grow smaller and sharper. She laid one narrow taloned hand on my arm. "Can I trust you, Mr. Archer?"

"Not if you murdered Hugh."

"I didn't; I swear I didn't. Hilary did."

"But you were there last night."

"No."

"I think you were. There was a charcoal sketch on the easel, and you posed for it, didn't you?"

Her nerves were badly strained, but she tried to be coquettish. "How would you know?"

"The way you carry your body. It reminds me of the picture."

"Do you approve?"

"Listen, Mrs. Turner. You don't seem to realize that that sketch is evidence, and destroying it is a crime."

"I didn't destroy it."

"Then where did you put it?"

"I haven't said I took it."

"But you did."

"Yes, I did," she admitted finally. "But it isn't evidence in this case. I posed for it six months ago, and Hugh had it in his studio. When I heard he was dead this afternoon, I went to get it, just to be sure it wouldn't turn up in the papers. He had it on the easel for some reason, and had ruined it with a beard. I don't know why."

"The beard would make sense if your story was changed a

little. If you quarreled while Hugh was sketching you last night, and you hit him over the head with a metal fist. You might have drawn the beard yourself, to cover up."

"Don't be ridiculous. If I had anything to cover up I would have destroyed the sketch. Anyway, I can't draw."

"Hilary can."

"Go to hell," she said between her teeth. "You're just a little stinker like the rest of them."

She walked emphatically to the house. I followed her into the long, dim hallway. Halfway up the stairs to the second floor she turned and flung down to me: "I hadn't destroyed it, but I'm going to now."

There was nothing I could do about that, and I started out. When I passed the door of the living room, the Admiral called out, "Is that you, Archer? Come here a minute, eh?"

He was sitting with Alice on a semicircular leather lounge, set into a huge bay window at the front of the room. He got up and moved toward me ponderously, his head down like a charging bull's. His face was a jaundiced yellow, bloodless under the tan.

"You're entirely wrong about the Chardin," he said. "Hilary Todd had nothing to do with stealing it. In fact, it wasn't stolen. I removed it from the gallery myself."

"You denied that this morning."

"I do as I please with my own possessions. I'm accountable to no one, certainly not to you."

"Dr. Silliman might like to know," I said with irony.

"I'll tell him in my own good time."

"Will you tell him why you took it?"

"Certainly. Now, if you've made yourself sufficiently obnoxious, I'll ask you to leave my house."

"Father." Alice came up to him and laid a hand on his arm. "Mr. Archer has only been trying to help."

"And getting nowhere," I said. "I made the mistake of assuming that some of Hugh's friends were honest."

"That's enough!" he roared. "Get out!"

Alice caught up with me on the veranda. "Don't go away mad. Father can be terribly childish, but he means well."

"I don't get it. He lied this morning, or else he's lying now."

"He isn't lying," she said earnestly. "He was simply playing

a trick on Dr. Silliman and the trustees. It's what happened to
Hugh afterwards that made it seem important."

"Did you know that he took the picture himself?"

"He told me just now, before you came into the house. I made
him tell you."

"You'd better let Silliman in on the joke," I said unpleasantly.
"He's probably going crazy."

"He is," she said. "I saw him at the gallery this afternoon, and
he was tearing his hair. Do you have your car?"

"I came up here in a taxi."

"I'll drive you down.'"

"Are you sure you feel up to it?"

"It's better when I'm doing something," she said.

An old black sedan was standing in the drive beside the
house. We got in, and she backed it into the street and turned
downhill toward the center of town.

Watching her face, I said, "Of course you realize I don't
believe his story."

"Father's, you mean?" She didn't seem surprised. "I don't
know what to believe, myself."

"When did he say he took the Chardin?"

"Last night. Hugh was working on the mezzanine. Father
slipped away and took the picture out to the car."

"Didn't Hugh keep the door locked?"

"Apparently not. Father said not."

"But what possible reason could he have for stealing his own
picture?"

"To prove a point. Father's been arguing for a long time that
it would be easy to steal a picture from the gallery. He's been
trying to get the board of trustees to install a burglar alarm. He's
really hipped on the subject. He wouldn't lend his Chardin to
the gallery until they agreed to insure it."

"For twenty-five thousand dollars," I said, half to myself.
Twenty-five thousand dollars was motive enough for a man to
steal his own picture. And if Hugh Western witnessed the theft,
there was motive for murder. "Your father's made a pretty good
story out of it. But where's the picture now?"

"He didn't tell me. It's probably in the house somewhere."

"I doubt it. It's more likely somewhere in Walter Hendryx'
house."

She let out a little gasp. "What makes you say that? Do you know Walter Hendryx?"

"I've met him. Do you?"

"He's a horrible man," she said. "I can't imagine why you think he has it."

"It's purely a hunch."

"Where would he get it? Father wouldn't dream of selling it to him."

"Hilary Todd would."

"Hilary? You think Hilary stole it?"

"I'm going to ask him. Let me off at his shop, will you? I'll see you at the gallery later."

The *Closed* sign was still hanging inside the plate glass, and the front door was locked. I went around to the back of the shop by the alley. The door under the stairs was standing partly open. I went in without knocking.

The living room was empty. The smell of alcohol rose from the stain on the wall where Sarah had smashed her glass. I crossed the passage to the door on the other side. It, too, was partly open. I pushed it wider and went in.

Hilary Todd was sprawled face down on the bed, with an open suitcase crushed under the weight of his body. The silver handle of his ice pick stood up between his shoulder blades in the center of a wet, dark stain. The silver glinted coldly in a ray of light which came through the half-closed Venetian blinds.

I felt for his pulse and couldn't find it. His head was twisted sideways, and his empty dark eyes stared unblinking at the wall. A slight breeze from the open window at the foot of the bed ruffled the hair along the side of his head.

I burrowed under the heavy body and went through the pockets. In the inside breast pocket of the coat I found what I was looking for: a plain white business envelope, unsealed, containing $15,000 in large bills.

I was standing over the bed with the money in my hand when I heard someone in the hallway. A moment later Mary appeared at the door.

"I saw you come in," she said. "I thought—" Then she saw the body.

"Someone killed Hilary."

"*Killed Hilary?*" She looked at the body on the bed and then at me. I realized that I was holding the money in plain view. "What are you doing with that?"

I folded the bills and tucked them into my inside pocket. "I'm going to try an experiment. Be a good girl and call the police for me."

"Where did you get that money?"

"From someone it didn't belong to. Don't tell the sheriff about it. Just say that I'll be back in half an hour."

"They'll want to know where you went."

"And if you don't know, you won't be able to tell them. Now do as I say."

She looked into my face, wondering if she could trust me. Her voice was uncertain: "If you're sure you're doing the right thing."

"Nobody ever is."

I went out to my car and drove to Foothill Drive. The sun had dipped low over the sea, and the air was turning colder. By the time I reached the iron gates that cut off Walter Hendryx from ordinary mortals, the valley beyond them was in shadow.

The burly man came out of the gatehouse as if I had pressed a button, and up to the side of the car. "What do you want?" He recognized me then, and pushed his face up to the window. "Beat it, chum. I got orders to keep you away from here."

I restrained an impulse to push the face away, and tried diplomacy. "I came here to do your boss a favor."

"That's not the way he feels. Now blow."

"Look here." I brought the wad of bills out of my pocket, and passed them back and forth under his nose. "There's big money involved."

His eyes followed the moving bills as if they hypnotized him. "I don't take bribes," he said in a hoarse and passionate whisper.

"I'm not offering you one. But you should phone down to Hendryx, before you do anything rash, and tell him there's money in it."

"Money for him?" There was a wistful note in his voice. "How much?"

"Fifteen thousand, tell him."

"Some bonus." He whistled. "What kind of a house is he

building for you, bud, that you should give him an extra fifteen grand?"

I didn't answer. His question gave me too much to think about. He went back into the gatehouse.

Two minutes later he came out and opened the gates. "Mr. Hendryx'll see you. But don't try any funny stuff or you won't come out on your own power."

The maid was waiting at the door. She took me into a big rectangular room with French windows on one side, opening on the terrace. The rest of the walls were lined with books from floor to ceiling—the kind of books that are bought by the set and never read. In front of the fireplace, at the far end, Hendryx was sitting half submerged in an overstuffed armchair, with a blanket over his knees.

He looked up when I entered the room and the firelight danced on his scalp and lit his face with an angry glow. "What's this? Come here and sit down."

The maid left silently. I walked the length of the room and sat down in an armchair facing him. "I always bring bad news, Mr. Hendryx. Murder and such things. This time it's Hilary Todd."

The turtle face didn't change, but his head made a movement of withdrawal into the shawl collar of his robe. "I'm exceedingly sorry to hear it. But my gatekeeper mentioned the matter of money. That interests me more."

"Good." I produced the bills and spread them fanwise on my knee. "Do you recognize this?"

"Should I?"

"For a man that's interested in money, you're acting very coy."

"I'm interested in its source."

"I had an idea that you were the source of this particular money. I have some other ideas. For instance, that Hilary Todd stole the Chardin and sold it to you. One thing I have no idea about is why you would buy a stolen picture and pay for it in cash."

His false teeth glistened coldly in the firelight. Like the man at the gate, he kept his eyes on the money. "The picture wasn't stolen. I bought it legally from its rightful owner."

"I might believe you if you hadn't denied any knowledge of it this afternoon. I think you knew it was stolen."

His voice took on a cutting edge: "It was not." He slipped his blue-veined hand inside his robe and brought out a folded sheet of paper, which he handed me.

It was a bill of sale for the picture, informal but legal, written in longhand on the stationery of the San Marcos Beach Club, signed by Admiral Johnston Turner, and dated that day.

"Now may I ask you where you got hold of that money?"

"I'll be frank with you, Mr. Hendryx. I took it from the body of Hilary Todd, when he had no further use for it."

"That's a criminal act, I believe."

My brain was racing, trying to organize a mass of contradictory facts. "I have a notion that you're not going to talk to anyone about it."

He shrugged his shoulders. "You seem to be full of notions."

"I have another. Whether or not you're grateful to me for bringing you this money, I think you should be."

"Have you any reason for saying that?" He had withdrawn his eyes from the money on my knee and was looking into my face.

"You're in the building business, Mr. Hendryx?"

"Yes." His voice was flat.

"I don't know exactly how you got this money. My guess is that you gouged it out of home-buyers, by demanding a cash side-payment in addition to the appraised value of the houses you've been selling to veterans."

"That's a pretty comprehensive piece of guesswork, isn't it?"

"I don't expect you to admit it. On the other hand, you probably wouldn't want this money traced to you. The fact that you haven't banked it is an indication of that. That's why Todd could count on you to keep this picture deal quiet. And that's why you should be grateful to me."

The turtle eyes stared into mine and admitted nothing. "If I were grateful, what form do you suggest my gratitude should take?"

"I want the picture. I've sort of set my heart on it."

"Keep the money instead."

"This money is no good to me. Dirty money never is."

He threw the blanket off and levered himself out of the chair.

"You're somewhat more honest than I'd supposed. You're offering, then, to buy the picture back from me with that money."

"Exactly."

"And if I don't agree?"

"The money goes to the Intelligence Unit of the Internal Revenue Bureau."

There was silence for a while, broken by the fire hissing and sputtering in an irritable undertone.

"Very well," he said at length. "Give me the money."

"Give me the picture."

He waded across the heavy rug, moving his feet a few inches at a time, and pressed a corner of one of the bookcases. It swung open like a door. Behind it was the face of a large wall safe. I waited uncomfortably while he twirled the double dials.

A minute later he shuffled back to me with the picture in his hands. The boy in the blue waistcoat was there in the frame, watching the apple, which looked good enough to eat after more than two hundred years.

Hendryx' withered face had settled into a kind of malevolent resignation. "You realize that this is no better than blackmail."

"On the contrary, I'm saving you from the consequences of your own poor judgment. You shouldn't do business with thieves and murderers."

"You still insist the picture was stolen?"

"I think it was. You probably know it was. Will you answer one question?"

"Perhaps."

"When Hilary Todd approached you about buying this picture, did he claim to represent Admiral Turner?"

"Of course. You have the bill of sale in your hand. It's signed by the Admiral."

"I see that, but I don't know his signature."

"I do. Now, if you have no further questions, may I have my money?"

"One more: Who killed Hugh Western?"

"I don't know," he said heavily and finally.

He held out his brown hand with the palm upward. I gave him the sheaf of bills.

"And the bill of sale, if you please."

"It wasn't part of the bargain."

"It has to be."

"I suppose you're right." I handed it to him.

"Please don't come back a third time," he said as he rang for the maid. "I find your visits tiring and annoying."

"I won't come back," I said. I didn't need to.

I parked in the alley beside the art gallery and got out of the car with the Chardin under my arm. There was talk and laughter and the tiny din of cutlery in the restaurant patio beyond the hedge. On the other side of the alley a light was shining behind the barred window of Silliman's office. I reached up between the bars and tapped on the window. I couldn't see beyond the closed Venetian blinds.

Someone opened the casement. It was Alice, her blond head aureoled against the light. "Who is it?" she said in a frightened whisper.

"Archer." I had a sudden, rather theatrical impulse. I held up the Chardin and passed it to her edgewise between the bars. She took it from my hands and let out a little yelp of surprise.

"It was where I thought it would be," I said.

Silliman appeared at her shoulder, squeaking, "What is it? What is it?"

My brain was doing a double take on the action I'd just performed. I had returned the Chardin to the gallery without using the door. It could have been stolen the same way, by Hilary Todd or anyone else who had access to the building. No human being could pass through the bars, but a picture could.

Silliman's head came out the window like a gray mop being shaken. "Where on earth did you find it?"

I had no story ready, so I said nothing.

A gentle hand touched my arm and stayed, like a bird alighting. I started, but it was only Mary.

"I've been watching for you," she said. "The sheriff's in Hilary's shop, and he's raving mad. He said he's going to put you in jail, as a material witness."

"You didn't tell him about the money?" I said in an undertone.

"No. Did you really get the picture?"

"Come inside and see."

As we turned the corner of the building, a car left the curb in front of it, and started up the street with a roar. It was Admiral Turner's black sedan.

"It looks like Alice driving," Mary said.

"She's gone to tell her father, probably."

I made a sudden decision, and headed back to my car.

"Where are you going?"

"I want to see the Admiral's reaction to the news."

She followed me to the car. "Take me."

"You'd better stay here. I can't tell what might happen."

I tried to shut the door, but she held on to it. "You're always running off and leaving me to make your explanations."

"All right; get in. I don't have time to argue."

I drove straight up the alley and across the parking lot to Rubio Street. There was a uniformed policeman standing at the back door of Hilary's shop, but he didn't try to stop us.

"What did the police have to say about Hilary?" I asked her.

"Not much. The ice pick had been wiped clean of fingerprints, and they had no idea who did it."

I went through a yellow light and left a chorus of indignant honkings at the intersection behind me.

"You said you didn't know what would happen when you got there. Do you think the Admiral—" She left the sentence unfinished.

"I don't know. I have a feeling I soon will, though." There were a great many things I could have said. I concentrated on my driving.

"Is this the street?" I asked her finally.

"Yes."

My tires shrieked on the corner, and again in front of the house. She was out of the car before I was.

"Stay back," I told her. "This may be dangerous."

She let me go up the walk ahead of her. The black sedan was in the drive with the headlights burning and the left front door hanging open. The front door of the house was closed but there was a light behind it. I went in without knocking.

Sarah came out of the living room. All day her face had been going to pieces, and now it was old and slack and ugly. Her bright hair was ragged at the edges, and her voice was ragged. "What do you think you're doing?"

"I want to see the Admiral. Where is he?"

"How should I know? I can't keep track of any of my men."
She took a step toward me, staggered, and almost fell.

Mary took hold of her and eased her into a chair. Her head
leaned limply against the wall, and her mouth hung open. The
lipstick on her mouth was like a rim of cracked dry blood.

"They must be here."

The single shot that we heard then was an exclamation point
at the end of my sentence. It came from somewhere back of the
house, muffled by walls and distance.

I went through into the garden. There were lights in the
gardener's cottage, and a man's shadow moved across the window. I ran up the path to the cottage's open door, and froze
there.

Admiral Turner was facing me with a gun in his hand. It was
a heavy-caliber automatic, the kind the Navy issued. From its
round, questioning mouth a wisp of blue smoke trailed. Alice
lay face down on the carpeted floor between us.

I looked into the mouth of the gun, into Turner's granite face.
"You killed her."

But Alice was the one who answered. "Go away." The words
came out in a rush of sobbing that racked her prostrate body.

"This is a private matter, Archer." The gun stirred slightly in
the Admiral's hand. I could feel its pressure across the width of
the room. "Do as she says."

"I heard a shot. Murder is a public matter."

"There has been no murder, as you can see."

"You don't remember well."

"I have nothing to do with that," he said. "I was cleaning my
gun, and forgot that it was loaded."

"So Alice lay down and cried? You'll have to do better than
that, Admiral."

"Her nerves are shaken. But I assure you that mine are not."
He took three slow steps towards me, and paused by the girl on
the floor. The gun was very steady in his hand. "Now go, or I'll
have to use this."

The pressure of the gun was increasing. I put my hands on the
doorframe and held myself still. "You seem to be sure it's loaded
now," I said.

Between my words I heard the faint, harsh whispering of

shifting gravel on the garden path behind me. I spoke up loudly, to drown out the sound.

"You had nothing to do with the murder, you say. Then why did Todd come to the beach club this morning? Why did you change your story about the Chardin?"

He looked down at his daughter as if she could answer the questions. She made no sound, but her shoulders were shaking with inner sobbing.

As I watched the two of them, father and daughter, the pattern of the day came into focus. At its center was the muzzle of the Admiral's gun, the round blue mouth of death.

I said, very carefully, to gain time, "I can guess what Todd said to you this morning. Do you want me to dub in the dialogue?"

He glanced up sharply, and the gun glanced up. There were no more sounds in the garden. If Mary was as quick as I thought, she'd be at a telephone.

"He told you he'd stolen your picture and had a buyer for it. But Hendryx was cautious. Todd needed proof that he had a right to sell it. You gave him the proof. And when Todd completed the transaction, you let him keep the money."

"Nonsense! Bloody nonsense." But he was a poor actor, and a worse liar.

"I've seen the bill of sale, Admiral. The only question left is why you gave it to Todd."

His lips moved as if he was going to speak. No words came out.

"And I'll answer that one, too. Todd knew who killed Hugh Western. So did you. You had to keep him quiet, even if it meant conniving at the theft of your own picture."

"I connived at nothing." His voice was losing its strength. His gun was as potent as ever.

"Alice did," I said. "She helped him to steal it this morning. She passed it out the window to him when Silliman and I were on the mezzanine. Which is one of the things he told you at the beach club, isn't it?"

"Todd has been feeding you lies. Unless you give me your word that you won't repeat those lies, not to anyone, I'm going to have to shoot you."

His hand contracted, squeezing off the automatic's safety. The tiny noise it made seemed very significant in the silence.

"Todd will soon be feeding worms," I said. "He's dead, Admiral."

"Dead?" His voice had sunk to an old man's quaver, rustling in his throat.

"Stabbed with an ice pick in his apartment."

"When?"

"This afternoon. Do you still see any point in trying to shoot me?"

"You're lying."

"No. There's been a second murder."

He looked down at the girl at his feet. His eyes were bewildered. There was danger in his pain and confusion. I was the source of his pain, and he might strike out blindly at me. I watched the gun in his hand, waiting for a chance to move on it. My arms were rigid, braced against the doorframe.

Mary Western ducked under my left arm and stepped into the room in front of me. She had no weapon, except her courage.

"He's telling the truth," she said. "Hilary Todd was stabbed to death today."

"Put down the gun," I said. "There's nothing left to save. You thought you were protecting an unfortunate girl. She's turned out to be a double murderess."

He was watching the girl on the floor. "If this is true, Allie, I wash my hands of you."

No sound came from her. Her face was hidden by her yellow sheaf of hair. The old man groaned. The gun sagged in his hand. I moved, pushing Mary to one side, and took it away from him. He didn't resist me, but my forehead was suddenly streaming with sweat.

"You were probably next on her list," I said.

"No."

The muffled word came from his daughter. She began to get up, rising laboriously from her hands and knees like a hurt fighter. She flung her hair back. Her face had hardly changed. It was as lovely as ever, on the surface, but empty of meaning, like a doll's plastic face.

"I was next on my list," she said dully. "I tried to shoot myself when I realized you knew about me. Father stopped me."

"I didn't know about you until now."

"You did. You must have. When you were talking to Father in the garden, you meant me to hear it all—everything you said about Hilary."

"Did I?"

The Admiral said with a kind of awe: "You killed him, Allie. Why did you want his blood on your hands? Why?" His own hand reached for her, gropingly, and paused in midair. He looked at her as if he had fathered a strange, evil thing.

She bowed her head in silence. I answered for her: "She'd stolen the Chardin for him and met his conditions. But then she saw that he couldn't get away, or if he did he'd be brought back, and questioned. She couldn't be sure he'd keep quiet about Hugh. This afternoon she made sure. The second murder comes easier."

"No!" She shook her blond head violently. "I didn't murder Hugh. I hit him with something, I didn't intend to kill him. He struck me first, he *struck* me, and then I hit him back."

"With a deadly weapon, a metal fist. You hit at him twice with it. The first blow missed and left its mark on the doorframe. The second blow didn't miss."

"But I didn't mean to kill him. Hilary knew I didn't mean to kill him."

"How would he know? Was he there?"

"He was downstairs in his flat. When he heard Hugh fall, he came up. Hugh was still alive. He died in Hilary's car, when we were starting for the hospital. Hilary said he'd help me to cover up. He took that horrible fist and threw it into the sea.

"I hardly knew what I was doing by that time. Hilary did it all. He put the body in Hugh's car and drove it up the mountain. I followed in his car and brought him back. On the way back he told me why he was helping me. He needed money. He knew we had no money, but he had a chance to sell the Chardin. I took it for him this morning. I had to. Everything I did, I did because I had to."

She looked from me to her father. He averted his face from her.

"You didn't have to smash Hugh's skull," I said. "Why did you do that?"

Her doll's eyes rolled in her head, came back to me, glinting with a cold and deathly coquetry. "If I tell you, will you do one thing for me? One favor? Give me father's gun for just a second?"

"And let you kill us all?"

"Only myself," she said. "Just leave one shell in it."

"Don't give it to her," the Admiral said. "She's done enough to disgrace us."

"I have no intention of giving it to her. And I don't have to be told why she killed Hugh. While she was waiting in his studio last night, she found a sketch of his. It was an old sketch, but she didn't know that. She'd never seen it before, for obvious reasons."

"What kind of a sketch?"

"A portrait of a nude woman. She tacked it up on the easel and decorated it with a beard. When Hugh came home he saw what she'd done. He didn't like to have his pictures spoiled, and he probably slapped her face."

"He hit me with his fist," Alice said. "I killed him in self-defense."

"That may be the way you've rationalized it. Actually, you killed him out of jealousy."

She laughed. It was a cruel sound, like vital tissue being ruptured. "Jealousy of *her*?"

"The same jealousy that made you ruin the sketch."

Her eyes widened, but they were blind, looking into herself. "Jealousy? I don't know. I felt so lonely, all alone in the world. I had nobody to love me, since my mother died."

"It isn't true, Alice. You had me." The Admiral's tentative hand came out and paused again in the air, as though there were an invisible wall between them.

"I never had you. I hardly saw you. Then Sarah took you. I had no one, no one until Hugh. I thought at last that I had some one to love me, that I could count on—"

Her voice broke off. The Admiral looked everywhere but at his daughter. The room was like a cubicle in hell where lost souls suffered under the silent treatment. The silence was finally broken by the sound of a distant siren. It rose and expanded until its lamentation filled the night.

Alice was crying, with her face uncovered. Mary Western came forward and put her arm around her. "Don't cry." Her voice was warm. Her face had a grave beauty.

"You hate me, too."

"No. I'm sorry for you, Alice. Sorrier than I am for Hugh."

The Admiral touched my arm. "Who was the woman in the sketch?" he said in a trembling voice.

I looked into his tired old face and decided that he had suffered enough. "I don't know."

But I could see the knowledge in his eyes.

Dead Game

Harold Q. Masur

I was the only passenger getting off the bus at Clawson's Cove on one of the myriad somnolent, sweltering and deserted inlets that scallop Florida's perimeter along the Gulf of Mexico. I carried my bag across the street to an airconditioned diner.

"Hamburger," I said. "Medium rare."

The girl behind the counter looked at me, shook her head sympathetically, and called out my order. "Just get off the bus?" she asked.

"Uh-huh."

"You may be the only tourist in town this time of year."

"I'm not really a tourist," I said. "Is there a decent hotel nearby?"

"Only the Everglades. But it's three miles down the road and even now, off-season, it's ridiculously expensive. So if you don't have a car I guess the old Mansion House around the corner is your best bet."

A bell summoned her to the kitchen. The hamburger she brought me was surprisingly good. She had a winsome face, warm and friendly.

"Do you live in Clawson's Cove?" I asked.

"All my life. I was born here. And this splendid four-star establishment is owned and operated by my Uncle Dan." She cocked her head. "Tell me something. How in the world did you get so thin?"

"Prison," I told her.

At first she was startled, then she smiled uncertainly. "You're pulling my leg. That's no prison pallor. Why, you're burned darker than any of those tourists who migrate down here all winter to broil themselves black. If you—" She stopped as the door opened and her face went blank.

A heavy man lumbered up to the counter, a leathery redneck, hard-bitten, barrel-chested, with a sheriff's star on his shirt and a large gun in a loose holster. His pale eyes gave me a quick appraisal and lost interest. The girl drew a cup of coffee for him and then came back to stand in front of me.

"The prison," I explained, "was in North Vietnam. Four long years, and most of the time I sat behind barbed wire. Plenty of sun and not much food. Picked up one of those tropical fevers, so after I got back they kept me in a hospital until about a week ago."

She was genuinely solicitous. "Didn't they feed you in the hospital?"

I smiled. "Sure. But that fever must have changed my metabolism."

"Well," she said stoutly, "you're entitled to a vacation. How long will you be staying in Clawson's Cove?"

"Day or two. I'm on my way to the Keys, but I thought I'd stop off first and see Martha Crawley. Do you know her?"

The diner congealed into sudden silence. Even the kitchen noises stopped. The sheriff came over and swiveled me around. "You got a name, Mister?"

"Harry Kane," I said.

"What's your business with Martha Crawley?"

"Well, now, Sheriff, I'm not sure I care to discuss it."

"Would you care to spend a couple of weeks on the county road?"

"On what charge?"

"Vagrancy."

"Sheriff, the United States Army owed me quite a lot of back pay when they brought me home and I've got a substantial piece of it in my wallet. Vagrancy won't wash."

"We're flexible here, Mister. I'll find something that'll stick."

I believed him. "I'm not looking for trouble," I said. "I don't know Martha Crawley. I never met the lady, but I knew her grandson overseas, a GI named Pete Crawley. He was my best friend. We spent a lot of time together and he told me about his family. He said he was six years old the last time he'd seen his grandmother, a year before his father died. Then Pete's mother married an engineer who settled the family in Hawaii. Pete was drafted and shipped off to Saigon. That's where I met him. I was with him when word came that his parents had been killed in an auto accident. So Martha Crawley was his only living relative. He wrote to her a few times, promising to come back here after the war. But he never made it."

"Keep talking, Mister."

"Our squad was out on patrol one night when the Cong ambushed us. They knew a lot more about jungle warfare than we did. Cut us to pieces. Only a few of us made it back. Not Pete. Missing in action and presumed dead, the Army said. Then two weeks later I got caught in a raid. They marched me north and I sweated out the rest of the war in a prison camp. I had promised Pete that if anything happened to him I would try to make it back to Clawson's Cove one day and visit his grandmother."

"You're too late, Mister. Martha Crawley is dead."

I blinked at him. "I guess I should have phoned first." I turned to the girl. "When's the next bus out of here?"

"This is Saturday," she said. "Only one bus a day and none on Sunday."

"So I'm stuck here for the weekend?"

She nodded. The sheriff turned and marched out. "That," she told me with her lips compressed, "was Sheriff Luke Spence. He's not one of my favorite people. Nor anyone else's either."

"It's an elective office. Why do they vote for him?"

"Because he's Glen Barrett's cousin and Mr. Barrett backs him and Mr. Barrett gets what he wants in this town."

"How does he manage that?"

"Through the Clawson Bank and Trust Company which he owns—and the bank holds mortgages on most of the property in this area." She smiled wryly and offered her hand. "You handled yourself rather well, Harry Kane. I'm Lucy Hume."

We shook. "Hi, Lucy. Why is your sheriff so uptight about Martha Crawley?"

"Because he can't stand the gossip about what happened. You see, the bank foreclosed its mortgage on Martha's property. Three acres along the water. That's where the new hotel is, the Everglades I told you about. Builders had been trying to buy it for years, but Martha wouldn't sell. Said she was saving it for her grandson. But then she failed to meet the mortgage payments and Mr. Barrett foreclosed."

"And later sold that land at a profit?" That was inevitable.

"You better believe it."

"I don't understand, Lucy. Pete Crawley told me the old lady was well off. What happened to her money?"

"She lost it. Mr. Barrett had been managing her security portfolio for years in an investment advisory account she had at the bank. Then the bottom fell out of the market and she was cleaned out. Martha was a real scrapper. She complained to anyone who'd listen. She even came to my boss and demanded that he sue the bank."

"Your boss?"

"Rudy Menaker." She saw my puzzled expression and explained. "Oh, you think I work here. I'm only helping out this weekend because Uncle Dan's regular girl called in sick. I'm Mr. Menaker's secretary. He's the town's leading lawyer; its only lawyer as a matter of fact."

"And did your Mr. Menaker sue the bank?"

"No. He looked at the evidence and told her she couldn't possibly win. She didn't even have a case."

"I'd like to know what happened. Would Mr. Menaker talk to me?"

"The office is closed on Saturday, but he might see you at home. I'll try to arrange it." She went to a telephone, made the call and came back. "He'll see you in half an hour. Meantime, you can check into the Mansion House." She gave me directions.

I picked up my bag. "Do they have a nice restaurant at the Everglades?"

"Oh, yes, it's lovely."

"Would you have dinner with me this evening?"

"Harry, you don't have to—"

"Accept," her Uncle Dan called from the kitchen. "I can manage here without you."

There were summer stars in her smile. "All right. I'll pick you up at seven."

The Mansion House was a two-story building, faded and musty. I shaved and then walked three blocks to a medium-sized house of weathered shingles.

Rudy Menaker answered the doorbell himself, stepping out onto the veranda and indicating a pair of wicker chairs, lowering himself arthritically into one. A sour-faced old gent, exuding the rich aroma of bonded whiskey, he crossed his knees with a painful grunt. "Lucy tells me you're a friend of Martha Crowley's grandson, the one who got killed in Vietnam."

"My best friend, sir. I promised him I'd visit the old lady if anything happened to him."

"You're a couple of years too late. What do you want from me?"

"I understand she had some financial problems with the local bank and wanted you to sue."

"No way I could help, son. She claimed the bank had lost her money. I looked at the papers and she had a discretionary investment account. Mr. Barrett handled it just fine for a good many years. Times change. The economy here is going to hell in a handbasket. Nothing but problems; labor, energy, inflation, shortages, unemployment, you name it, we got it. What happened, son, it hammered the stock market right down through the floor into the basement. Cleaned out a lot of people. Martha Crawley wasn't the only one. Took a bath myself. Weren't nobody's fault. I told her she'd be wasting her time and what little money she had left."

"Weren't you also the bank's lawyer at that time, Mr. Menaker?"

His eyes narrowed. "Are you trying to tell me something, son?"

"Seems like you had a conflict of interest, Mr. Menaker. Maybe you should have suggested another lawyer."

"She came to me for an opinion. I gave it. She was free to do what she liked. Fact is, she did try to get someone to drive her to Palm City. Told everybody she was going to retain old Willis Saunders."

"What stopped her?"

"A heart attack. And not her first. Ask Doc Kramer. He took care of Martha Crawley."

"Who took care of her property?"

"The bank foreclosed on the land and the public administrator sold off her household effects."

"What happened to the proceeds?"

"Barely enough to cover tax arrears and a few debts. Now, if you'll excuse me . . ." He stood up and walked into the house.

I went looking for a public telephone and found a Dr. Edward Kramer listed in the book. A passerby gave me directions.

As I entered the doctor's waiting room a small angry boy shot out of the office and a short portly man appeared in the doorway holding a hypodermic syringe.

"Allergy," he explained. "Been treating that little feller for years and I can't make him believe there are no vital organs in the target area. Come on in. Sit." He surveyed me critically and shook his head. "Too thin. Too much sun. Can't understand you tourists. Always dieting and sunbathing Charred skeletons. You'd better put some meat on that frame, boy. Eat. And stay the hell out of the sun. It's overrated. Now take off your shirt and let's have a look."

"I'm not a patient, Doctor."

He frowned. "You ought to be. So . . . what's on your mind?"

He heard me out, the creases deepening, the benevolence shading into vigilance. He sat in silence for a long moment.

"That Rudy Menaker," he said finally, "too much booze. Ruining his health. Brain insult. Liver dysfunction. Won't take advice. How about you, Mr. Kane? Can you take advice?"

"If it's sensible."

"That's the only kind I dispense. Forget Martha Crawley. Go on about your business."

"Are you telling me to leave town?"

"Yes. There's nothing here for you except trouble."

"Something puzzles me, Doctor. Soon as I mention Martha Crawley's name, people turn edgy. Sheriff Spence; Rudy Menaker; you; and I shudder to think of my reception if I walk in on Mr. Glen Barrett at the bank. You seem intimidated, Doctor."

He was suddenly agitated. He paced once around the room,

then faced me, his jaw set. "All right, boy. Ask me specific questions."

"Did Martha Crawley die a natural death?"

"Yes and no."

"Too cryptic, Doctor."

"She came to me with chest pains some time back. Angina symptoms. I examined her. Hypertension, arteriosclerosis. I prescribed nitroglycerin, digitalis, heparin. They kept her going for two more years. I warned her to take it easy. But she had money troubles with the bank and was all wrought up. Then one night she called me, barely able to speak. I got out of bed and drove over. I got there too late. She was gone. All right. An old woman with a bad heart. People her age die all the time. But something seemed wrong and it bothered me."

"What, Doctor?"

"She always kept her drugs on a night table beside her bed. That night they were missing. I couldn't find them anywhere, not even in the bathroom cabinet. Martha was not senile. She understood her dependence on those drugs. So where were they? What happened to them?"

"Did you mention this to the sheriff?"

"He made light of it. Said she had probably swallowed her last pills and thrown the bottles away, intending to renew her prescriptions the following day."

"Would she let her supply run that low?"

"I can't argue with Luke Spence. I've had to patch up too many injuries because of the man's excessive zeal. Perhaps cruelty would be a better term. We've had confrontations. I never win. Now I steer clear of him." He looked past me and saw another patient in the waiting room. "Just keep your guard up, boy."

I found a visitor waiting for me in my room at the Mansion House. Sheriff Spence sat on the bed, staring at me with flat-eyed truculence. He stood up and came close, his voice harshly accusing. "You just came from Doc Kramer's. Now tell me you're sick."

"Are you really worried about my health, Sheriff?"

"I'm worried about your nose. You keep poking it into places it don't belong."

"I needed some medical advice."

"Legal advice too? Is that why you're bothering Rudy Menaker?"

"Have I broken the law, Sheriff?"

The bull neck inched out of his collar. His voice thickened. "Keep it up, Mister. Keep pushing me and you won't be able to leave on Monday. I'm telling you for the last time. Stay away from Kramer. Leave Rudy Menaker alone. Keep your nose out of our business. You understand what I'm telling you?"

"I read you loud and clear, Sheriff."

He bulled his way past me and slammed the door behind him. My years in the Cong prison camp would seem like a picnic compared to custody under Sheriff Luke Spence. I glanced at my watch and saw that I had just enough time to shower and change my clothes before meeting Lucy Hume.

She arrived at dusk, driving a five-year-old compact, her smile warming me instantly. When we reached the Everglades I could see why the hotel people had been willing to wait for that particular site. A pair of flamingos glided along a natural lagoon near the entrance and there were formal plantings of flame vine, hibiscus, and bougainvillea.

"That section there," Lucy told me, "is just about where Martha's house stood."

We sat in candlelight and dined and talked. Finally, over coffee, she asked me if Mr. Menaker had been any help.

"I seldom expect candor from lawyers," I told her. "But even so, he let something slip. He mentioned the name of Martha's doctor."

"Dr. Ed." Lucy laughed. "He brought me into this world and saw me through all the usual childhood afflictions. Did you talk to him?"

"Yes."

"Crusty but lovable, isn't he? And he makes house calls too." She turned serious. "Harry, whatever you're trying to prove, I want to help."

"Sheriff Spence wouldn't like that."

"I don't care. All the more reason."

I thought about it for a moment. "What happened to the papers Martha showed Mr. Menaker?"

"She demanded them back so she could take them to Willis Saunders in Palm City."

I asked her to brief me on Saunders.

"I guess he's the best-known lawyer in these parts. We elected him to Congress for seven terms. Now he's back in private practice. I phoned him a few times on matters involving our office and his."

I thought it would be fitting if Saunders finally saw those papers. "Lucy, do you have any friends at the bank?"

"I have Tommy Hume."

"Sounds like a relative."

"He is. Tommy's my first cousin. He's the bank's auditor."

"Would he do you a favor?"

"Does he have to break any rules?"

"Only bend them a little."

"Suppose you tell me what you're after, Harry."

"Copies of the latest investment transactions Mr. Barrett made for Martha Crawley."

"Aren't those things confidential?"

"Not really. They'd be available from the brokerage firm in any event. But it would save me a lot of time and trouble."

"Tommy's working at the bank this weekend. I'll call him when I get home."

When I walked over to the diner for lunch on Sunday she handed me an envelope. It held Xeroxed copies of confirmation slips covering the brokerage transactions I'd requested. I glanced through them and asked if I could borrow her car after lunch.

"What's on your agenda?"

"A trip to Palm City for a talk with Mr. Willis Saunders."

"May I see your operator's license?"

"It's long expired."

"Then I guess I'd better drive."

I grinned at her. "When can you leave?"

"Any time she likes," her Uncle Dan called from the kitchen. "Business is lousy."

Palm City was northeast through swamp country. Saw grass stretched out on both sides of the narrow road. Clouds had scudded in from the Gulf and the sky was now dark and overcast. There was moisture in the air. Mangrove and palm hammocks were so dense at times that we seemed isolated from the world. Lucy drove carefully, concentrating on the road.

An hour later we moved out onto dry land and passed a small citrus grove. Cypress draped with Spanish moss stood tall. The road widened into a broad avenue lined with coconut palms. Palm City. We continued beyond the old courthouse and a small mission church to the other side of town.

Lucy had phoned ahead and Willis Saunders was expecting us. A slender man in his seventies with a shock of snowy hair and a bright sardonic glint in pale eyes, he gave Lucy a courtly bow and escorted us into a long cool living-room.

He turned to me and said, "Now, young man, what is this urgency that could not hold until office hours on Monday?"

He listened to me with single-minded total absorption. I told him everything that happened since I had alighted from the bus at Clawson's Cove the previous day. Then I handed him the brokerage slips and he studied them, his white eyebrows rising higher and higher.

Finally he looked up. His voice was sharp. "Are you telling me that Glen Barrett bought this unholy mess of speculative garbage for the trust account of an elderly widow?"

"You're holding the proof, Mr. Saunders."

"And nobody called him on it until you appeared?"

"Mrs. Crawley intended to, but she died."

His mouth tightened, distaste curdling into sour contempt. "Outrageous! A wanton dissipation of assets. It violates the 'prudent man' rule which limits fiduciaries to the most conservative investments for funds entrusted to their care. To seasoned blue chips. These transactions represent ventures of such a precarious and speculative nature they constitute a flagrant violation of responsibility."

"Is it actionable?"

"My dear young man, Mrs. Crawley could have sued the bank from here to Key West and back again."

"Mr. Menaker advised her to the contrary."

"Rudy Menaker is a fool. He had no business advising her at all. He was and is counsel for the bank. A definite conflict of interest." Saunders studied me, pinching the bridge of his nose. "Are you implying that Barrett bought this junk deliberately, so that Mrs. Crawley would lose her money and default on her mortgage, thus permitting him to foreclose and then sell off the land at a profit?"

"Not implying, Mr. Saunders. Asserting it outright."

He shook his head. "Too bad the old lady left no heirs."

"Why?"

"Because the aggrieved parties are all dead. Who will sue?"

He stroked his jaw. "I'd like some time to look into this."

"How much time? The local sheriff wants me out of Clawson's Cove on tomorrow's bus."

"Luke Spence?"

"Yes, sir."

"I've heard of the man. A troglodyte. I have no clout in his bailiwick, so I suggest you come back here to Palm City on Monday." He looked at Lucy. "Does Rudy Menaker know about your visit here?"

"No, sir," she said. "I've decided to give Mr. Menaker notice. I don't think I care to work for him any longer."

He beamed at her. "Miss Hume, my secretary is retiring next month. I believe Palm City has more to offer a young woman than Clawson's Cove. Would you consider moving here?"

She smiled. "Let me think about it."

He accompanied us to the door. It had not yet begun to rain. We decided to stay in Palm City for dinner. We wandered around, window-shopping, and then found a small seafood grill that served fresh pompano.

By the time we were ready to leave, it was dark and drizzling. Lucy drove slowly through the plaza and past the citrus grove and back into the Glades where heavy mist floated over the marshland, cutting visibility. No cars passed in either direction. Darkness brings its own sense of fear to unfamiliar terrain. This was an unreal world, eerie and silent.

I think I heard the deep-throated rumble of the huge diesel engine before its high beams came glaring up out of the night behind us. A deafening horn blast shattered the silence, sustained, unnerving. I turned my head and saw the ghostlike tractor-trailer closing in fast, barreling wildly down the dark slick road.

Lucy glanced nervously into the rearview mirror. "Why is he driving so fast?"

"Maybe he's trying to kill himself. Quick, turn on your emergency flasher."

She fumbled at the dashboard. "Harry," she said thinly, "he's not pulling over into the passing lane."

"Pull away from him! Step on the gas!"

"I—I can't see far enough ahead." Sudden panic edged her voice. "He's almost on top of us."

The diesel's engine filled our ears. The great solid bumper rammed hard into the compact's rear and our heads whiplashed. I heard the trunk compartment crumple. We lurched and pitched sideways almost out of control, almost over the shoulder. Lucy fought the wheel. I reached over to help her. She was quaking and ashen but she held on, dead game.

We had the car under control when a sledgehammer blow rocked us again. I saw the pressure gauge flash red. Concussion had cracked the pan. We were losing oil. Without lubricant the engine would freeze and he'd have us for sure. I felt helpless and impotent—and responsible for Lucy.

The third blow spun us into a skid that sent the car over the shoulder to a shuddering stop, our front wheels caught in brackish muck. The diesel went roaring past while we hung there in teetering balance.

"Is he gone?" Lucy asked in a small gargling, scared whisper.

"I think so."

I was wrong. We heard him in reverse gear as he came backing up the road—to finish us off. I yanked at the door and tumbled out, hauling Lucy after me. We scuttled across the road and crouched down among the saw grass. The diesel kept backing, going past us. He needed room to accelerate.

Then he braked and changed gears, revving the engine. He started forward, gathering momentum, hurtling down the road. Under his headlights I saw a bluish-green reflection, our own oil spill shining on the slippery blacktop. The diesel swung hard and caught the compact a solid blow that smashed it over the shoulder and into the swamp. In that instant, as the driver straightened out, the diesel's tires lost traction on the oil slick —an irresistible force, mass times velocity, a stumbling leviathan careening and fishtailing out of control. It slammed sideways over the shoulder into a mangrove tree and jacknifed high with a crunch of tortured metal. Sparks flew and, as the whole vast bulk somersaulted ponderously, a sheet of orange flame blossomed against the night with a muted roar.

We saw the bulky figure of a man struggle out of the shattered cab, clothes ablaze, face illuminated by the flames—Sheriff Luke Spence, his feet entangled in mangrove roots, unable to move. I started toward him, but the intense heat drove me back. He fell then, smoldering down into the saw grass.

Lucy clung to me. "Is he—"

"Yes," I said. "Nobody could survive that heat."

"Why was he trying to kill us?"

"Not us. Me. You just happened to be along. He did not like my probing in Clawson's Cove. First, because the bank's transactions would not hold up under scrutiny; and second, because he had something far worse than Barrett's fraud to conceal. He knew Martha planned on taking her case to Willis Saunders, and she had to be stopped. Somehow, he managed to make off with her drugs, knowing it would be fatal, intending to return them after her body was discovered. But Dr. Kramer got there first and saw they were missing. Spence was sure I'd been told and it worried him enough to learn my real identity."

She stared at me, oblivious to the drizzling rain.

"The name is Crawley," I said. "Pete Crawley. My guess is that Spence found some letters I'd written to my grandmother. All he had to do was check the handwriting against my signature on the Mansion House register, and that pegged me for him. He was afraid I'd blow the works. There was too much at stake. I had to be canceled. So he tailed us into Palm City and he waited to finish us on the way back."

"But where could Spence get a tractor like that?"

"Lucy, there must be one very disgruntled trucker locked up in the Clawson's Cove jail on some minor traffic violation. Spence planned on releasing him soon as he got back, hoping the rig would be far away by tomorrow morning."

"Pete Crawley," she said wonderingly. "Why were you listed as missing in action?"

"Because I'd been wounded and I was hiding out in the jungle when the Cong took me. I'd picked up one of those tropical fevers and my memory was gone. They lost my dog tags in some primitive field hospital. After I came home, the Army shrinks lined it all up for me, and I found a letter from my grandmother mailed to my last APO address, telling me about her problems with the bank. So I came down here incognito to find out what happened."

She searched my face. "And now? What are you going to do now?"

"I'm going to retain Mr. Willis Saunders to sue the bank. That foreclosure involved fraud. Who knows, maybe the hotel people have a defective title. We may find ourselves in the resort business."

"We?"

"Sure. You've been working in your uncle's diner, so you know a little about food. And I can take a correspondence course in hotel management."

Reaction set in. Lucy began to laugh and cry at the same time, a small touch of delayed hysteria. She stopped suddenly. "You're crazy." Then she wailed, "I'm soaking wet. How are we going to get home?"

"Walk," I said. "With the kind of lunatics they have around here, it's safer than driving."

No Such Thing As a Vampire

Richard Matheson

In the early autumn, Madame Alexis Gheria awoke one morning to a sense of utmost torpor. For more than a minute, she lay inertly on her back, her dark eyes staring upward. How wasted she felt. It seemed as if her limbs were sheathed in lead. Perhaps she was ill. Petre must examine her and see.

Drawing in a faint breath, she pressed up slowly on an elbow. As she did, her nightdress slid, rustling to her waist. How had it come unfastened? she wondered, looking down at herself.

Quite suddenly, Madame Gheria began to scream.

In the breakfast room, Dr. Petre Gheria looked up, startled, from his morning paper. In an instant, he had pushed his chair back, slung his napkin on the table and was rushing for the hallway. He dashed across its carpeted breadth and mounted the staircase two steps at a time.

It was a near hysterical Madame Gheria he found sitting on the edge of her bed looking down in horror at her breasts. Across the dilated whiteness of them, a smear of blood lay drying.

Dr. Gheria dismissed the upstairs maid who stood frozen in the open doorway, gaping at her mistress. He locked the door and hurried to his wife.

"Petre!" she gasped.

233

"Gently." He helped her lie back across the bloodstained pillow.

"Petre, what *is* it?" she begged.

"Lie still, my dear." His practiced hands moved in swift search over her breasts. Suddenly, his breath choked off. Pressing aside her head, he stared down dumbly at the pinprick lancinations on her neck, the ribbon of tacky blood that twisted downward from them.

"My *throat,*" Alexis said.

"No, it's just a—" Dr. Gheria did not complete the sentence. He knew exactly what it was.

Madame Gheria began to tremble. "Oh, my God, my *God,*" she said.

Dr. Gheria rose and foundered to the wash basin. Pouring in water, he returned to his wife and washed away the blood. The wound was clearly visible now—two tiny punctures close to the jugular. A grimacing Dr. Gheria touched the mounds of inflamed tissue in which they lay. As he did, his wife groaned terribly and turned her face away.

"Now listen to me," he said, his voice apparently calm. "We will not succumb, immediately, to superstition, do you hear? There are any number of—"

"I'm going to die," she said.

"Alexis, do you hear me?" He caught her harshly by the shoulders.

She turned her head and stared at him with vacant eyes. "You know what it is," she said.

Dr. Gheria swallowed. He could still taste coffee in his mouth.

"I know what it appears to be," he said, "and we shall—not ignore the possibility. However—"

"I'm going to die," she said.

"Alexis!" Dr. Gheria took her hand and gripped it fiercely. *"You shall not be taken from me,"* he said.

Solta was a village of some thousand inhabitants situated in the foothills of Romania's Bihor Mountains. It was a place of dark traditions. People, hearing the bay of distant wolves, would cross themselves without a thought. Children would gather garlic buds as other children gather flowers, bringing them home for the windows. On every door there was a painted cross, at every throat a metal one. Dread of the vampire's blighting was as normal as the dread of fatal sickness. It was always in the air.

Dr. Gheria thought about that as he bolted shut the windows of Alexis' room. Far off, molten twilight hung above the mountains. Soon it would be dark again. Soon the citizens of Solta would be barricaded in their garlic-reeking houses. He had no doubt that every soul of them knew exactly what had happened to his wife. Already the cook and upstairs maid were pleading for discharge. Only the inflexible discipline of the butler, Karel, kept them at their jobs. Soon, even that would not suffice. Before the horror of the vampire, reason fled.

He'd seen the evidence of it that very morning when he'd ordered Madame's room stripped to the walls and searched for rodents or venomous insects. The servants had moved about the room as if on a floor of eggs, their eyes more white than pupil, their fingers twitching constantly to their crosses. They had known full well no rodents or insects would be found. And Gheria had known it. Still, he'd raged at them for their timidity, succeeding only in frightening them further.

He turned from the window with a smile.

"There now," he said, "nothing alive will enter this room tonight."

He caught himself immediately, seeing the flare of terror in her eyes.

"Nothing at *all* will enter," he amended.

Alexis lay motionless on her bed, one pale hand at her breast, clutching at the worn silver cross she'd taken from her jewel box. She hadn't worn it since he'd given her the diamond-studded one when they were married. How typical of her village background that, in this moment of dread, she should seek protection from the unadorned cross of her church. She was such a child. Gheria smiled down gently at her.

"You won't be needing that, my dear," he said, "you'll be safe tonight."

Her fingers tightened on the crucifix.

"No, no, wear it if you will," he said. "I only meant that I'll be at your side all night."

"You'll stay with me?"

He sat on the bed and held her hand.

"Do you think I'd leave you for a moment?" he said.

Thirty minutes later, she was sleeping. Dr. Gheria drew a chair beside the bed and seated himself. Removing his glasses, he massaged the bridge of his nose with the thumb and forefinger of his left hand. Then, sighing, he began to watch his wife. How incredibly beautiful she was. Dr. Gheria's breath grew strained.

"There is no such thing as a vampire," he whispered to himself.

There was a distant pounding. Dr. Gheria muttered in his sleep, his fingers twitching. The pounding increased; an agitated voice came swirling from the darkness. "Doctor!" it called.

Gheria snapped awake. For a moment, he looked confusedly toward the locked door.

"Dr. Gheria?" demanded Karel.

"What?"

"Is everything all right?"

"Yes, everything is—"

Dr. Gheria cried out hoarsely, springing for the bed. Alexis' nightdress had been torn away again. A hideous dew of blood covered her chest and neck.

Karel shook his head.

"Bolted windows cannot hold away the creature, sir," he said.

He stood, tall and lean, beside the kitchen table on which lay the cluster of silver he'd been polishing when Gheria had entered.

"The creature has the power to make of itself a vapor which can pass through any opening however small," he said.

"But the cross!" cried Gheria. "It was still at her throat—untouched! Except by—blood," he added in a sickened voice.

"This I cannot understand," said Karel, grimly. "The cross should have protected her."

"But why did I see nothing?"

"You were drugged by its mephitic presence," Karel said. "Count yourself fortunate that you were not, also, attacked."

"I do not count myself fortunate!" Dr. Gheria struck his palm, a look of anguish on his face. "What am I to do, Karel?" he asked.

"Hang garlic," said the old man. "Hang it at the windows, at the doors. Let there be no opening unblocked by garlic."

Gheria nodded distractedly. "Never in my life have I seen this thing," he said, brokenly. "Now, my own wife . . ."

"I have seen it," said Karel. "I have, myself, put to its rest one of these monsters from the grave."

"The stake—?" Gheria looked revolted.

The old man nodded slowly.

Gheria swallowed. "Pray God you may put this one to rest as well," he said.

"Petre?"

She was weaker now, her voice a toneless murmur. Gheria bent over her. "Yes, my dear," he said.

"It will come again tonight," she said.

"No." He shook his head determinedly. "It cannot come. The garlic will repel it."

"My cross didn't, she said. "You didn't."

"The garlic will," he said. "And see?" He pointed at the bed-side table. "I've had black coffee brought for me. I won't sleep tonight."

She closed her eyes, a look of pain across her sallow features.

"I don't want to die," she said. "Please don't let me die, Petre."

"You won't," he said. "I promise you; the monster shall be destroyed."

Alexis shuddered feebly. "But if there is no way, Petre," she murmured.

"There is always a way," he answered.

Outside, the darkness, cold and heavy, pressed around the house. Dr. Gheria took his place beside the bed and began to wait. Within the hour, Alexis slipped into a heavy slumber. Gently, Dr. Gheria released her hand and poured himself a cup of steaming coffee. As he sipped it, hotly bitter, he looked around the room. Door locked, windows bolted, every opening sealed with garlic, the cross at Alexis' throat. He nodded slowly to himself. It will work, he thought. The monster would be thwarted.

He sat there, waiting, listening to his breath.

Dr. Gheria was at the door before the second knock.

"Michael!" He embraced the younger man. "Dear Michael, I was sure you'd come!"

Anxiously, he ushered Dr. Vares toward his study. Outside, darkness was just falling.

"Where on earth are all the people of the village?" asked Vares. "I swear I didn't see a soul as I rode in."

"Huddling, terror-stricken, in their houses," Gheria said, "and all my servants with them save for one."

"Who is that?"

"My butler, Karel," Gheria answered. "He didn't answer the door because he's sleeping. Poor fellow, he is very old and has been doing the work of five." He gripped Vares' arm. "Dear Michael," he said, "you have no idea how glad I am to see you."

Vares looked at him worriedly. "I came as soon as I received your message," he said.

"And I appreciate it," Gheria said. "I know how long and hard a ride it is from Cluj."

"What's wrong?" asked Vares. "Your letter only said—"

Quickly, Gheria told him what had happened in the past week.

"I tell you, Michael, I stumble at the brink of madness," he said. "Nothing works! Garlic, wolfsbane, crosses, mirrors, running water—useless! No, don't say it! This isn't superstition nor imagination! This is *happening*! A vampire is destroying her! Each day she sinks yet deeper into that—deadly torpor from which—"

Gheria clenched his hands. "And yet I cannot understand it," he muttered, brokenly, "I simply cannot understand it."

"Come, sit, sit." Doctor Vares pressed the older man into a chair, grimacing at the pallor of him. Nervously, his fingers sought for Gheria's pulse beat.

"Never mind me," protested Gheria. "It's Alexis we must help." He pressed a sudden, trembling hand across his eyes. "Yet how?" he said.

He made no resistance as the younger man undid his collar and examined his neck.

"You, too," said Vares, sickened.

"What does that matter?" Gheria clutched at the younger man's hand. "My friend, my dearest friend," he said, "tell me that it is not I! Do *I* do this hideous thing to her?"

Vares looked confounded. *"You?"* he said. "But—"

"I know, I know," said Gheria, "I, myself, have been attacked. Yet nothing follows, Michael! What breed of horror is this which cannot be impeded? From what unholy place does it emerge? I've had the countryside examined foot by foot, every grave-yard ransacked, every crypt inspected! There is no house within the village that has not been subjected to my search. I tell you, Michael, there is nothing! Yet, there *is* something—something which assaults us nightly, draining us of life. The village is engulfed by terror—and I as well! I never see this creature, never hear it! Yet, every morning, I find my beloved wife—"

Vares' face was drawn and pallid now. He stared intently at the older man.

"What am I to do, my friend?" pleaded Gheria. "How am I to save her?"

Vares had no answer.

.   .   .

"How long has she—been like this?" asked Vares. He could not remove his stricken gaze from the whiteness of Alexis' face.

"For days," said Gheria. "The retrogression has been constant."

Dr. Vares put down Alexis' flaccid hand. "Why did you not tell me sooner?" he asked.

"I thought the matter could be handled," Gheria answered, faintly. "I know now that it—cannot."

Vares shuddered. "But, surely—" he began.

"There is nothing left to be done," said Gheria. "Everything has been tried, *everything!*" He stumbled to the window and stared out bleakly into the deepening night. "And now it comes again," he murmured, "and we are helpless before it."

"Not helpless, Petre." Vares forced a cheering smile to his lips and laid his hand upon the older man's shoulder. "I will watch her tonight."

"It's useless."

"Not at all, my friend," said Vares, nervously. "And now you must sleep."

"I will not leave her," said Gheria.

"But you need rest."

"I cannot leave," said Gheria. "I will not be separated from her."

Vares nodded. "Of course," he said. "We will share the hours of watching then."

Gheria sighed. "We can try," he said, but there was no sound of hope in his voice.

Some twenty minutes later, he returned with an urn of steaming coffee which it was barely possible to smell through the heavy mist of garlic fumes which hung in the air. Trudging to the bed, Gheria set down the tray. Dr. Vares had drawn a chair up beside the bed.

"I'll watch first," he said. "You sleep, Petre."

"It would do no good to try," said Gheria. He held a cup beneath the spigot and the coffee gurgled out like smoking ebony.

"Thank you," murmured Vares as the cup was handed to him. Gheria nodded once and drew himself a cupful before he sat.

"I do not know what will happen to Solta if this creature is not destroyed," he said. "The people are paralyzed by terror."

"Has it—been elsewhere in the village?" Vares asked him.

Gheria sighed exhaustedly. "Why need it go elsewhere?" he said. "It is finding all it—craves within these walls." He stared despondently at Alexis. "When we are gone," he said, "it will go elsewhere. The people know that and are waiting for it."

Vares set down his cup and rubbed his eyes.

"It seems impossible," he said, "that we, practitioners of a science, should be unable to—"

"What can science effect against it?" said Gheria. "Science which will not even admit its existence? We could bring, into this very room, the foremost scientists of the world and they would say—my friends, you have been deluded. There is no vampire. All is mere trickery."

Gheria stopped and looked intently at the younger man. He said, "Michael?"

Vares' breath was slow and heavy. Putting down his cup of

untouched coffee, Gheria stood and moved to where Vares sat slumped in his chair. He pressed back an eyelid, looked down briefly at the sightless pupil, then withdrew his hand. The drug was quick, he thought. And most effective. Vares would be insensible for more than time enough.

Moving to the closet, Gheria drew down his bag and carried it to the bed. He tore Alexis' nightdress from her upper body and, within seconds, had drawn another syringe full of her blood; this would be the last withdrawal, fortunately. Stanching the wound, he took the syringe to Vares and emptied it into the young man's mouth, smearing it across his lips and teeth.

That done, he strode to the door and unlocked it. Returning to Vares, he raised and carried him into the hall. Karel would not awaken; a small amount of opiate in his food has seen to that. Gheria labored down the steps beneath the weight of Vares' body. In the darkest corner of the cellar, a wooden casket waited for the younger man. There he would lie until the following morning when the distraught Dr. Petre Gheria would, with sudden inspiration, order Karel to search the attic and cellar on the remote, nay fantastic possibility that—

Ten minutes later, Gheria was back in the bedroom checking Alexis' pulse beat. It was active enough; she would survive. The pain and torturing horror she had undergone would be punishment enough for her. As for Vares . . .

Dr. Gheria smiled in pleasure for the first time since Alexis and he had returned from Cluj at the end of the summer. Dear spirits in heaven, would it not be sheer enchantment to watch old Karel drive a stake through Michael Vares' damned cuckolding heart!

A Piece of the World

Steve O'Connell

Unfortunately the elastic band broke. It was an ordinary black mask which is slipped over the upper part of the face. I had purchased it at a novelty store the day before, but evidently it had been on the shelves for a long time. I sighed as it fluttered to the floor, but I kept the gun steady.

The bartender and the four patrons stared at me. My Uncle Eldridge did not stare. He closed his eyes.

Well, I thought wearily, I might just as well go through with it. I spoke to the bartender. "Empty the till into this paper bag. And do not attempt anything rash. I will kill you if you do."

He rang up a No Sale and did as he was told. My uncle and the other patrons had their hands in the air. Two of them wore sport shirts. The other two were in suit-coats and hats, and their eyes were narrow as they watched me. I had the feeling they were just waiting for the slightest lack of attention on my part.

I moved the gun in their direction. "Take your wallets out of your pockets and put them on the bar. But be careful. Very careful."

They did as I directed, including my uncle. I dropped the wallets into the paper bag. "Now all of you stand with your faces against the wall. And keep your hands up."

242

The bartender came from around the bar and joined the others.

I took the paper bag and backed toward the rear door. On the way I picked up the briefcase my uncle had left on a stool. It contained thousands of dollars.

Outside, I quickly closed the door and began running. It was my intention to travel through a few alleys and then merge into the night street crowds. By the time I reached the first street, I was already puffing. I wasn't used to quite so much exercise.

A squad car was parked at the curb.

I stopped in my tracks.

The two officers appeared to be having cigarettes and idle conversation. Apparently they hadn't noticed me.

I had just about made up my mind to stroll as casually as possible past them, when behind me came the sound of running feet and police whistles. The two policemen looked up and saw me.

I'm afraid I panicked. I dashed across the street and into the next alley. I don't know how many fences I climbed or how many dark passageways I stumbled through in the next ten minutes. Eventually I threw away the paper bag, but I still clung to the briefcase. From the converging sounds of the police whistles and the whines of the sirens, it appeared to me that the entire police department must have been alerted.

Finally I found myself huddled in the dark corner of an alley, completely out of breath and utterly at a loss about what to do next.

Seventy-five feet ahead, a huge semi-trailer stood parked against the unloading platform at the rear of a supermarket. The driver and two men in white aprons came out of the exit. They appeared to listen to the sirens and then evidently they made up their minds to investigate. They trotted down to the farther end of the alley and stood there looking to the right and the left, trying to pinpoint the excitement.

The lighted doorway seemed to beckon like a sanctuary. I took a deep breath, dashed past the semi, up the stairs of the unloading platform and into the rear of the store.

The area I entered was evidently used for storage, for a wall separated it from the store proper and hundreds of cases of goods were stacked about.

I glanced into the store itself. It was lighted, though it was at least an hour after closing. Evidently the men I had seen were the employees who restocked the shelves during the night hours.

Where could I hide? Certainly not in the store. My eyes fell on the stack of one-hundred-pound sugar bags that reached almost to the ceiling. There appeared to be some kind of a trap door up there. I scrambled up the bags until I reached it. Apparently it hadn't been opened in years, for it took considerable effort before it yielded and moved up. I pulled myself quickly into the darkness and lay there trying to regain my breath.

After a while I noticed a small shaft of light from a slight crack beside the trapdoor. I put my eye to it and peered down.

The truck driver and the two stockboys returned. Someone called up from the basement. "What was all the noise about?"

The truck driver shrugged. "I don't know. We'll probably read about it in the papers tomorrow."

The men finished unloading the truck by eleven and it was driven away. I crawled to another shaft of light a dozen feet or so farther on and watched as the stockboys wheeled the stacks of cartons to appropriate positions in the aisles. There they cut open the cases, stamped the prices on the individual cans and boxes, and stacked them on the shelves.

By four o'clock in the morning they had finished. They removed the empty cartons from the aisles and swept up. Before they left the store, they turned out all but a few strategic lights here and there.

I waited another half an hour before I opened the trap door and let myself down. One light had been left on in the rear storeroom and I could see a telephone on the wall. I went to it and dialed.

My uncle recognized my voice immediately. "You fool!"

"I'm sorry," I said. "The elastic band broke. But don't worry. I read somewhere that witnesses are very unreliable, and probably the people in the bar gave five different descriptions of me. And with yours, that would be six."

"You idiot," Uncle Eldridge said. "I had to *identify* you."

"Identify me? I don't understand."

"Look," he said, "it just so happened that two of the people in the bar were off-duty detectives. The second your mask fell, they had your face fixed solid in their minds. So what could I do? From the size of the army chasing you, I thought they'd get you for sure. And then what could I say? That I hadn't been able to recognize my own nephew? I had to protect myself and think about you later."

I felt exceedingly disappointed. "What will I do now?"

"Where are you?"

"In a supermarket."

He swore.

"It's all right," I said. "The place is closed and nobody knows I'm here. I could probably hide here for days."

"Have you got the briefcase?"

"Yes."

"Then stay put. I'll think of something. I'll have to get you out of town tomorrow. Out of the state, maybe the country."

"But, Uncle," I said. "I don't like traveling. As a matter of fact, I detest it."

"I don't care what you detest." He was quiet for a few seconds. "What really worries me is what I will tell Big Mac now."

Over the phone, I thought I heard the buzzer of Uncle Eldridge's apartment and I wondered who would be calling on him at that hour of the morning. His voice became tense. "Look, stay put. Don't call me for a couple of days." He hung up.

I put the receiver back on the hook and went to the employees' lavatory where I washed the dust and grime from my face.

I would have to stay here at least forty-eight hours and that meant I ought to provide myself with some food. I put on one of the white aprons hanging on a peg and picked up an empty carton. If some early morning passerby happened to see me in the store, he would probably think I was one of the stockboys.

A supermarket these days seems to be a combination grocery store, meat market, drugstore, variety shop, and considerably more. I wandered through the aisles feeling almost like a small boy released in a candy shop. I supplied myself with the essentials—milk, bread, and cold cuts and a few other items, including an imported Edam.

I also picked up a flashlight and batteries. By the time I ascended the stack of sugar bags, my box was rather heavy. I closed the trapdoor behind me and turned on the flashlight.

The area I stood in appeared to be approximately nine feet high, twenty feet in depth, and stretched across the entire width of the store. Apparently another establishment had preceded the supermarket in this building, and this space had been used for storage. But now it was empty and thick with dust.

The beam of my flashlight located a number of empty light sockets on the ceiling. I decided I might as well get some light bulbs too. I was about to lift the trap-door when I heard a noise down below. I turned off my flashlight and put my eye to the crack.

The rear door opened slowly and a rather thin man cautiously peered in. Then he pocketed his key, entered, and closed the door behind him. He took the precaution of making certain that he was the only person in the building. Then he emptied several large trash boxes against one wall. He removed a candle from his pocket, lit it, and set it among the scrap paper at the base of the pile. He stepped back, viewed the arrangement and smiled.

My eyes widened. A firebug! The candle would burn down to the trash in half an hour or so and the store would soon be ablaze.

He regarded his handiwork once again and then quietly let himself out the back door.

I waited five minutes and then descended. I extinguished the candle and threw it aside. Really, I thought, the incredibly strange people who inhabit this earth!

I went into the store and got some light bulbs and a broom. After eating, I swept my loft a bit. Then I extinguished the lights and lay down on the floor, using the briefcase as a pillow. I closed my eyes and attempted to sleep.

Uncle Eldridge is a collector and he works for Big Mac. I don't know exactly what it's all about, but he goes to different places in the city at night and each one of them gives him money.

Why had he chosen me for this particular scheme? I would have considered myself a most unlikely candidate. I suppose it was because we are related and he thought he could turn to me in time of trouble.

"There'll be at least thirty thousand in the briefcase," Uncle Eldridge had said. "And five of that is yours. You could use five thousand, couldn't you? Maybe travel a little?"

But I didn't care for travel. On my yearly vacation I go nowhere except to the library and back to my one-room apartment.

"No, Uncle," I said. "I wouldn't want any of the money."

His eyes flickered. "Well, thanks, Fred. As a matter of fact, I owe the syndicate thirty thousand, not twenty-five. The extra five will square things right up to the zero mark."

"How could you possibly owe that much money?"

He shrugged. "Just one of those things that happen, Fred. The horses all run against me. So now I got to cover or be covered, if you know what I mean."

"But I'd think that surely Big Mac would give one of his own employees more time to pay the money back? Did you ask him?"

Uncle Eldridge cleared his throat. "It's like this, Fred. I didn't do the betting with Big Mac. I went down to St. Louis weekends and that's where I owe it." He patted me on the shoulder. "You and I have nobody else in this world but ourselves. You can't let me down, Fred. It means my life, and I'm not kidding."

I sighed. "All right. But frankly I dread the entire thing."

And now I lay here in the darkness. I am a bookkeeper. I rise at seven. I shower, I shave, I dress, I prepare my own breakfast. At eight I leave for work. It is a journey which requires almost an hour and four transfers. At six I am back in my apartment. There follows another hour for making and eating the evening meal.

And then seven to eleven, I read, I listen to music, and I think. Four hours out of every twenty-four, I live.

"It'll be easy," Uncle Eldridge had said. "You just walk in, point the gun, and take everybody's wallet. And my briefcase."

"But you don't intend to tell the police there was nearly thirty thousand dollars in the briefcase?"

"Certainly not. They'll start asking questions about how I happened to be carrying all that kind of money and that could lead to trouble. All they got to know is that it was a simple bar hold-up and the briefcase went with my wallet."

"What will you tell Big Mac?"

"The same thing. It was an ordinary heist and I was unlucky enough to be there. And if he don't swallow that, I'll remind him that a lot of punks know I'm a collector and it could be one of them decided to make a strike."

"And you think he'll believe that?"

"Look," Uncle Eldridge said. "In his business you got to think suspicious and I expect him to. So he'll brood over three things. One: Was it just a hold-up? Two: Or was it really a hi-jack job by some punk who knew the score? And three: Is the collector trying to pull something?"

"And when he gets to number three?"

"He might even get a little physical. But I can take a few bumps for thirty grand, and I'll keep blinking innocent like he never saw before. So he'll remember that I been working for him three years and I been clean. Finally he'll say to himself, 'All right. I'll let it go this time. But if anything like this happens again, the blood's going to flow.' "

"He'll do that after losing thirty thousand dollars?"

Uncle Eldridge snorted. "To him thirty grand is toothpick money. The only thing that might really bother him is the principle of the thing—like somebody in the organization having the nerve to rob him."

I became aware of the sound of voices below and went to the peephole which gave me a panoramic view of the entire store. It was almost eight and various clerks were arriving to start the day.

The hours which followed were long, though I did catnap often. At nine in the evening the supermarket closed and, as in the previous night, the stockboys took over and worked until four in the morning.

After they left, I went downstairs. I washed up and donned the white apron. I made several trips from the store to my sanctuary, during which I transferred more food, an extension cord, a small table lamp, a bridge table, and a folding chair. I browsed a bit at the magazine and bookstand and selected half a dozen pocket books. My eyes turned to the newspaper stacks and I saw my picture on the front page of one of them.

The article consisted of two columns down at the bottom of the page. *Nephew Robs Uncle, Two Detectives.* It told about what had happened and how the two detectives were now suspended, pending an investigation.

There was a quote by Uncle Eldridge. "I don't know what got into the boy. He's been trying to borrow a couple of hundred from me for the last month, but I had to turn him down. He got pretty mad about it and maybe he thought he'd get the money this way. All I had was about twenty bucks but he could have had that if I'd known he was so desperate."

I was upstairs arranging the extension cord and the lamp when I heard the noise below. I switched off the lights and crept quietly to the trapdoor.

It was that man again. He glared about, then once again, he emptied the trash containers against the wall. This time he lit two candles and placed them in the midst of the paper. He moved about, apparently testing for drafts, and then satisfied, he left.

I sighed, went down, and snuffed out the two candles. I searched through the manager's desk until I found his name, address, and phone number, and then I dialed. "Mr. Nelson?"

From the muddle of his voice, it was obvious he had been awakened. "Yeah?"

"Sir," I said. "I'm afraid someone is attempting to burn down your store. You better investigate."

He growled. "Is this some kind of a practical joke? You have any idea what time this is?"

"I'm sorry, sir," I said. "But this is almost the only time of the day I can call. And it isn't a practical joke."

He seemed to wake up. "Who is this?"

"Just say I am a friend of the supermarket. This individual has already made two attempts to burn down your store. Somehow they failed. But I have the suspicion he will try again tomorrow. Somewhere around five o'clock in the morning, I believe." I hung up and went back upstairs.

During the day and evening, I read two books. I lay down to sleep at ten and woke about three in the morning, a bit stiff. The floor is not exactly the most comfortable place to sleep. I went to the trapdoor, removed the plug, and looked down.

The stockboys moved about quite industriously, because the manager was present, I imagine. In a corner, he conferred with two uniformed policemen and two other men, possibly detectives.

At four o'clock the stockboys had finished and they left. The manager and the policemen began arranging places of concealment for themselves.

One of the detectives clambered up the sugar stack. For a moment I thought we looked eye to eye, and that all was lost. But he turned his back to the trapdoor, arranged several of the sacks in the form of a barricade and crouched behind them.

All of us waited. By my watch, it was five after five when the rear door was unlocked and opened.

It was the punctual firebug, and this time he had apparently lost faith in candles. He carried a gasoline can, and he appeared to be exceedingly vexed. Once again he piled trash against the wall. He poured gasoline on the accumulation and reached into his pocket. He brought out a book of matches.

Directly below me the detective rose to his feet. "Hold it! This is the police! You're under arrest!"

The police converged upon the unfortunate individual, and within a matter of seconds the bewildered man was handcuffed. One of the officers observed the manager's astonishment. "You know him?"

The manager nodded. "I fired him for loafing on the job."

By the time the excitement had died down and everyone had gone, it was almost daylight. I went down and dialed Uncle Eldridge.

"Why didn't you call?" he demanded.

"You told me not to."

"Well, never mind that now. Where are you?"

"Still in the supermarket."

"I mean which one? What's the address?'

I scratched my head. "I don't know the address, and there don't seem to be any numbers on the show windows."

"You can't be too far from Eighth and Hadley. That's where the bar was. So listen. I want you to go over to Ninth, between Hadley and Atkinson. Wait in the alley on the even numbered side of the street. And don't forget the briefcase."

I thought I heard someone coughing while Uncle Eldridge was speaking. "Are you alone? I heard somebody cough."

"It's the TV," he said. "One of them early morning programs."

I looked up at the window high in the storeroom. "It's just about daylight, Uncle. Don't you think there's a good chance the police might pick me up if I went out now? Ninth and Hadley could be a dozen blocks from here."

He didn't answer for a second and I thought I heard the TV in the background again. Then he said, "All right, we'll play it safe and certain. You be there tomorrow when it's still dark. What time can you make it?"

"I think five o'clock would be about the right time," I said. "The stockboys don't quit until four or a little after."

"Be there," Uncle Eldridge said, and he hung up.

The next morning the stockboys quit at their usual time. I waited ten minutes and then picked up the briefcase.

The phone downstairs rang. I glanced about to see if I'd left anything, then turned off the lights, and opened the trap door. I went down the sugar bags and to the door.

The phone was still ringing. I was about to leave anyway, so why not? I picked up the receiver. "Hello?"

There was a slight delay, then, "Is that you, Fred?"

"Yes," I said. "How did you know I was here?"

"I didn't. I just looked in the phone book and called every supermarket around Hadley. But luckily I got to you in time."

"I'm just about to leave, Uncle."

"Forget that. Some of Big Mac's boys would be waiting to pick you up and what they got in mind for you is fatal."

"But, Uncle, you were the one who told me to ..."

"Look, Fred, when you got a couple of guys lighting matches and not for cigarettes, you get to telling them the truth eventually."

"You told them about us?"

"Not exactly. I said I didn't know you were going to pull the heist, and that I was going to talk you into bringing back the money."

"And Big Mac believed you?"

"I wouldn't bet a dime on it. But, at least, he put me on the shelf until he could get his hands on you." Uncle Eldridge was talking fast. "They left Red Bronson to see that I stayed put, but Red's attention wandered. Right now he's on the floor of my apartment wrapped up with all the clothesline I could steal from my landlady. Now that I know where you are, I'll pick you up in five minutes. I'm only a few blocks from there. Meet me at the rear of the store."

I sat down on some cartons and waited. I heard the car pull into the alley and stop, the motor idling. I pressed the bar that unlocked the rear door from the inside. It swung open and the stop at its base lowered and held it ajar.

Uncle Eldridge had his car parked at the loading platform and he was alone.

I stooped down and handed him the briefcase through the open window. "Where will we go?"

He shrugged. "How do I know? The world's a big place."

I stared out into the darkness.

"Hurry it up," Uncle Eldridge snapped. "We haven't got all day."

I wondered what would happen now. A thousand miles away, would I get another bookkeeping job and live four hours a day? And then I shook my head. "No. You go on."

He frowned. "Are you crazy?"

"Maybe," I said. "But I'm not going with you."

He regarded me for a few seconds. "All right. Have it your way. I haven't got time to argue. But I always did think you were a little nuts." He put the car into gear and it roared down the alley.

I went back into the store and closed and locked the rear door. Upstairs, I turned on the lamp and picked up a book.

Yes, the world was a big place, much too big for me. But here it was warm and just my size.

Easy Mark

Talmage Powell

The two youths at the front corner table marked me from the moment I strolled into the psychedelic, nether-world decor of the Moons of Jupiter.

I was surely a sudden out-of-kilter detail on the scene. My appearance stamped me as the most reprehensible of straights: businessman, establishment man; specter from the far side of the generation gap. Fortyish, brushed with gray at the temples, lean, conditioned from regular workouts, I was smoothly barbered, tailored in a two-hundred-dollar suit of English cut, with coordinated shirt and necktie.

A cool young hostess, blonde and topless, decided I was for real. She smiled a greeting to take me in tow and threaded a way through a dimly lighted, pot-smoke-hazed broken field of tables and hovering, pale faces. In passing, I drew a few glances, ranging from the sullen to the amused. Empty, bored young eyes lifted, noted the stranger, and dropped again to contemplation of existence and a world they had rejected. I was of no more real interest than the movement of a shadow—except to the pair at the corner table. They studied every detail about me as I was seated and ordering a drink.

On the bandstand a four-piece rock group, as hairy as dusty and moth-eaten young gorillas, suddenly assailed the senses

253

with electronic sound. The lighting came and went like a Gehenna fire, swirling faces from corpse-green to paranoid purple to jaundice yellow, cycling and recycling until the brain swam and burst from the brew of shattering sound and color.

Throughout the hard-rock number I had the impression that I was being discussed by the pair at the corner table. Their faces in the ghoulish glow turned toward me, turned away, drew close over the table as words blanketed by the music were exchanged.

The music shimmered to a long-drawn wail against a mad rhythmic background and slipped eerily to silence. The lighting settled to a twilight. There was a shifting of bodies and a ripple of applause.

I lifted my drink, covertly watching the pair rise from the corner table. I sensed a decision, and my palms became a little damp as they came toward me.

Their shadows streamed across my table. Suddenly they stopped.

"Hi, pops."

The taller, huskier one had spoken. I looked up. He was a strapping youth with a heavy-boned face lurking behind a heavy growth of thick black beard and wiry tresses that fell to his thick neck. He wore nondescript poplin slacks, dirty and wrinkled, and a leather vest that partially covered his massive, hairy chest. His swarthy, bare arms were corded and muscled like a weight lifter's.

The companion beside him was as tall, but much thinner, a fine-boned fellow. Tangled, unwashed locks of yellow and a sparse beard graced a narrow, almost delicate face and high-domed head. The smoldering eyes of a decadent poet peered from the shadows of large sockets. The thin-lipped mouth was faintly quirked, as if sardonic amusement was an habitual reaction.

"We sensed a loneliness," the poet said, "and would offer a friendly ear if you'd care to rap. Peace." He had a thin, nasal voice. His jerky delivery and the embers in his eyes were clues to a good high on drugs. Clad in a rumpled tie-dyed gaucho shirt that hung loose about greasy ducks, he slipped with unreal movements into a chair across the table.

"I'm Cleef," he said, "and my boon companion is known as Willis."

Willis wiped a palm across his leather vest and extended his hand. "Into the pudding, man."

I saw no alternative at the moment but to shake his hand. His grip was modestly powerful. He pumped my hand once, then eased into the chair at my left.

"Pudding?" I inquired.

"As your group would put it," Cleef-the-poet said, "welcome to the club."

"I see. Well, thanks. Buy you fellows a drink?"

Willis' heavy mouth curled gently. "You're out of sight, pops. We don't ruin the belly with booze. But you might blow the price of a joint."

He lifted a muscle-lumped arm and signaled a waitress who was moving from a nearby table. She served them joints from an innocent-looking package bearing the brand name of a well-known cigarette. As Willis and Cleef fired the reefers, I ordered a second double Scotch. I figured I needed it.

Cleef drew deeply, half closing his eyes and holding the smoke until his lungs burned for air. Willis was a more conservative pothead, less greedy, less desperate for a turn-on. He puffed, inhaled, exhaled.

"What brings you to a place like this, pops?" Willis asked conversationally.

My gaze roamed the unreality of the room, returned to Willis' dark face. My shoulders made a vague movement. "I'm really not sure," I said.

"Hung-up man, ice cream man," the poet suggested.

"Ice cream?" I asked.

"Now and then user of drugs," Willis explained. "Ice cream habit."

I nodded, grinned slightly. "Thanks for the translation, but I haven't an ice cream habit. Just an occasional Scotch does it for me."

"Translate, extrapolate," Cleef rhymed. "Rap across the gap."

Willis reached and patted the back of my hand. "We'll try to talk your lingo, pops."

"Thanks. It would be less awkward."

The waitress came with my drink. Willis elaborately mused on her thin face and slender topless figure. The gesture on his part was almost pathetically obvious, a cover-up for his quick assessment of the thick wallet from which I paid the tab.

I lifted the Scotch. "Cheers." I rolled the first drops under my tongue for the taste. The liquor dispelled a little of the clammy chill inside me.

I set the glass down and studied it a moment. "I guess it was because of Camilla," I said finally.

"Come again?" Willis said.

"The reason I came in here," I said. "Dear Camilla . . . about the same age as some of the young women in here . . . early twenties . . . very beautiful."

Willis chuckled, eyes brightening. "Well, what do you know! The old boy has got himself a chick!"

"Straight man buys anything his little heart desires," Cleef said lazily.

I couldn't help the angry look I shot across the table. "It wasn't that way at all!"

"Easy, pops," Willis suggested mildly.

I lifted the glass and threw the remainder of the drink down my throat. "Well, it wasn't!"

"So okay."

"I want you to understand."

"Sure, pops. Don't blow your mind."

I took out a spotless Irish linen handkerchief and brushed the cold needles from my forehead. "Blow my mind . . . Sonny, that's just what I did, with Camilla. Couldn't eat, couldn't sleep, couldn't live without her. Went crazy if she glanced at another man. Never wanted her out of my sight . . ."

"Zap!" mumbled the poet. "What a king-sized hangup."

My vision cleared slightly. "At last you have voiced a truth. I became a different man, totally different, a stranger to myself."

"How'd you meet such a chick?" Willis asked with genuine interest.

I drew a breath. "In a place much like this. I—My wife had died. I was, you might say, in loose-ends bachelorhood. One evening I was entertaining a business client and his wife."

"How deadly dull," decided Cleef.

"She, the client's wife, had heard of a place similar to this one," I said, as if the poet hadn't interrupted. "She wanted to see the sights. She insisted we go, as a lark."

"But you, not the fellowship, were the bugs under the microscope," Cleef intoned sagely.

"Shut up." Willis glowered a look at his companion. "Let the man talk. Go on, pops."

"Go on?" I sagged morosely. "Where is there to go, after Camilla? With Camilla you have been all the way."

Willis' eyes glinted with a grain of fresh respect. "Tough, pops."

"Lovely while it lasted," I amended. "I met her that night, on the lark. We grooved, as I believe you would put it." I broke off, numbly, trying to relate the experience in my own mind to the "straight" sitting at the table with Cleef and Willis. "Then she turned me off. It was nightmare. I pleaded. She reviled. I begged—and Camilla laughed . . ."

"And she split the scene?" Willis finished.

"Yes," I said, squeezing my eyes tight and seeing her face against the darkness; lovely face, mask-like face; face that could become cruel, unendurably cruel. "Yes, she split the scene." I wrapped it up in a whisper.

Willis scratched his beard and gave his head a short shake. "Who'd have believed it?" He lifted his eyes and looked about the Moons of Jupiter. "So it was the thought of Camilla that brought you in tonight?"

"You might say that," I agreed. I washed the final drop of Scotch from the glass against my lips. "You see, after Camilla, my home town was unbearable. I left. I've wandered, for a long way. It hasn't been easy."

"Looking for another Camilla," the poet said. "I should write about you, man, if it all wasn't so corny." Cleef half stood, drugged eyes flicking about the room. "Is she here tonight? Another Camilla? Do you see another Camilla, man?"

"There will never be another Camilla, sonny," I said. "Once is enough."

"So now you wander some more, pops?" Willis asked.

"Perhaps."

"Why don't we wander together, pops? Have a ball? Cleef

and I have rapped about blowing this town. We'd like to see California, New Orleans, Miami when the chill winds blow."

"Dust to salve the itch in our feet," the poet supplied.

"That's right, pops," Willis nodded. "We yearn to roam. You got a car and dough."

"Sorry," I said, suddenly very sober, "but I don't think ..."

"Man," Willis said, "you just think about Camilla." His heavy face had changed, hardened. He lifted his right hand almost to tabletop level. I saw the glint of dusky light on six inches of gleaming switchblade. I sat very still. This was the decision the pair had made when I'd strolled in and they'd pegged me for an easy mark.

"Let's go, pops," Willis said.

"All right," I swallowed drily. "I won't resist. You won't have to hurt me."

"That's good, pops. We don't want to hurt you. We're not stupid. Just the dough and the car, that's all."

We rose from the table and walked out of the Dantean room and onto a parking lot, Willis close behind me with the tip of the knife against my back.

"It's the sporty little car right over there," I said. "Please . . . careful with the knife." I eased the wallet from my pocket, stripped it of cash, several hundred dollars, and handed the money to Willis.

His big hand closed over the bread. "Thanks, pops. And look, you ought to be more careful, wandering into places like the Moons of Jupiter."

"Seeking adventure, you found it," the poet surmised.

I handed the car keys to Willis. "That's it. You have got it. You've stripped me clean."

"So long, pops."

I saw the flash of his big fist. Conditioned as I was, even after Camilla, I could have handled him—both of them, Cleef posing no problem in a rough-and-tumble.

I took the punch on the chin, rolling with it just enough to keep from being knocked blotto. My knees crumpled. I fell on the darkly shadowed asphalt, stunned but not unconscious.

I heard Willis say: "That'll hold him while we split the scene."

I heard the poet intone: "Hail the open road!"

I heard the rush of their feet, the starting of the car, the sigh of engine as the car took them from the parking lot.

I got up and dusted myself off in time to see the taillights vanish around a distant street corner.

Good-bye Camilla's car . . . Bought with my money, but she'd done the shopping, chosen the model. Not even a fingerprint to connect the car to me; I'd wiped them away before entering the Moons of Jupiter.

I strolled to the street in order to find a taxicab several blocks from the scene.

Good-bye, Camilla . . .

I still had the smallest catch in my throat. I hadn't really meant to kill her when I struck her in that final moment of insane rage.

Farewell, Camilla . . . It was hard to cover my tracks and get rid of you, the evidence. I wonder when they will find you in the trunk of the car? California? New Orleans? At some service station in Alabama when the attendant moves from gas pump to the rear of the car and catches the first whiff of the ripening smell?

As for you, easy marks, you know not from where I came, or where I go, or even my name.

So enjoy the ride . . .

Proof of Guilt

Bill Pronzini

I've been a city cop for thirty-two years now, and during that time I've heard of and been involved in some of the weirdest, most audacious crimes imaginable—on and off public record. But as far as I'm concerned, the murder of an attorney named Adam Chillingham is *the* damnedest case in my experience, if not in the entire annals of crime.

You think I'm exaggerating? Well, listen to the way it was.

My partner Jack Sherrard and I were in the Detective Squadroom one morning last summer when this call came in from a man named Charles Hearn. He said he was Adam Chillingham's law clerk, and that his employer had just been shot to death; he also said he had the killer trapped in the lawyer's private office.

It seemed like a fairly routine case at that point. Sherrard and I drove out to the Dawes Building, a skyscraper in a new business development on the city's south side, and rode the elevator up to Chillingham's suite of offices on the sixteenth floor. Hearn, and a woman named Clarisse Tower, who told us she had been the dead man's secretary, were waiting in the anteroom with two uniformed patrolmen who had arrived minutes earlier.

According to Hearn, a man named George Dillon had made a 10:30 appointment with Chillingham, had kept it punctually, and had been escorted by the attorney into the private office at that exact time. At 10:40 Hearn thought he heard a muffled explosion from inside the office, but he couldn't be sure because the walls were partially sound-proofed.

Hearn got up from his desk in the anteroom and knocked on the door and there was no response; then he tried the knob and found that the door was locked from the inside. Miss Tower confirmed all this, although she said she hadn't heard any sound; her desk was farther away from the office door than was Hearn's.

A couple of minutes later the door had opened and George Dillon had looked out and calmly said that Chillingham had been murdered. He had not tried to leave the office after the announcement; instead, he'd seated himself in a chair near the desk and lighted a cigarette. Hearn satisfied himself that his employer was dead, made a hasty exit, but had the presence of mind to lock the door from the outside by the simple expediency of transferring the key from the inside to the outside— thus sealing Dillon in the office with the body. After which Hearn put in his call to Headquarters.

So Sherrard and I drew our guns, unlocked the door, and burst into the private office. This George Dillon was sitting in the chair across the desk, very casual, both his hands up in plain sight. He gave us a relieved look and said he was glad the police had arrived so quickly.

I went over and looked at the body, which was sprawled on the floor behind the desk; a pair of French windows were open in the wall just beyond, letting in a warm summer breeze. Chillingham had been shot once in the right side of the neck, with what appeared by the size of the wound to have been a small-caliber bullet; there was no exit wound, and there were no powder burns.

I straightened up, glanced around the office, and saw that the only door was the one which we had just come through. There was no balcony or ledge outside the open windows—just a sheer drop of sixteen stories to a parklike, well-landscaped lawn which stretched away for several hundred yards. The nearest building was a hundred yards distant, angled well to the right. Its roof was about on a level with Chillingham's office, it being a lower structure than the Dawes Building; not much of the roof was visible unless you peered out and around.

Sherrard and I then questioned George Dillon—and he claimed he hadn't killed Chillingham. He said the attorney had been standing at the open windows, leaning out a little, and that all of a sudden he had cried out and fallen down with the bullet in his neck. Dillon said he'd taken a look out the windows, hadn't seen anything, checked that Chillingham was dead, then unlocked the door and summoned Hearn and Miss Tower.

When the coroner and the lab crew finally got there, and the doc had made his preliminary examination, I asked him about the wound. He confirmed my earlier guess—a small-caliber bullet, probably a .22 or .25. He couldn't be absolutely sure, of course, until he took out the slug at the post-mortem.

I talked things over with Sherrard and we both agreed that it was pretty much improbable for somebody with a .22 or .25 caliber weapon to have shot Chillingham from the roof of the nearest building; a small caliber like that just doesn't have a range of a hundred yards and the angle was almost too sharp. There was nowhere else the shot could have come from—except from inside the office. And that left us with George Dillon, whose story was obviously false and who just as obviously had killed the attorney while the two of them were locked inside this office.

You'd think it was pretty cut and dried then, wouldn't you? You'd think all we had to do was arrest Dillon and charge him with homicide, and our job was finished. Right?

Wrong.

Because we couldn't find the gun.

Remember, now, Dillon had been locked in that office—except for the minute or two it took Hearn to examine the body and slip out and relock the door—from the time Chillingham died until the time we came in. And both Hearn and Miss Tower swore that Dillon hadn't stepped outside the office during that minute or two. We'd already searched Dillon and he had nothing on him. We searched the office—I mean, we *searched* that office—and there was no gun there.

We sent officers over to the roof of the nearest building and down onto the landscaped lawn; they went over every square inch of ground and rooftop, and they didn't find anything. Dillon hadn't thrown the gun out the open windows then, and there was no place on the face of the sheer wall of the building where a gun could have been hidden.

So where was the murder weapon? What had Dillon done with it? Unless we found that out, we had no evidence against him that would stand up in a court of law; his word that he *hadn't* killed Chillingham, despite the circumstantial evidence of the locked room, was as good as money in the bank. It was up to us to prove him guilty, not up to him to prove himself innocent. You see the problem?

We took him into a large book-filled room that was part of the Chillingham suite—what Hearn called the "archives"—and sat him down in a chair and began to question him extensively. He was a big husky guy with blondish hair and these perfectly guileless eyes; he just sat there and looked at us and answered in a polite voice, maintaining right along that he hadn't killed the lawyer.

We made him tell his story of what had happened in the office a dozen times, and he explained it the same way each time— no variations. Chillingham had locked the door after they entered, and then they sat down and talked over some business. Pretty soon Chillingham complained that it was stuffy in the room, got up, and opened the French windows; the next thing Dillon knew, he said, the attorney collapsed with the bullet in him. He hadn't heard any shot, he said; Hearn must be mistaken about a muffled explosion.

I said finally, "All right, Dillon, suppose you tell us why you came to see Chillingham. What was this business you discussed?"

"He was my father's lawyer," Dillon said, "and the executor of my father's estate. He was also a thief. He stole three hundred and fifty thousand dollars of my father's money."

Sherrard and I stared at him. Jack said, "That gives you one hell of a motive for murder, if it's true."

"It's true," Dillon said flatly. "And yes, I suppose it does give me a strong motive for killing him. I admit I hated the man, I hated him passionately."

"You admit that, do you?"

"Why not? I have nothing to hide."

"What did you expect to gain by coming here to see Chillingham?" I asked. "Assuming you didn't come here to kill him."

"I wanted to tell him I knew what he'd done, and that I was going to expose him for the thief he was."

"You tell him that?"

"I was leading up to it when he was shot."

"Suppose you go into a little more detail about this alleged theft from your father's estate."

"All right." Dillon lit a cigarette. "My father was a hard-nosed businessman, a self-made type who acquired a considerable fortune in textiles; as far as he was concerned, all of life revolved around money. But I've never seen it that way; I've always been something of a free spirit and to hell with negotiable assets. Inevitably, my father and I had a falling-out about fifteen years ago, when I was twenty-three, and I left home with the idea of seeing some of the big wide world—which is exactly what I did.

"I traveled from one end of this country to the other, working at different jobs, and then I went to South America for a while. Some of the wanderlust finally began to wear off, and I decided to come back to this city and settle down—maybe even patch things up with my father. I arrived several days ago and learned then that he had been dead for more than two years."

"You had no contact with your father during the fifteen years you were drifting around?"

"None whatsoever. I told you, we had a falling-out. And we'd never been close to begin with."

Sherrard asked, "So what made you suspect Chillingham had stolen money from your father's estate?"

"I am the only surviving member of the Dillon family; there are no other relatives, not even a distant cousin. I knew my father wouldn't have left me a cent, not after all these years, and I didn't particularly care; but I *was* curious to find out to whom he had willed his estate."

"And what did you find out?"

"Well, I happen to know that my father had three favorite charities," Dillon said. "Before I left, he used to tell me that if I didn't 'shape-up,' as he put it, he would leave every cent of his money to those three institutions."

"He didn't, is that it?"

"Not exactly. According to the will, he left two hundred thousand dollars to each of two of them—the Cancer Society and the Children's Hospital. He also, according to the will, left three hundred and fifty thousand dollars to the Association for Medical Research."

"All right," Sherrard said, "so what does that have to do with Chillingham?"

"Everything," Dillon told him. "My father died of a heart attack—he'd had a heart condition for many years. Not severe, but he fully expected to die as a result of it one day. And so he did. And because of this heart condition his third favorite charity—the one he felt the most strongly about—was the Heart Fund."

"Go on," I said, frowning.

Dillon put out his cigarette and gave me a humorless smile. "I looked into the Association for Medical Research and I did quite a thorough bit of checking. It doesn't exist; there *isn't* any Association for Medical Research. And the only person who could have invented it is or was my father's lawyer and executor, Adam Chillingham."

Sherrard and I thought that over and came to the same conclusion. I said, "So even though you never got along with your father, and you don't care about money for yourself, you decided to expose Chillingham."

"That's right. My father worked hard all his life to build his fortune, and admirably enough he decided to give it to charity at his death. I believe in worthwhile causes, I believe in the work being done by the Heart Fund, and it sent me into a rage to realize they had been cheated out of a substantial fortune which could have gone toward valuable research."

"A murderous rage?" Sherrard asked softly.

Dillon showed us his humorless smile again. "I didn't kill Adam Chillingham," he said. "But you'll have to admit, he deserved killing—and that the world is better off without the likes of him."

I might have admitted that to myself, if Dillon's accusations were valid, but I didn't admit it to Dillon. I'm a cop, and my job is to uphold the law; murder is murder, whatever the reasons for it, and it can't be gotten away with.

Sherrard and I hammered at Dillon a while longer, but we couldn't shake him at all. I left Jack to continue the field questioning and took a couple of men and re-searched Chillingham's private office. No gun. I went up onto the roof of the nearest building and searched that personally. No gun. I took my men down into the lawn area and supervised another minute search. No gun.

I went back to Chillingham's suite and talked to Charles Hearn and Miss Tower again, and they had nothing to add to what they'd already told us; Hearn was "almost positive" he had heard a muffled explosion inside the office, but from the legal point of view that was the same as not having heard anything at all.

We took Dillon down to Headquarters finally, because we knew damned well he had killed Adam Chillingham, and advised him of his rights and printed him and booked him on suspicion. He asked for counsel, and we called a public defender for him, and then we grilled him again in earnest. It got us nowhere.

The F.B.I. and state check we ran on his fingerprints got us nowhere either; he wasn't wanted, he had never been arrested, he had never even been printed before. Unless something turned up soon in the way of evidence—specifically, the missing murder weapon—we knew we couldn't hold him very long.

The next day I received the lab report and the coroner's report and the ballistics report on the bullet taken from Chillingham's neck—.22 caliber, all right. The lab's and coroner's findings combined to tell me something I'd already guessed: the wound and the calculated angle of trajectory of the bullet did not entirely rule out the remote possibility that Chillingham had been shot from the roof of the nearest building. The ballistics report, however, told me something I hadn't guessed—something which surprised me a little.

The bullet had no rifling marks.

Sherrard blinked at this when I related the information to him. "No rifling marks?" he said. "Hell, that means the slug wasn't fired from a gun at all, at least not a lawfully manufactured one. A homemade weapon, you think, Walt?"

"That's how it figures," I agreed. "A kind of zip gun probably. Anybody can make one; all you need is a length of tubing or the like and a bullet and a grip of some sort and a detonating cap."

"But there was no zip gun, either, in or around Chillingham's office. We'd have found it if there was."

I worried my lower lip meditatively. "Well, you can make one of those zips from a dozen or more small component parts, you know; even the tubing could be soft aluminum, the kind you can break apart with your hands. When you're done using it, you can knock it down again into its components. Dillon had enough time to have done that, before opening the locked door."

"Sure," Sherrard said. "But then what? We *still* didn't find anything—not a single thing—that could have been used as part of a homemade zip."

I suggested we go back and make another search, and so we drove once more to the Dawes Building. We re-combed Chillingham's private office—we'd had a police seal on it to make sure nothing could be disturbed—and we re-combed the surrounding area. We didn't find so much as an iron filing. Then we went to the city jail and had another talk with George Dillon.

When I told him our zipgun theory, I thought I saw a light flicker in his eyes; but it was the briefest of reactions, and I couldn't be sure. We told him it was highly unlikely a zipgun using a .22 caliber bullet could kill anybody from a distance of a hundred yards, and he said he couldn't help that, *he* didn't know anything about such a weapon. Further questioning got us nowhere.

And the following day we were forced to release him, with a warning not to leave the city.

But Sherrard and I continued to work doggedly on the case; it was one of those cases that preys on your mind constantly, keeps you from sleeping well at night, because you know there has to be an answer and you just can't figure out what it is. We ran checks into Chillingham's records and found that he had made some large private investments a year ago, right after the Dillon will had been probated. And as George Dillon had claimed, there was no Association for Medical Research; it was a dummy charity, apparently set up by Chillingham for the explicit purpose of stealing old man Dillon's $350,000. But there was no definite proof of this, not enough to have convinced Chillingham of theft in a court of law; he'd covered himself pretty neatly.

As an intelligent man, George Dillon had no doubt realized that a public exposure of Chillingham would have resulted in nothing more than adverse publicity and the slim possibility of disbarment—hardly sufficient punishment in Dillon's eyes. So he had decided on what to him was a morally justifiable homicide. From the law's point of view, however, it was nonetheless Murder One.

But the law still had no idea what he'd done with the weapon, and therefore, as in the case of Chillingham's theft, the law had no proof of guilt.

As I said, though, we had our teeth into this one and we weren't about to let go. So we paid another call on Dillon, this time at the hotel where he was staying, and asked him some questions about his background. There was nothing more immediate we could investigate, and we thought that maybe there was an angle in his past which would give us a clue toward solving the riddle.

He told us, readily enough, some of what he'd done during the fifteen years since he'd left home, and it was a typical drifter's life: lobster packer in Maine, ranch hand in Montana, oil worker in Texas, road construction in South America. But there was a gap of about four years which he sort of skimmed over without saying anything specific. I jumped on that and asked him some direct questions, but he wouldn't talk about it.

His reluctance made Sherrard and me more than a little curious; we both had that cop's feeling it was important, that maybe it was the key we needed to unlock the mystery. Unobtrusively we had the department photographer take some pictures of Dillon; then we sent them out, along with a request for information as to his whereabouts during the four blank years, to various law enforcement agencies in Florida—where he'd admitted to being just prior to the gap, working as a deckhand on a Key West charter-fishing boat.

Time dragged on, and nothing turned up, and we were reluctantly forced by sheer volume of other work to abandon the Chillingham case; officially, it was now buried in the Unsolved File. Then, three months later, we had a wire from the Chief of Police of a town not far from Fort Lauderdale. It said they had tentatively identified George Dillon from the pictures we'd sent and were forwarding by airmail special delivery something which might conceivably prove the nature of Dillon's activities during at least part of the specified period.

Sherrard and I fidgeted around waiting for the special delivery to arrive, and when it finally came I happened to be the only one of us in the Squadroom. I tore the envelope open and what was inside was a multicolored and well-aged poster, with a picture of a man who was undeniably George Dillon depicted on it. I looked at the picture and read what was written on the poster at least a dozen times.

It told me a lot of things all right, that poster did. It told me exactly what Dillon had done with the homemade zipgun he had used to kill Adam Chillingham—an answer that was at once fantastic and yet so simple you'd never even consider it. And it told me there wasn't a damned thing we could do about it now, that we couldn't touch him, that George Dillon actually had committed a perfect murder.

I was brooding over this when Jack Sherrard returned to the Squadroom. He said, "Why so glum, Walt?"

"The special delivery from Florida finally showed up," I said, and watched instant excitement animate his face. Then I saw some of it fade while I told him what I'd been brooding about, finishing with, "We simply can't arrest him now, Jack. There's no evidence, it doesn't exist any more; we can't prove a thing. And maybe it's just as well in one respect, since I kind of liked Dillon and would have hated to see him convicted for killing a crook like Chillingham. Anyway, we'll be able to sleep nights now."

"Damn it, Walt, will you tell me what you're talking about!"

"All right. Remember when we got the ballistics report and we talked over how easy it would be for Dillon to have made a zipgun? And how he could make the whole thing out of a dozen or so small component parts, so that afterward he could break it down again into those small parts?"

"Sure, sure. But I still don't care if Dillon used a hundred components, we didn't find a single one of them. Not one. So what, if that's part of the answer, did he do with them? There's not even a connecting bathroom where he could have flushed them down. What did he do with the damned zipgun?"

I sighed and slid the poster—the old carnival sideshow poster —around on my desk so he could see Dillon's picture and read the words printed below it: STEAK AND POTATOES AND APPLE PIE IS OUR DISH; NUTS, BOLTS, PIECES OF WOOD, BITS OF METAL IS HIS!

YOU HAVE TO SEE IT TO BELIEVE IT: THE AMAZING MR. GEORGE, THE MAN WITH THE CAST-IRON STOMACH.

Sherrard's head jerked up and he stared at me open-mouthed.

"That's right," I said wearily. "He *ate* it."

The Operator

Jack Ritchie

Inside the police station, I found the Motor Vehicle Section and approached the sergeant.

He took his time about going through some papers on his desk, but finally he looked up. "Well?"

I cleared my throat. "I'd like to report the theft of an automobile."

He yawned, opened a desk drawer, and reached for some forms.

"It was a 1963 Buick," I said. "Four door. The body is dark green and the top cream."

He looked up. "Buick?"

"Yes. I parked it on the bluff above the lake, on Lincoln Drive. I just got out for a minute or two and walked around. When I came back, it was gone."

"The license number?"

I rubbed the back of my neck for a moment. "Oh, yes. E20–256."

He looked at the civilian clerk at the next desk. They both grinned.

"As soon as I found that my car was gone," I said, "I flagged down a taxi and came here. This is the right place to report this, isn't it?"

"Yeah. It's the right place." He turned to the clerk. "Fred."

Fred left his desk and came over. He had a slip of paper in his hand.

The sergeant glanced at it and then looked up again. "Let's see your ignition keys."

"Ignition keys?" I reached into my right trouser pocket. Then I tried my left. I began patting my other pockets. Finally I smiled sheepishly. "I guess I must have lost them."

"No, mister. You didn't *lose* them." His face lost the grin. "Don't you know that it's against the law to leave your ignition keys in an unlocked car?"

I shifted uneasily. "But I was gone for just a minute."

"You were gone a lot longer than that, mister. The boys in the squad even took the trouble to look for you. They couldn't find you any place around there."

I frowned. "The boys in the squad?"

"That's right. They waited fifteen minutes, and then one of them had to drive the car away."

"A *policeman* took my car?"

"He didn't steal it. If that's what you mean. He just took it to the police garage for your own protection." His eyes became cold. "Mister, did you know that in eighty percent of automobile thefts, the owner left his keys in the ignition?"

"Well . . . I guess I read something about that, but . . ."

"No buts," he snapped. "It's people like you who make it possible for the punks to steal cars."

I bristled. "Wouldn't it have been simpler just to lock the car and take the ignition keys? And maybe leave a note under the windshield wiper?"

"Sure it would be simpler, but it wouldn't teach people like you anything. But *this* you'll remember." He seemed to relent a little. "It's just your tough luck, mister. We've got orders to crack down this week and haul away any car if we can't find the owner. You should have read about it in the papers." He reached into another drawer this time and came out with a smaller form. "Like I said, it's against the law to leave your keys in the ignition. The fine is twenty-five dollars."

"*Twenty-five* dollars?"

"You can pay right here or take it to court. So far that's never done anybody any good. Just adds twelve dollars and ten cents to the tariff. That's costs."

I exhaled slowly. "I'll pay here." I took out my wallet and put two tens and a five on his desk.

"Let's see your driver's license."

I put the wallet on the desk in front of him.

He filled out the form, shoved it toward me, and pointed. "Sign here."

I signed. "Where can I pick up the car?"

He tore off the stub along the perforated line and handed it to me. "Your receipt. Show that to the sergeant in the basement garage. He'll let you have your car and keys."

Seven minutes later I drove out of the garage.

It was a clean car and handled nicely.

I wondered whom it belonged to.

Earlier that morning, I had parked my car where the Lincoln Driveway arched down to the lake front.

It had been cool and only a scattering of cars were parked along the drive. I lit a cigarette and walked easy, taking in the automobiles I passed. Some of them were occupied, and the empty ones appeared to be locked.

And then I came to the 1963 Buick. It was parked two hundred yards from the nearest other car, and the keys were in the ignition.

I investigated the paths near the car and saw no one. At the bluff's edge, I looked down.

A man and a woman strolled along the beach far below and it seemed a good bet that they belonged to the Buick. Even if they started back right now, it would take them fifteen minutes to get up the twisting path to the top.

I walked back toward the Buick and was almost there when I saw the squad car parked behind it.

Both cops were out of their car. The taller one glanced my way. "Your car, Mister?"

"No. But I wish it was." I kept walking and got back to my car ten minutes later.

I looked back the long drive. One of the cops was still at the Buick, but the other had disappeared.

I watched. Five minutes later the tall cop reappeared. I guessed that he'd been looking for the owner of the Buick and hadn't found him down there on the beach.

He got into the Buick and pulled away. The squad car followed.

I turned on my ignition and kept about two blocks behind them. They took the Buick to the downtown police headquarters, and it disappeared into the basement garage.

I parked my car and slowly smoked a cigarette. The tall cop finally came out of the basement drive and got back into the squad car. It drove away.

I thought it over and then grinned. I opened my glove compartment and took out the wallet that had once belonged to somebody named Charles Janik.

I got out of the car and went into the police station.

I drove the Buick the half mile to Joe's Garage, and he opened the doors when I blew the horn. I eased the car to the pair of doors at the rear of the shop and into the room no legitimate customer of Joe's ever saw.

In twenty-four hours the Buick would have a different paint job, the motor block number would be changed, and it would leave here with a new set of license plates. By tomorrow afternoon it would be across the state line and on a used car lot.

Joe closed the door behind us and looked the car over. "Nice buggy."

I nodded. "Cost me twenty-five dollars."

He didn't get that. "Where did you pick it up?"

I grinned. "You'll probably read about it in the papers this afternoon."

We went into his office.

"I'll phone in," Joe said. "You should get your money in the mail tomorrow."

"Have it sent to the Hotel Meredith in St. Louis."

"Taking a vacation?"

"You might say that."

But it was more than a vacation. After what I'd just done, every cop in the city would have a complete description of me down to the last button.

I phoned for a taxi and took it back to where I'd parked my own car.

At my apartment I packed a suitcase and then drove to St. Louis. The trip took three hours, and I checked in at the Meredith at two-thirty in the afternoon.

The clerk swiveled the register back so he could read my name. "How long are you staying, Mr. Hagen?"

"I don't know. It all depends."

Maybe I would stay three or four weeks before I thought it was cool enough to go back. Or maybe I wouldn't have to go back at all—if I got the telephone call I was hoping for.

The story got into the St. Louis evening papers, all about the man who walked into a police station and stole a car. The newspapers seemed to think it was hilarious, but the police didn't, especially not the sergeant I'd talked to. He had been suspended.

I stuck to my room and the phone call came the next afternoon. It was a voice I'd never heard before.

"Hagen?"

"That's right."

He wanted to be a little more sure he had the right party. "Joe says we owe you some money for the last errand."

"Send it here."

He seemed to relax. "I see you got into the papers."

"Not my picture."

He laughed slightly. "Some people would give a lot to have it."

I waited, because I didn't think he had called just to congratulate me.

"The man in Trevor Park wants to talk to you," he said. "You know who I mean."

"I know."

"Eight tonight." He hung up.

I got to the main gates of Trevor Park at about seven-thirty.

You couldn't call Trevor Park a town. It had no stores or gas stations and the big houses were far apart and not even numbered. But it was a place of trees and acres and money. It had its walking guards to keep the ordinary people out and a private police force to help them.

The cop at the gate came to my window.

"Hagen," I said.

He checked the clipboard he carried and nodded. "Mr. Magnus is expecting you."

"Which is his place?"

"The fourth one on your right."

The fourth one on my right didn't come up until half a mile later. There was another gate at the entrance but it was open. Another two hundred yards brought me to a circle driveway in front of a three-story Tudor.

Eventually I found myself in a large study facing two men.

Mac Magnus was big and graying at the temples. Looking at him you would have thought he was born to the clothes he wore. He was that far away from where he had started.

The other man was tall and thin, with shrewd gray eyes, and when he spoke I recognized his voice as the one I'd heard on the phone. His name was Tyler.

We got drinks served on a tray, and Magnus looked me over. "Did you read about yourself?"

"In St. Louis. Page three."

He indicated some newspapers on the desk. "You did better than that locally."

I walked over and glanced down. The front page, bottom. There was a picture of the unhappy sergeant too, but I didn't think he would save it for his scrapbook.

When I looked up, Magnus was still studying me.

"I suppose you know you cut your own throat," he said.

I shrugged.

"You'll never be able to go back. At least, not for a long time. Right now if you passed even a rookie patrolman, he'd look you over sharp and wonder if he should have a talk with you."

I sipped my drink. "There are other cities."

Tyler spoke now. "Hagen, just why did you take a chance like that in the first place?"

"I just wondered if it could be done. And so I tried."

But that hadn't been the real reason. I stole the Buick in the way I did because I wanted someone up high to notice me. I didn't want to be doing nothing but stealing cars the rest of my life.

Magnus glanced at Tyler. "I still think it was a fool thing to do."

"Maybe," I said.

My eyes went around the room taking in the expensive furnishings. "The car racket must be good, if you can afford all this."

Magnus laughed softly. "Not that good, Hagen. But I'm like a supermarket. I got all departments. The canned goods, the fresh vegetables, the meat counters, the frozen foods. Hot cars is just a little counter somewhere in the back of the store."

But I had known that too. Magnus had his finger in everything that paid. He *was* everything. He was on the top, and safe.

Magnus looked at Tyler. "He's got your okay?"

Tyler nodded.

Magnus went to the map on the wall and pointed. "Ever been there?"

I looked at the dot. "No."

"It's a medium-type city of about two hundred thousand. I don't have a big operation there, but I want you to report to Sam Binardi."

"I go to work for him?"

"No. You replace him."

"You don't like him any more?"

Mangus selected a cigar from a humidor. "Don't get any movie ideas, Hagen. Sam's sixty-five and worried about his ulcers. He wants to retire to one of those colonies in Florida and play golf all day." He lit the cigar. "Like I said, Hagen, it's not a big operation, so don't get excited. And you can thank Tyler for the promotion. He seems to think you got something— nerve, maybe—but as far as I'm concerned you're still only a second lieutenant, and that's way down on the ladder."

I decided to find out just where Tyler stood in the organization. "Tyler's second-in-command?"

Magnus laughed. "There *is* no second-in-command. You might say that Tyler's my personnel and recruitment officer. And that's only for the operating personnel. Not the bookkeepers. He's got his job, and I don't want him to know any more than that."

I reported to Sam Binardi the next day.

Sam was a small, florid man with nervous gestures, and his office was on the second floor of a toy factory.

He shook hands. "Tyler phoned. Said you were taking over."

He indicated a cabinet. "If you want a drink, help yourself. I don't drink myself. Bad for the stomach."

"Later, maybe."

He looked me over. "They're sending them up young these days. I been in this business forty years—thirty before I got to sit behind this desk." He sighed and looked at some papers. "Well, let's get at it. We've got ninety-six people on the payroll, and they're all good men."

"Counting the toy factory?"

"No. That's legitimate. Thirty-two employees. Mr. Swenson is the supervisor." He looked down at the papers again. "The real business is organized into four divisions. D–1. That's all the gambling, including the bookies. D–2. Junk. Riordan in charge. He's not hooked himself, so you can depend on him. D–3. Mable Turley. The girls like her. And D–4. Cars."

"What do I do? Just sit here?"

"Most of the time. There's the toy factory to consider, too. That'll keep you busy a couple of hours a day." He beamed. "We cleared twenty-eight thousand last year. Mostly because of the Dottie Dee dolls. Ever see one?"

"No."

"I'll show you around the factory later." He got up and went to the city map on the wall. "This is our territory. Everything north of the river, including the suburbs."

I looked at the map. The river divided the city into two almost equal sections. "What about the south side of the city?"

Binardi shook his head. "We leave that alone. That's Ed Willkie's territory. We mind our business and he minds his. That way we got no trouble." He came back to the desk. "We got a treaty like. There's no sense in fighting. I play golf with Ed twice a week."

He sat down. "I'll be in every day for about a month to break you in."

I phoned Captain Parker and we arranged a meeting at the Lyson Motel just outside of Reedville.

Walt Parker listened to what I had to say and then grinned. "So it was you who stole the car?"

"I had to get attention from the right people some way. This fell into my lap."

Parker agreed. "You could be stealing cars for twenty years and maybe never got noticed by Magnus. You got away with five cars so far?"

"Including the Buick."

He nodded. "They ship them to a place called Karl's Used Cars in Hainsford. Just across the state line. We could clamp down, but there's no point to that now. We're after bigger things. So we dip into the fund, buy up the cars for real, and store them in the garage for now. After this is all over, we'll make the adjustments with the owners or their insurance companies."

"Pretty rough on the fund."

"If this all works out, everyone will forgive us."

"What about the sergeant?"

"In a way he's got it coming, considering how he let you get away with what you did. But we'll pass the word to the chief, and it won't be too hard on him."

Parker sat down on one of the beds. "So now you're a second lieutenant in the operation?"

"It's still a long way from the top. Magnus won't be handing me any secrets for some time yet."

"At least it's a toe hold. Magnus has got himself a great big organization. I would't be surprised if it covered every one of the fifty states and Puerto Rico for frosting. And this isn't the type of operation where you carry the bookkeeping under your hat or in a little black notebook. There's got to be a central bookkeeping headquarters, and we're out to find it. It's the only way we can really nail Magnus."

Parker lit a cigar. "We know how Magnus runs the operation. Take Binardi's, for instance—it's just like any of the hundreds of others Magnus controls. Once every month Magnus has a crew come in to microfilm Binardi's books. The film is mailed to a box number. Somebody picks it up and mails it somewhere else. Maybe it goes through five or six hands before it reaches the bookkeeping headquarters. But Magnus has so many safeguards on the way that we've never been able to follow the mail all the way through.

"And when the film gets to headquarters, half a dozen or more trusted accountants get to work on it—and hundreds of

others like it—and Magnus gets to know how much he made
and where and when and by whom.

"Magnus' empire is like a head of hair. We can snip off a little
here and there—maybe even give him a crew cut—but the
roots are still there. We've got to get at those roots, and our best
bet is to find out where in these whole blessed United States he's
hidden that bookkeeping headquarters."

After a month, Sam Binardi left for Florida, and I was left to
play golf with Ed Willkie on Tuesday and Thursday afternoons.

Willkie was in his fifties, tanned, and played in the eighties.
His wife was dead, but he had a twelve-year-old son named Ted.

I learned that Willkie's organization was long-established and
conservative. Everybody waited patiently for his promotion.
There was no idea of mutiny. Everyone took his orders from
Boss Willkie and didn't feel frustrated about it.

On a Tuesday afternoon, two months later, when I pulled up
in front of Willkie's house, I noticed Ted duck back behind the
garage.

I was about to ring Willkie's doorbell, but then I changed my
mind. I went to the garage and found Ted hiding behind it.
"Aren't you supposed to be in school?"

He glanced uneasily toward the house. "There's no school
today."

"On a Tuesday?"

He didn't meet my eyes. "Well . . . I didn't feel so good. So I
stayed home."

"But your father doesn't know that?"

Ted didn't say anything.

"Do you play hookey a lot?"

"You're not going to tell my father?"

"No. I never cared much for school myself. How do you get
away with skipping school?"

He grinned. "I write the excuses and sign Dad's name."

"What do you do when you skip school? You go somewhere
special?"

His eyes brightened. "Mostly I go down to the lake and watch
the boats. They have races almost every day now. There's a big
one Thursday afternoon."

"And I suppose you'll be there?"

He grinned. "I guess so."

I went back to the front door and pressed the button. Willkie and I drove to the Wildwood course. He shot an eighty-two, and I came in with a seventy-six.

The next morning I left the office for an inspection trip of my territory. I found the two big men I thought I could use and had them report to my office in the afternoon.

I came right to the point. "I've got a little job for you."

They looked at each other a little uneasily. "Job?"

"It's about the simplest thing you've ever done in your lives. I just want you to sit in the back seat of my car. I'm going to pick up Ed Willkie tomorrow afternoon. I'll drive the three of you a couple of blocks, and then I want you to get out. Go back to work and forget everything."

They looked at each other again and then the bigger one spoke. "Just that? Nothing else?"

"Nothing else."

"I don't get it."

"You're not supposed to. Just do as you're told."

He had one more question. "You don't expect us to do any rough stuff: I mean . . . well . . . those days are gone. I got a wife and . . ."

"No rough stuff. Nothing but what I told you. I'll pick both of you up at noon on the corner of Sixth and Wells."

At noon Thursday I packed my golf bag in the trunk of the car and stopped at Sixth and Wells. We drove on to Ed Willkie's big house, and I honked the horn.

Willkie came down the walk carrying his golf clubs. He opened the car door. "A foursome today?"

"No," I said. "Just giving them a lift."

I drove two blocks and then pulled to the curb. The two men got out of the back seat.

When I pulled back into traffic, Willkie asked, "Who were they?"

"Just a couple of friends from Chicago."

After the eighteenth hole, Willkie and I went to the clubhouse. We got some cokes and sandwiches at the counter and took a table near the window overlooking the first tee.

I glanced at my watch. "As soon as you're through eating, Ed, you'd better call a meeting of your division heads."

Willkie took a bite of his sandwich. "Why?"

"I want you to make the announcement that you're retiring because of your health. And you're appointing me to take your place."

His eyes narrowed. "You're crazy."

"No. You'll make the announcement if you ever want to see your son alive again."

He stared at me unbelievingly.

I smiled. "Remember those two nice men who were in the car when I picked you up? They've got your son by now." I tried my sandwich. "He's perfectly safe, Willkie. And he will be. As long as you do what I say."

He glared at me for thirty seconds and then rose abruptly. He strode to the telephone booth. I followed and kept him from closing the door. "I'll listen. I wouldn't want you to say anything rash."

I watched him dial his home number. He got his house-keeper, Mrs. Porter.

"Amy," he said. "Is Ted there?"

"Why, no, Mr. Willkie. He came home for lunch and then went back to school."

Willkie hung up and began paging theough the phone book. I watched his finger run down the list of public schools. He dialed the number of Stevenson Grade and got the principal. "This is Edward Willkie. Is my son, Ted, in his class?"

It took about ten minutes for the principal to get the information. "No, he isn't Mr. Willkie. And I've been meaning to speak to you about the number of times . . ."

I touched the hook on the side of the telephone and disconnected us. "Are you satisfied, Willkie?"

His face was gray. "I want to speak to Ted. I want to be sure he's all right."

"I can't accommodate you, Ed. I don't know where they took him."

He didn't understand that.

"Self-preservation," I said. "If I knew, you might be able to beat it out of me. But this way it wouldn't do you any good."

I gave him another minute to think things over and then cracked down. "All right. Start phoning your division heads. Have them meet at your office."

By the time we got to his office on the third floor of a furniture factory, his chief lieutenants were waiting.

Willkie took a deep breath and made the announcement, and the reason for it. They seemed to believe him. He didn't look too healthy.

I watched their faces for signs of resentment over the fact that an outsider had been promoted over their heads. I didn't see any. If there were some, they kept it off their faces. And possibly they were just specialists in their line. None of them ever really expected to get the number one position.

When they were gone, Willkie turned to me. "Now do I get my boy back?"

"Not for a week. You'll be gone at least that long yourself."

I drove him to the airport and explained things on the way. "You'll take the first plane out of here to Los Angeles. You'll stay there one week. At the end of that time you can come back, and you'll get your son safe and sound. One week will give me enough time to consolidate everything here. By the time you come back you won't be able to do anything about anything." The smile left my face. "But if I were you, I wouldn't bother to come back at all. It might not be too healthy for either you or your son. Why not just send for him? I think he'll like California."

At the air terminal I bought him a nonstop ticket to L.A. and we walked to ramp 202. I glanced at the waiting passengers. They were all strangers to me, but I nodded to a heavy man whose luggage seemed to indicate that he collected hotel stickers. He nodded back, probably wondering who the hell I was.

I turned my back on him and spoke to Willkie. "See that big man all wrapped up in the light tan coat?"

His eyes flicked that way. "The one you nodded to?"

"That's right. When you get to Los Angeles, I want you to follow him."

"Follow him?"

I nodded. "Check in at the same hotel he does. Stay there one whole week. He'll always be somewhere around to see that you do."

"He's one of your . . . ?"

"Don't talk to him. And don't try to buy him. He doesn't know any more than his part of the job. And remember, no phone calls to anyone. I don't want you arranging things behind my back. Remember, we've got your son. Don't even try phoning your home. If you do, I'll know about it. Mrs. Porter has orders to . . ." I stopped and shrugged irritably as though I'd revealed something.

Willkie must have felt surrounded. He certainly looked that way.

Ten minutes later, I watched him walk up the ramp and disappear into the plane. He was still wearing his golf cap and sports shirt. He looked small.

When the plane took off, I phoned Mrs. Porter and told her that Willkie would be gone for a week and not to worry. It was a business trip.

I expected a telephone call that night, but it didn't come until eight days later. Tyler told me to report to Magnus right away.

When I pulled into the circle drive in front of Magnus' house I noticed a dark-haired girl on the lawn near the lake. She had set up an easel and was painting. She gave me only a momentary glance and returned to her work.

Her picture was in the Mac Magnus file. Valerie Magnus. Twenty-three. His only child.

Tyler and Magnus were waiting for me in the study.

Magnus let me stand for a while and then he said. "I hear you took over the south side."

I nodded.

"That was eight days ago," Magnus said. "Why didn't you let me know?"

"I wanted to be sure the merger would take."

"Did it?"

"Willkie could come back today, and I don't think anybody would listen to him."

Magnus went to the humidor. He took out a cigar, looked it over, and finally lit it. He walked to the TV set and tapped it with a knuckle. "If I turn the thing on I'll probably find somebody giving a spiel about soap. The talk will be that there's only one thing you're supposed to use when you do your washing. Soap. Don't use harsh detergents."

He tapped the set again. "And if I turn to another channel, I'll probably find somebody else pushing detergents. Detergents are the new, the modern thing. Don't use old-fashioned inefficient soaps."

I noticed that Tyler was smiling.

Magnus went on. "What most people don't know is that the *same* company ... the same *syndicate* ... manufactures the soap *and* the detergent. They really don't give a damn *which* you buy ... as long as you buy one. The money all goes into the same pocket."

He waited for that to sink in and then he said, "Willkie works for me too."

I blinked. "Binardi didn't say anything to me about that."

"Binardi didn't *know* that. And Willkie doesn't know that Binardi worked for me either. I wanted it that way."

Tyler spoke. "Divide and rule. Empires are built that way."

Magnus held up a hand. "I don't want one finger to know what the other's doing, but I want to control the hand." He took a deep puff of his cigar. "Tyler, I'm beginning to think that you made a mistake about Hagen."

Tyler rubbed his jaw. "Hagen, how many people helped you pull this off?"

"None." And I told them all about it.

Magnus was impressed in spite of himself. "Damn. You scared Willkie silly. He didn't do a thing but stay in that L.A. hotel for a week. When he got up enough nerve, finally, to phone his home, he found that his son hadn't been kidnapped at all. The next thing he did was to phone me." Magnus glared at me. "I told Willkie to come right back. And as for you, Hagen, I want you to get back to the north side and *stay* on the north side."

Tyler stepped forward. "I've been thinking, Mac. If Willkie scared that easy, maybe he's not the right man for the job."

"He was scared because of his kid," Magnus said.

"Sure. But he still shouldn't have waited eight days before he told us what happened to his organization. Do you want somebody like that working for you?"

Magnus worked on the idea for half a minute. "Tell Willkie he's through. He should have reported."

Tyler nodded. "And as long as the district's consolidated, why not leave it that way?"

Magnus showed teeth. "And I suppose you mean leave Hagen in charge?"

"Why not? I'd say he can handle the job. He has been, as a matter of fact. And it would cut down on overhead."

Magnus looked as though his arm had been twisted, but he said, "All right, Hagen, you got it." Then he glowered. "But if you get any other fancy ideas, you'd better clear them with me *before* you do anything."

Outside the house, I stopped for a moment to watch Magnus' daughter. Her back was toward me, and she was still at her easel. She was slim, but from the picture in the files, you could hardly call her pretty. I had the suspicion that she did a lot of painting mostly because there was nothing else to do with her time.

I wondered what kind of a part she played as Magnus' daughter. Did he try to keep her ignorant of what he was? It seemed almost impossible that she could fail to know about him. Maybe she knew a lot more than he thought.

It was tempting to walk over there, admire her painting, and introduce myself. But on the other hand, I thought that if I were that direct, and Magnus heard about it, I'd be broken down to private.

And yet, it might pay to know her.

I went to the left rear wheel of my car and let the air out of the tire. The wind came off the lake, and I didn't think she could hear the hiss.

I got the jack and handle from my trunk and made some noise doing it.

As I jacked up the car, I covertly glanced her way. She had turned and was watching.

When I pried off the hub cap, I allowed the iron to slip and strike my knuckles. I jerked to my feet, holding the fingers of my left hand. I walked stiffly in a circle, cursing softly. It hurt more than I had anticipated.

That brought her over. "Are you hurt?"

"No. I always dance this way."

She looked down at the jacked-up wheel. "I can get somebody to change that for you."

"Thanks. But I think I can manage as soon as my wound heals." I flexed the hand. "Nothing seems to be broken." I knelt down and began removing the bolts from the wheel. "Do you work here?"

"Would I be sitting on the lawn painting second-rate pictures if I did?"

"Why not? I imagine you'd get time off and all the free scenery you can eat. No reason why a maid can't paint."

"I'm Magnus' daughter."

"Oh," I said. I removed one bolt from the wheel. Then the next. And the next.

"You're still allowed to talk to me," she said acidly.

I shrugged but still said nothing. I removed the fourth bolt.

She took an exasperated breath. "I suppose you work for my father?"

I nodded. The fifth bolt came off, and I removed the wheel. I went to the trunk for the spare. She followed me. "You just don't talk to anybody at all? Is that it?"

I took the spare out of the trunk, and when I straightened, we were eye to eye. I kept it that way for about ten seconds, then I smiled faintly. "Let me put it this way. You're country club and I'm corner tavern. Kismet."

"I am *not* country club. As a matter of fact, we've never even been invited to join the one in Trevor Park."

I grinned. "Why not just buy the place? Your father ought to be able to do that."

"Of course he could. But you just don't *do* things like that. You've got to be *asked*. It makes all the difference in the world."

"To you?" I was mildly curious.

"No. I really don't care much one way or the other. But it does bother Dad."

I rolled the wheel to the side of the car. "Why doesn't he just send the club a five-thousand-dollar gift? But make it anonymous."

"Anonymous? What good would that do?"

"The members of the board, or whoever runs the place, won't be able to send the money back, because they won't know who gave it to them. So they'll think, 'Well, now, that's nice, and we do need a new bar.' And they'll spend it.

I began tightening the bolts. "That's the first hook. A month later, your father ought to send another five thousand. Again anonymous. Keep that up for four or five months."

She was interested. "And then?"

"And then *stop* sending money. But by now they'll be accustomed to getting the money regularly. They'll be wondering how they ever got along without it. They've begun to depend on it. As a matter of fact, they wouldn't have started building that new swimming pool if they hadn't expected the dollar rain to continue."

I tapped the hubcap into place. "And then let it leak out that your Dad is the one who's been sending all that beautiful cash —out of the goodness of his heart, and in the spirit of general neighborliness."

I looked up at her. "And so there'll be a meeting of the board, and nobody will say anything direct about money, but someone will clear his throat and say 'Everybody in Trevor Park belongs to the country club, except Mr. Magnus. Now I was thinking, isn't that just a little inhospitable?'

"And somebody else will say, 'After all, he's never been convicted of anything. There are just rumors. And this *is* America, isn't it? We shouldn't convict a man just on hearsay.'

"And they'll all feel good, and American, and virtuous, and besides they still need another five thousand to finish that swimming pool. And the next thing you know a delegation will call on your father, and within another six months he'll be the chairman of the Annual Dance Committee."

She grinned when I finished. "I'll be sure to tell Dad."

And don't forget to mention who gave you the idea, I thought. I put the spare in the trunk and wiped my hands on a rag. This time I looked at her longer, bolder. I grinned faintly. "I still wish you only worked here."

Then I got into my car and drove away, not pausing to look back.

I thought I had played things just about right. I didn't press the situation, yet I thought that she would spend some time thinking about me.

After I told Captain Parker how I'd taken over Willkie's territory, he frowned. "But we know that both Binardi and Willkie worked for Magnus. It's in the files we gave you to study. You should have remembered that."

I grinned. "I did."

"Then why ... ?"

"Because it was time for me to get noticed again. To move up another notch. And I did just that."

Parker rubbed his jaw. "What did Magnus think about it?"

"He wasn't too happy at first, and maybe he's not enthusiastic now. But the point is that he was impressed."

Parker sighed. "You have a lot of luck."

"Maybe so. Tyler seems to think I've got possibilities. As a matter of fact, I might not have been able to make it if Tyler hadn't been on my side."

Parker still looked unhappy. "Why don't you let us know before you do any of these crazy things?"

"I never really *know* what I'm going to do next. I make plans and wait for the situation. If it doesn't show up, I forget them. But if it does come up, I have to act fast."

Something else bothered Parker. "We can have you stealing cars, because we're working on a bigger thing. But this kidnapping . . ."

"There wasn't any kidnapping."

"Not actually, I suppose, but still if Willkie had some other trade and could be in a position to complain, you'd get yourself into trouble we couldn't get you out of."

He took an envelope out of his pocket. "Your check. If you'll endorse it, I'll bank it for you."

I looked at it. One month's pay. Twenty years from now the figures probably wouldn't be much different.

I turned it over and signed my real name.

When I got back to the city, I had Willkie's chief clerk bring in the books. I went over them, hoping to find something wrong, something I could run to tell Magnus about and get another gold star in my record, but the books were clean.

I did notice something else though. Even if there were nothing wrong with the books, the handwriting had changed abruptly eighteen months ago.

I called the clerk back into the office and wanted to know why.

"That was when Fielding retired, sir," he said. "And I took over the job. Is there something wrong with the books?"

"No."

"Fielding was a very sick man, sir. His kidneys. You might say that he didn't exactly retire; he just wanted to spend his declining days in a warmer climate. California, Sir."

"How is he getting along?"

The clerk sighed. "I received a letter from his wife last week. Fielding passed away."

When the clerk was gone, I lit a cigarette and mulled things over. What the hell, I thought finally, you can't hurt a dead man.

I studied Fielding's handwriting and for a while considered trying to imitate it. But I gave that up. I didn't think anybody was going to be comparing handwriting anyway.

I got some blank paper and copied two of the pages from the account books Fielding had filled out. I kept the items the same, but I changed the figures.

I folded the paper and rubbed it on the floor a few times. I wanted to make it look at least eighteen months old, but it wouldn't have to pass a laboratory test.

At one o'clock I made a call to Magnus' place in Trevor Park. I got a formal voice. "This is the Magnus residence."

"Could I speak to Mr. Magnus?"

"He isn't here, sir. He won't be home until five. Do you wish to leave a message?"

"No." I hung up. Perhaps it was just as well Magnus wasn't in. While I was working on this, I might as well keep something else going too. And make it seem accidental.

I phoned the Magnus place again.

"The Magnus residence," the butler said again.

I hung up without saying a word. Five minutes later I called again and did the same thing.

Eventually the butler would get tired of picking up the phone and having no one to talk to. I thought he'd go to somebody and complain. And since Magnus wasn't there, it would be Valerie.

He must have been a patient man. It wasn't until twelve calls later that I finally heard Valerie's voice.

"Who *is* this?" she demanded.

"I'd like to speak to Mr. Magnus."

"Have you been phoning every five minutes and then hanging up?"

"Why, no. I just got to my office and . . ." I stopped. "The voice is familiar. Is this the girl who paints?"

"Hagen? Pete Hagen?"

"I didn't think I left the name."

"You didn't. I asked Dad." She laughed lightly. "He sent the first five thousand to the country club. He liked the idea."

"Good. Can I talk to him?"

"He's not here right now."

"Tell him I'll be there around five."

"Now look, Pete ... Hagen. Nobody just *says* that he's coming here. That much I know. You wait until ...."

I hung up.

At a little after five, the patient butler showed me into the study once again. Tyler was with Magnus, and they had evidently just returned from a golf course.

Magnus glowered, but held himself in until the butler closed the door. "Damn it, Hagen, nobody, *nobody* calls up and tells me he's coming here. If I want to see anybody here, *I'm* the one who does the inviting."

"I thought I ought to see you personally. I don't know how clear your phone line is."

He seemed to go along with that precaution, but he still wasn't happy. "All right. What is it?"

I took the sheets out of my pocket. "While I was going over Willkie's books, I found this. It must have slipped behind one of the shelves."

Magnus glanced at them. "So?"

"I checked these with the ledgers and found the right pages. The items are identical, but the figures are different. It looks like you were being taken, Magnus. For about five hundred a week."

He wouldn't believe that. "I have those books checked every month."

"There's nothing wrong with the books. The juggling takes place *before* the entries themselves are made."

He frowned. "Willkie?"

"No. A clerk Willkie used to have, Fielding. I compared the handwriting and it checks."

The name Fielding meant nothing to Magnus or Tyler. He was just another one of hundreds of clerks.

"I thought I'd let you know before I did anything about it," I said. "You told me you wanted things that way."

He studied me. "*You* want to do something about it?"

I nodded. "Fielding retired eighteen months ago. To California. But that isn't good enough for us. I think I'll take a trip out there."

Magnus waited.

"At least we'd have his hide," I said. "If not the money. We can't let anybody in the organization get away with something like this."

"And you'd take care of that little thing yourself?"

"Sure. But I wanted to clear it with you first."

Tyler looked worried, and I thought he'd say something.

But Magnus laughed softly. "Thanks for volunteering. But all I need is Fielding's address. I've got a division that specializes in people like him."

And Magnus would arrange for Fielding to have visitors. But the visitors would discover that he had unfortunately died before they could see him.

But I had scored two points. For one, I could be trusted to keep the books honest. For another, so far as Magnus knew, I was willing to commit murder for the organization.

The phone on Magnus' desk rang and he picked it up. He listened for a minute and then hung up.

His eyes were thoughtful. "Benson's dead."

Tyler and I looked at each other. The name didn't mean a thing to either one of us.

"Heart attack," Magnus said. "Went just like that." He puffed his cigar and finally looked at Tyler. "You once mentioned that you had some kind of a degree in accounting?"

Tyler nodded.

Magnus let things ride for a quiet half a minute. Then he said. "Tyler, you got the job."

"The job?"

"Benson's job," Magnus said. "It's a promotion, Tyler. You'll be the only one beside me who knows where central bookkeeping ..." He stopped and looked my way. Evidently he had forgotten I was still there. "You can go now, Hagen."

Outside the room, I walked past doors to the front of the house. None of them opened.

I began to wonder about Valerie. I'd made the phone call specifically so that she'd know I'd be here, and when.

At my car I waited. Still nothing.

I'd been wrong before in my life, and this looked like another time.

I got into my car and drove down the winding drive.

Valerie waited at the gate. She gave the hitchhiker's sign, and I slowed the car to a stop.

She smiled. "Hello."

"Hello."

"How about a lift?"

I rubbed my hand along the steering wheel and tried to look uneasy. "Car break down?"

"No." She smiled. "Are you afraid of something?"

I took a breath. "No. Get in."

I waited until we were out of Trevor Park before I said anything. "How will you get back?"

"I'll take a taxi."

"Wouldn't it have been much simpler if you'd just take your car?"

"I walked down to get the mail. There wasn't any, so I decided to go to town. Flash of the moment type of thing."

"Does the mail come this late in the day?"

She looked at me. "Did you think that I deliberately waited for you to come along?"

I didn't say anything.

She stiffened. "You might as well stop right here. I'll *walk* the rest of the way."

I slowed the car down to about twenty and then stepped on the accelerator again. I sighed. "Care for a cigarette?" I took the pack and lighter out of my pocket and handed it to her.

She lit two cigarettes and passed one on to me. "Suppose I weren't Magnus' daughter?"

"Maybe I'd ask you for a date. Maybe."

"Why?"

"What do you mean, 'why'?"

Her eyes were level. "I have a mirror. People don't ask me for dates."

I stared at her as though I didn't have the faintest idea of what she was talking about.

"Watch the road," she said. But she had blushed, and she was pleased.

I got the car back into my lane. "You wouldn't happen to

know if there's a good restaurant in town? I haven't had anything to eat since breakfast."

"There's Henrich's"

After a while I asked, "Have you had dinner?"

"No."

This time when I looked at her, I smiled. And so did she.

In the restaurant we kept the talk small, but at coffee she said,
"I wish you didn't work for my father."

"He gives out nice money."

"No, he doesn't." She looked away. "As my father, I love him.
And he loves me. But I know what he does. What he is. I'm not
a little girl who thinks her father's in the investment business."

After I paid the check, I drove her back. At the entrance to
Magnus' estate, she touched my arm. "I'll get out here and walk
the rest of the way."

I had intended to stop here anyway. I didn't want Magnus to
see me with his daughter. But I made the motions of protest.
"I'll take you up to the house."

"No. I think it would be better if we just . . ."

"Sure," I said. "I guess you're right. We're both right. It's
better to say good-by."

"I didn't mean that," she said desperately. "I mean—just for
now."

I stopped the car, got out, and opened her door. She stepped
out, looking small and lonely.

It was evening, and a full pale moon hung in the sky. I looked
down at her. "I like that restaurant, Henrich's. I don't suppose
you'd like another lift to town? Say tomorrow night at eight?"

Her smile was sudden. "I'll be here. I will."

When I drove away, I glanced back. She still stood beside the
road, watching me.

I got back to my apartment at about nine. I made myself a stiff
drink and walked to the mirror. I looked about the way I felt.
A little dirty.

I went to the window and stared out over the lights of the
city. How long would it take before I found out where Magnus
kept that damn bookkeeper's nest? One year? Two?

And then what? Another assignment and a three-figure
check?

I took out my wallet and counted the money. Nineteen hundred dollars. And that was just spending money. Something you carried around to keep from feeling insecure. Just for odds and ends.

But I'd never had that much in my wallet before. I'd never expected to.

I had a good deal going here. Suppose I kept it that way?

Suppose I told Captain Parker to go to hell.

I swallowed half the drink.

There was a lot of money to be made with Magnus. A lot. But there was something else too. Just working for him was one thing, but suppose . . . suppose . . .

It could be done, I thought. Get Magnus to see me more often. Get *him* to invite me to his house. Like Tyler. Get Magnus to trust me completely. Depend on me.

Make it so that when he saw what was happening between Valerie and me, it wouldn't bother him at all. Maybe I could even get him to think that it was his own idea.

Yes. It would take time. But I could sell it.

And what about Parker?

There wasn't much he could really do except to let Magnus know why I had gotten into the organization in the first place.

How could I get Magnus really to believe that I'd switched sides? How could I convince him? How?

My phone rang.

It was Tyler. "Hagen? I'm at the Carson Hotel in Bellington. That's about an hour's drive north of where you are. I'd like to see you right away. Room 408."

When I got there and knocked, Tyler opened the door. I noticed a bottle and two glasses on the table.

Tyler patted me on the shoulder. "Come on in and help me celebrate."

I closed the door behind me. "Sure. Your promotion."

He grinned. "I just finished inspecting Magnus' central book-keeping headquarters. It's right here in Bellington. The front is the Spencer Insurance Agency. The complete books are there, Hagen. Everything."

I frowned. "I thought that kind of information was something you were supposed to keep under your hat."

Tyler laughed again. "There's no reason why I can't tell you, Hagen. We're both working for the same organization."

"I know. But . . ."

Tyler's face became serious. "Hagen, did you think that in something this big, Captain Parker would have only *one* man working on the job?"

I stared at him.

"There are at least a half dozen besides you and me, Hagen. I don't know who the others are, but I was told about you."

It took a little while for what he said to sink in. I shook my head. "Why didn't Parker tell me about you? Or the others?"

"Because if something went wrong, he didn't want any single man to pull down all the rest."

"But still he told *you* about me."

"Because I was in a position to help you along. Did you think that you alone made all your luck? You might still be stealing cars if I hadn't been there to keep calling you to Magnus' attention.

He poured whiskey into two glasses. "I've been on this assignment for five years, Hagen. And that's a long, long time. But it looked like I'd gotten into a dead end. So my instructions were to help you along whenever I could—try to get you to the top, and maybe you could do what I hadn't been able to. And then this good thing came along. Benson died. Luck? Sure. But it wasn't luck that I was up there for Magnus to tap on the shoulder."

I took one of the glasses and almost emptied it. "Have you told Captain Parker about the books?"

"Not yet. I phoned his office and got referred to his home. But his daughter told me that Parker and his wife went out for the evening. She didn't know where they went. I left a message for him to call here just as soon as he gets home." Tyler lifted his glass in a toast. "Parker will get his squads busy, and we ought to have this thing wrapped up before morning."

I stared at the liquor in my glass. No one knew about the books yet, but Tyler.

He frowned slightly. "About this clerk, Fielding. We've got to stop that. We don't want anything to happen to him."

"Fielding died about two weeks ago."

Tyler grinned slowly. "You're a smart operator, Hagen. For a while there you had me worried. Murder's going too far."

Is it? I smiled faintly to myself.

I would kill tyler. I would kill him and tell Magnus who he was. What he had been.

And then I would tell him who *I* was—and that I'd changed sides.

Even then he might not believe me—until I told him I knew where central bookkeeping headquarters was and hadn't gone to the department with the information.

I reached for the bottle and filled my glass.

"Easy on the liquor, Hagen," Tyler said. "You want to be on your feet for the raid, don't you?"

"Sure." But I took another long drink.

The phone on the table rang. When Tyler picked it up, his back was toward me.

I slipped the .38 out of my holster, leveled it at Tyler's back.

Tyler spoke into the mouthpiece. "Parker?"

I found myself perspiring. Just one shot, and it would all be over. It could be as simple as that. My finger touched the trigger.

And then I closed my eyes.

No. I couldn't do it.

I cursed myself for being a fool. A sucker. But I slipped the .38 back into the holster.

Someday I would figure out why a badge was more important than a million dollars, but I didn't want to work on it now.

When Tyler was through he turned. "It's all set. Parker's getting the wheels moving. He's even going to pick up Magnus tonight."

A reflective haze came into Tyler's eyes, and he grinned wryly. "There's a lot of money to be made with Magnus. There were times . . . well . . . you know . . . there were times when I was a little tempted to change sides."

I pulled a cigarette slowly from my pack. "Yeah. I know what you mean."

I parked and waited outside the car. The road ahead was white with moonlight.

There wasn't any reason for being here, I thought. Not now.

I glanced at my watch. Eight-fifteen.

Then I heard the footsteps, and in a moment Valerie stood at the gates.

She was a nobody now, I told myself savagely. She didn't mean millions. She didn't mean information I wanted.

And yet I was here.

She walked slowly to the car. "Why did you come?"

"I don't know." Was it pity?

"Everything was planned, wasn't it? Meeting me? Talking to me?"

"Yes, I planned it."

"You didn't have to come back now," she said. "Everything has been done."

"I know."

"Did you travel all this way just to say good-by?"

I touched her face lightly, and she began to cry.

I held her and I knew why I'd come back.

The Other Celia

Theodore Sturgeon

If you live in a cheap enough rooming house and the doors are made of cheap enough pine, and the locks are old-fashioned single-action jobs and the hinges are loose, and if you have a hundred and ninety lean pounds to operate with, you can grasp the knob, press the door sidewise against its hinges, and slip the latch. Further, you can lock the door the same way when you come out.

Slim Walsh lived in, and was, and had, and did these things partly because he was bored. The company doctors had laid him up—not off, up—for three weeks (after his helper had hit him just over the temple with a fourteen-inch crescent wrench) pending some more X-rays. If he was going to get just sick-leave pay, he wanted to make it stretch. If he was going to get a big fat settlement—all to the good; what he saved by living in this firetrap would make the money look even better. Meanwhile, he felt fine and had nothing to do all day.

"Slim isn't dishonest," his mother used to tell Children's Court some years back. "He's just curious."

She was perfectly right.

Slim was constitutionally incapable of borrowing your bathroom without looking into your medicine chest. Send him into your kitchen for a saucer and when he came out a minute later,

299

he'd have inventoried your refrigerator, your vegetable bin, and (since he was six feet three inches tall) he would know about a moldering jar of maraschino cherries in the back of the top shelf that you'd forgotten about.

Perhaps Slim, who was not impressed by his impressive size and build, felt that a knowledge that you secretly use hair-restorer, or are one of those strange people who keeps a little mound of unmated socks in your second drawer, gave him a kind of superiority. Or maybe security is a better word. Or maybe it was an odd compensation for one of the most advanced cases of gawking, gasping shyness ever recorded.

Whatever it was, Slim liked you better if, while talking to you, he knew how many jackets hung in your closet, how old that unpaid phone bill was, and just where you'd hidden those photographs. On the other hand, Slim didn't insist on knowing bad or even embarrassing things about you. He just wanted to know things about you, period.

His current situation was therefore a near-paradise. Flimsy doors stood in rows, barely sustaining vacuum on aching vacuum of knowledge; and one by one they imploded at the nudge of his curiosity. He touched nothing (or if he did, he replaced it carefully) and removed nothing, and within a week he knew Mrs. Koyper's roomers far better than she could, or cared to. Each secret visit to the rooms gave him a starting point; subsequent ones taught him more. He knew not only what these people had, but what they did, where, how much, *for* how much, and how often. In almost every case, he knew why as well.

Almost every case. Celia Sarton came.

Now, at various times, in various places, Slim had found strange things in other people's rooms. There was an old lady in one shabby place who had an electric train under her bed; used it, too. There was an old spinster in this very building who collected bottles, large and small, of any value or capacity, providing they were round and squat and with long necks. A man on the second floor secretly guarded his desirables with the unloaded .25 automatic in his top bureau drawer, for which he had a half-box of .38 cartridges.

There was a (to be chivalrous) girl in one of the rooms who kept fresh cut flowers before a photograph on her night table

—or, rather, before a frame in which were stacked eight photographs, one of which held the stage each day. Seven days, eight photographs: Slim admired the system. A new love every day and, predictably, a different love on successive Wednesdays. And all of them movie stars.

Dozens of rooms, dozens of imprints, marks, impressions, overlays, atmospheres of people. And they needn't be odd ones. A woman moves into a room, however standardized; the instant she puts down her dusting powder on top of the flush tank, the room is *hers.* Something stuck in the ill-fitting frame of a mirror, something draped over the long-dead gas jet, and the samest of rooms begins to shrink toward its occupant as if it wished, one day, to be a close-knit, form-fitting, individual integument as intimate as a skin.

But not Celia Sarton's room.

Slim Walsh got a glimpse of her as she followed Mrs. Koyper up the stairs to the third floor. Mrs. Koyper, who hobbled, slowed any follower sufficiently to afford the most disinterested witness a good look, and Slim was anything but disinterested. Yet for days he could not recall her clearly. It was as if Celia Sarton had been—not invisible, for that would have been memorable in itself—but translucent or, chameleonlike, drably reradiating the drab wall color, carpet color, woodwork color.

She was—how old? Old enough to pay taxes. How tall? Tall enough. Dressed in . . . whatever women cover themselves with in their statistical thousands. Shoes, hose, skirt, jacket, hat.

She carried a bag. When you go to the baggage window at a big terminal, you notice a suitcase here, a steamer-trunk there; and all around, high up, far back, there are rows and ranks and racks of luggage not individually noticed but just *there.* This bag, Celia Sartons' bag, was one of them.

And to Mrs. Koyper, she said—she said— She said whatever is necessary when one takes a cheap room; and to find her voice, divide the sound of a crowd by the number of people in it.

So anonymous, so unnoticeable was she that, aside from being aware that she left in the morning and returned in the evening, Slim let two days go by before he entered her room; he simply could not remind himself about her. And when he did, and had inspected it to his satisfaction, he had his hand on the knob, about to leave, before he recalled that the room was, after all, occupied. Until that second, he had thought he was giving one of the vacancies the once-over. (He did this regularly; it gave him a reference point.)

He grunted and turned back, flicking his gaze over the room. First he had to assure himself that he was in the right room, which, for a man of his instinctive orientations, was extraordinary. Then he had to spend a moment of disbelief in his own eyes, which was all but unthinkable. When that passed, he stood in astonishment, staring at the refutation of everything his—hobby—had taught him about people and the places they live in.

The bureau drawers were empty. The ashtray was clean. No toothbrush, toothpaste, soap. In the closet, two wire hangers and one wooden one covered with dirty quilted silk, and nothing else. Under the grime-gray dresser scarf, nothing. In the shower stall, the medicine chest, nothing and nothing again, except what Mrs. Koyper had grudgingly installed.

Slim went to the bed and carefully turned back the faded coverlet. Maybe she slept in it, but very possibly not; Mrs. Koyper specialized in unironed sheets of such a ground-in gray that it wasn't easy to tell. Frowning, Slim put up the coverlet again and smoothed it.

Suddenly he struck his forehead, which yielded him a flash of pain from his injury. He ignored it. "The bag!"

It was under the bed, shoved there, not hidden there. He looked at it without touching it for a moment, so that it could be returned exactly. Then he hauled it out.

It was a black gladstone, neither new nor expensive, of that nondescript rusty color acquired by untended leatherette. It had a worn zipper closure and was not locked. Slim opened it. It contained a cardboard box, crisp and new, for a thousand virgin sheets of cheap white typewriter paper surrounded by a glossy bright blue band bearing a white diamond with the legend: *Nonpareil the writers friend 15% cotton fiber trade mark registered.*

Slim lifted the paper out of the box, looked under it, riffled a thumbful of the sheets at the top and the same from the bottom, shook his head, replaced the paper, closed the box, put it back into the bag and restored everything precisely as he had found it. He paused again in the middle of the room, turning slowly once, but there was simply nothing else to look at. He let himself out, locked the door, and went silently back to his room.

He sat down on the edge of his bed and at last protested, "Nobody *lives* like that!"

His room was on the fourth and topmost floor of the old house. Anyone else would have called it the worst room in the place. It was small, dark, shabby and remote and it suited him beautifully.

Its door had a transom, the glass of which had many times been painted over. By standing on the foot of his bed, Slim could apply one eye to the peephole he had scratched in the paint and look straight down the stairs to the thirdfloor landing. On this landing, hanging to the stub of one of the ancient gas jets, was a cloudy mirror surmounted by a dust-mantled gilt eagle and surrounded by a great many rococo carved flowers. By careful propping with folded cigarette wrappers, innumerable tests and a great deal of silent mileage up and down the stairs, Slim had arranged the exact tilt necessary in the mirror so that it covered the second floor landing as well. And just as a radar operator learns to translate glowing pips and masses into aircraft and weather, so Slim became expert at the interpretation of the fogged and distant image it afforded him. Thus he had the comings and goings of half the tenants under surveillance without having to leave his room.

It was in this mirror, at twelve minutes past six, that he saw Celia Sarton next, and as he watched her climb the stairs, his eyes glowed.

The anonymity was gone. She came up the stairs two at a time, with a gait like bounding. She reached the landing and whirled into her corridor and was gone, and while a part of Slim's mind listened for the way she opened the door (hurriedly, rattling the key against the lock-plate, banging the door open, slamming it shut), another part studied a mental photograph of her face.

What raised its veil of the statistical ordinary was its set purpose. Here were eyes only superficially interested in cars, curbs, stairs, doors. It was as if she had projected every important part of herself into that empty room of hers and waited there impatiently for her body to catch up. There was something in the room, or something she had to do there, which she could not, would not, wait for. One goes this way to a beloved after a long parting, or to a deathbed in the last, precipitous moments. This was not the arrival of one who wants, but of one who needs.

Slim buttoned his shirt, eased his door open and sidled through it. He poised a moment on his landing like a great moose sensing the air before descending to a waterhole, and then moved downstairs.

Celia Sarton's only neighbor in the north corridor—the spinster with the bottles—was settled for the evening; she was of very regular habits and Slim knew them well.

Completely confident that he would not be seen, he drifted to the girl's door and paused.

She was there, all right. He could see the light around the edge of the ill-fitting door, could sense that difference between an occupied room and an empty one, which exists however silent the occupant might be. And this one *was* silent. Whatever it was that had driven her into the room with such headlong urgency, whatever it was she was doing (*had* to do) was being done with no sound or motion that he could detect.

For a long time—six minutes, seven—Slim hung there, open-throated to conceal the sound of his breath. At last, shaking his head, he withdrew, climbed the stairs, let himself into his own room and lay down on the bed, frowning.

He could only wait. Yet he *could* wait. No one does any single thing for very long. Especially a thing not involving movement. In an hour, in two—

It was five. At half-past eleven, some faint sound from the floor below brought Slim half-dozing, twisting up from the bed and to his high peephole in the transom. He saw the Sarton girl come out of the corridor slowly, and stop, and look around at nothing in particular, like someone confined too long in a ship's cabin who has emerged on deck, not so much for the lungs' sake, but for the eyes'. And when she went down the stairs, it was easily and without hurry, as if (again) the important part of her was in the room. But the something was finished with for now and what was ahead of her wasn't important and could wait.

Standing with his hand on his own doorknob, Slim decided that he, too, could wait. The temptation to go straight to her

room was, of course, large, but caution also loomed. What he
had tentatively established as her habit patterns did not include
midnight exits. He could not know when she might come back
and it would be foolish indeed to jeopardize his hobby—not
only where it included her, but all of it—by being caught. He
sighed, mixing resignation with anticipatory pleasure, and went
to bed.

Less than fifteen minutes later, he congratulated himself with
a sleepy smile as he heard her slow footsteps mount the stairs
below. He slept.

There was nothing in the closet, there was nothing in the
ashtray, there was nothing in the medicine chest nor under the
dresser scarf. The bed was made, the dresser drawers were
empty, and under the bed was the cheap gladstone. In it was
the box containing a thousand sheets of typing paper surrounded by a glossy blue band. Without disturbing this, Slim
riffled the sheets, once at the top, once at the bottom. He
grunted, shook his head and then proceeded, automatically but
meticulously, to put everything back as he had found it.

"Whatever it is this girl does at night," he said glumly, "it
leaves tracks like it makes noise."

He left.

The rest of the day was unusually busy for Slim. In the morning he had a doctor's appointment, and in the afternoon he
spent hours with a company lawyer who seemed determined to
(a) deny the existence of any head injury and (b) prove to Slim
and the world that the injury must have occurred years ago. He
got absolutely nowhere. If Slim had another characteristic as
consuming and compulsive as his curiosity, it was his shyness;
these two could stand on one another's shoulders, though, and
still look upward at Slim's stubbornness. It served its purpose.
It took hours, however, and it was after seven when he got
home.

He paused at the third-floor landing and glanced down the
corridor. Celia Sarton's room was occupied and silent. If she
emerged around midnight, exhausted and relieved, then he
would know she had again raced up the stairs to her urgent,
motionless task, whatever it was . . . and here he checked himself. He had long ago learned the uselessness of cluttering up his

busy head with conjectures. A thousand things might happen; in each case, only one would. He would wait, then, and could.

And again, some hours later, he saw her come out of her corridor. She looked about, but he knew she saw very little; her face was withdrawn and her eyes wide and unguarded. Then, instead of going out, she went back into her room.

He slipped downstairs half an hour later and listened at her door, and smiled. She was washing her lingerie at the handbasin. It was a small thing to learn, but he felt he was making progress. It did not explain why she lived as she did, but indicated how she could manage without so much as a spare handkerchief.

Oh, well, maybe in the morning.

In the morning, there was no maybe. He found it, he found it, though he could not know what it was he'd found. He laughed at first, not in triumph but wryly, calling himself a clown. Then he squatted on his heels in the middle of the floor (he would not sit on the bed, for fear of leaving wrinkles of his own on those Mrs. Koyper supplied) and carefully lifed the box of paper out of the suitcase and put it on the floor in front of him.

Up to now, he had contented himself with a quick riffle of the blank paper, a little at the top, a little at the bottom. He had done just this again, without removing the box from the suitcase, but only taking the top off and tilting up the banded ream of *Nonpareil-the-writers-friend.* And almost in spite of itself, his quick eye had caught the briefest flash of pale blue.

Gently, he removed the band, sliding it off the pack of paper, being careful not to slit the glossy finish. Now he could freely riffle the pages, and when he did, he discovered that all of them except a hundred or so, top and bottom, had the same rectangular cut-out, leaving only a narrow margin all the way around. In the hollow space thus formed, something was packed.

He could not tell what the something was, except that it was pale tan, with a tinge of pink, and felt like smooth untextured leather. There was a lot of it, neatly folded so that it exactly fitted the hole in the ream of paper.

He puzzled over it for some minutes without touching it again, and then, scrubbing his fingertips against his shirt until he felt that they were quite free of moisture and grease, he gently worked loose the top corner of the substance and unfolded a layer. All he found was more of the same.

He folded it down flat again to be sure he could, and then brought more of it out. He soon realized that the material was of an irregular shape and almost certainly of one piece, so that folding it into a tight rectangle required care and great skill. Therefore he proceeded very slowly, stopping every now and then to fold it up again, and it took him more than an hour to get enough of it out so that he could identify it.

Identify? It was completely unlike anything he had ever seen before.

It was a human skin, done in some substance very like the real thing. The first fold, the one which had been revealed at first, was an area of the back, which was why it showed no features. One might liken it to a balloon, except that a deflated balloon is smaller in every dimension than an inflated one. As far as Slim could judge, this was life-sized—a little over five feet long and proportioned accordingly. The hair was peculiar, looking exactly like the real thing until flexed, and then revealing itself to be one piece.

It had Celia Sarton's face.

Slim closed his eyes and opened them, and found that it was still true. He held his breath and put forth a careful, steady forefinger and gently pressed the left eyelid upward. There was an eye under it, all right, light blue and seemingly moist, but flat.

Slim released the breath, closed the eye and sat back on his heels. His feet were beginning to tingle from his having knelt on the floor for so long.

He looked all around the room once, to clear his head of strangeness, and then began to fold the thing up again. It took a while, but when he was finished, he knew he had it right. He replaced the typewriter paper in the box and the box in the bag, put the bag away and at last stood in the middle of the room in the suspension which overcame him when he was deep in thought.

After a moment of this, he began to inspect the ceiling. It was made of stamped tin, like those of many old-fashioned houses. It was grimy and flaked and stained; here and there, rust showed through, and in one or two places, edges of the tin sheets had sagged. Slim nodded to himself in profound satisfaction, listened for a while at the door, let himself out, locked it and went upstairs.

He stood in his own corridor for a minute, checking the position of doors, the hall window, and his accurate orientation of the same things on the floor below. Then he went into his own room.

His room, though smaller than most, was one of the few in the house which was blessed with a real closet instead of a rickety off-the-floor wardrobe. He went into it and knelt, and grunted in satisfaction when he found how loose the ancient, unpainted floorboards were. By removing the side baseboard, he found it possible to get to the air-space between the fourth floor and the third-floor ceiling.

He took out boards until he had an opening perhaps fourteen inches wide, and then, working in almost total silence, he began cleaning away dirt and old plaster. He did this meticulously, because when he finally pierced the tin sheeting, he wanted not one grain of dirt to fall into the room below. He took his time and it was late in the afternoon when he was satisfied with his preparations and began, with his knife, on the tin.

It was thinner and softer than he had dared to hope; he almost overcut on the first try. Carefully he squeezed the sharp steel into the little slot he had cut, lengthening it. When it was somewhat less than an inch long, he withdrew all but the point of the knife and twisted it slightly, moved it a sixteenth of an inch and twisted again, repeating this all down the cut until he had widened it enough for his purposes.

He checked the time, then returned to Celia Sarton's room for just long enough to check the appearance of his work from that side. He was very pleased with it. The little cut had come through a foot away from the wall over the bed and was a mere pencil line lost in the baroque design with which the tin was stamped and the dirt and rust that marred it. He returned to his room and sat down to wait.

He heard the old house coming to its evening surge of life, a voice here, a door there, footsteps on the stairs. He ignored them all as he sat on the edge of his bed, hands folded between his knees, eyes half closed, immobile like a machine fueled, oiled, tuned and ready, lacking only the right touch on the right control. And like that touch, the faint sound of Celia Sarton's footsteps moved him.

To use his new peephole, he had to lie on the floor half in and half out of the closet, with his head in the hole, actually below floor level. With this, he was perfectly content, any amount of discomfort being well worth his trouble—an attitude he shared with many another ardent hobbyist, mountain-climber or speleologist, duck-hunter or bird-watcher.

When she turned on the light, he could see her splendidly, as well as most of the floor, the lower third of the door and part of the washbasin in the bathroom.

She had come in hurriedly, with that same agonized haste he had observed before. At the same second she turned on the light, she had apparently flung her handbag toward the bed; it was in mid-air as the light appeared. She did not even glance its way, but hastily fumbled the old gladstone from under the bed, opened it, removed the box, opened it, took out the paper, slipped off the blue band and removed the blank sheets of paper which covered the hollowed-out ream.

She scooped out the thing hidden there, shaking it once like a grocery clerk with a folded paper sack, so that the long limp thing straightened itself out. She arranged it carefully on the worn linoleum of the floor, arms down at the side, legs slightly apart, face up, neck straight. Then she lay down on the floor, too, head-to-head with the deflated thing. She reached up over her head, took hold of the collapsed image of herself about the region of the ears, and for a moment did some sort of manipulation of it against the top of her own head.

Slim heard faintly a sharp, chitinous click, like the sound one makes by snapping the edge of a thumbnail against the edge of a fingernail.

Her hands slipped to the cheeks of the figure and she pulled at the empty head as if testing a connection. The head seemed now to have adhered to hers.

Then she assumed the same pose she had arranged for this other, letting her hands fall wearily to her sides on the floor, closing her eyes.

For a long while, nothing seemed to be happening, except for the odd way she was breathing, very deeply but very slowly, like the slow-motion picture of someone panting, gasping for breath after a long hard run. After perhaps ten minutes of this, the breathing became shallower and even slower, until, at the end of the half hour, he could detect none at all.

Slim lay there immobile for more than an hour, until his body shrieked protest and his head ached from eyestrain. He hated to move, but move he must. Silently he backed out of the closet, stood up and stretched. It was a great luxury and he deeply enjoyed it. He felt moved to think over what he had just seen, but clearly and consciously decided not to—not yet, anyway.

When he was unkinked, again, he crept back into the closet, put his head in the hole and his eye to the slot.

Nothing had changed. She still lay quiet, utterly relaxed, so much so that her hands had turned palm upward.

Slim watched and he watched. Just as he was about to conclude that this was the way the girl spent her entire nights and that there would be nothing more to see, he saw a slight and sudden contraction about the region of her solar plexus, and then another. For a time, there was nothing more, and then the empty thing attached to the top of her head began to fill.

And Celia Sarton began to empty.

Slim stopped breathing until it hurt and watched in total astonishment.

Once it had started, the process progressed swiftly. It was as if something passed from the clothed body of the girl to this naked empty thing. The something, whatever it might be, had to be fluid, for nothing but a fluid would fill a flexible container in just this way, or make a flexible container slowly and evenly flatten out like this. Slim could see the fingers, which had been folded flat against the palms, inflate and move until they took on the normal relaxed curl of a normal hand. The elbows shifted a little to lie more normally against the body. And yes, it was a body now.

The other one was not a body any more. It lay foolishly limp in its garments, its sleeping face slightly distorted by its flattening. The fingers fell against the palms by their own limp weight. The shoes thumped quietly on their sides, heels together, toes pointing in opposite directions.

The exchange was done in less than ten minutes and then the newly filled body moved.

It flexed its hands tentatively, drew up its knees and stretched its legs out again, arched its back against the floor. Its eyes flickered open. It put up its arms and made some deft manipulation at the top of its head. Slim heard another version of the soft-hard click and the now-empty head fell flat to the floor.

The new Celia Sarton sat up and sighed and rubbed her hands lightly over her body, as if restoring circulation and sensation to a chilled skin. She stretched as comfortingly and luxuriously as Slim had a few minutes earlier. She looked rested and refreshed.

At the top of her head, Slim caught a glimpse of a slit through which a wet whiteness showed, but it seemed to be closing. In a brief time, nothing showed there but a small valley in the hair, like a normal parting.

She sighed again and got up. She took the clothed thing on the floor by the neck, raised it and shook it twice to make the clothes fall away. She tossed it to the bed and carefully picked up the clothes and deployed them about the room, the undergarments in the washbasin, the dress and slip on a hanger in the wardrobe.

Moving leisurely but with purpose, she went into the bathroom and, except from her shins down, out of Slim's range of vision. There he heard the same faint domestic sounds he had once detected outside her door, as she washed her underclothes. She emerged in due course, went to the wardrobe for some wire hangers and took them into the bathroom. Back she came with the underwear folded on the hangers, which she hooked to the top of the open wardrobe door. Then she took the deflated integument which lay crumpled on the bed, shook it again, rolled it up into a ball and took it into the bathroom.

Slim heard more water-running and sudsing noises, and, by ear, following the operation through a soaping and two rinses. Then she came out again, shaking out the object, which had apparently just been wrung, pulled it though a wooden clothes-hanger, arranged it creaselessly depending from the crossbar of the hanger with the bar about at its waistline, and hung it with the others on the wardrobe door.

Then she lay down on the bed, not to sleep or to read or even to rest—she seemed very rested—but merely to wait until it was time to do something else.

By now, Slim's bones were complaining again, so he wormed noiselessly backward out of his lookout point, got into his shoes and a jacket, and went out to get something to eat. When he came home an hour later and looked, her light was out and he could see nothing. He spread his overcoat carefully over the hole in the closet so no stray light from his room would appear in the little slot in the ceiling, closed the door, read a comic book for a while, and went to bed.

The next day, he followed her. What strange occupation she might have, what weird vampiric duties she might disclose, he did not speculate on. He was doggedly determined to gather information first and think later.

What he found out about her daytime activities was, if anything, more surprising than any wild surmise. She was a clerk in a small five-and-ten on the East Side. She ate in the store's lunch bar at lunchtime—a green salad and a surprising amount of milk—and in the evening she stopped at a hot-dog stand and drank a small container of milk, though she ate nothing.

Her steps were slowed by then and she moved wearily, speeding up only when she was close to the rooming house, and then apparently all but overcome with eagerness to get home and . . . into something more comfortable. She was watched in this process, and Slim, had he disbelieved his own eyes the first time, must believe them now.

So it went for a week, three days of which Slim spent in shadowing her, every evening in watching her make her strange toilet. Every twenty-four hours, she changed bodies, carefully washing, drying, folding and putting away the one she was not using.

Twice during the week, she went out for what was apparently a constitutional and nothing more—a half-hour around midnight, when she would stand on the walk in front of the rooming house, or wander around the block.

At work, she was silent but not unnaturally so; she spoke, when spoken to, in a small, unmusical voice. She seemed to have no friends; she maintained her aloofness by being uninteresting and by seeking no one out and by needing no one. She evinced no outside interests, never going to the movies or to the park. She had no dates, not even with girls. Slim thought she did not sleep, but lay quietly in the dark waiting for it to be time to get up and go to work.

And when he came to think about it, as ultimately he did, it occurred to Slim that within the anthill in which we all live and have our being, enough privacy can be exacted to allow for all sorts of strangeness in the members of society, providing the strangeness is not permitted to show. If it is a man's pleasure to sleep upsidedown like a bat, and if he so arranges his life that no one ever sees him sleeping, or his sleeping-place, why, bat-like he may sleep all the days of his life.

One need not, by these rules, even *be* a human being. Not if the mimicry is good enough. It is a measure of Slim's odd personality to report that Celia Sarton's ways did not frighten him. He was, if anything, less disturbed by her now than he'd been before he had begun to spy on her. He knew what she did in her room and how she lived. Before, he had not known. Now he did. This made him much happier.

He was, however, still curious.

His curiosity would never drive him to do what another man might—to speak to her on the stairs or on the street, get to know her and more about her. He was too shy for that. Nor was he moved to report to anyone the odd practice he watched every evening. It wasn't his business to report. She was doing no harm as far as he could see. In his cosmos, everybody had a right to live and make a buck if they could.

Yet his curiosity, its immediacy taken care of, did undergo a change. It was not in him to wonder what sort of being this was and whether its ancestors had grown up among human beings, living with them in caves and in tents, developing and evolving along with *homo sap* until it could assume the uniform of the smallest and most invisible of wage-workers. He would never reach the conclusion that in the fight for survival, a species might discover that a most excellent characteristic for survival among human beings might be not to fight them but to join them.

No, Slim's curiosity was far simpler, more basic and less informed than any of these conjectures. He simply changed the field of his wonderment from *what* to *what if?*

So it was that on the eighth day of his survey, a Tuesday, he went again to her room, got the bag, opened it, removed the box, opened it, removed the ream of paper, slid the blue band off, removed the covering sheets, took out the second Celia Sarton, put her on the bed and then replaced paper, blue band, box-cover, box, and bag just as he had found them. He put the folded thing under his shirt and went out, carefully locking the door behind him in his special way, and went upstairs to his room. He put his prize under the four clean shirts in his bottom drawer and sat down to await Celia Sarton's homecoming.

She was a little late that night—twenty minutes, perhaps. The delay seemed to have increased both her fatigue and her eagerness; she burst in feverishly, moved with the rapidity of near-panic. She looked drawn and pale and her hands shook. She fumbled the bag from under the bed, snatched out the box and opened it, contrary to her usual measured movements, by inverting it over the bed and dumping out its contents.

When she saw nothing there but sheets of paper, some with a wide rectangle cut from them and some without, she froze. She crouched over that bed without moving for an interminable two minutes. Then she straightened up slowly and glanced about the room. Once she fumbled through the paper, but resignedly, without hope. She made one sound, a high, sad whimper, and, from that moment on, was silent.

She went to the window slowly, her feet dragging, her shoulders slumped. For a long time, she stood looking out at the city, its growing darkness, its growing colonies of lights, each a symbol of life and life's usages. Then she drew down the blind and went back to the bed.

She stacked the papers there with loose uncaring fingers and put the heap of them on the dresser. She took off her shoes and placed them neatly side by side on the floor by the bed. She lay down in the same utterly relaxed pose she affected when she made her change, hands down and open, legs a little apart.

Her face looked like a death-mask, its tissues sunken and sagging. It was flushed and sick-looking. There was a little of the deep regular breathing, but only a little. There was a bit of fluttering contractions at the midriff, but only a bit. Then— nothing.

Slim backed away from the peephole and sat up. He felt very bad about this. He had been only curious; he hadn't wanted her to get sick, to die. For he was sure she had died. How could he know what sort of sleep-surrogate an organism like this might require, or what might be the results of a delay in changing? What could he know of the chemistry of such a being? He had thought vaguely of slipping down the next day while she was out and returning her property. Just to see. Just to know *what if.* Just out of curiosity.

Should he call a doctor?

She hadn't. She hadn't even tried, though she must have known much better than he did how serious her predicament was. (Yet if a species depended for its existence on secrecy, it would be species-survival to let an individual die undetected.) Well, maybe not calling a doctor meant that she'd be all right, after all. Doctors would have a lot of silly questions to ask. She might even tell the doctor about her other skin, and if Slim was the one who had fetched the doctor, Slim might be questioned about that.

Slim didn't want to get involved with anything. He just wanted to know things.

He thought, "I'll take another look."

He crawled back into the closet and put his head in the hole. Celia Sarton, he knew instantly, would not survive this. Her face was swollen, her eyes protruded, and her purpled tongue lolled far—too far—from the corner of her mouth. Even as he watched, her face darkened still more and the skin of it crinkled until it looked like carbon paper which has been balled up tight and then smoothed out.

The very beginnings of an impulse to snatch the thing she needed out of his shirt drawer and rush it down to her died within him, for he saw a wisp of smoke emerge from her nostrils and then—

Slim cried out, snatched his head from the hole, bumping it cruelly, and clapped his hands over his eyes. Put the biggest size flash-bulb an inch from your nose, and fire it, and you might get a flare approaching the one he got through his little slot in the tin ceiling.

He sat grunting in pain and watching, on the insides of his eyelids, migrations of flaming worms. At last they faded and he tentatively opened his eyes. They hurt and the after-image of the slot hung before him, but at least he could see.

Feet pounded on the stairs. He smelled smoke and a burned, oily unpleasant something which he could not identify. Someone shouted. Someone hammered on a door. Then someone screamed and screamed.

It was in the papers next day. Mysterious, the story said. Charles Fort, in *Lo!*, had reported many such cases and there had been others since—people burned to a crisp by a fierce heat which had nevertheless not destroyed clothes or bedding, while leaving nothing for autopsy. This was, said the paper, either an unknown kind of heat or heat of such intensity and such brevity that it would do such a thing. No known relatives, it said. Police mystified—no clues or suspects.

Slim didn't say anything to anybody. He wasn't curious about the matter any more. He closed up the hole in the closet the same night, and next day, after he read the story, he used the newspaper to wrap up the thing in his shirt drawer. It smelled pretty bad and, even that early, was too far gone to be unfolded. He dropped it into a garbage can on the way to the lawyer's office on Wednesday.

They settled his lawsuit that afternoon and he moved.

An Evening
in Whitechapel

Nancy C. Swoboda

The fog billowed through the narrow cobbled streets and around the corners to wrap Whitechapel in a clammy gray shroud. Even the ribald noises coming from the pub were muffled by the cottonlike mist. The girl standing close to the dimly glowing gas lamp waited for one last possible customer before everything shut down and the night became dangerous. Petulantly, she walked over and peered through the mullioned windows where the men sat laughing and warm, swilling down their pints.

As she went back to her post under the gas lamp she stopped to listen. There were running footsteps coming her way out of the fog. Her eyes grew large, and she could barely make her legs propel her around and to the safety of the pub. When the figure emerged from the swirling mist she sank against the wall and blew out her breath in a sigh of relief. It was a woman of about her own age and, judging from her dress and make-up, the same profession.

"Coo! I must be dotty to be flitting about in this stuff. Now, don't get huffy, dearie. I'm not trying to take your spot. I bloody well swear *he* was after me!"

The first woman, having just regained her composure, went white. "You mean, the Ripper? Oh gawd! Where?"

"I work the area near the Three Sisters pub, and let me tell you, ducks, in this fog, no man's going to dally. There ain't a bobby in sight over there."

"But, they're supposed to be protecting us!"

"Not for a hundred quid would I turn another trick this night. And you'd be smart if you'd close up shop yourself."

"Maybe you're right. Business is off. The men are even spooked for fear they'll get accused of being Jack by just looking sideways at the likes of us."

"Now you're being smart. I've got m'self a pint of brandy here. Want to share it?"

"Why not? Where shall we go?"

"The name's Cleo, dearie. Whose flat's closest?"

"Mine's Mavis. I live four blocks down over on Heathridge."

"Worthley Mews is mine."

"I'm closest. Let's get out of here. I've got the willies. He won't attack two, will he?"

"Never has that I've heard of. Bloody good luck I ran into you. Let's go."

They linked arms and plunged into the fog. The four blocks seemed full of darting shadows and stealthy footfalls, and when they got to Mavis' flat alive, there was real cause to celebrate with the brandy. She lived on the second floor of a frame building, and the stairway ran up the outside. She didn't stop to fish out her key until they were both all the way to the top.

"Whew!" Mavis threw open the door, and they scurried in.

When Mavis turned up the lamps, a cozy little place came to light. There was a sitting room, bedroom and bath, and a small kitchen. The way she had decorated it did not belie the profession of the woman.

"Say luv, I like your digs. It's real homey." Cleo took off her cape and plopped down into an overstuffed chair.

"I never had a home of my own, so this is it. Shall I make us a cuppa to wash down the brandy?"

"Goodo. I'll open the bottle."

Mavis brought the tea and two glasses to the little table in the sitting room, and they drew their chairs up to the business at hand. A coal fire glowed in the grate, and before long they were both mellow and warm.

The contrasting girls—Mavis, pretty, blonde and buxom,

Cleo, dark, thin and intense—watched the fire together, their thoughts hidden from the dancing orange light on their faces.

Mavis poured another healthy slug of brandy into her glass and broke the silence. "And what brought you into our ranks m'lady?" She smiled wryly.

"You might say it was me dear old Daddy."

"You can't mean it." Mavis blinked wide blue eyes.

"I could say it was the likes of you, as well." Cleo's eyes grew darker. "But then, Daddy always had an eye for the ladies. Only looked . . . until *she* came along."

"She?"

"Waltzed into our shop one day, and he went bonkers. It was plain what she was, and he couldn't resist."

"What kind of shop, dearie?"

"A butcher shop. We lived in a flat above. Ate well and all worked together . . . until . . ." Cleo pinched her lips together and began to pound a fist on her knee slowly.

"Now, now. More brandy?" Mavis soothed.

Cleo took a deep breath, and her face relaxed; her hands met and folded in her lap. "A drop."

"So your old man ran off with her. But why did you . . . ?"

"Mum and I tried to keep the shop going, but it needed a man. Ever tried waltzing with a side of beef?"

Mavis giggled and took a large drink from her glass.

Cleo fixed her giddy companion with a look of total disgust. "It wasn't so funny for a young girl with no education, no relatives to help . . . a not-so-pretty girl who only knew how to grind meat and cut roasts."

"Coo. I'm sorry. I wasn't laughing at you. So that's when you took to the street?"

"Can you think of any other profession that brings in as much? I tried not to let Mum know what I was about, but you know how hard that would be. She just sort of dried up inside. Died last winter."

Mavis straightened up as if to shake off the brandy's hazy effects and tried to offer a philosophical question. "Who's to blame, then? Dear old Daddy? The tart who ran off with him? Or you for becoming what you are?"

Cleo stared into the fire as she spoke. Her voice was low and emotional. "You are to blame. I am to blame. Our kind is to blame. Mum never put it on me for what I had to do. I promised her I'd make it right."

Mavis shrugged as if to accept her share of guilt. "I never had a family to get hurt or cry over. Did scullery work until I found my favors to the men paid more, and frankly dearie, I like the men."

"Who's the bloke in the picture over there? Guess it isn't your pop." Cleo pointed at a distinguished-looking man with a handlebar mustache in a gold-filigreed frame.

"That's a gentleman friend of mine. He's got a family, but we've got an understanding. He lives his life, and I live mine. We just have a regular arrangement."

"Neat. Does he give you a little for the pot?"

"Enough so's if I don't feel up to being out on the street I don't have to worry about bed and board."

"Shades of dear old Daddy," Cleo snorted. "Next thing you know he'll be wanting to leave his shoes under your bed permanent."

"Who knows, ducks? Who knows? You got a nice flat, Cleo? I hope you've got a nice flat." Mavis was becoming maudlin from the hot tea and brandy combination.

"It's fit enough. Digs ain't much for me. Speaking of digs . . . I'd better tootle off pretty soon." She got up and drew aside a lace curtain. "A bit thick."

Mavis got up and looked out. "Not in that pea souper! I won't let you. You can jolly well put up here till dawn."

"It's for sure no one's waiting by the hearth. I guess I could stay. I don't relish the thought of running into old Jack. This is his kind of night, all right." Cleo shuddered and dropped the curtain.

"It's settled. I'll get you a pillow and a robe."

"No. This overstuffed is super. I can sleep sitting up quite nicely. Don't bother. Just get yourself easy. Here. Finish the last of the bottle, and call it a night."

Mavis changed into her gown, came out and downed the last of the brandy and went weaving back into her bedroom.

"Good night, Cleo," she called over her shoulder. "See you in the morning."

"Good night, Mavis. Good night."

It was not long before Mavis was snoring evenly and deeply.

It was so much better when the victim didn't have to be subdued. Just get on with it.

Later, Cleo stepped back to look at her work. Satisfied, she wiped the butcher knife on the bedclothes. For a moment she paused, looked up and said softly, "The Ripper's done in another one for you, Mum. Rest easy."

With the knife again sheathed on the outer side of her thigh, Cleo put on her cape and went fearlessly out into the Whitechapel fog.

Wile Versus Guile

Arthur Train

It was a mouse by virtue of which Ephraim Tutt had leaped into
fame. It is true that other characters famous in song and story
—particularly in "Mother Goose"—have similarly owed their
celebrity in whole or part to rodents, but there is, it is submitted, no other case of a mouse, as mouse *per se*, reported in the
annals of the law, except Tutt's mouse, from Doomsday Book
down to the present time.

Yet it is doubtful whether without his mouse Ephraim Tutt
would ever have been heard of at all, and same would equally
have been true if when pursued by the chef's gray cat the
mouse aforesaid had jumped in another direction. But as luck
would have it, said mouse leaped foolishly into an open casserole upon a stove in the kitchen of the Comers Hotel, and Mr.
Tutt became in his way a leader of the bar.

It is quite true that the tragic end of the mouse in question
has nothing to do with our present narrative except as a side-
light upon the vagaries of the legal career, but it illustrates how
an attorney, if he expects to succeed in his profession, must be
ready for anything that comes along—even if it be a mouse.

The two Tutts composing the firm of Tutt & Tutt were both,
at the time of the mouse case, comparatively young men. Tutt
was a native of Bangor, Maine, and numbered among his child-

hood friends one Newbegin, a commercial wayfarer in the shingle and clapboard line; and as he hoped at some future time to draw Newbegin's will or to incorporate for him some business venture Tutt made a practise of entertaining his prospective client at dinner upon his various visits to the metropolis, first at one New York hostelry and then at another.

Chance led them one night to the Comers, and there amid the imitation palms and imitation French waiters of the imitation French restaurant Tutt invited his friend Newbegin to select what dish he chose from those upon the bill of fare; and Newbegin chose kidney stew. It was at about that moment that the adventure which has been referred to occurred in the hotel kitchen. The gray cat was cheated of its prey, and in due course the casserole containing the stew was borne into the dining room and the dish was served.

Suddenly Mr. Newbegin contorted his mouth and exclaimed: "Heck! A mouse!"

It was. The head waiter was summoned, the manager; the owner. Guests and garçons crowded about Tutt and Mr. Newbegin to inspect what had so unexpectedly been found. No one could deny that it was mouse—cooked mouse; and Newbegin had ordered kidney stew. Then Tutt had had his inspiration.

"You shall pay well for this!" he cried, frowning at the distressed proprietor, while Newbegin leaned piteously against a papier-mâché pillar. "This is an outrage! You shall be held liable in heavy damages for my client's indigestion!"

And thus Tutt & Tutt got their first case out of Newbegin, for under the influence of the eloquence of Mr. Tutt a jury was induced to given him a verdict of one thousand dollars against the Comers Hotel, which the Court of Appeals sustained in the following words, quoting verbatim from the learned brief furnished by Tutt & Tutt, Ephraim Tutt of counsel:

"The only legal question in the case, or so it appears to us, is whether there is such a sale of food to a guest on the part of the proprietor as will sustain a warranty. If we are not in error, however, the law is settled and has been since the reign of Henry the Sixth. In the Ninth Year Book of that Monarch's reign there is a case in which it was held that 'if I go to a tavern to eat, and the taverner gives and sells me meat and it corrupted, whereby I am made very sick, action lies against him without any express warranty, for there is a warranty in law'; and in the time of Henry the Seventh the learned Justice Keilway said, 'No man can justify selling corrupt victual, but an action on the case lies against the seller, whether the victual was warranted to be good or not.' Now, certainly, whether mouse meat be or be not deleterious to health a guest at a hotel who orders a portion of kidney stew has the right to expect, and the hotel keeper impliedly warrants, that such dish will contain no ingredients beyond those ordinarily placed therein."

"A thousand dollars!" exulted Tutt when the verdict was rendered. "Why, anyone would eat mouse for a thousand dollars!"

The Comers Hotel became in due course a client of Tutt & Tutt, and the mouse which made Mr. Tutt famous did not die in vain, for the case became celebrated throughout the length and breadth of the land, to the glory of the firm and a vast improvement in the culinary conditions existing in hotels.

"Come in, Mr. Barrows! Come right in! I haven't seen you for —well, how long is it?" exclaimed Mr. Tutt, extending a long welcoming arm toward a human scarecrow upon the threshold.

"Five years," answered the visitor. "I only got out day before yesterday. Fourteen months off for good behavior."

He coughed and put down carefully beside him a large dress-suit case marked E. V. B., Pottsville, N.Y.

"Well, well!" sighed Mr. Tutt. "So it is. How time flies!"

"Not in Sing Sing!" replied Mr. Barrows ruefully.

"I suppose not. Still, it must feel good to be out!"

Mr. Barrows made no reply but dusted off his felt hat. He was but the shadow of a man, an old man at that, as was attested by his long gray beard, his faded blue eyes, and the thin white hair about his fine domelike forehead.

"I forget what your trouble was about," said Mr. Tutt gently. "Won't you have a stogy?"

Mr. Barrows shook his head.

"I ain't used to it," he answered. "Makes me cough." He gazed about him vaguely.

"Something about bonds, wasn't it?" asked Mr. Tutt.

"Yes," replied Mr. Barrows; "Great Lakes and Canadian Southern."

"Of course! Of course!"

"A wonderful property," murmured Mr. Barrows regretfully. "The bonds were perfectly good. There was a defect in the foreclosure proceedings which made them a permanent underlying security of the reorganized company—under The Northern Pacific R. R. Co. vs. Boyd; you know—but the court refused to hold that way. They never will hold the way you want, will they?" He looked innocently at Mr. Tutt.

"No," agreed the latter with conviction, "they never will!"

"Now those bonds were as good as gold," went on the old man; "and yet they said I had to go to prison. You know all about it. You were my lawyer."

"Yes," assented Mr. Tutt, "I remember all about it now."

Indeed it had all come back to him with the vividness of a landscape seen during a lightning flash—the crowded court, old Doc Barrows upon the witness stand, charged with getting money on the strength of defaulted and outlawed bonds—picked up heaven knows where—pathetically trying to persuade an unsympathetic court that for some reason they were still worth their face value, though the mortgage securing the debt which they represented had long since been foreclosed and the money distributed.

"I'd paid for 'em—actual cash," he rambled on. "Not much, to be sure—but real money. If I got 'em cheap that was my good luck, wasn't it? It was because my brain was sharper than other folks'! I said they had value and I say so now—only nobody will believe it or take the trouble to find out. I learned a lot up there in Sing Sing too," he continued, warming to his subject. "Do you know, sir, there are fortunes lying all about us? Take gold, for instance! There's a fraction of a grain in every ton of sea water. But the big people don't want it taken out because it would depress the standard of exchange. I say it's a conspiracy—and yet they jailed a man for it! There's great mineral deposits all about just waiting for the right man to come along and develop 'em."

His lifted eye rested upon the engraving of Abraham Lincoln over Mr. Tutt's desk. "There was a man!" he exclaimed inconsequently; then stopped and ran his transparent, heavily veined old hand over his forehead. "Where was I? Let me see. Oh, yes —gold. All those great properties could be bought at one time

or another for a song. It needed a pioneer! That's what I was—
a pioneer to find the gold where other people couldn't find it.
That's not any crime; it's a service to humanity! If only they'd
have a little faith—instead of locking you up. The judge never
looked up the law about those Great Lakes bonds! If he had he'd
have found out I was right! I'd looked it up. I studied law once
myself."

"I know," said Mr. Tutt, almost moved to tears by the sight
of the wreck before him. "You practised upstate, didn't you?"

"Yes," responded Doc Barrows eagerly. "And in Chicago too.
I'm a member of the Cook County bar. I'll tell you something!
If the Supreme Court of Illinois hadn't been wrong in its law I'd
be the richest man in the world—in the whole world!" He
grabbed Mr. Tutt by the arm and stared hard into his eyes.
"Didn't I show you my papers? I own seven feet of water front
clean round Lake Michigan all through the city of Chicago. I got
it for a song from the man who found out the flaw in the original
title deed of 1817; he was dying. 'I'll sell my secret to you,' he
says, 'because I'm passing on. May it bring you luck!' I looked
it all up and it was just as he said. So I got up a corporation—
The Chicago Water Front and Terminal Company—and sold
bonds to fight my claim in the courts. But all the people who
had deeds to my land conspired against me and had me arrested! They sent me to the penitentiary. There's justice for
you!"

"That was too bad!" said Mr. Tutt in a soothing voice. "But
after all what good would all that money have done you?"

"I don't want money!" affirmed Doc plaintively. "I've never
needed money. I know enough secrets to make me rich a dozen
times over. Not money but justice is what I want—my legal
rights. But I'm tired of fighting against 'em. They've beaten me!
Yes, they've beaten me! I'm going to retire. That's why I came
in to see you, Mr. Tutt. I never paid you for your services as my
attorney. I'm going away. You see my married daughter lost her
husband the other day and she wants me to come up and live
with her on the farm to keep her from being lonely. Of course
it won't be much like life in Wall Street—but I owe her some
duty and I'm getting on—I am, Mr. Tutt, I really am!"

He smiled.

"And I haven't seen Louisa for three years—my only daughter. I shall enjoy being with her. She was such a dear little girl! I'll tell you another secret"—his voice dropped to a whisper— "I've found out there's a gold mine on her farm, only she doesn't know it. A rich vein runs through her cow pasture. We'll be rich! Wouldn't it be fine, Mr. Tutt, to be rich? Then I'm going to pay you in real money for all you've done for me—thousands! But until then I'm going to let you have these—all my securities; my own, you know, every one of them.

He placed the suitcase in front of Mr. Tutt and opened the clasps with his shaking old fingers. It bulged with bonds, and he dumped them forth until they covered the top of the desk.

"These are my jewels!" he said. "There's millions represented here!" He lifted one tenderly and held it to the light, fresh as it came from the engraver's press—a thousand dollar first-mortgage bond of The Chicago Water Front and Terminal Company. "Look at that! Good as gold—if the courts only knew the law."

He took up a yellow package of valueless obligations, upon the top of which an old-fashioned locomotive, from whose bell-shaped funnel the smoke poured in picturesque black clouds, dragging behind it a chain of funny little passenger coaches, drove furiously along beside a rushing river through fields rich with corn and wheat amid a border of dollar signs.

"The Great Lakes and Canadian Southern," he crooned lovingly. "The child of my heart! The district attorney kept all the rest—as evidence, he claimed, but some day you'll see he'll bring an action against the Lake Shore or the New York Central based on these bonds. Yes, sir! They're all right!"

He pawed them over, picking out favorites here and there and excitedly extolling the merits of the imaginary properties they represented. There were the repudiated bonds of Southern states and municipalities; of railroads upon whose tracks no wheel had ever turned; of factories never built except in Doc Barrows' addled brain; of companies which had defaulted and given stock for their worthless obligations; certificates of oil, mining and land companies; deeds to tracts now covered with skyscrapers in Pittsburgh, St. Louis and New York—each and every one of them not worth the paper they were printed on except to some crook who dealt in high finance. But they were exquisitely engraved, quite lovely to look at, and Doc Barrows gloated upon them with scintillating eyes.

"Ain't they beauties?" he sighed. "Some day—yes, sir!—some day they'll be worth real money. I paid it for some of 'em. But they're yours—all yours."

He gathered them up with care and returned them to the suitcase, then fastened the clasps and patted the leather cover with his hand.

"They are yours, sir!" he exclaimed dramatically.

"As you say," agreed Mr. Tutt, "there's gold lying round everywhere if we only had sense enough to look for it. But I think you're wise to retire. After all, you have the satisfaction of knowing that your enterprises were sound even if other people disagreed with you."

"If this was 1819 instead of 1919 I'd own Chicago," began Doc, a gleam appearing in his eye. "But they don't want to upset the status quo—that's why I haven't got a fair chance. But they needn't worry! I'd be generous with 'em—give 'em easy terms—long leases and nominal rents."

"But you'll like living with your daughter, I'm sure," said Mr. Tutt. "It will make a new man of you in no time."

"Healthiest spot in northern New York," exclaimed Doc. "Within two miles of a lake—fishing, shooting, outdoor recreation of all kinds, an ideal site for a mammoth summer hotel."

Mr. Tutt rose and laid his arms round old Doc Barrows' shoulders.

"Thank you a thousand times," he said gratefully, "for the securities. I'll be glad to keep them for you in my vault." His lips puckered in a stealthy smile which he tried hard to conceal.

"Louisa may want to repaper the farmhouse some time," he added to himself.

"Oh, they're all yours to keep!" insisted Doc. "I want you to have them!" His voice trembled.

"Well, well!" answered Mr. Tutt. "Leave it that way; but if you ever should want them they'll be here waiting for you."

"I'm no Indian giver!" replied Doc with dignity. "Give, give, give a thing—never take it back again."

He laughed rather childishly. He was evidently embarrassed.

"Could—could you let me have the loan of seventy-five cents?" he asked shyly.

Down below, inside a doorway upon the other side of the street, Sergeant Murtha of the Detective Bureau waited for Doc Barrows to come out and be arrested again. Murtha had known Doc for fifteen years as a harmless old nut who had rarely succeeded in cheating anybody, but who was regarded as generally undesirable by the authorities and sent away every few years in order to keep him out of mischief. There was no danger that the public would accept Doc's version of the nature or value of his securities, but there was always the chance that some of his worthless bonds—those bastard offsprings of his cracked old brain—would find their way into less honest but saner hands. So Doc rattled about from penitentiary to prison and from prison to madhouse and out again, constantly taking appeals and securing writs of habeas corpus, and feeling mildly resentful, but not particularly so, that people should be so interfering with his business. Now as from force of long habit he peered out of the doorway before making his exit; he looked like one of the John Sargent's prophets gone a little madder than usual—a Jeremiah or a Habakkuk.

"Hello, Doc!" called Murtha in hearty, friendly tones. "Hie spy! Come on out!"

"Oh, how d'ye do, captain!" responded Doc. "How are you? I was just interviewing my solicitor."

"Sorry," said Murtha. "The inspector wants to see you."

Doc flinched.

"But they've just let me go!" he protested faintly.

"It's one of those old indictments—Chicago Water Front or something. Anyhow— Here! Hold on to yourself!"

He threw his arms around the old man, who seemed on the point of falling.

"Oh, captain! That's all over! I served time for that out in Illinois!" For some strange reason all the insanity had gone out of his bearing.

"Not in this state," answered Murtha. New pity for this poor old wastrel took hold upon him. "What were you going to do?"

"I was going to retire, captain," said Doc faintly. "My daughter's husband—he owned a farm up in Cayuga County—well, he died and I was planning to go up there and live with her."

"And sting all the boobs?" grinned Murtha not unsympathetically. "How much money have you got?"

"Seventy-five cents."

"How much is the ticket?"

"About nine dollars," quavered Doc. "But I know a man down on Chatham Square who might buy a block of stock in the Last Chance Gold Mining Company; I could get the money that way."

"What's the Last Chance Gold Mining Company?" asked Murtha sharply.

"It's a company I'm going to organize. I'll tell you a secret, Murtha. There's a vein of gold runs right through my daughter Louisa's cow pasture—she doesn't know anything about it—"

"Oh, hell!" exclaimed Murtha, "Come along to the station. I'll let you have the nine bones. And you can put me down for half a million of the underwriting."

That same evening Mr. Tutt was toasting his carpet slippers before the sea-coal fire in his library, sipping a hot toddy and rereading for the eleventh time the "Lives of the Chancellors" when Miranda, who had not yet finished washing the few dishes incident to her master's meager supper, pushed open the door and announced that a lady was calling.

"She said you'd know her sho' enough, Mis' Tutt," grinned Miranda, swinging her dishrag, " 'cause you and she used to live tergidder when you was a young man."

This scandalous announcement did not have the startling effect upon the respectable Mr. Tutt which might naturally have been anticipated, since he was quite used to Miranda's forms of expression.

"It must be Mrs. Effingham," he remarked, closing the career of Lord Eldon and removing his feet from the fender.

"Dat's who it is!" answered Miranda. "She's downstairs waitin' to come up."

"Well, let her come," directed Mr. Tutt, wondering what his old boarding-house keeper could want of him, for he had not seen Mrs. Effingham for more than fifteen years, at which time she was well provided with husband, three children and a going business. Indeed, it required some mental adjustment on his part to recognize the withered little old lady in widow's weeds and rusty black with a gold star on her sleeve who so timidly, a moment later, followed Miranda into the room.

"I'm afraid you don't recognize me," she said with a pitiful attempt at faded coquetry. "I don't blame you, Mr. Tutt. You don't look a day older yourself. But a great deal has happened to me!"

"I should have recognized you anywhere," he protested gallantly. "Do sit down, Mrs. Effingham, won't you? I am delighted to see you. How would you like a glass of toddy? Just to show there's no ill-feeling!"

He forced a glass into her hand and filled it from the teakettle standing on the hearth, while Miranda brought a sofa cushion and tucked it behind the old lady's back.

Mrs. Effingham sighed, tasted the toddy and leaned back deliciously. She was very wrinkled and her hair under the bonnet was startlingly white in contrast with the crêpe of her veil, but there were still traces of beauty in her face.

"I've come to you, Mr. Tutt," she explained apologetically, "because I always said that if I ever was in trouble you'd be the one to whom I should go to help me out."

"What greater compliment could I receive?"

"Well, in those days I never thought that time would come," she went on. "You remember my husband—Jim? Jim died two years ago. And little Jimmy—our eldest—he was only fourteen when you boarded with us—he was killed at the Front last July." She paused and felt for her handkerchief, but could not find it. "I still keep the house; but do you know how old I am, Mr. Tutt? I'm seventy-one! And the two older girls got married long ago and I'm all alone except for Jessie, the youngest—and I haven't told her anything about it."

"Yes?" said Mr. Tutt sympathetically. "What haven't you told her about?"

"My trouble. You see, Jessie's not a well girl—she really ought to live out West somewhere the doctor says—and Jim and I had saved up all these years so that after we were gone she would have something to live on. We saved twelve thousand dollars—and put it into Government bonds."

"You couldn't have anything safer, at any rate," remarked the lawyer. "I think you did exceedingly well."

"Now comes the awful part of it all!" exclaimed Mrs. Effingham, clasping her hands. "I'm afraid it's gone—gone forever.

I should have consulted you first before I did it, but it all seemed so fair and above-board that I never thought."

"Have you got rid of your bonds?"

"Yes—no—that is, the bank has them. You see I borrowed ten thousand dollars on them and gave it to Mr. Badger to invest in his oil company for me."

Mr. Tutt groaned inwardly. Badger was the most celebrated of Wall Street's near-financiers.

"Where on earth did you meet Badger?" he demanded.

"Why, he boarded with me—for a long time," she answered. "I've no complaint to make of Mr. Badger. He's a very handsome polite gentleman. And I don't feel altogether right about coming to you and saying anything that might be taken against him—but lately I've heard so many things—"

"Don't worry about Badger!" growled Mr. Tutt. "How did you come to invest in his oil stock?"

"I was there when he got the telegram telling how they had found oil on the property; it came one night at dinner. He was tickled to death. The stock had been selling at three cents a share, and, of course, after the oil was discovered he said it would go right up to ten dollars. But he was real nice about it —he said anybody who had been living there in the house could share his good fortune with him, come in on the ground floor, and have it just the same for three cents. A week later there came a photograph of the gusher and almost all of us decided to buy stock."

At this point in the narrative Mr. Tutt kicked the coal hod violently and uttered a smothered ejaculation.

"Of course I didn't have any ready money," explained Mrs. Effingham, "but I had the bonds—they only paid two percent and the oil stock was going to pay twenty—so I took them down to the bank and borrowed ten thousand dollars on them. I had to sign a note and pay five percent interest. I was making the difference—fifteen hundred dollars every year."

"What has it paid?" demanded Mr. Tutt ironically.

"Twenty percent," replied Mrs. Effingham. "I get Mr. Badger's check regularly every six months."

"How many times have you got it?"

"Twice."

"Well, why don't you like your investment?" inquired Mr. Tutt blandly. "I'd like something that would pay me twenty percent a year!"

"Because I'm afraid Mr. Badger isn't quite truthful, and one of the ladies—that old Mrs. Channing; you remember her, don't you—the one with the curls?—she tried to sell her stock and nobody would make a bid on it at all—and when she spoke to Mr. Badger about it he became very angry and swore right in front of her. Then somebody told me that Mr. Badger had been arrested once for something—and—and— Oh, I wish I hadn't given him the money, because if it's lost Jessie won't have anything to live on after I'm dead—and she's too sick to work. What do you think, Mr. Tutt? Do you suppose Mr. Badger would buy the stock back?"

Mr. Tutt smiled grimly.

"Not if I know him! Have you got your stock with you?"

She nodded. Fumbling in her black bag she pulled forth a flaring certificate—of the regulation kind, not even engraved—which evidenced that Sarah Maria Ann Effingham was the legal owner of three hundred and thirty thousand shares of the capital stock of the Great Geyser Texan Petroleum and Llano Estacado Land Company.

Mr. Tutt took it gingerly between his thumb and forefinger. It was signed ALFRED HAYNES BADGER, Pres., and he had an almost irresistible temptation to twist it into a spill and light a stogy with it. But he used a match instead, while Mrs. Effingham watched him apprehensively. Then he handed the stock back to her and poured out another glass of toddy.

"Ever been in Mr. Badger's office?"

"Oh, yes!" she answered. "It's a lovely office. You can see 'way down the harbor—and over to New Jersey. It's real elegant."

"Would you mind going there again? That is, are you on friendly terms with him?"

Already a strange, rather desperate plan was half formulated in his mind.

"Oh, we're perfectly friendly," she smiled. "I generally go down there to get my check."

"Whose check is it—his or the company's?"

"I really don't know," she answered simply. "What difference would it make?"

"Oh, nothing—except that he might claim that he'd loaned you the money."

"Loaned it? To me?"

"Why, yes. One hears of such things."

"But it is my money!" she cried, stiffening.

"You paid that for the stock."

She shook her head helplessly.

"I don't understand these things," she murmured. "If Jim had been alive it wouldn't have happened. He was so careful."

"Husbands have some uses occasionally."

Suddenly she put her hands to her face.

"Oh, Mr. Tutt! Please get the money back from him. If you don't something terrible will happen to Jessie!"

"I'll do my best," he said gently, laying his hand on her fragile shoulder. "But I may not be able to do it—and anyhow I'll need your help."

"What can I do?"

"I want you to go down to Mr. Badger's office tomorrow morning and tell him that you are so much pleased with your investment that you would like to turn all your securities over to him to sell and put the money into the Great Geyser Texan Petroleum and Llano Estacado Land Company."

He rolled out the words with unction.

"But I don't!"

"Oh, yes, you do!" he assured her. "You want to do just what I tell you, don't you?"

"Of course," she answered. "But I thought you didn't like Mr. Badger's oil company."

"Whether I like it or not makes no difference. I want you to say just what I tell you."

"Oh, very well, Mr. Tutt."

"Then you must tell him about the note, and that first it will have to be paid off."

"Yes."

"And then you must hand him a letter which I will dictate to you now."

She flushed slightly, her eyes bright with excitement.

"You're sure it's perfectly honest, Mr. Tutt? I wouldn't want to do anything unfair!"

"Would you be honest with a burglar?"

"But Mr. Badger isn't a burglar!"

"No—he's only about a thousand times worse. He's a robber of widows and orphans. He isn't man enough to take a chance at housebreaking."

"I don't know what you mean," she sighed. "Where shall I write?"

Mr. Tutt cleared a space upon his desk, handed her a pad and dipped a pen in the ink while she took off her gloves.

"Address the note to the bank," he directed.

She did so.

"Now say: 'Kindly deliver to Mr. Badger all the securities I have on deposit with you, whenever he pays my note. Very truly yours, Sarah Maria Ann Effingham.'"

"But I don't want him to have my securities!" she retorted.

"Oh, you won't mind! You'll be lucky to get Mr. Badger to take back your oil stock on any terms. Leave the certificate with me," laughed Mr. Tutt, rubbing his long thin hands together almost gleefully. "And now as it is getting rather late perhaps you will do me the honor of letting me escort you home."

It was midnight before Mr. Tutt went to bed. In the first place he had felt himself so neglectful of Mrs. Effingham that after he had taken her home he had sat there a long time talking over the old lady's affairs and making the acquaintance of the phthisical Jessie, who turned out to be a wistful little creature with great liquid eyes and a delicate transparent skin that foretold only too clearly what was to be her future. There was only one place for her, Mr. Tutt told himself—Arizona; and by the grace of God she should go there, Badger or no Badger!

As the old lawyer walked slowly home with his hands clasped behind his back he pondered upon the seeming mockery and injustice of the law that forced a lonely, half-demented old fellow with the fixed delusion that he was a financier behind prison bars and left free the sharp slick crook who had no bowels or mercies and would snatch away the widow's mite and leave her and her consumptive daughter to die in the poorhouse. Yet such was the case, and there they all were! Could you blame people for being Bolsheviks? And yet old Doc Barrows was as far from a Bolshevik as anyone could well be.

Mr. Tutt passed a restless night, dreaming, when he slept at all, of mines from which poured myriads of pieces of yellow gold, of gushers spouting columns of blood-red oil hundreds of feet into the air, and of old-fashioned locomotives dragging picturesque trains of cars across bright green prairies studded with cacti in the shape of dollar signs. Old Doc Barrows was with him, and from time to time he would lean toward him and whisper, "Listen, Mr. Tutt, I'll tell you a secret! There's a vein of gold runs right through my daughter's cow pasture!"

When Willie next morning at half past eight reached the office he found the door already unlocked and Mr. Tutt busy at his desk, up to his elbows in a great mass of bonds and stock certificates.

"Gee!" he exclaimed to Miss Sondheim, the stenographer, when she made her appearance at a quarter past nine. "Just peek in the old man's door if you want to feel rich! Say, he must ha' struck pay dirt! I wonder if we'll all get a raise?"

But all the securities on Mr. Tutt's desk would not have justified even the modest advance of five dollars in Miss Sondheim's salary, and their employer was merely sorting out and making an inventory of Doc Barrows' imaginary wealth. By the time Mrs. Effingham arrived by appointment at ten o'clock he had them all arranged and labeled; and in a special bundle neatly tied with a piece of red tape were what on their face were securities worth upward of seventy thousand dollars. There were ten of the beautiful bonds of the Great Lakes and Canadian Southern Railroad Company with their miniature locomotives and fields of wheat, and ten equally lovely bits of engraving belonging to the long-since defunct Bluff Creek and Iowa Central, ten more superb lithographs issued by the Mohawk and Housatonic in 1867 and paid off in 1882, and a variety of gorgeous chromos of Indians and buffaloes, and of factories and steamships spouting clouds of soft-coal smoke; and on the top of all was a pile of the First Mortgage Gold Six Per Cent obligations of the Chicago Water Front and Terminal Company —all of them fresh and crisp, with that faintly acrid smell which though not agreeable to the nostrils nevertheless delights the banker's soul.

"Ah! Good morning to you, Mrs. Effingham!" Mr. Tutt cried, waving her in when that lady was announced. "You are not the only millionaire, you see! In fact, I've stumbled into a few barrels of securities myself—only I didn't pay anything for them."

"Gracious!" cried Mrs. Effingham, her eyes lighting with astonishment. "Wherever did you get them? And such exquisite pictures! Look at that lamb!"

"It ought to have been a wolf!" muttered Mr. Tutt. "Well, Mrs. Effingham, I've decided to make you a present—just a few pounds of Chicago Water Front and Canadian Southern—those over there in the pile; and now if you say so we'll just go along to your bank."

"Give them to me!" she protested. "What on earth for? You're joking, Mr. Tutt."

"Not a bit of it!" he retorted. "I don't make any pretensions as to the value of my gift, but they're yours for whatever they're worth."

He wrapped them carefully in a piece of paper and returned the balance to Doc Barrows' dress-suit case.

"Aren't you afraid to leave them that way?" she asked, surprised.

"Not at all! Not at all!" he laughed. "You see there are fortunes lying all about us everywhere if we only know where to look. Now the first thing to do is to get your bonds back from the bank."

Mr. Thomas McKeever, the popular loan clerk of the Mustardseed National, was just getting ready for the annual visit of the state bank examiner when Mr. Tutt, followed by Mrs. Effingham, entered the exquisitely furnished boudoir where lady clients were induced by all modern conveniences except manicures and shower baths to become depositors. Mr. Tutt and Mr. McKeever belonged to the same Saturday evening poker game at the Colophon Club, familiarly known as The Bible Class.

" 'Morning, Tom," said Mr. Tutt. "This is my client, Mrs. Effingham. You hold her note, I believe, for ten thousand dollars secured by some government bonds. She has a use for those bonds and I thought that you might be willing to take my indorsement instead. You know I'm good for the money."

"Why, I guess we can accommodate her, Mr. Tutt!" answered the Chesterfieldian Mr. McKeever. "Certainly we can. Sit down, Mrs. Effingham, while I send for your bonds. See the morning paper?"

Mrs. Effingham blushingly acknowledged that she had not

seen the paper. In fact, she was much too excited to see anything.

"Sign here!" said the loan clerk, placing the note before the lawyer.

Mr. Tutt indorsed it in his strange, humpbacked chirography.

"Here are your bonds," said Mr. McKeever, handing Mrs. Effingham a small package in a manila envelope. She took them in a half-frightened way, as if she thought she was doing something wrong.

"And now," said Mr. Tutt, "the lady would like a box in your safe-deposit vaults; a small one—about five dollars a year—will do. She has quite a bundle of securities with her, which I am looking into. Most if not all of them are of little or no value, but I have told her she might just as well leave them as security for what they are worth, in addition to my indorsement. Really it's just a slick game of ours to get the bank to look after them for nothing. Isn't it, Mrs. Effingham?"

"Ye-es!" stammered Mrs. Effingham, not understanding what he was talking about.

"Well," answered Mr. McKeever, "we never refuse collateral. I'll put the bonds with the note—" His eye caught the edges of the bundle. "Great Scott, Tutt! What are you leaving all these bonds here for against that note? There must be nearly a hundred thousand dol—"

"I thought you never refused collateral, Mr. McKeever!" challenged Mr. Tutt sternly.

Twenty minutes later the exquisite blonde who acted as Mr. Badger's financial accomplice learned from Mrs. Effingham's faltering lips that the widow would like to see the great man in regard to further investments.

"How does it look, Mabel?" inquired the financier from behind his massive mahogany desk covered with a six by five sheet of plate glass. "Is it a squeal or a fall?"

"Easy money," answered Mabel with confidence. "She wants to put a mortgage on the farm."

"Keep her about fourteen minutes, tell her the story of my philanthropies, and then shoot her in," directed Badger.

So Mrs. Effingham listened politely while Mabel showed her the photographs of Mr. Badger's home for consumptives out in

Tyrone, New Mexico, and of his wife and children, taken on the porch of his summer home at Seabright, New Jersey; and then, exactly fourteen minutes having elapsed, she was shot in.

"Ah! Mrs. Effingham! Delighted! Do be seated!" Mr. Badger's smile was like that of the boa constrictor about to swallow the rabbit.

"About my oil stock," hesitated Mrs. Effingham.

"Well, what about it?" demanded Badger sharply. "Are you dissatisfied with your twenty percent?"

"Oh, no!" stammered the old lady. "Not at all! I just thought if I could only get the note paid off at the Mustardseed Bank I might ask you to sell the collateral and invest the proceeds in your gusher."

"Oh!" Mr. Badger beamed with pleasure. "Do you really wish to have me dispose of your securities for you?"

He did not regard it as necessary to inquire into the nature of the collateral. If it was satisfactory to the Mustardseed National it must of course exceed considerably the amount of the note.

"Yes," answered Mrs. Effingham timidly; and she handed him the letter dictated by Mr. Tutt.

"Well," replied Mr. Badger thoughtfully, after reading it, "what you ask is rather unusual—quite unusual, I may say, but I think I may be able to attend to the matter for you. Leave it in my hands and think no more about it. How have you been, my dear Mrs. Effingham? You're looking extraordinarily well!"

Mr. McKeever had about concluded his arrangements for welcoming the state bank examiner when the telephone on his desk buzzed, and on taking up the receiver he heard the ingratiating voice of Alfred Haynes Badger.

"Is this the Loan Department of the Mustardseed National?"

"It is," he answered shortly.

"I understand you hold a note of a certain Mrs. Effingham for ten thousand dollars. May I ask if it is secured?"

"Who is this?" snapped McKeever.

"One of her friends," replied Mr. Badger amicably.

"Well, we don't discuss our clients' affairs over the telephone. You had better come in here if you have any inquiries to make."

"But I want to pay the note," expostulated Mr. Badger.

"Oh! Well, anybody can pay the note who wants to."

"And of course in that case you would turn over whatever collateral is on deposit to secure the note?"

"If we were so directed."

"May I ask what collateral there is?"

"I don't know."

"There is some collateral, I suppose?"

"Yes."

"Well, I have an order from Mrs. Effingham directing the bank to turn over whatever securities she has on deposit as collateral, on my payment of the note."

"In that case you'll get 'em," said Mr. McKeever gruffly. "I'll get them out and have 'em ready for you."

"Here is my certified check for ten thousand dollars," announced Alfred Haynes Badger a few minutes later. "And here is the order from Mrs. Effingham. Now will you kindly turn over to me all the securities?"

Mr. McKeever, knowing something of the reputation of Mr. Badger, first called up the bank which had certified the latter's check, and having ascertained that the certification was genuine he marked Mrs. Effingham's note as paid and then took down from the top of his roll-top desk the bundle of beautifully engraved securities given him by Mr. Tutt. Badger watched him greedily.

"Thank you," he gurgled, stuffing them into his pocket. "Much obliged for your courtesy. Perhaps you would like me to open an account here?"

"Oh, anybody can open an account who wants to," remarked Mr. McKeever dryly, turning away from him to something else.

Mr. Badger fairly flew back to his office. The exquisite blonde had hardly ever before seen him exhibit so much agitation.

"What have you pulled this time?" she inquired dreamily. "Father's daguerreotype and the bracelet of mother's hair?"

"I've grabbed off the whole bag of tricks!" he cried. "Look at 'em! We've not seen so much of the real stuff in six months.

"Ten—twenty—thirty—forty—fifty— By gad!—sixty—seventy!"

"That are they?" asked Mabel curiously. "Some bonds—what?"